C0-AQV-508

Lamed Vav

R. SHLOMO ALWAYS USED TO SAY:

There are many stories
about the lamed-vav *(lah-med vav)* tzaddikim,
the thirty-six holy people in whose merit the world exists.
You know, sometimes the state of the world seems so low that
G-d despairs of His creation.
Still, these thirty-six are so important to Him
that for their sake alone He keeps the whole operation going.

Some people say that in every generation
there are lamed-vav tzaddikim *who serve the whole world.*
Others say there are thirty-six such holy people in chutz la'aretz,
outside of Israel, thirty-six more in Eretz Yisrael,
and still another thirty-six in the Holy City of Jerusalem.

But on one thing everybody agrees:
the lamed-vav tzaddikim *are all hidden people.*
Nobody knows who they are...

Lamed Vav

a collection of the favorite stories of

Rabbi Shlomo Carlebach
ztz'l

compiled and illustrated by
Tzlotana Barbara Midlo

Copyright © 2005/5765
By Tzlotana Barbara Midlo
Email: lamedvav@netvision.net.il

All rights reserved.
No part of this publication may be translated, reproduced, stored in a retrieval system
or transmitted, in any form or by any means, electronic, mechanical, photocopying,
recording or otherwise, without prior permission in writing from the copyright holder.

This book is presented in cooperation with - and under license given by - the Carlebach family.

Library of Congress Cataloging-in-Publication Data

Carlebach, Shlomo.
Lamed Vav: a collection of the favorite stories of Rabbi Shlomo Carlebach / told and
illustrated by Tzlotana Barbara Midlo.
p. cm.
ISBN 1-931681-65-1
1. Zaddikim--Anecdotes. 2. Hasidim--Legends. 3. Legends, Jewish. 4. Jewish parables.
5. Hasidic parables. I. Midlo, Tzlotana Barbara. II. Title.
BM532.C3722 2005
296.1'9--dc22

                              2005018513

Printed in Israel

Distributed by: Israel Book Shop
                501 Prospect Street, Lakewood, NJ 08701
                Tel: (732) 901-3009 Fax: (732) 901-4012 Email: isrbkshp@aol.com

Design and layout: Yehudit Abinun
                Argaman Studio, Jerusalem   Email: jabinun@netvision.net.il

IN LOVING MEMORY OF

DAVID HERTZBERG z"l
Mayim Chaim Dovid Hillel ben Shraga Feivel and Rivka

What can you say about the one who knew the secret of holy laughter…?

Sarah, Chana and Akiva

and

SARA ROTHKOPF z"l
Sara bat Eliezer and Rachel

"Sara Rothkopf (née Baum) was born February 15, 1912, in Lodz, Poland. Her mother had been born in Kozhnitz and her father, a sofer, a scribe, was an Amshinover chasid. In their backyard, the Kozhnitzer Rebbe held court. My mother told many stories about her experiences with the Holy Kozhnitzer. Once, when her sister Leah was seriously ill, the Rebbe happened to stop by. He called into the room, 'A refuah shleimah, a complete recovery' three times. And her sister immediately began feeling better.

"Another time the Rebbe was walking down the street when a crowd gathered and began making fun of him. 'Come with me to the mikvah,' he entreated one of the scoffers. But the man refused. While the Rebbe was still in the mikvah, someone informed him this same man had just been hit by a wagon and killed.

"The Rebbe sighed, 'I tried to rescue him…'

"This was the world into which my mother was born … and then it was abruptly and brutally swept away. First, her husband was arrested and killed for eating a potato in a field. Then, while she was interned in the Lodz Ghetto, her two sons — my unknown brothers, Moshe Aaron and Eliezer — were taken from her, never to be seen again.

"Later, her mother was herded into a wagon for deportation to a concentration camp. My grandmother pleaded, 'Come with me!' As my mother tried to board the wagon, a man came out of the crowd crying, 'If you go, you will die with the rest!' — and pulled my mother off. The wagon drove away, and the man disappeared. Eliahu HaNavi, Elijah the Prophet, had performed another miracle.

"My mother and her sister were finally taken to Auschwitz. Leah was sickly and feeble, so my mother volunteered to make the long walk to get both their meager daily rations of dry bread and water so that her sister could rest. One day, when she returned, Leah was on the other side of the barbed wire fence, pleading, 'Save me, please save me!' A guard started beating Leah savagely with the butt of his rifle, while my mother stood there, helpless.

"One Passover in Auschwitz, my mother and a friend refused to eat chametz. Instead, they hoarded their bread. When their stash was found, they were accused of stealing, and the guards began to beat her friend. My mother begged them to stop, explaining that the bread had not been stolen … it was only the accumulation of their Passover rations. Somehow, the Nazis believed her and let her friend live.

"When Auschwitz was evacuated, my mother was transferred to a factory in Austria, from which she was liberated on or about Passover, 1945. After three years she married my father, Yehudah Leib (Leon) Rothkopf, a Sochatchover chasid – who had also lost his wife and children. My sister Rose was born in a DP camp in Regensburg, and I was later born in New York."

"If I had to sum up the essence of my mother's life in one motto, it would be, 'Never give up!' This was also the underlying message of my Rebbe, R. Shlomo Carlebach, who – through teachings and stories like the ones in this book – brought my mother's destroyed world back to life. And this too was the legacy of my dearest friend and brother, R. Dovid Hertzberg. Through all his suffering he never stopped giving us strength with his joy in life … and with his jokes.

"Together, my mother, R. Dovid'l and R. Shlomo sent us this message: 'Don't ever give up! G-d depends on you, your children and grandchildren depend on you, the whole world depends on you. You are the nekudah, the point, the link that ties past to present, Heaven to earth – that spurns evil and supplants it with good…'

"R. Shlomo blessed my mother and Dovid'l, and they both blessed him. R. Dovid loved my mother and R. Shlomo, and they both loved him. They all three had the utmost kavod, respect, for each other. We've all been blessed by having passed their way…"

"May their memories continue to bless and protect all of Israel…"

Moshe and Tziporah Rothkopf
Shira and Leah

Rose and Joe Falowitz
Jesse, Lisa and Michael

WITH HEARTFELT THANKS TO

R. Shlomo *ztz'l's* family:
Neila, Neshama and Nedara

Susan Yael Mesinai
Yehudit Abinun

Steve Amdor, David Staloff, Leah and Michael Golomb,
Dina and Ben Tzion Solomon, Emunah Witt, Gedaliah Fleer,
Shalom Brodt, Alifa Sa'adia, Akiva Unger, Frieda Jacobowitz and
Sarah Ben Zakkai.

And most special thanks to my father,
Moise S. Steeg, for everything.

———————————

You know, anybody who really loves his children, mamash, loves everyone in the world. It has to be ... there is no other way.

Because – did you ever watch little children, the way they are with other people? Maybe sometimes they're shy, maybe sometimes they're friendly. But however they react at first, they're always ready to open their hearts.

So if you're really connected to your children, then through them – if you look at the world through their eyes – you forget what hatred is. All you know is their openness and their love...

This book is dedicated to:

Reb Shlomo ztz'l's children,
Neshama and Nedara

My children,
Miriam and Aaron Leibowitz

Their children,
Yedidya Yehuda Chiya, Ashrina Chein,
Ma'ayana Emunah and Nadiv Yeshaya Yaacov Leibowitz

And all of G-d's children, young and old, everywhere.

Contents

Contents

A little More
Light from the Sun

Reb Shlomo on Story-telling

*Everybody knows the Holy R. Shlomo Carlebach ztz'l as our generation's
"sweet singer of Israel." Today,* Yidden *everywhere in the world* daven *and celebrate
to the strains of his uplifting* niggunim. *But R. Shlomo was more than a vocalist,
more than a "dancing Rebbe," as he was sometimes called. He was an extremely
insightful teacher, giving over the deepest depths of the Torah in his own inimitable
style. And punctuating his songs at concerts and his teachings at study sessions,
there were always stories – stories about* tzaddikim, *about the Rebbes – chasidic
stories, Jewish stories…*

*But R. Shlomo didn't tell stories merely to provide extra entertainment at his
performances or a moment of lightness to break an intense learning. His tales were
vehicles for giving over profound insights, the inside of the inside of the Torah.
Storytelling, for him, wasn't an art form. It was a form of prayer, prayer wrapped
in the garment of a seemingly simple narrative. Hidden within each story of* Yidden
*of another time, struggling with – and overcoming – the obstacles of exile, are the
seeds of our own strength in dealing with our troubled world.*

*I once had the opportunity to speak to R. Shlomo about his love of, and gift
for, storytelling. And he shared with me his thoughts about the role of stories in our
lives…*

A story, R. Shlomo began, has the power to change us. After we
hear or read it, it's as if we become new, subtly different than
we were before. And he gave an example:

Suppose you go to a class on how important it is not to talk
about other people. Maybe the lesson is full of heavy *musar*, stressing
that if you gossip about others, you're *mamash* the lowest of the low. And
if – G-d forbid – you're already somebody who talks about people, you'd
better fix yourself fast – or else…!

Now really, how many of us can claim that we never talk about
others? So when we leave the class, how do we feel? Pretty down, right?
Maybe discouraged, upset with ourselves. Okay, in former good days
perhaps such a lecture would inspire its audience to do *teshuvah*. People
then were maybe stronger, and could handle such heavy words. But today
we're living in such a broken world. We already know, even if we can't
always admit it, that we're not really on the level. And the last thing we
need is for somebody to make us feel smaller. We're broken enough, we
don't need anybody to break us more…

Or perhaps the teaching will have a different effect. Maybe the speaker is really eloquent, his message extremely powerful. So we get very inspired and decide that from that moment on, we will *mamash* never ever say anything about another human being. But what usually happens when we walk out of the lecture? Sadly enough, despite our best intentions, a few days – or weeks – or hours – or even a few minutes later, there we are again, gossiping about others. Do you know what our problem is? It's so hard to break old habits, to have self-control. Even when we want to, we can't always – or even often – do it. We're just too weak…

And this is where stories come in. Suppose that somebody tells us a story about a *Yid* who worked on himself his whole life until he *mamash* reached the level of never talking about other people. What do you think will happen to us? Maybe, just maybe, when we open our mouths to say something about another person, we'll see in our minds an image of this *Yiddele*. And maybe, just maybe, that will at least make us stop and think about what we're about to do.

And this is the whole thing. A story doesn't just give over a teaching … and it certainly doesn't bring us down. In fact, just the opposite: a good story has the power to raise us up to a different level. It can give us what we need the most … it can give us so much strength.

A good story does more than give us moral instruction or warn us about the consequences of our mistakes. It gives us an example of a *Yiddele* who is struggling, just like we are. But in the end – *gevalt*! He or she *mamash* succeeds in accomplishing just what we are striving for. So we think, "If this person could do it, maybe I can too." And this gives us the strength to try again…

You know, for us *Yidden* there are two kinds of miracles – let's call them "G-d miracles" and "Jew miracles." We all know about the miracles that the Master of the World performed for *Am Yisrael* … like the Exodus from Egypt and the splitting of the Red Sea. But did you ever think about the level that Abraham reached when he was ready to obey the *Ribbono Shel Olam* and bring up his only son as a sacrifice? Or that of Isaac when he was prepared to die for G-d on the altar? That kind of commitment, that kind of faith, can only be called a "Jew miracle."

Everybody knows that the *Ribbono Shel Olam* is always performing miracles for us *Yidden*. But in our days, after the destruction of the Temple,

His miracles are often hidden, and we aren't always so much aware of them. Instead, we see more of the miracles that Jews do themselves.

Can you imagine what a miracle it was that a *Yiddele* could be in a place like Auschwitz and still find a way to light candles on Chanukah, to dance and sing in honor of the Holy Shabbos? Or, when a young *yeshivah* student is so tired he's about to faint and he still makes himself sit down and learn the Talmud – or a poor *Yid* gives his last penny to a beggar even poorer than himself… *Gevalt!* – are these the highest "Jew miracles!"

And you know, so many Jews today are coming back to *Yiddishkeit.* Some people think their return is a miracle from G-d. But really, it's the greatest "Jew miracle."

And this is the thing about stories. A good story has a little bit of both sides, of the "G-d miracles" and the "Jew miracles." But do you know how a story gives us so much strength? By reminding us that we're all *mamash* capable of performing the highest kinds of miracles.

Stories have the unbelievable ability to take us back to the beginning. As the Holy Rizhiner says, how does the Torah, the Five Books of Moses, start? With the Master of the World telling us stories…

A story has the strength to cleanse us completely. We feel like it transports us back to the day we were born. And suddenly we're as pure as we were when we first came down from Heaven.

That's why even people we don't like so much sometimes become our friends through stories. Because a story can wash away all of the dirt that has accumulated inside us and stopped up our hearts and souls. When these blocks are dissolved, we forget about hate … and even dislike. Because the way we understand things has changed. We ask ourselves, "What do I really know?"

Yesterday we looked at certain people, and we were sure they were wrong. We thought they could never be our friends. Now we see these people with new eyes, and we realize they were right. And we were also right. We were both right – each in our own way. So what reason do we have to argue or fight? And suddenly we know that – not only will we now be friends, but on the inside of the inside, we were actually friends the whole time…

Everything we understand derives from our consciousness. But a story comes from a higher place – from our imagination. And not only that. The *Heilige* R. Nachman of Breslov says that it is stories themselves that awaken the highest, holiest levels of our imagination.

Stories seem simple, they seem just to be giving over a tale, an event. They seem clear. They have a beginning, a middle, and an end. But as we listen or read, we realize that stories have many levels, many layers of meaning. They are strange and familiar at the same time. They tease us, invite us to play with them, to turn them inside out to discover all the things, hidden and revealed, that they are actually saying.

And while we wrestle with their meanings, stories – *mamash* without our even realizing it – enter into the deepest depths of our being where other forms of teaching can't reach. There they begin to do their holy work. They open up our closed places, they wake up our imagination. And – *gevalt, gevalt!* Something new begins to happen inside us. Stories fill us with new light – and new life.

Then the Holy R. Nachman says something else. Our imagination is freest when we dream. So we never dream in terms of ideas, theories, or philosophies. Our dreams are always in the form of stories.

A good story increases our knowledge, but is deeper than that knowledge. It comes from beyond our consciousness, but flows into our conscious awareness. The power of a story reaches beyond our minds, penetrates even deeper than our hearts. It *mamash* touches our souls…

The world places its greatest value on knowledge, especially scientific knowledge. But all the holy "hippies"– the young people who dropped out of college in the 1960's and 70's to search for a different kind of life – you know, some people thought they were beautiful, while others thought they were completely off. The truth is, maybe they were both at the same time. But the thing is, they wanted something holier, something more profound, than the knowledge they were getting. It wasn't enough for them to have the information to, let's say, build a space station, or go on a rocket to the moon. They wanted something else, which you can get from stories. Because in the end, the most important knowledge is not scientific, or even mystical. It's to know what life is all about.

And that's the essence of a story – understanding life.

When we seek knowledge, information, it's because we want to learn something we don't already know. But with a story, it's just the opposite. What we want is to know what we already know, the knowledge that is already hidden deep inside our hearts.

Of course, it's true that we have to keep learning all our lives. We always need to acquire more information, additional insights – especially when it comes to Torah. But our biggest problem isn't lack of knowledge. The Master of the World gives us everything we need to know in order to serve Him … which, after all, is what our lives are really about. G-d isn't stingy when it comes to giving us knowledge.

Our problem is that we don't believe we know what we know. And the truth is, if we had just an inkling of how much knowledge we actually have, it would *mamash* change our lives.

The thing is, we think knowledge has to come from our heads, from our logical minds. But there are also other ways of knowing, ways that some people call by names like "intuition" or "instinct". And at this point in our conversation R. Shlomo shook his head with a smile, and gave a personal example…

Once R. Shlomo was supposed to go to a certain place, which he didn't name. His heart told him not to go, and his head told him he had a responsibility, a commitment, which he really had to honor. He couldn't decide whether to follow his heart or to listen to his head, so he just waited. And he was praying: "Master of the World, please send me a sign. Show me whether or not to go."

One night, R. Shlomo was walking down Broadway in New York City, and he passed a movie theater. Now, he was very preoccupied with the problem of his impending trip, and anyway, he wasn't really interested in movies. But somehow he glanced up at the billboard announcing the current film. And, he said, a shiver ran through him. Because what was playing? A film called "Trouble all the Way." Talk about a sign!

So what did R. Shlomo do? He went on the trip anyway. The problem, he said, was that he didn't trust his own deep inside knowledge. The whole thing proved good for him in the long run – and also bad, because it occupied a lot of his time and *mamash* did cause him a lot of trouble. But in a certain way, it was one of the most important experiences of his life, because he learned an important lesson – to believe in himself…

Do you think, R. Shlomo asked me, that the Jews in Europe at the time of the Second World War had no idea what was coming – that they didn't realize it was going to be "trouble all the way?" They knew, but they didn't trust their own knowledge...

But the big Rebbes, the holy people – ah, they really knew what they knew. They trusted themselves and their own knowledge. And that is the power of telling stories about *tzaddikim*, about the Holy Masters. It can fix our own self-doubts, by reminding us of what we already know.

When R. Shlomo told a story, he often interrupted his narrative to exhort his listeners: "Sweetest friends, now open your hearts!" But what, he asked me, did that expression, "open your hearts," really mean? Not, he insisted, that one should invite everybody to dump all of their garbage on our heads. We don't have to let everyone and everything in, no matter how rotten, no matter how low. But what "open your hearts" does mean is to suspend rational skepticism and be ready to accept the unexpected. To relate to the story ... to relate to life ... by feeling, as well as – maybe even instead of – thinking. To listen, to LIVE, with the heart as well as the mind...

What do we remember when we think back on our lives? Not facts handed down by our parents or grandparents. Our lives are wonderful, marvelous, complicated stories. And you know, it's very strange. We can go up to any stranger on the street and talk about politics, or the latest basketball scores. Facts we can discuss with anyone. But we only tell stories to people we love...

Everybody knows how much children connect to stories. Because most little children don't yet know that there's anybody in the world who doesn't love them. They're still living in Paradise, where everybody is telling each other stories...

Sometimes you walk into a house and you want to see what relationship the parents there have with their children. And one way to find out is to talk to the children themselves. So you go up to a little boy of six or seven, and ask some questions. And – *gevalt*! He can tell you all the facts of life, or the latest news headlines. It's the same thing with his little sister. Obviously their parents have given over a lot of information to them. But really, is that the sign of a close relationship?

Closeness is telling your little ones stories as they're falling asleep. Or, when the weather is bad and they can't go outside to play, drawing your children close beside you and telling them their favorite tales. And you know, maybe the most special stories are not those that parents tell their children. Maybe it's the stories their children tell to THEM.

If we only love somebody a little, then we try to come up with a really good story to tell. But with people we love the most, we can say something as simple as: "I woke up late this morning, skipped breakfast, and was still late for work." And not only do they listen — they're totally fascinated and involved. Because they know the story is our way of speaking to them from the deepest depths of our hearts…

A good story has to connect to all our emotions. It has to reach not only the place of our laughter, it also has to touch the fountain of our tears. Because it's not only *simchah*, not only joy, that connects us to the Messiah. Everybody knows that there are two days of the year when we're closest to *Mashiach*. Yes, one of them is Purim, when we're laughing. But the other is Tisha B'Av, when we're *mamash* crying from the deepest depths of our hearts and souls.

And that's another reason why children love stories. When they're small, children are absolutely one with their feelings. When they're happy, they're completely filled with joy, and they laugh with the purest delight. And when they're sad, for no matter how trivial a reason, they cry and wail like their hearts are *mamash* broken. Until, that is, they get older, and we want them to "grow up." Then we tell them not to get so carried away with their feelings. We want them to "be mature," which means cutting their emotions in half.

But "half" isn't enough in the world anymore. For anything to reach us in the deepest depths, we need the "all." And when it comes to emotions, the "all" is crying AND laughing at the same time.

So, R. Shlomo explained, when you read or hear a good story, there should be times when you are *mamash* moved to laugh out loud. But there should also be moments when there are tears in your eyes. A good story has to reach all of your feelings, the inside of the inside of your soul.

How, I wondered, did R. Shlomo come to realize the incredible power of stories? And what was the source of the wondrous tales he so often told?

The first thing I had to understand, R. Shlomo said, was that he had an amazingly good memory. He only had to hear or read a story a few times before he could repeat it from beginning to end. And the second thing was – he *mamash* couldn't remember a time when stories weren't part of his life. When he and his brother and sister were small, his mother always read to them when they went to bed. But the real storyteller of the family was his father. Every Friday night R. Naftali took R. Shlomo and his twin brother, R. Eli Chaim, for long walks, enchanting them with the family narratives he told. And it was in this way that R. Shlomo first experienced a story's ability to transport a listener to a different time, a different place – *mamash*, to another world.

And then there were the Rebbes. R. Shlomo and R. Eli Chaim often visited the great *chasidic* courts where, particularly on the Sabbath, they heard the Holy Masters tell the most amazing tales … especially the Bobover Rebbe, R. Shlomo Halberstam – the most unbelievable storyteller R. Shlomo ever met. It was from the Bobover, R. Shlomo told us, that he learned many of his favorite stories.[1]

Of course, R. Shlomo often gave over some of his own personal experiences, ones that he found particularly significant – although no such narratives are included in this volume. And there were also ordinary people, often complete strangers, who came up to him on their own initiative. Maybe they'd been to one of his concerts, or maybe to one of his lessons. However it happened, they somehow knew he loved stories, and wanted to tell him one of their favorites – or a tale about someone in their family.[2] And here he gave an example:

Once R. Shlomo was having a meal in a restaurant in Tel Aviv, when a *Yiddele* came up to him and said, "Let me tell you a story about my uncle…"

It was 1938 or 1939, and Poland was already a living hell for Jews. People were desperately trying to leave the country, but really, the only safe way out was to have a false passport. Some industrious *Yidden* banded together to learn how to copy the writing so they could forge the papers. But, you know, passports have a certain style, a particular system of numbers. Unless you do it exactly right, anybody trying to use it is bound to be caught. And in Poland at that time, being caught meant certain death. So what the Jews of Poland needed most were old passports from many different countries, so they could study the form and the systems.

Now this man's uncle, a *chasid* of the *Heilige* Alexander Rebbe, was part of an underground group assigned to buy, borrow, or steal old passports. One day he was unbelievably successful. He *mamash* collected one hundred and fifty passports from many different places. He was so happy, thinking about all the frightened people these papers would help. But as he was hurrying back to his headquarters, with all the passports in a packet under his arm – *gevalt, gevalt!* He was stopped by the Polish police!

"Jew!" the head policeman shouted. "Give us your package, and show us your identity papers."

"But officer," the poor *Yid* replied, "Really, you're making a big mistake. I was just going home from work and…"

"What? Do you really think we're that stupid?" the officer interrupted him. "We know what you're doing, you filthy liar." He grabbed the packet and ripped it open, revealing the piles and piles of passports. "What have we here?" he asked with a sneer. "I think we'll take these. And as for you…"

"Please, I have a wife and children. Let me at least go home and explain what's happened. If I just don't show up, they'll be frantic. They'll think I'm dead…"

"Which you soon will be if you don't tell us everything about your organization," the policeman interrupted again. "We want the names of your leaders, the addresses of your offices. But – for some reason I'm in a generous mood today. All right, go home now to your family. But you'd better show up for questioning first thing tomorrow. Here's where to go…" He scribbled something on a scrap of paper and handed it to the *Yid*. "And don't even think about trying to run away. We know who you are and where to find you. And it won't just be you who will suffer but also your family…"

The officer turned away, and the poor *Yiddele* immediately ran home, more terrified than he'd ever been in his life. He knew one thing for sure: if he went to the police station as he'd been instructed, he'd be tortured for what he knew, and then he'd be shot. Because dealing in false passports, especially if you were a Jew, was a very heavy offense. But he also knew the policeman's threat had been for real – if he tried to run away he would be risking the lives of his wife and children. He didn't know what to do, so he went to his Rebbe, the Holy Alexander, for help.

Now, R. Shlomo explained, the Holy R. Yitzhak Menachem Mendel Danziger of Alexander was *mamash* the holiest of the holy. His father passed away when he was still young, and he was supposed to become the Rebbe. But he refused. "I'm not fit to be a Rebbe," he said. "I'm really not ready. I'm not nearly old enough. And besides, I have very bad eyesight. I won't be able to read the notes, the *kvittlach*, that people will give me with all their requests…"

But his father's *chasidim* said, "We don't care about all that. You're the only one we want. Please, be our Rebbe!" And they begged him so much that he finally agreed.

One day R. Yitzhak told his own son this story. His son immediately asked him, "So, what happened? You never seem to have any trouble reading people's *kvittlach*. How do you do it?"

And the Holy Alexander answered, *"Gevalt, gevalt!* I want you to know, as soon as I became a Rebbe, G-d opened all the gates, and I could see from one end of the world to the other!"

But do you know the holiest thing about the *Heilige* Alexander? He already had passports for himself and his family that would get them out of Poland safely. And all his friends and followers were begging him to use them and leave before it was too late. But he wouldn't go. He said, "How could I do such a thing? I've given my whole life to my people here in Poland. And if the end, G-d forbid, has to come, at my last moment I want to be among them too."

So the *Yid* in the coffee shop continued his narrative:

My uncle ran to the *Heilige* Alexander and told him the whole story about the police and his passports. Then he cried, "Rebbe, please tell me what to do!"

R. Yitzhak closed his eyes and sat still for a moment. Then he looked at my uncle and shook his head. "My dearest friend, I'm so sorry, but I don't know what to tell you. If you go tomorrow, you're right – the police will torture you and finally kill you. And if you don't go, they'll kill both you and your family. And there's nothing I can do to help you. *Oy vey, oy vey…*"

And suddenly the Rebbe buried his head in his hands and started sobbing from the deepest depths of his heart. He cried so hard that his whole body was trembling. And this went on for a long time, with his body shaking more and more. My uncle started getting worried. He ran to the Holy Alexander's son and said:

"Please, come fast! Your father is crying so much, I'm afraid he'll make himself sick!"

The Rebbe's son hurried to his father's side. "Please, father, stop crying," he begged. "I know how much you care, but it won't do your poor *chasid* any good if you do damage to yourself."

But the Alexander just cried even harder. Then, a few minutes later, he suddenly stopped crying and sat up. He looked at my uncle, smiled and said, "It's all right now. You can go to the police tomorrow – nothing will happen to you. Because Heaven just opened the gates of mercy…"

My uncle went to the police station early the next morning. And who was the first person he saw as he went in the door? The same officer who had stopped him on the street. But the man didn't seem to recognize him. "Can I help you?" he asked.

For a moment my uncle didn't know what to say. Then he had an idea. "Uh, I'm here to pick up my passports."

"Your passports? Of course, just a moment … let's see, where did I put them? Oh yes, here they are…" and he handed my uncle his package full of passports.

My uncle thanked him, and went on his way to help Jews escape from the Nazis.

And that, R. Shlomo said with a smile, is a story that he heard from a stranger in a coffee shop!

Besides the tales he learned from his family, or Rebbes and other *Yidden*, R. Shlomo told us he found many of his best stories in Holy Books[3] …

Who first opened up for R. Shlomo the wonderful world of books? The same person who introduced him to the incredible power of stories: his father. R. Naftali had one of the best libraries in Vienna – he *mamash* had thousands of books. R. Shlomo loved being in that library … he loved not only the books' contents, but their very appearance, their leathery smell. And it was in that library, from his earliest childhood, that his lifelong passion for books was born.

Sadly enough, the family had to leave behind all these precious *s'farim*, many of which had been passed down from his grandfather,

R. Shlomo Carlebach, when they left Austria. But R. Shlomo and his brother never lost their love of reading. All they wanted as gifts for their *Bar Mitzvah* were books. And when R. Shlomo was a poor *yeshivah* student, any extra money he had always went for books. There was even a time, he admitted wryly, when he was afraid to show his face on the East Side of New York because he owed so much money to the booksellers there.

And why did R. Shlomo collect as many *s'farim* as he could? He was, he told me, always searching for new and better stories. Because he maybe had to read as many as a hundred *chasidishe* stories before he found the special tale he knew he had to pass on to others…

Sometimes people would come up to R. Shlomo and say, "You know, I was at your concert last night and that story you gave over … well, I don't like to say bad things, but I just read it in a book, and you told it wrong." But, he explained, there was a very simple reason for the discrepancy. He'd found that sometimes the same story is told in a number of books, but about different Rebbes. Or the details of the same story in two different *s'farim* aren't exactly the same. So it wasn't that he'd made a mistake. He'd only given over one version.

And more than that. R. Shlomo had his own unique approach to storytelling. Once, he said, he picked up a book of stories written exactly as they had been told by old *chasidic Yidden*. He read a few pages and then put the book down, because he couldn't connect to it. He simply couldn't relate to the style, the way the stories were given over.

Every generation, he explained, has its own patterns of speech, its own special language. You know, today everybody is translating R. Nachman from Yiddish or Hebrew into English. But it doesn't work if you translate it the way it was said maybe fifty years ago. The world has changed too much since then. It isn't what our generation needs to hear.

A good story, even if it took place hundreds of years ago, has to seem to happen right now, today. Because a *chasidic* story – or one about other *tzaddikim* – is *mamash* an experience. It has to have something real about it – the deepest kind of reality.

Sometimes we meet a person who tells the same tale over and over again. (I remember this happening often with R. Shlomo himself.) Now, if we were only interested in information, we'd become impatient with this repetition and say, "I heard this already. Tell me something new." But strangely enough, we don't seem to mind. In fact, we often appreciate the story more each time it's told. Because while we're hearing (or reading) it, it's *mamash* happening. And not only that: it seems to be happening to us. We find ourselves inside the narrative. This is the most special thing about a good story – it's something with which everybody can identify.

And this is the whole thing. Sometimes people think that for a story to be good, it has to have a lot of violence, or romance – or, even better, a combination of both. But this isn't what storytelling is about. A story has to happen, it has to be real to us. And then, while it's happening, we come alive.

This is why, R. Shlomo said, his stories usually had a strong taste of the present, even when he was talking about the time of the Holy Baal Shem Tov. And this also explains his unique linguistic blend of Yiddish and "hip" expressions. Not that he intentionally made alterations in the story. The changes just seemed to evolve on their own once he began sharing the tale with others.

The truth was, he explained, after he read a story and began to give it over, he never looked at it in the book again. Something happened – he admitted he couldn't explain just what – and he began to tell the tale as he experienced it at the moment, right now, today. And he didn't want to feel guilty because he hadn't stuck strictly to the original version.[4]

R. Shlomo saw a story as a living entity, like a plant, a bush, or maybe a tree. He believed that, like other organic things, a tale has to grow – to blossom and bear its fruit. And that as he told the story in his own characteristic way, he was helping this process along. He was adding a few more leaves, a few more flowers … a few drops of rain, a little more light from the sun…

I want to add here a few words about my own experience of writing this book…

Everybody knows, as R. Shlomo would say, how difficult it is to translate spoken words into a written form. Really, it's not the words that are the problem: words are the same, spoken or written. But the way they are spoken, the tone of voice, the hand gestures, the facial expressions – all these speak as much as the words themselves. How can one capture these in the starkness of printed words on a page?

And if this is true in general, how much more is it true of our beloved R. Shlomo and his telling of stories. Our Rebbe gave over his tales with great fervor, with deep emotion, with gentleness and with fire. He said so much more than words with his voice, he spoke so much with his eyes and his hands – and, of course, with his melodies...

I had originally hoped to present these stories in at least an approximation of R. Shlomo's own voice. But ultimately this proved to be impossible. I was terribly discouraged, almost in despair. I wondered if this book was even worth publishing if it wasn't presented in R. Shlomo's own – if edited – words.

Then one morning I found myself reading a transcript of one of R. Shlomo's teachings on an entirely different subject. And it was as if the Rebbe himself had sent me the answer to my dilemma. He was talking about different levels of beauty and, as I remember it, he said:

Suppose someone gives over a profound and inspiring lesson, and his students receive it enthusiastically. That's very satisfying, very beautiful. But then suppose that one of the students tells over that same teaching to the Rebbe, but in the student's own words, from his own heart. Ah, R. Shlomo said. That's real beauty, so much deeper.

So I have written these stories in my own words, from my own heart. I have told them from my memory both of R. Shlomo as he related them, as well as of the stories themselves. I have always tried to preserve the flavor of R. Shlomo's speech: his distinctive cadence, his unique phraseology. In truth, this wasn't all that difficult, since his well-remembered "Shlomo-isms" are an integral part of my own way of speaking. And anyone who knew him well surely remembers that R. Shlomo insisted that, when we repeated his stories or teachings, we do so as accurately as possible.

I have even tried to emulate R. Shlomo's style by including "teachings" before, after, and sometimes within the text of the stories, as he was wont to do.

But you know, not many of us can claim to be "clear vessels," transmitting remembered information without alteration. Somehow our own imaginations get involved, our own vision. And so it was with me

– and also with R. Shlomo himself, as he explained above. Working as I was from memory, it's likely my own image of and involvement with the stories supplied details which R. Shlomo didn't actually include, or even an interpretation here and there which he didn't explicitly offer.

Just as R. Shlomo gave over – in his own style, his own way – stories he heard from his Rebbes, so too have I transmitted tales I heard from my Rebbe – at least in part – in my own style and my own way. I pray that I have faithfully followed R. Shlomo's tradition in whatever changes I have made, that maybe I've helped these stories grow in a beautiful and holy way. Because the truth is, it seemed to me that I could hear our Rebbe whispering in my ear as I worked, telling me the stories, how to write them down. And it is my deepest wish that you will pause from time to time as you read and try to see R. Shlomo… And that you will *mamash* hear in my words an echo of his own voice, telling these stories to you.

Still, I want to make a clear disclaimer. All these stories I received from R. Shlomo, and for this gift I will be indebted to him all my life. And all the "teaching" material is derived from his holy insights and deep wisdom. But the words are mine, not his. And the responsibility for any errors – or even deviations from the original versions – is also not his, but mine as well.

A word about the title: One night I sat down and made a list of those stories of R. Shlomo's that I remembered. Then for some reason I counted them. And there were exactly thirty-six stories. "*Gevalt!*" I thought. "How perfect. The number of stories must be just that, thirty-six – in Hebrew, *lamed-vav* [5] – and that must also be the title!"

The truth is, after that night I kept remembering more and more stories. So in the end this book includes many more than I first envisioned. Still I have maintained my original concept by organizing the tales into thirty-six chapters. Because, for me, the number "thirty-six" has a double significance…

First, it suggests the *lamed-vav tzaddikim*, the thirty-six holy people who sustain the world and who figure so prominently in many of these stories. And the salient feature of these *tzaddikim* is their hidden-ness — to the casual observer they appear at best ordinary, or at worst, grotesque or even sinful.

We all know how little R. Shlomo received during his lifetime of the recognition he so richly deserved. Here was a great Torah scholar, a Rabbi who brought literally thousands of estranged Jews back to *Yiddishkeit*. And he was laughed at by some, shunned by others. Only now that he is in *Gan Eden* is his greatness finally beginning to be appreciated. How concealed, how unassuming, was our dearest R. Shlomo. And how fitting that this volume honoring him has a title and number of chapters referring to his hidden holiness.

And the number thirty-six has another significance for me as well. In Hebrew, each letter represents a number (as above, where "*lamed*" is 30 and "*vav*" is 6). And there is a method of studying Hebrew words, based on the numerical values of their letters, which is called *gematria*.

The *gematria* of the Hebrew word for life, *chai*, is eighteen, so that the number thirty-six is twice *chai*, two times life. This made me think of R. Shlomo's two lives: his life here in this world – which to our everlasting sorrow has ended – and his life now in the World to Come. And it seemed appropriate to allude in the title of this book to both of R. Shlomo's lives, because those of us who loved him still hear R. Shlomo speaking to us from the Beyond, and still feel him illuminating our lives with his wisdom, his goodness and his love…

It is my greatest honor and deepest joy to have the privilege of sharing these stories with R. Shlomo's friends. But there are also tears in my eyes as I write, because his own story ended so soon, and the storyteller left us so suddenly.

I know that, like myself, none of us will ever forget him.

And sometimes when I walk in the Holy City of Jerusalem in the darkness of night, I look up at the sky, and see R. Shlomo's face shining among the stars. And I know, with absolute certainty, that from his throne in the highest Heavens, R. Shlomo is still telling us stories…

1. For example, R. Shlomo said that he heard all of the stories included here about the Sanzer Rebbe (See "The Sun Will Yet Rise Again" – p. 311) from the Rebbe of Bobov. Another story, "Neighbor Above, Neighbor Below" (p. 237) he specifically attributed to R. Abraham Yaakov of Sadygore.

2. Among the stories in this volume which R. Shlomo said he heard from an anonymous "someone" are "The Munkatcher Passport" (p. 93), told to him by the nephew of the main character; "One Last Chance," (p. 37), related by an unnamed *chasid* who had heard it from his father; and "A Real Jew" (p. 153), given over to him by an elderly Jew from B'nai Brak whose grandfather had actually been present at one of the Sokolover Rebbe's annual feasts.

3. For example, R. Shlomo identified the source of the story "Chatzkele Lekoved Shabbos" (p. 245) as the introduction to R. Berele Uschpitziner's own *sefer*, *The Three Shepherds*.

4. By some "holy coincidence" I recently purchased a book on the Holy Apter Rav – *The Heschel Tradition* (by Moshe A. Braun, Jason Aronson publishers, c. 1997.) And in it (p. 205) I found a story included in this volume – "The Holy Apter's Accounts" (p. 163) – that differed from R. Shlomo's version in many ways, but was still clearly identifiable as the same tale. And in *A Chassidic Journey* (based on *Shalsheles Boston* (Hebrew) by Meir Valach, translated by Eliezer Stone, Feldheim Publishers, c. 2002, pp. 30, 32, 33) I discovered several anecdotes about R. Dovid Lelover which are similar - but not identical - to those included in "The Way of Loving Kindness" (p. 277).

5. In Hebrew, the letter "*lamed*" represents the number 30, and "*vav*" represents 6. So together they equal 36.

You Never Know

Illustration: _____

"'But if you so much as open this door ... I will mamash *strangle you with these,' he said, curling his fingers into massive fists..."*

"Schwartzer Wolf"

We rely so much on our own senses for our perceptions of the world. We trust what we see with our eyes, what we understand with our minds. So we think we know who other people are and what the events of our lives are really about.

But the truth is, so much of what we see – or think we understand – is only the tip of the iceberg, the outside of the outside. How much do we know ... how much CAN we know ... about the deepest depths of another human being? How much do we understand ... how much can we understand ... of the Divine Wisdom and Purpose hidden in all the events of our lives? Or how our simplest actions reverberate in the highest Heavens? Here's an unbelievable story:

The Holy R. Avraham Bornstein of Sochatchov, the Avnei Nezer, was such a big genius that when he was only a small child he was already answering questions that his father's most brilliant students couldn't even understand. He mamash *had one of the greatest minds in the world.*

When the Sochatchover reached his bar mitzvah, *he married the daughter of R. Menachem Mendel of Kotzk. But a year later, sadly enough, he got very sick, and no one could do anything to help him. So his father went to the Heilige Kotzker Rebbe and begged him: "Rebbe, I'm so afraid for my son. Please pray for him. You know how much he has learned, how devoted he is to Torah. Surely if someone as holy as you reminds Heaven of his greatness, he will be found worthy, and he will live!"*

But the Kotzker only answered, "Ach, you call him learned? You call him devoted? What he's done is nothing. Nothing!"

The Sochatchover's father was amazed. "Rebbe, what are you saying? My son is only fourteen years old, yet he already knows the whole Torah by heart!"

But the Kotzker just shook his head, muttering under his breath, "He's done nothing. Nothing at all." And no matter how much the distraught father praised his son and tried to convince the Rebbe how accomplished the Sochatchover really was, the Kotzker did nothing but criticize him. R. Avraham's father just couldn't understand what was going on.

A few days later, the most miraculous thing happened. The Sochatchover recovered completely. His father was overjoyed, but he was still troubled about his meeting with the Rebbe of Kotzk. So he said to his son, " I know your father-in-law, the Kotzker, is a great Rebbe and a very holy man. But to tell you the truth, I mamash *don't understand him. I went to him with so much respect to ask him to pray for you. And I praised you so much; I was sure that if he reminded the Heavenly Court of your learning and knowledge you would be found worthy of the greatest miracles. But he wouldn't even listen to me. No matter what I said he just replied, 'You call that learning? It's nothing, nothing at all.'"*

The Sochatchover laughed. "Gevalt, father, is the Kotzker holy! Gevalt, is he wise! You thought that by praising me you would help me. But really, the opposite was true. You see, every person comes into this world to accomplish one special task, to make one special fixing. And once he has done this, there is no longer any need for him to stay here in olam hazeh.

"My father-in-law knew that I had only come into this world to learn Torah, and that if Heaven thought I had already learned everything I needed to know, there was no way to save my life. So when he kept answering, 'What, you call this learning? It's nothing!' he was actually saying to Heaven, 'R. Avraham has only begun to accomplish his task. His work isn't finished yet – there is so much more he needs to learn. Heavenly Court, You have to give him more time.'

"And this, Father, is what saved my life..."

So you see – what do we know? You never know...

The Funeral
of the Drunken Tailor

Our Rabbis teach us that the First Holy Temple was destroyed because the Jews of that time were guilty of the three cardinal sins: idol worship, the spilling of blood, and sexual immorality. And what about the Second Beis HaMikdash? Why did it fall to the Romans? Because the Yidden hated each other without reason. And so, our Sages conclude, senseless hatred is as terrible as the three worst sins in the world.

Why do we hate other people? Because we think we know everything about them – who they are, why they do what they do. Parents think, "These are my children, so I know what's going on with them." But sadly enough, much of the time we're totally wrong...

We so misjudge each other. That's why the Torah says that if we hate people, or even if we're only angry – we have to try to find a way to tell them, to talk to them about it. Because really, it might only be a misunderstanding.

Sometimes we meet people who seem to us a little bit crude, a little bit impure – certainly not holy. So we want to knock them off. But the truth is, we have no idea what a Yiddele might be doing when we're not looking. So the Holy Baal Shem Tov tells us that, even when we see others doing wrong, we have to believe that in the inside of their insides they're really the holiest of holy ... and deserving of the greatest miracles.

Everybody is created in G-d's Image. What does this mean? That just as G-d is so Deep, so Hidden – just as we can't see G-d – so too we can't really know what's going on in the depths of other people. And unless we love them with all our hearts, we'll never know...

So we have to remember: don't ever judge. Because you never know...

wo hundred years ago, in the city of Koretz, all the Jews were good, G-d fearing *Yidden*. They all kept Shabbos and ate only kosher food. They all *davened* three times a day. All, that is, except one – the tailor, the *schneider*. Avramele never went to the synagogue or to buy kosher meat. He never joined the Jews of Koretz in their community gatherings. The only place people ever saw him was in the local *cretchma* late at night, drunk. So Avramele was a total outcast. Okay, if people's clothes were torn they had to go to him; after all, he was the only tailor in town. But other than that, nobody ever spoke to him. And nobody cared about him at all.

Now, the rabbi of Koretz at that time was R. Pinchas Shapiro, one of the three greatest students of the Holy Baal Shem Tov. One day, after the morning prayers, R. Pinchas saw that a crowd of people had gathered in a corner of the *shul*. The *shammes* was trying to get a *minyan* together for something, but nobody wanted to join. R. Pinchas hurried over: "What's all this commotion? What's going on here?"

The *shammes* looked embarrassed. "It's nothing, Rebbe. Don't bother yourself about it."

But R. Pinchas insisted: "Tell me. I want to know."

"Well … it's just that the most disgusting Jew in the city – really, the lowest of the low – died today, and nobody wants to go to the funeral."

R. Pinchas stared at the *shammes*. "I didn't know there were any disgusting Jews in Koretz," he said coldly. "Just who in our city is considered so unworthy that no one will do the *mitzvah* of accompanying him to his final resting place?"

So the *shammes* told him, "Avramele the *schneider*, the tailor…"

R. Pinchas turned very pale. The people around him were afraid he might faint on the spot. To everybody's amazement, he started crying, *mamash* from the deepest depths of his heart. "I can't believe it," he sobbed. "*Gevalt, gevalt*! My dearest friend, the tailor, has left the world! What time is his *levaiyah*? I, for one, will certainly be there…"

Word quickly spread throughout Koretz that the Holy R. Pinchas was going to the funeral of Avramele the *schneider*. Now, everybody knew that the Rebbe never went to a funeral unless it was for a *tzaddik*, a holy man. So all the Jews of the city jumped to the conclusion that Avramele hadn't been just a tailor; he had been a *lamed-vav tzaddik*, one of the thirty-six hidden holy people. And suddenly everybody wanted to go to his funeral.

So all the *Yidden* of Koretz turned out for Avramele's *levaiyah*. Everybody was yelling and praying, "Tailor, please forgive us for the way we talked about you. We didn't know you were so holy… *Schneider*, please bless us…" All the mothers were begging, "Holy Avramele, please pray for our children … please bless my daughter Malka to get married … don't forget my daughter Sarah, she needs a good husband…" Everyone was crying. R. Pinchas walked right behind the casket, with big tears rolling down his holy cheeks. And you know, our rabbis tell us that if you want to know how important a person is in Heaven, look at his funeral. The funeral of Avramele the tailor was *mamash* a *gevalt*!

Now, on that particular day the Rebbe R. Yaivah, also a top student of the Holy Baal Shem Tov, happened to be in Koretz visiting his good friend R. Pinchas. And, of course, he also went to the funeral. He watched the whole scene quietly, not saying a word, but after the funeral was over he went up to R. Pinchas and said,

"R. Pinchas'l, my dear friend, what's going on here? Maybe you can fool the whole city into thinking that the tailor was holy. But you and I know better: he was really just what he seemed, a simple Jew, maybe even a little bit sinful. So tell me the truth. Why did you mourn him so much? What did he do to deserve such a funeral?"

"Ah, R. Yaivah," R. Pinchas sighed. "Really, we know so little about other people. Let me tell you the story…"

Do you remember the orphan girl, Feigele, who grew up in my house? My wife and I adopted her when she was only a baby, and took care of her like she was our own daughter. Well, six months ago she turned fourteen and was ready to get married. So we arranged a match for her with another orphan – a good boy, the sweetest of the sweet – from a nearby city. And we borrowed money from every single person we know to make her a beautiful *chuppa*. The wedding was a few weeks ago. And just minutes before the ceremony was supposed to start, Feigele's groom came running up to me and said,

"Rebbe, there's something you forgot! You didn't buy me a new *tallis*, a new prayer shawl." Because, you know, it's the custom for the bride to give her groom a new prayer shawl.

I said, "*Oy*, Eli, you're right. But please have mercy! I just can't get you a new prayer shawl right now. A *tallis* costs ten rubles, and not only don't I have a single penny left – I don't even know anybody I can borrow the money from. Let me get it for you in a few weeks."

But Eli was *mamash* crying. "Rebbe," he begged. "Everybody will laugh at me if I don't have a new *tallis*."

Again, I knew he was right. And he had nobody else in the world but me. How could I refuse him? So I said, "Okay, Eli. I'll do my best. Wait here, maybe G-d will open the gates for me."

I started walking down the street, trying to think of someone – anyone – from whom I could get the money for Eli's *tallis*. I didn't know where to go or what to do, so I decided that I'd just go up to the first house with a light on and ask for the money. Soon afterwards I saw a light in a window, so I just went right up to the house and knocked on the door. And – it was the tailor's house.

When Avramele opened the door and saw me standing there, his face lit up with joy. "Rebbe," he stammered, "I never dreamed you'd come to visit me. It's such an honor … I know I don't deserve it … thank you for coming. You know, I love you so much, I'd do anything for you…"

Gevalt, he made me feel so good!

"Sweet tailor," I said. "You know, the orphan Feigele is getting married tonight. And I need ten rubles to buy a new prayer shawl for her groom."

The tailor's face fell. "*Oy*, Rebbe," he almost whispered. "I wish I could help you, but you know how poor I am." And I did know. Then he said slowly, "But – I think I could give you one ruble."

I smiled at him. "*Schneider*," I said. "Thank you so much for whatever you can do. May the Master of the World bless you with everything."

The tailor gave me the one ruble, and I left. I still didn't know where to get the rest of the money, but somehow I felt lighter. I had so much more hope. I was walking slowly down the street, wondering where else to go, when suddenly I heard someone running after me. I stopped and waited. It was the tailor. And as he came up beside me, I saw that he was *mamash* crying like his heart was broken.

"Avramele!" I exclaimed. "What hurts you so much? How can I help you?"

"Rebbe," he sobbed. "G-d knows how poor I am. But from time to time I've managed to save a few pennies, and now I have – exactly nine rubles left. Holy Master, it's my whole life's savings. But if I gave it all to you … if I gave you all of my money now … do you think…" and he started crying so hard he could hardly speak. "… Do you think that I might … that maybe I could … have a place in the Coming World?"

I put my hands on Avramele's head, and I said, "Holy Tailor, I know how poor you are, I really do. But Feigele is waiting, her groom Eli is waiting – for them every minute is an eternity. If you do this great *mitzvah* and give all your money to me now, it will be because of you that their wedding will take place. And I swear to you by the G-d of Abraham, Isaac and Jacob, by the G-d of our Four Holy Mothers, that you will have a place in the World to Come…"

"And so," R. Pinchas told R. Yaivah, "I went to Avramele's funeral. And I cried as I walked behind his coffin. Because I could see that his soul was wrapped in the *tallis* he had bought with his last ten rubles for the groom of the orphan Feigele."

You know, we think we're so perceptive. We trust so much in what we see. But the truth is, if we only see with our eyes, we're sometimes mamash *blind. Because we can't penetrate to the deepest depths. Can we ever see in what kind of prayer shawl other people's souls are wrapped?*

We need to look at each other in a different way, not only with our eyes, but also with our hearts. And most of all we have to remember: no matter how wise we think we are, we never know

The Bookbinder

The Talmud says that when we learn, we should always say the words out loud. Otherwise we'll forget. Because actually uttering the words fixes the Torah in our souls.

The Holy Ishbitzer Rebbe has an even deeper teaching: When you kiss something, you don't speak. Because what happens with a kiss is beyond any words...

here was once a bookbinder named Moshe who lived in the city of Premishlan. Now Moshele was a quiet, unassuming person, and everybody thought that he was just a very simple *Yid*. But a few weeks after Moshe left this world, the Holy R. Meir of Premishlan went up to Heaven to speak to R. Shmuel Shmelke of Nikolsburg, one of the teachers of the Seer of Lublin. And whom did he find sitting next to the *Heilige* R. Shmelke on High but Moshele the bookbinder!

"Moshele!" R. Meir blurted out in surprise. "How is it that you are sitting here?"

Everyone in Heaven shouted at R. Meir, "Please, have a little respect! Didn't you hear the Heavenly Voice decree that from now on this man is to be called REB Moshe?"

Now, everybody knows that the *Heilige* Premishlaner was so humble that he never used the word "I." He always referred to himself in the third person. So now he tried again: "R. Meir is terribly sorry, REB Moshele. But he doesn't understand. He thought he knew you well, but he never realized you were a Rebbe."

"Please, Holy Master," Reb Moshele replied. "Don't apologize. To tell you the truth, I really was just a simple bookbinder, not a learned man. To me it was a great honor simply to prepare the holy books that others would use in their study. But let me ask you, do you know how to bind a book? You always have to trim the edges of the pages to make the sides of the book straight. These cut pieces just fall down to the floor. But of course, you only cut off the parts of each page that have no writing on them.

"All day I would trim the pages and bind them together. Then every night I would lie down on the floor and gather up all the edges I'd cut off. Of course, I thought these pieces were blank. Yet, blank or not, I kept remembering they HAD come from holy books. So I'd reverently kiss every scrap of paper, take them all to the cemetery, and bury them, as is fitting for fragments of holy *s'farim*.

"Two weeks ago, when I came up here to Heaven, all those pieces of paper were waiting for me. For the first time I could see what was really written on them. And so, as my reward for honoring them, I'm now sitting next to R. Shmuel Shmelke."

You know, paper with writing on it is holy. But it's not as holy as paper that appears blank. When you find this kind of holy paper, hold it up. Look at it with the light of a candle. But not the glow of a regular candle. With the light of the candle of your soul...

On this blank paper find your name, your father's name, your great-great-great grandfather's name. See how you are connected to all the Yidden in every place and in every time, all the way back to Avraham Avinu. Then imagine how it feels to find the names of your children – of your great-great grandchildren – on that blank piece of paper...

Let the day be soon when the writing on all the blank paper will be revealed...

One Last Chance

Imagine for a moment that you are sitting in a room, and there's a very bad smell. Completely turns you off, right? But if you sit there long enough, you get so used to the odor that it no longer bothers you.

It's the same thing on a spiritual level. We can reach the point where we no longer know the difference between the sweet fragrance of good and the rancid stench of evil. We've grown so accustomed to the foul smells of this world we don't even notice them any more...

he Holy R. Naftali Ropschitzer was at one time a follower of R. Mordechai of Neshchiz. Now, every good *chasid* always wanted to spend the holidays with his Rebbe. So the Ropschitzer liked to go to the Neshchizer for all the *Yomim Tovim*. But one year, as R. Naftali prepared to leave after Purim, R. Mordechai called him over and said, "Do me a favor. Don't come back for Pesach."

The Ropschitzer was appalled. Not to be with his Rebbe for Passover? Impossible! But, since Pesach was still four weeks away, he knew he had time to figure out a way to be invited back for the holiday.

R. Naftali thought and thought, and finally came up with a plan. A few days before Pesach he returned to Neshchiz, and went straight to the kitchen to help R. Mordechai's *Rebbetzin*, because he knew that thousands of people would be coming to the Neshchizer for Passover, and the *Rebbetzin* could use all the help she could get.

The Ropschitzer made himself absolutely indispensable to R. Mordechai's wife. Then, after working for several days, he said to her, "I've been so happy helping you. And I can't stop thinking about how special, how exalted, Pesach will be here in Neshchiz. I just wish I could stay to celebrate it with you.

The *Rebbetzin* was surprised. "What are you talking about? You're always here for the holidays."

"Well, this year your holy husband, my Rebbe, made it clear he doesn't want me around. But let me tell you, I'll really miss being with him! It's so important to me ... do you think maybe you could...?"

The *Rebbetzin* took the hint and asked R. Mordechai to let the Ropschitzer stay for Pesach. "I *mamash* need R. Naftali, he's such a help to me…" She begged and pleaded until finally the Neshchizer had to relent:

"All right, enough already. If it means so much to you, he can stay. But I'm warning you, he's going to make a lot of trouble for me."

The morning before Passover, the whole community of Neshchiz burned all their leftover bread to fulfill the *mitzvah* of removing and destroying all their *chametz* before the start of the festival. But you know, before Pesach we're not just burning bread. We're wiping out evil from the world – and from inside ourselves. We're cleaning out the deepest depths of our being.

After all the *chametz* was destroyed, the Ropschitzer felt completely cleansed. So he went to the *Beis Midrash* to learn. He was totally engrossed in his *sefer* when suddenly his nose began to twitch. The most terrible odor was seeping into the room. Then the door to the *Beis Midrash* burst open, and a *shlepper* came in. He was ragged and filthy, but worst of all, he *mamash* smelled awful! The Holy Ropschitzer was proud of his ability to tell the difference between a good smell and a bad one, and to him this man reeked of pure evil. R. Naftali thought he must have already committed just about every sin in the world, and was eager to do the few remaining *aveiras* he might have missed.

The *shlepper* came over to R. Naftali and said, "I've come to see the Rebbe."

It *mamash* took all of the Ropschitzer's strength not to hold his nose against the man's stench. He thought, "There's no way I'll allow this person in to see my Rebbe. The Holy Neshchizer just cleansed himself and the whole world of every trace of evil, and now this repulsive *shlepper* wants to defile him with his very presence. No way!" So he said to the visitor, "I refuse to take you to the Rebbe in the condition you're in. You stink of sin, you're *mamash* disgusting! Go home and wash yourself. Burn your *chametz* and do *teshuvah*, repent for all your wrongdoings. Then maybe come back. But the way you are now – how could you have the *chutzpah* to think of disturbing the Holy Neshchizer?"

Without another word, the *shlepper* turned around and walked out of the *Beis Midrash*. And the Ropschitzer went back to his learning, promptly forgetting about the whole incident.

A few minutes later the door to the *Beis Midrash* flew open again, and R. Mordechai Neshchizer ran into the room. "Did anyone just come in here?" he asked the Ropschitzer breathlessly. He seemed very anxious, but R. Naftali didn't notice. He answered carelessly,

"No. At least not anybody worth mentioning."

The Neshchizer looked at him angrily. "I didn't ask you if anyone was here who you thought was worth knowing. I asked you – and I'm asking you again – did anyone, anyone at all, just come into this *Beis Midrash*?"

The Ropschitzer still didn't get it. He said, "Well, now that you mention it, there was this awful *shlepper* who had the most terrible odor … really, such a disgusting person…"

R. Mordechai was *mamash* beside himself. "*Gevalt*! I knew this would happen if I let you stay. What did you do?"

"What was I supposed to do? I couldn't let such a low person in to see you. I threw him out!"

The Neshchizer's face flushed red with rage, and his voice quivered with anger. He looked the Ropschitzer right in the eye and said, "If you don't find that man and bring him back to me, I never want to see you again!"

The Ropschitzer couldn't understand what was happening. All he'd done was try to protect the Holy Neshchizer. So what had he done wrong? But he couldn't bear the thought of losing his Rebbe, so he dashed out of the *Beis Midrash* and ran all over the city, looking for the *shlepper*. Finally he found him … in the local tavern, drunk. The man looked and smelled worse than ever. But this time R. Naftali spoke to him with utmost respect, as if he were the holiest person in the world:

"My sweetest friend, please forgive me for the way I treated you before. I was so absorbed in my learning, I wasn't really paying attention. Please come back with me now to the Holy Neshchizer … I'll personally take you to see him…"

But the *shlepper* didn't even look at him. He didn't want anything to do with someone who had insulted him so terribly, and he wasn't about to go anywhere with the Ropschitzer. So he completely ignored him, and went on with his drinking.

So R. Naftali tried again: "Listen, my dear *Yid*, let me tell you the truth. The *Heilige* R. Mordechai really wants to see you. And he's so angry with me for kicking you out … if I don't bring you to him he'll never speak to me again. So I'm *mamash* begging you – please come back with me!"

But the *shlepper* still wouldn't budge.

The Ropschitzer had no choice. He picked the *Yiddele* up, and carried him over his shoulder all the way back to the Neshchizer.

R. Mordechai was overjoyed to see the *shlepper*. He hugged and kissed him, saying: "Where have you been? I've been waiting for you. *Gevalt*, I'm so happy to see you!"

Suddenly he remembered that the Ropschitzer was also standing there. But if R. Naftali expected the Rebbe to thank him for bringing the *Yiddele* back, he was sadly mistaken. R. Mordechai dismissed him curtly: "You can go now." Then he put his arm around the *shlepper* and led him into his house.

All of Pesach R. Mordechai was cold and distant to the Ropschitzer. But the *shlepper* was always at the Rebbe's side. And he looked like a new man. He was fresh and clean, he was wearing a new *bekeshe*, a new robe, and a new *shtreimel*. And he was *mamash* shining from one end of the world to the other.

After the holiday, the Neshchizer called the Ropschitzer into his private room. "It's time I explained things to you," he said. "You see, this man was not always a disgusting *shlepper*. Once he was one of my top students. What a level he was on – in his learning, his *midos*, his *davening*. He could have been a great Rebbe. Still he was only human, like all of us, and, sadly enough, he once made a big mistake. He knew I was aware of what he'd done, and was too ashamed to face me. So he left Neshchiz without a word, and could never muster up the courage to come back. And after that, for him it was just downhill all the way…

"Time went by, but I never stopped thinking about this student. So on Purim I *davened* all day that *Hashem* should bring him back. The *Ribbono Shel Olam* had mercy on me, and I saw prophetically that he'd come on the day before Pesach. But I also saw that you would be learning in the *Beis Midrash* when he arrived, and that you would throw him out.

"I knew that when this man decided to come to see me, he considered it his last chance. He thought, 'If the Holy Rebbe accepts me without saying anything about what I did, that will be my sign that my sin has been forgiven in Heaven, and I will stay in Neshchiz. But if his *chasidim* judge me harshly and send me away, I'll know that Heaven still considers me guilty. Then I'll leave Neshchiz and never come back.'

"That's why I told you not to come here for Pesach. I wanted you out of the way. And now you know, Naftali Ropschitzer. You were so quick to judge that you almost robbed this man of the chance G-d gave him to become whole again…"

Gevalt, we always have to be so careful. Many times we meet people – and we don't like how they look, we don't like how they smell. We want to turn them away. But instead we have to welcome everyone with an open heart: "My sweetest friend, I'm so glad to see you…"

Because when you meet somebody, you never know: It may be his last try. It may be his last chance to come back

But Nobody Knows

You know, it's really very sad. Everybody says they're searching for the truth. But would they recognize real emes *if it hit them in the face?*

Today all the doctors in the world are looking for a cure for cancer. Imagine that the top cancer specialist receives a letter. It's from a little Eskimo in Alaska who writes: "I'm just a simple Eskimo and I make my living catching whales. I have discovered that a certain part of the whale can be used to cure cancer, and I'd like to come to the next meeting of the International Association of Cancer Doctors to tell you about what I've found."

What do you think would happen? Do you think that all these important doctors, with all their MD's and PhD's, would ever invite a primitive Eskimo – who probably never even finished school – to their meeting? So what if his discovery might save millions of lives…?

Now imagine that a top official at the United Nations gets a letter from a notorious murderer who says: "I've found a way to bring peace to the world!" Of course he would immediately be invited to address the International Convention of Lovers of Peace. And if anybody had the chutzpah *to complain – "But this man is a mass murderer!" – he'd immediately be shouted down: "How can you judge this man so harshly? He's talking about peace! And who knows more about how to bring peace to the world than a murderer?"*

Let's face it. People very often can't tell the good from the bad. All they really notice is if someone's tie matches his shirt…

ne of the greatest Rebbes in Eastern Europe around one hundred and fifty years ago was the Ohr HaMeir, The Shining Light – one of the top students of the Holy Seer of Lublin. Just to give you an idea how sensitive he was – once while he was travelling, he stopped at an inn for the night. The innkeeper recognized that he was a Rebbe, and gave him the best room, with an especially comfortable bed and a big clock hanging on the wall. But the Ohr HaMeir couldn't sleep; he spent the whole night pacing around in his room. And the sound of his heavy footsteps echoing through the flimsy wooden *cretchma* kept the innkeeper awake as well. So finally the poor man knocked on the Ohr HaMeir's door to find out what was going on.

"Holy Master, I couldn't help but hear that you're still awake. What's the matter? Is there something wrong with the room, with the bed?"

"No, everything here is just fine. But let me ask you something. This clock in here, did it by any chance once belong to the *Heilige* Seer of Lublin?"

"Yes, as a matter of fact it did. The Holy Seer's son once stayed here, and I accepted this clock in lieu of payment. How did you know? And what does that have to do with your not sleeping?"

The Ohr HaMeir answered, "Let me tell you, there are two kinds of clocks. Most clocks mark the passage of time. When this kind of clock chimes the hour, it's like it is saying: 'One more hour has passed, you have one hour less in your life.' And if you understand its message you think, '*Oy vey*, who needs this?' And you go to sleep so you won't have to think about what the clock is telling you.

"But this clock – ah! It's a different thing altogether. With every tick it is saying, 'One second closer, one minute closer, one hour closer to the coming of the Messiah.' There is only one clock in the world that keeps time this way – that of the Holy Seer of Lublin. And once I recognized it and its message, I got so excited – how could I possibly sleep?"

One day the Holy Ohr HaMeir realized that he'd never in his life visited a certain nearby city. And for some reason he knew that he had to go there right away. So he told his driver to bring the wagon, and they took off. The trip didn't take long, and as they drove into town, the Rebbe kept looking around as if he were searching for something. Suddenly he noticed a man standing by the side of the road, leaning against a tree. He said to his driver, "Stop the wagon right here. I want to talk to that man."

Now, news of the Ohr HaMeir's visit had traveled faster than the Rebbe himself. All the top officials of the city had heard he was coming, and had come out to greet him. They saw the carriage come into town, and hurried toward it. And when they saw where it had stopped, they ran even faster.

"*Heilege* Rabbi," they called as they approached the wagon. "Holy Master, we are here to welcome you to our humble city. Let us escort you to our reception area and offer you a little something to eat, to drink. Then maybe we could…"

"Thank you very much," the Ohr HaMeir interrupted them. "I'll be with you in a minute. There's something I have to do first." And he turned toward the man by the side of the road.

The officials looked at each other uneasily. "Rebbe," they said. "Forgive us for interfering but the truth is, you shouldn't talk to that man. He has a very bad reputation. It's *mamash* beneath you to have anything to do with him. Please, come with us now…"

"But I want to talk to him," the Ohr HaMeir interrupted them again. "And really, you know, this has nothing to do with you." He turned again to the *Yiddele*: "Please, friend, join me on my wagon. We have something to discuss."

Now the officials were really upset. "Rebbe," they complained. "We can't believe you're doing this. You're demeaning yourself by even being seen with this man. We really must insist…"

This time the Ohr HaMeir completely ignored them. He turned to the *Yiddele*, who had climbed up beside him, and asked, "My dearest friend, do you have children?"

"Yes, I have a son of twenty and a daughter of fourteen."

"How perfect! Your girl is just the right age. You know, I myself have a son of fifteen. I think our children should get married!"

The officials of the city couldn't believe their ears. The Rebbe hadn't even asked the man his name. He didn't know his age, where he lived, how he made his living. Nothing! And already he was arranging a match for his son? They felt they had to speak up, so they said,

"Rebbe, we didn't mean to eavesdrop, but we couldn't help hearing … You know, this is all going much too fast. You don't know anything about this man. Please listen to us – his daughter isn't on the level to marry into a holy family like yours!"

But the Ohr HaMeir was adamant. "I know what I'm doing. I have a good nose for people, and I trust my own judgment!"

Still the welcoming committee wouldn't leave him alone. They were so insulted that he was ignoring their advice that finally the Ohr HaMeir proposed a compromise: "Okay, enough of this! I'll tell you what I'll do. Let's make a little test. Bring me twenty children. If they like this man, then my son will marry his daughter. If they don't, then I promise I won't have anything more to do with him." And the townspeople agreed … because everybody knows that children are absolutely THE best judges of character.

So the next day, all of the important people in the city – the chief rabbi, the mayor, the president of the *shul* – escorted the Ohr HaMeir and the strange *Yiddele* to a room in the city hall. They waited in silence for a few minutes. Then the door to the room flew open, and twenty children ran in, shouting and laughing. And to whom did they run? Not to the local leaders, whom they'd known all their lives. Not even to the Holy Ohr HaMeir. They ran straight to the *Yiddele*.

The Ohr HaMeir laughed out loud. "*Gevalt!*" he cried. "I knew it! You see, I was right. Okay, I've fulfilled our agreement. Now you do the same. No more arguments. My son is going to marry this man's daughter, and that's final!"

Now, the Holy R. Baruch Asher – *mamash*, one of the greatest of the Rebbes – had lived in this same city. And his widow, his *Rebbetzin*, still had a house there. Everybody knew that to R. Baruch Asher, every Jew was a *tzaddik*, a holy person. He greeted everyone – from the greatest Rebbe to the simplest *Yid* – in the same way. "Holy Master," he would say. And "Holy Water Carrier" or "Holy Tailor." No *Yid* was too low … or too sinful … for R. Baruch to pay him honor.

Once a group of rabbis came to R. Baruch Asher. A certain thief had been stealing from all the people in town, and they wanted the Rebbe to curse the man. They knew that R. Baruch had great power, and could make this little thief *mamash* disappear.

"I can't believe what you're saying!" R. Baruch cried, when they told him their plan. "You really expect me to curse the Holy Moshele?"

"But Rebbe," the rabbis exclaimed. "We all know Moshele isn't the slightest bit holy. He's a thief!"

R. Baruch looked at them for a long minute. Then he said, "Come with me." He turned around and led the way down the narrow steps to his basement. There he pointed to a barrel filled with what seemed to be rainwater.

"Do you see this?" he demanded. "These are the tears I shed begging G-d that I should never see evil in another human being. And you want these tears – my prayers for all these years – to have been for nothing because you are annoyed by a common thief?"

Before going home to arrange his son's wedding, the Ohr HaMeir went to pay his respects to R. Baruch Asher's *Rebbetzin*. She greeted him warmly: "Rebbe, I'm so happy to see you. Let me wish you *mazel tov*. I heard your son is getting married. And I also heard about the commotion you caused. It was just as my holy husband predicted. Let me tell you the story:

"Many years ago, everybody started talking about this man whose daughter you've chosen for your son. Some people decided they didn't like him, so they told all kinds of stories about him, saying he had done terrible things. They *mamash* put him to shame. Things got so bad that once they even tied him to the back of a wagon and dragged him through the streets of the city, with everyone jeering at him, spitting on him, and calling him names.

"My husband was sitting at our window at the time, and he saw everything that happened. He turned to me, and his eyes were filled with tears. He said, 'That man is completely innocent of everything people are saying about him. He's really very holy. But nobody knows…

"'Someday, when I am no longer in this world, a great rabbi will come to our city. The Rebbe will see this man, and he will choose his daughter as a wife for his son. And that will be your sign that what I say today is true: This *Yiddele* is – and always has been – the purest of the pure, the holiest of the holy…'"

The Talmud says that G-d can forgive us for all the sins in the world except saying bad things about another person. The worst aveira *we can do is tear people down.*

You know, G-d created every human being, endowed him with potential, and gave him a certain task, a certain kind of life. And G-d planted in every person – in the inside of his insides – a spark of His own Holiness.

How then do we have the audacity, the chutzpah, *to enter where even G-d trembles? For, as the Ibn Ezra teaches, when we tear a person down, it's not just that we hurt his feelings. We are* mamash *ripping apart his soul…*

The Knife
of Avraham Avinu

You know, we want so much to be holy. We try to keep all the mitzvos, *and to avoid the kinds of people, the kinds of places — even the kinds of thoughts — that we think will bring us down.*

But sadly enough, sometimes we are blinded by our own prejudices and preconceptions. Too often we judge things only by their outsides. And then our thoughts — even about the highest ideals in the world — won't lift us up. Just the opposite. They can mamash *bring us down to the lowest levels in the world…*

verybody knows that all the big Rebbes kept every *mitzvah* in the highest way. But each Holy Master had one particular commandment that he observed with special fire, with particular love … and which he took great care to perfect. For one, perhaps, it was *davening*; for another it was learning Torah day and night. Or maybe the Rebbe had special concentration when he put on *tefillin*, or when he shook the *lulav* on Sukkos.

When it came to the *Heilige* R. Yehudah Tzvi Hirsch of Stretyn, the top student of the Holy R. Uri of Strelisk, his special *mitzvah* was *kashrus*, observing the dietary laws. He was so strict about keeping kosher that he would *mamash* never eat in another person's house. He personally examined every bit of food that was brought into his home and — not only would he not eat meat unless it was prepared by his own kosher butcher — he even insisted on supervising the *shochet* during the *shechitah*, the ritual slaughtering.

One day the Holy Stretyner announced to his *chasidim*: "Bring the wagon. We're going for a ride."

All of his followers jumped into the carriage with their Rebbe, and they drove for a long time. Finally they reached a little village far from their home, one they'd never visited before. And on the main street of the town they saw a small rundown building that seemed to be some kind of a restaurant… At least it had a sign outside that said: "Meat. Eat here or take out."

"Quick! Stop here!" the Stretyner cried. "I'm hungry. Let's get a little snack."

The *chasidim* were shocked. The Rebbe never ate out anywhere, even in the house of a close friend or another Rebbe. Could he really have said he wanted to eat in this strange place in the middle of nowhere? They thought maybe the long ride in the hot sun had affected his mind – or, at least, they'd misunderstood him.

"Uh, Rebbe," one of them ventured, as the wagon began to slow down. "We're not sure we heard you correctly. Did you really say...?"

"That I want to eat something here?" the Stretyner finished for them. "Yes! Stop immediately!" The wagon jerked to a halt and, without another word, the Rebbe climbed down and walked toward the building, his *chasidim* following reluctantly behind him.

Inside, there was a woman taking orders for the meat. "Well, hi there," she greeted them with a smile and a wink. "So glad to see you! What'll you have?" She behaved – and was dressed – in such an immodest way that the *chasidim* were too embarrassed to look at her. They stared out the window, at the stains on the floor, the cracks in the walls … at anything but this woman. But the Stretyner seemed to like her immediately. And he treated her like he would the holiest *rebbetzin* – with utmost *kavod,* with the greatest honor:

"My sweetest young lady, could we have the privilege of ordering some of your excellent meat?"

"Sure, that's what we're here for, you know. Meat for how many?"

The *chasidim* couldn't believe how she spoke to R. Yehudah – so familiarly, without a trace of respect. Didn't she realize she was dealing with a great and holy man? But the Rebbe seemed undisturbed as he answered her with a smile, "A big order for myself and all of my students."

The woman showed them to a large table, and went to get their food. The table was streaked with grease and caked with dirt. The *chasidim* couldn't hide their distaste. "Rebbe," one began, "if you're really so hungry, I think there's another place just down the road…"

The Stretyner silenced him with a look. And just then the woman brought their meat. Now the *chasidim* really didn't know what to do. There was no way they would eat in such a place – obviously it couldn't be kosher. On the other hand – to their astonishment – R. Yehudah had already begun to eat heartily, and to refuse the food in an obvious way would only shame their Rebbe. Some of them noticed a dog begging under the table and slipped him their meat. Others hid the food in their pockets until they could go outside and find a garbage can. Only the Stretyner enjoyed the meal.

Suddenly the door to the kitchen burst open, and a man strode into the room. He had long wild hair and a strong fierce face. And he was playing with a knife that he had in his hand, tossing it up and then snatching it out of the air. The waitress went to his side: "Guys, I want you to meet my husband, the *shochet* and the owner of this restaurant."

The *chasidim* were *mamash* terrified. To them the man looked like a gangster … or worse. And to think they had almost eaten meat slaughtered by this thug! They pushed back their chairs, ready to run out. But the Rebbe, quietly and respectfully, stood up and offered the man his hand. The *shochet* seemed to notice the Stretyner for the first time: "Why, hello Rabbi. It's so nice to see you."

R. Yehudah *mamash* began to tremble. He said, in a strangely pleading voice, "Please, sir, could I speak to you alone for a few minutes."

"Well, I'm really very busy, but I guess I can spare a little time."

The Rebbe went with the man into a back room. He stayed only five minutes, and when he came out, his eyes were red and swollen. He walked silently back to the table where the *chasidim* were anxiously waiting, and sat down only long enough to say the blessing after his meal. Then he signaled his students and they all left, with the strange couple following behind them. As the Stretyner climbed onto the wagon, he turned and waved to the *shochet* and his wife. And they waved back at him. Then the wagon drove away.

R. Yehudah and his followers rode in silence for several hours. Only as they approached Stretyn did the Rebbe speak: "Okay, tell me the truth. Who ate the meat?"

The *chasidim* looked at each other. They *mamash* didn't know what to say. Finally one of them stammered, "Uh, Rebbe … you see … the fact is, I really wasn't feeling well … my stomach…"

"I have this weakness for starving animals," another chimed in. "So when I saw this poor dog I just had to…"

"Enough!" the Rebbe silenced them. "I know you didn't eat, and I know why. But let me tell you something. It's important to know when things are high and when they are low. But that isn't enough. The deepest secret of life is to be able to find the highest of the high even in what seems like the lowest place in the world…

"Now listen to me. When Abraham went up onto Mount Moriah to sacrifice Isaac, he carried with him a special knife. That knife has been preserved until today, entrusted to the care of the head of the *lamed-vav tzaddikim* of each generation. I don't think I need to tell you how holy it is.

"The owner of that restaurant is the leader of the thirty-six hidden holy people of our time. The meat that he served us – that you wouldn't eat – had been slaughtered with the Knife of Avraham Avinu. And I was begging him to let me touch that knife.

"The *tzaddik* said he was sorry, but he couldn't do as I asked. The only one who can touch the knife … besides him, of course … is Eliahu HaNavi, Elijah the Prophet. But he said he could let me see it. So while we were alone in his room he showed me the knife, and I saw that engraved on it were the words: *Ma'acheles shel Avraham Avinu* – the knife of our Father Abraham."

The *chasidim* couldn't believe what they were hearing. What had they done! Not only hadn't they had faith in their Rebbe. Worse – they had relied on their own ideas of what holiness should look like, should feel like. They had gotten hung up on appearances, and so they had missed their chance, *mamash*, to taste real holiness.

So the *chasidim* decided that after they'd escorted the Stretyner home, they were going right back to the restaurant to see that holy knife. They went through the motions of putting the horses away until they saw the Rebbe disappear into the *Beis Midrash*. Then they jumped back onto the wagon and took off. They returned to the same village, to the same street, but in the place where the restaurant had stood, there was only a decrepit, boarded up shack. It seemed to be completely empty; there was no sign of life … or of the *shochet* and his wife. The *chasidim* couldn't understand it. So they asked some people passing by,

"What happened to the meat restaurant, the butcher shop that was right here? We had a meal there just hours ago."

And the people told them, "The restaurant? Oh, it went out of business a long time ago. That place has been deserted for years…"

The Bakers

The Holy Apter Rav, R. Avraham Yehoshua Heschel, had a son named R. Yitzhak Meir. One day R. Meir said to his father, "You know, we're *mamash* blessed to be living in Poland. Here there are so many holy Rebbes, so many *tzaddikim*, to guide us in our service of G-d and to lift our souls up to Heaven. But in Germany there is absolutely nobody. How do the German Jews survive?"

And his father answered, "You'll see, Yitzhak Meir. You'll see…"

Of course, as the son of the Rebbe, Yitzhak Meir spent all his time learning Torah. Nobody expected him to work. Still, even a Rebbe's son has to eat. So his father sent him two rubles every Friday, to support him.

The Friday after this conversation, R. Meir didn't receive his usual two rubles. But he wasn't too worried; he still had a little left from the week before. "I guess my father was so busy with other people's problems that he just forgot," he thought. "He'll probably pay me double next time." But the next week there was also no money. And by the third week, when again the money didn't come, R. Meir was *mamash* desperate.

Now the Apter Rav was so holy that you couldn't just walk in and remind him to send you money, even if you were his son. So R. Yitzhak Meir went to a fellow *chasid* and said, "I know it's a lot to ask, but could you please go to my father and find out why he hasn't been sending me my two rubles?"

The *chasid* was very reluctant: "I've never been alone with your holy father before. How can I ask him for money, even for you?" But R. Meir begged him so much, he finally agreed to go. He knocked timidly on the Rebbe's door, and when the *Heilige* Apter answered he said shyly, "Rebbe, I really hate to bother you … I know you're busy, you have so many important things to deal with… But, you see, your son asked me to come to you. It's about his two rubles a week. He doesn't understand why you've forgotten him…"

The Apter Rav barely looked up from his learning. "So, Yitzhak Meir thinks I'm going to support him all his life? Go back to my son and tell him it's time he started taking care of himself."

The *chasid* was shocked. "But Rebbe," he cried. "All R. Meir knows about is learning Torah. He doesn't know anything about earning a living!"

"So it's time he learned," the Apter said. "But I guess I should help him get started." He thought for a minute, then left the room. When he returned, he handed the *chasid* some rubles and said, "Give this to Yitzhak Meir. It's the last money he's going to get from me. Tell him I said he should go immediately to Italy and use these rubles to buy *esrogim* for Sukkos. Between Rosh Hashanah and Yom Kippur he should go to Germany; there he can sell the *esrogim* for a lot of money, and live from the profit for the rest of the year."

The *chasid* ran right back to R. Yitzhak Meir and delivered his father's message. R. Meir was *mamash* beside himself! He couldn't bear the thought of not being with his holy father for the High Holy Days. But he knew he had no choice. "Oh well," he consoled himself. "At least I'll be back by Sukkos."

So R. Meir went to Italy and bought *esrogim*. Then, as his father had instructed, he went to Germany, to Leipzig. And the Apter was right: R. Meir sold his entire stock for an unbelievable profit. So, feeling very rich – and also very pleased with himself – he hired a special carriage to take him back to Apt right after Yom Kippur. He was determined to make the trip in four days, even if he had to travel day and night, so he wouldn't miss one minute of the Sukkos holiday in his father's *sukkah*.

But the day before Yom Kippur it started raining. And it rained all of Yom Kippur, the entire next night, and all of the day after that. Floods washed away most of the roads, and the rest were rivers of mud. The driver told him, "There's no way we can travel in this weather. It's no use. We'll have to wait…"

It not only rained, it *mamash* poured until the day before Sukkos. By then R. Meir knew that even if they started right away, he'd never make it back to Apt in time. Like it or not, he'd have to spend the holiday in Germany.

So the first night of Sukkos, R. Yitzhak Meir, feeling very sorry for himself, went to the synagogue in Leipzig. He found a place in the last row and just sat there, with his eyes closed, daydreaming about Sukkos in Apt. He was so lost in his thoughts that when he finally opened his eyes and looked around, he saw that he was the only person left in the *shul*. Because on top of everything else, in his misery he'd forgotten that – unlike in Poland – in Germany *davening* takes all of two minutes!

"*Oy gevalt*," he thought. "Now what do I do?" He'd been so busy thinking about the beauty of Sukkos in Apt that he'd missed his chance to be invited to a meal in somebody's *sukkah*. And eating in the *sukkah* is the most important *mitzvah* of the holiday.

"*Oy, Ribbono Shel Olam*!" he wailed silently. "Master of the World, what's going on here? I never wanted to come to Germany in the first place … it was all my father's idea. It isn't my fault that it rained like mad and I got stuck here in Leipzig, with no friends and no *sukkah*. Now, if all of that wasn't bad enough, I don't even have a place to go for the holiday meal!" Suddenly he was angry. "Okay, *Ribbono Shel Olam*. There's nothing I can do about this mess. If You don't want me to eat in a *sukkah*, then that's the way it will be. I'll just sit here in this *shul* all night. " And he leaned back in his seat and closed his eyes again.

A few minutes later R. Meir heard someone come into the synagogue. He opened his eyes and turned around. The *Yid* who had entered seemed to be a baker: at least he was covered from head to toe with flour. Yitzhak Meir watched him head toward the front of the *shul*; then he shut his eyes again and started to slouch back down in his seat. But when the man started *davening* – so loudly that his voice carried all the way to the back row where R. Meir was sitting – he sat upright. He couldn't believe his ears. The man, *mamash*, said everything wrong! To begin with, he started with the first line of the weekday prayers, not the holiday ones. Then he got the rest of the service completely out of order. And he mispronounced almost every word. It all sounded so funny that R. Meir could barely keep himself from laughing out loud. At least, he thought, this *Yid* was cheering him up!

When the baker finally finished praying and started to leave, R. Meir knew this was his last chance. He hurried up to him and said, "Excuse me, but I'm a stranger in Leipzig. Do you think I could go home with you and eat in your *sukkah*?"

"I have to warn you," the man replied. "There's a strong wind tonight, and my *sukkah* is high up on my roof. If it didn't blow down already, I'm happy to have you. If it did, we're both out of luck!"

So R. Yitzhak Meir went with the baker to his house. But what a house … a rundown shack with broken windows and the door hanging off its hinges. The baker led the way to the roof up a shaky ladder with every other rung missing. And when they finally got to the top, there was the *sukkah* – if you could really call it that. It was in worse shape than the house; the wind blew in through all the cracks, and it shuddered and shook with every gust. There were no decorations, only a three-legged table and some broken stools. R. Meir couldn't help but compare it to his father's *sukkah* in Apt – so strong, so elegant, so holy. To think he had to spend Sukkos in such a place! But he knew it was this or nothing. So he went in, and sat down on a stool that looked so weak, it was *mamash* a miracle it didn't collapse under his weight.

Now you know, on Sukkos, before we eat, we say a special prayer inviting the Seven Holy Shepherds – Abraham, Isaac, Jacob, Moses, Aaron, Joseph and King David – to come to our *sukkah*. The first night our special guest is Avraham Avinu, the second it's Yitzhak, and so on through the week.

The baker put a bottle of wine and some *challah* and fish on the table, then stood in the doorway to invite the holy guests. He opened his big prayer book to welcome Abraham, but he couldn't find the place. He just stood there, flipping through the pages, until finally R. Meir had to help him. At last he started reading the greeting, but again every other word was a mistake. Eventually he managed to say, "Holy Avraham Avinu, our Holy Father Abraham, please be my guest in the *sukkah* tonight."

Just then R. Meir heard footsteps coming across the roof. And a *Yiddele*, also covered with flour, entered the *sukkah*. His host stood up to greet him: "Thank you so much for coming…" He turned to R. Meir: "I want you to meet my friend, Abraham the baker."

But Yitzhak Meir was barely paying attention. He was far away, imagining himself in the *sukkah* in Apt. There he'd be sitting next to his *heilige* father, and would be surrounded by holy, exalted people – rabbis and scholars – instead of sharing a drafty *sukkah* with two dusty bakers. He barely said hello to the other guest.

The first baker made *Kiddush* and said the blessing over the bread. He served a little herring. Then he turned to the other baker, and the two of them talked in hushed tones all night. But R. Meir didn't bother to taste the meager food. And he didn't even try to hear, much less take part in, the bakers' conversation. What could they be talking about anyway, the temperature in the oven? All he could think about was Apt: the sumptuous feast they would be having, the exalted Torah they would be learning…

R. Meir had no choice but to stay with the baker for both days of Sukkos. He couldn't sleep at all the first night, with the *sukkah* rattling and shaking in the wind. And he sat hunched miserably in a corner all of the next day. The second night he automatically found the baker the right place in his *siddur*, and then drifted away in thought so quickly he barely heard the baker invite Yitzhak Avinu into the *sukkah*: "Tonight, please let my special guest be our Father Isaac." And he hardly glanced up when again there were footsteps, and his host introduced another flour-covered baker – this one so tall he almost hit his head coming in the low door: "Please meet my friend, Yitzhak the baker." All he could see was a vision of the *sukkah* in Apt: himself sitting next to his father at the elegant table, singing all the special holiday songs at the top of his lungs, revelling in the joy of the festival. Oh, how he wished he were home!

The third night, maybe Yitzhak Meir's body was sitting in a wretched *sukkah* on a rooftop in Leipzig. But in his mind he was already on the road. He didn't even notice when again a guest came in – another baker, this one named Yaacov. He was too busy planning how he would leave at first light the next morning, and drive like crazy to get back to Apt by the last day of Sukkos. "At least I'll have one day to sit in a real *sukkah*," he thought…

So early the next morning R. Meir got onto his wagon, and drove day and night. On Hoshana Rabba, the last day of the festival, he finally arrived in Apt, and went right away to find his father.

Now a very special thing happened with some of the really big *tzaddikim*. The minute the Rebbe gave you his hand, suddenly your eyes, your heart and your mind were opened, and you saw and understood everything.

The Apter Rav was overjoyed that his son had finally come home. He gave him his hand and said with a smile, "So, Yitzhak Meir, what do you think about Germany now?"

Suddenly Yitzhak Meir was back on a rooftop in Leipzig, in a broken-down *sukkah* with the wind blowing in. And he saw the three guests – three *shleppers* covered with flour – with new eyes. Abraham, Isaac and Jacob – the three Holy Fathers themselves. *Gevalt*!

Then the Apter Rav said to his son, "You see, Yitzhak Meir, it is possible to sit, *mamash*, in a place of utmost holiness, and not even be there!"

Two Glasses of Tea
and
A Load of Lumber

Everybody talks about finding his or her "soulmate." But what does the word "soulmate" really mean?

My soulmate is the one person in the world without whom I cannot live. Even the first time we meet, I feel like I've already known him or her for a thousand years. I mamash can't imagine there was a time when we thought we were strangers. Because suddenly it's clear to both of us that we were always part of each other's hearts.

You know, I can pray for something like a new house or a fancy car. Still, at the same time that I'm asking G-d to help me get what I want, I know where I can find it myself. I can go to a real estate agent or a car dealer. But when I pray for my soulmate, do I have any idea where he or she might be? My bashert might be in France, in Japan, in South Africa, in India, or right next door. How do I know? It takes G-d to bring us together. And the way He does it is the greatest miracle in the world.

Sometimes we meet a person who we mamash think might be our soulmate. Yet we hesitate. We don't want to jump into anything right away. We have to think about it first, weigh the pros and cons, consult other people – our brothers or sisters, our best friend, even strangers on the street:

"You know, I just met this wonderful man, this gevaldig woman – do you think I should get married?"

Do you know what the problem is? We think we met this other person by chance. We don't – we can't – believe that we met because of our prayers. Here I am, living in Jerusalem, and I'm begging G-d to send me the one person in the world who will fill my heart and complete my soul. And then I meet this amazing man or woman, who maybe is visiting here from Canada, at a friend's Shabbos table. Dare I believe that we are connected?

But if you believe in miracles, if you are tuned into the way G-d is taking care of you and leading you in your life, then you understand the truth. The Gemorah says that when G-d created the world, it was mamash an incredible miracle. But it doesn't compare to the miracles He performs to bring two soulmates together.

All the Rebbes say that finding your soulmate is as hard as crossing the Red Sea. So often we think we'll never find the right person for us, because nobody we meet really fits. Oy, there are misfits everywhere – like we were at the Red Sea.

With the water on one side of us, the wild animals all around us, and the Egyptians behind us, it seemed there was no place for us...

That's how we sometimes feel. And we cry, "Gevalt, Ribbono Shel Olam, I was born in the wrong time. There is no place for me, nowhere for me to go. There is no one like me anywhere!"

Then suddenly G-d opens the gates, and takes the whole thing into His own hands...

he Holy Alshich, Rabbi Moshe ben Chaim, got married when he was very young, only fourteen years old. Now the Alshich HaKodesh had a special custom: he would wake up every day at three o'clock in the morning to learn. And his wife, because she loved him so much, would get up at the same time, to serve him tea. She would fix the tea and put it on the table very quietly, so she wouldn't disturb him.

Sadly enough, after only three years, the Holy Alshich's wife left the world. And his mother felt so bad for her son: "He may be holy and learned, but he's only seventeen, and now he's all alone. It must be so hard for him, with no one to help him." She prayed day and night that he would marry again soon, but in the meantime, she wanted to do something to make the Holy Alshich's life easier. So she decided to bring him his tea when he got up early to learn.

But after a few months, the Alshich's mother realized she was too old for this. She *mamash* didn't have the strength to get up every day at three o'clock in the morning. So she started looking for someone she could hire to bring her son his tea.

Now, in the house next to the Alshich there lived a water carrier, a simple but pious *Yiddele*. And he had a daughter who was a little younger than the Holy Alshich. R. Moshe's mother liked this girl, and decided to ask her to take care of the tea. She gave her simple instructions:

"All you have to do is make the tea and put it on the table next to my son. But above all, be very quiet about it. Don't interrupt his learning."

Early the next morning the Holy Alshich burst into his mother's room and *mamash* woke her up: "Mother, tell me fast! Who brought me my tea this morning?"

"Why, Bracha Feigele, the water carrier's daughter."

Without another word the Holy Alshich ran to the house next door and knocked loudly. When the water carrier sleepily answered, he asked to speak to his daughter. And as soon as she appeared, the Holy Alshich demanded, "Why did you put two glasses of tea on my table this morning?"

Bracha Feigele seemed surprised by his question. "It seemed like the right thing to do – to bring one glass for you, and one for the man you were learning with."

"*Gevalt!*" the Holy Alshich cried. "I can't believe this! My wife prepared my tea for three years, yet she never made two cups. My mother took care of the tea for several months, and she only brought one glass. But you! Right away, the first night, you could see that I was learning with Eliahu HaNavi, Elijah the Prophet. So answer me fast – will you marry me?"

Because obviously, she was his real soulmate!

Our Rabbis teach that, forty days before a person is born, a bas kol – *a Heavenly voice – calls out whom he or she is to marry. Why? Because,* gevalt, *is life deep! Relationships between people are so deep. And only the Master of the World – the One, the Only One Who Knows the deepest depths of every human being – can make the right match between two people. Here's another story:*

he Holy Baal Shem Tov had a *chasid* who was a lumberjack. He was a simple but good man, sincerely devoted to *Hashem*. And as his lumber business was prosperous, when his only son reached marriageable age, a number of excellent matches were proposed for him. But there was a problem. As soon as the boy saw a prospective bride, he would collapse in a dead faint.

His father brought in all the doctors in the area to try to help his son. But the doctors not only couldn't heal him – they couldn't even find out what was the matter. Finally the *chasid* went to the Holy Baal Shem Tov for advice. But the Rebbe only said:

"Don't worry. When he meets the right one, he will not faint."

Now, this *chasid* made his living by chopping down trees in the forest, cutting them up into lumber, and casting them into a nearby river. The strong flow of the stream would carry the logs to the town at the bottom of the mountain, where his agent would sell them. Only when the lumber had been sold in the city would the lumberjack be paid for his work.

One winter, the *chasid* managed to cut more trees than usual. He was very excited, thinking he'd make a big profit. But soon after he had put all the logs into the river, there was a terrible storm. It rained so hard that the river overflowed its banks and the water flooded the countryside, carrying off the lumber. All the wood was lost, and with it the lumberjack's dreams of prosperity. In fact, until he delivered another load to the city, he had no money at all. What would his family live on in the meantime? So, being the good *chasid* that he was, he again went to the Holy Baal Shem Tov for help.

The *Besht* looked at him for a long moment, then said quietly, "I'm afraid I can't help you. You'll have to become a beggar."

The *chasid's* eyes filled with tears. He was ashamed to think he'd fallen so low that he'd have to ask other people for money. "Please, Rebbe," he cried. "Isn't there anything else I can do?" But the Holy Baal Shem only shook his head. And the *chasid* knew he had no choice.

So the former lumberjack began to travel all over Poland, begging in all the towns and villages. He felt so broken, but he had one solace: whenever he had time, he'd stop in the local *Beis Midrash* and learn Torah.

One day he came to a large town some distance from his home. He made his rounds, begging for money, and then, as usual, went to the local House of Study. He was sitting there, engrossed in his learning, when a prominent resident of that particular city – whose house the *chasid* had visited earlier in the day – came over to him. "You know," he said, "I've been watching you. When I saw you before, I thought you seemed different from most of the *shleppers* who come to town. And now I'm sure of it. Tell me, how much do you earn a day begging?"

The *chasid* was embarrassed. "Not much," he murmured. "Maybe a ruble, a ruble and a half."

"I have an offer for you," the man said. "I am quite wealthy, and have a thriving business. But my business affairs take up so much of my time that I no longer learn as much Torah as I'd like. And a house without Torah is such an empty place… So I'll make a deal with you. I'll pay you two and a half rubles a day just to sit and learn in my home. And whenever you want, you can take your pay and go back to your family."

And of course the *chasid* immediately agreed.

For several weeks the former lumberjack happily learned Torah in the businessman's house. He became quite fond of the *Yiddele's* whole family, especially his lovely daughter – who reminded him of his own children. Then, late one night, he heard the rich man and his wife talking in hushed tones in their bedroom. And he realized that the woman was crying. So the next morning at breakfast he said to them,

"I don't mean to intrude on your private affairs, but last night – well, I couldn't help overhearing that … uh … it seemed to me you're upset about something. And you've both been so kind to me … I was wondering if there is anything I can to do help you…"

The businessman and his wife, after some hesitation, told him that their daughter had just reached the right age to get married. All the matchmakers were trying to find a husband for her, but every time she was introduced to an eligible man, she fainted. And nobody had been able to help her overcome this problem.

The *chasid* smiled sadly to himself. "I understand the difficulty quite well," he said, thinking of his son. "You know, I am a follower of the great Rebbe, the Holy Baal Shem Tov. Just the other day I was thinking about returning home and going to see him. Why don't you and your daughter come with me? Maybe the Rebbe can help her."

So the *chasid* and the businessman and his family set out the next day, and within two weeks they were standing before the Holy Baal Shem Tov. But strangely, when the Rebbe saw them he said, "I'll be happy to talk to you, but first…" He turned to his *chasid*: "Please, go get your wife and son. Ask them to wait in the next room, then come back to me and we'll discuss everything."

The *chasid* couldn't understand his Rebbe's request, but of course he did as he was told. He brought his wife and son, then returned to the Holy Baal Shem's private room where the businessman's family was waiting. The *Besht* listened quietly as the rich man explained their problem, and then he asked,

"Tell me, can you give your daughter a good dowry?"

"Oh yes," the businessman answered eagerly. "You know, until recently I barely made enough money to support my family. Then the greatest miracle happened. One morning, after a particularly bad winter rainstorm, we woke up to find our front yard covered with lumber. We had no idea where the wood had come from, and no way to return it to the original owner. So, after consulting a Rav, we sold it all to a lumberyard and made so much money that I was able to start my own business – which, thank G-d, is very profitable. So yes, we can provide well for our daughter."

The Holy Baal Shem Tov smiled. He said to his *chasid*, "Please bring in your wife and son." When they came into the room, the *chasid's* son looked at the businessman's daughter, and the rich man's daughter looked at the former lumberjack's son. And neither of them fainted.

"How great are the ways of *Hashem*!" the Baal Shem cried. Turning to his *chasid* he said, "You see, G-d brought it about that you should lose all your lumber, and that this man should be the one to find it and become rich. And everything that happened after that – your becoming a beggar and learning in his house – was only intended to bring your son and his daughter together. *Mazel Tov*!"

It Depends On
Your Point of View

Everybody knows there is Heaven, and then there's Hell. But there is also such a thing as living in Paradise – and also, G-d forbid, in the other place – right here in olam hazeh.

Sometimes, when I look at this world, I have to admit that a few things here and there are pretty good. But mostly I complain about this and I kvetch about that, and I find two million things about olam hazeh that are just plain rotten. And when this is the way I see the world, I might just as well already be in hell.

To be in Paradise is just the opposite. Yes, I see things in this world that maybe need fixing. But that's not where I focus my attention. Instead, I thank G-d every day, every moment of every day, for the great good He showers upon us – sometimes even hidden within what seems to be bad.

Ah, but to have this kind of vision that everything is good, the light inside us must be so strong, so deep, so holy…

ou know, in former not-so-good days, the government of Russia was always making harsh decrees against the Jews. *Gevalt!* Most *Yidden's* lives were so hard, so bitter. And the suffering! People would always look to their Rebbes for help, hoping their prayers could convince Heaven to bring some relief.

Once, when the Russian government issued a particularly heavy decree, the Holy R. Elimelech of Lizensk, The Noam Elimelech, began to cry and scream and shout to Heaven about all the troubles of the Jews in this world. Then he decided that this time, words weren't enough. So he announced a public fast, and he himself didn't eat or drink for three days. Yet the decree remained in place. R. Elimelech couldn't understand why Heaven wasn't responding, and – even more – why those holy *tzaddikim* already in the other world were keeping silent as well.

The next night, R. Elimelech, exhausted by his fasting, fell into a deep sleep. And his Rebbe, the exalted Maggid of Mezhirech, came to him from the upper world in a dream. The Noam Elimelech asked him, "Holy Master, how can you be silent at a time like this, when there is such a terrible decree against the Jews?"

And the Maggid answered, "It is only from your perspective, below, that things look so bad. Here in Heaven we don't see troubles, we see only good. This is the world of truth; *mamash* nothing is hidden from us here.

I know the Heavenly reason for this decree, and I've not only accepted it, I've agreed to it. So how can I try to get the *Ribbono Shel Olam* to cancel it, as you ask in your prayers?"

"But Rebbe," R. Elimelech cried, "What should we do? Our lives are so hard, we suffer so much. Do you mean that we shouldn't pray, we shouldn't ask the Master of the World to help us, to take away our pain?"

"G-d forbid!" the Maggid cried. "G-d forbid you should ever stop praying! As long as you are in *olam hazeh* there's no other choice – you must act according to the way you understand your world. If you see things that you think are wrong, if you feel pain, you must fall down on the ground and beg the *Ribbono Shel Olam* for help. And, because of your prayers, the Merciful One may nullify the harsh decree, and find a different way to accomplish its hidden purpose.

"But you know, even in your world a person can reach the level that he can see the good in everything. The truth is, not many can attain this *madreigah*. But there was once such a *tzaddik* – R. Nachum Ish Gamzu. He *mamash* felt the pain of every *Yid*. But he always remembered there was another, higher point of view. And he was so holy that he could say, even about all the troubles of the world, '*Gam zu l'tovah*', this too is for the good…"

Imagine for a moment that you walk into a hospital and meet a doctor, a surgeon. He seems like a nice, normal person. But then you follow him into a big white room, and see him standing over someone lying on a table. He has a bloody knife in his hand. If you don't know what's going on you'll think: "Gevalt, this man is a murderer! I've got to call the police!"

What isn't apparent, at that moment, is that a healed man will later get off the table and have a new and better life…

The truth is, G-d is constantly operating on our world. But to us it sometimes seems cruel, because all we notice is the blood and the pain. We are only seeing the world with the eyes of below.

So we must fix our eyes. We must lift up our way of seeing, so we can begin to look around us with the eyes of above, the eyes of Heaven. And when we are able to perceive the world with the eyes of eternity – with the eyes of Mashiach – things look pretty good after all…

Schwartzer Wolf

The Talmud says that the lamed-vav tzaddikim *are even holier than the Prophets. A prophet only hears G-d speaking to him at certain times, under certain conditions. But the thirty-six hidden holy people are so high, so exalted, that they always hear G-d's Voice...*

Did you ever wonder how the day ends and the night comes in its place? It's really very simple. The Ribbono Shel Olam says "Goodnight" to the world. Then the sun sets, the sky gets dark, and the moon and stars come out. We don't hear anything. But – can you believe it? – the thirty-six, mamash, *hear G-d's Voice when He says "Goodnight" to the world.*

And in the morning? How does the night turn back into day? The Master of the World simply says "Good morning." And right away the moon and the stars give way to the light of the sun. We still don't hear a sound. But can you imagine the exalted way the lamed-vav tzaddikim *start their day? They* mamash *hear G-d wishing "Good morning" to all His creation...*

Everybody knows the *chasidic* Masters were on the absolutely most exalted level. And one of the greatest of them all was the *Heilige* R. Yisrael Hofstein, the Kozhnitzer Maggid. He was *mamash* the holiest of the holy.

One morning, there was a knock on the Maggid's door. And when he opened it, whom did he find standing there but the rabbi of the nearby town of Czenslochov, crying from the deepest depths of his heart.

"My dear Rabbi," R. Yisrael said, leading the man into his private room. "Please, sit down and tell me what hurts you so much. What can I do to help you?"

"I'm sorry, Rebbe," the rabbi sobbed. "But I'm *mamash* at the end. My wife and I have been married for so long, almost twenty years. But we've never been able to have children. And the pain of being without a child ... I just can't stand it any more...

"To tell you the truth, I'm really not much of a *chasid*. I've never been to a Rebbe before in my whole life. But I heard you are a really great rabbi, and that you can do miracles. So please, Holy Master, help us. If you pray for us, surely G-d will have mercy and we will have a baby."

The Kozhnitzer Maggid closed his eyes and sat very still, lost in the deepest concentration. Then after a moment he raised his head and looked at his visitor sadly. "My sweetest friend," he said, "I'm so sorry. I'm afraid all the Gates of Heaven are closed to you and your wife. And I'm not strong enough to open them."

"How can that be?" the rabbi cried. "You are so exalted, so holy. Surely you can do something to help us!"

But the Maggid just shook his head.

The rabbi started crying even harder. "Rebbe, I *mamash* can't bear to leave this world without children! Isn't there someone, somewhere, who can open the Gates for us…?"

"Well," R. Yisrael said thoughtfully, "there is one person. All the Gates of Heaven are open for him. But I have to warn you, it's not easy to see him. Tell me, my dear Rabbi, have you ever heard of a *Yid* who lives near your city who's called Schwartzer Wolf?"

"Schwartzer Wolf! You can't mean that disgusting woodcutter who lives in the forest! Why, he's so vulgar, so cruel, so brutal, nobody wants anything to do with him. He almost never comes to town or *davens* in our *shul*. But when he does, we fall all over ourselves trying to avoid him!"

"Yes, that's him," the Maggid said quietly. "I want you to know, the Schwartzer Wolf is the head of the *lamed-vav tzaddikim* of our generation. He's *mamash* the holiest man alive. If you can get him to invite you for even one meal of Shabbos and to give you his blessing … he's the only person I know who can open the Gates of Heaven for you…"

If the rabbi from Czenslochov had been afraid of the Schwartzer Wolf before, now he was *mamash* terrified! You know, it's one thing to be scared of somebody on a physical level. But the idea of approaching a *lamed-vav tzaddik* – much less the HEAD of the thirty-six holy people… The rabbi knew one thing for sure: he was absolutely not on the level. He would have to purify himself completely, do real *teshuvah*, before he could even think of being invited for Shabbos by somebody as holy as the Schwartzer Wolf.

So the rabbi rushed home to try to prepare himself. He went to the *mikvah* a hundred times a day. He recited the Psalms until he knew them all by heart. And he tried as hard as he could to repent; he *mamash* promised G-d everything in the world if only He would help him be worthy of the blessing of the Schwartzer Wolf.

Still the rabbi was afraid hat despite all his efforts, his *teshuvah* might not be enough. So, just in case, he came up with a little plan. He knew that the Schwartzer Wolf lived deep in the forest. If he appeared at the woodchopper's door two minutes before Shabbos, explaining that he'd gotten lost in the woods and couldn't make it back to town before the holy day began, the Schwartzer Wolf would just have to take him in. No G-d fearing *Yid* would turn him away under such circumstances, especially not a *tzaddik!*

So the next Friday afternoon the rabbi asked some townspeople directions to the Schwartzer Wolf's house, and plunged into the forest. He found the path he'd been told about, and after following it for what seemed like hours, finally saw in the distance a dirty, broken down shack. This must be it. The rabbi looked up at the sky. Ah – he was right on schedule. The sun was just going down. So, whispering a silent prayer, the rabbi knocked on the door of the house of the Schwartzer Wolf.

For a few minutes, nothing happened. Nobody came to the door, and the rabbi couldn't hear any sound in the house. He knocked again. Still nothing. "*Gevalt!*" he thought. "If there's nobody here, I'm *mamash* in trouble. I really will be lost in the forest with nowhere to go for Shabbos!"

The rabbi had just turned away from the house, trying to figure out what to do next, when a loud crash made him jump in fear. Trembling, he turned around. The door of the house had slammed open. The wife of the Schwartzer Wolf was standing there. And – *gevalt!* – she was the ugliest, most disgusting woman he had ever seen in his life! She had a baby on her hip, and three more children hanging onto her filthy, torn skirt. Usually the rabbi delighted in children. But these – they looked as obnoxious and repulsive as their mother did!

Now, everybody knows that the *lamed-vav tzaddikim* – and their exalted families – are so holy that they perfectly mirror whoever is looking at them. If when you see them you think they're disgusting, it's because you're disgusting. If they seem ugly, that means you're ugly – not just on the outside, but in the deepest depths. Only if you are pure and holy can you see their beauty and their light.

The rabbi of Czenslochov might not have been much of a *chasid*, but this much he knew – when he looked at the wife and children of the Schwartzer Wolf, everything he saw was really a reflection of himself. *Gevalt*, was he the lowest of the low! He was so ashamed that he wanted to run away. But then he thought of his wife – and how much they wanted children... So he managed to stammer, "Please, could I stay with you for Shabbos? I got lost in the forest, and I can't make it back to town in time..."

The woman screamed at him, and cursed him in the most vulgar language. Then she tried to slam the door in his face.

The rabbi had expected something like this, so he was ready. He managed to stick his foot in the door before it could close. "Please let me in," he begged the wife of the Schwartzer Wolf. "Where else can I go?"

She looked at him coldly, and at last she spoke. "My friend, there is no way you're spending Shabbos in this house. You've *mamash* put your life in danger just by knocking on the door. If my husband finds you here, he will kill you with his bare hands!" The rabbi began to look around him wildly, at the darkening sky and the unfamiliar thick forest. And his heart pounded with fear as he suddenly realized that if she wouldn't let him stay, he really did have nowhere else to go.

The rabbi's terror must have shown on his face, because the wife of the Schwartzer Wolf seemed to soften. "Okay," she said, suddenly relenting. "If you have to, you can stay in our stable. But let me warn you. Don't even think of coming near this house. There's no telling what my husband might do…"

As a precaution, the rabbi had brought two candles with him, and a little wine and bread. So he turned away from the shack and went into the stable. "What a way to spend the Holy Sabbath," he thought as he looked around. "In a smelly stable with a horse and two dogs, sleeping on dirty old hay. But at least I'm close to the house … and, after all, there are three meals on Shabbos. Maybe I can still find a way to get in…"

Now that the rabbi from Czenslochov knew who the Schwartzer Wolf really was, he understood why the woodchopper didn't *daven* in the *shul* with the rest of the *Yidden*. Obviously the *lamed-vav tzaddikim* had their own secret *minyan* somewhere in the forest, hidden from view. Late that Friday night, the rabbi heard heavy footsteps coming back from the woods. This had to be the Schwartzer Wolf! The rabbi could hear him going up the steps to his house, and his wife telling him about the stranger spending Shabbos in the stable. Then there was silence.

Suddenly, the door to the stable burst open, and the Schwartzer Wolf stalked in. And if the rabbi had been afraid of him before, now he was *mamash* frozen in fear. The man's hair and beard were wild and dirty; he was very tall, and looked incredibly strong. His eyes were crazed, and the expression on his face… Even though the rabbi knew the man was really very holy, still he trembled before the sheer power of his physical presence.

The Schwartzer Wolf went up to the rabbi and stood towering over him: "I want you to know, friend, that if it had been up to me, you'd still be wandering around in the forest. I'd have thrown you out in a minute. Since my wife let you in, you can stay. But if you so much as open this door – or even look out of the window – I will *mamash* strangle you with these," he said, curling his fingers into massive fists and shaking them at the rabbi. "And as soon as Shabbos is over, I want you out of my stable!" With this he spun around and walked out, slamming the door so hard that the whole building shook.

The rabbi sank to the floor and buried his face in his hands. He had never felt so broken in his life. So much for getting an invitation for Shabbos. So much for his hopes for a blessing. He knew what the Schwartzer Wolf had really been saying: "*Gevalt*, are you far away. You aren't even on the level to spend one night in the stable of my house!"

All that night the rabbi from Czenslochov poured out his heart to G-d: "Master of the World, please have mercy. Please help me become worthy enough for the Schwartzer Wolf to give me his blessing..." He *mamash* prayed harder than he ever had in his whole life. And by the first light of day, he was beginning to believe he'd really repented for everything he'd ever done wrong.

Early Shabbos morning the rabbi heard the Schwartzer Wolf going off to *daven* in the forest. Then there was absolute silence. All day he stayed in the stable, praying and waiting. Finally, in the late afternoon, he heard the *tzaddik* come back and go into his house. Then, again there was no sound. By now the rabbi was *mamash* desperate. It was getting later and later; he knew that time was running out. He kept trying to do teshuvah; he *davened* harder than ever: "*Ribbono Shel Olam*, if You only help me get this blessing, I promise You..." But there came a point when he didn't have anything else to promise G-d. And time kept passing ... it was getting darker and darker...

Suddenly the rabbi glanced out of the window of the stable. There in the night sky he could see the three stars that meant Shabbos was over. He hadn't gotten the blessing. He hadn't even made it into the house. It looked like he'd lost his one chance to have children.

The rabbi from Czenslochov sank to the ground, burying his head in his hands and sobbing from the depths of his broken heart. Then, all at once, he sat up, like he was waking from a bad dream. What a fool he'd been! He'd been depending on people to give him what he needed, people like the Kozhnitzer Maggid and the Schwartzer Wolf. Yes, they were the holiest of the holy, truly exalted. But he had forgotten the One on whom he should really rely… Again he started to cry, but this time he was crying out to G-d, the One Who is above everyone and everything else. And for the first time in his life, the rabbi from Czenslochov really prayed:

"*Ribbono Shel Olam*, there is nobody who can help me but You. I know I'm not worthy. But I'm *mamash* begging You – please have mercy. Please don't let me die without children…"

Just at that moment, he felt the gentle touch of a hand on his head. He looked up through his tears. It was the Schwartzer Wolf. And yet, he seemed like a different man. If yesterday he had seemed so gruesome, so frightening, today he was shining with holiness, *mamash* radiant with light. And he said, so kindly and sweetly, "My dearest friend, would you do me and my family the honor of joining us for the third meal of Shabbos?"

The rabbi went with the Schwartzer Wolf back to his house. And he couldn't believe his eyes. The shack too was completely different – it was clean and glowing. And his wife and children – if the day before they had seemed totally disgusting, now they were absolutely beautiful… The rabbi joined the family in the ritual hand washing, and they all ate some *challah* and fish. The rabbi was so lost in the exalted holiness of the moment that he could hardly swallow the food, much less open his mouth to ask for a blessing. But it really didn't matter, because the Schwartzer Wolf turned to him and said:

"My sweetest rabbi, I know why you came to my house. I know what's in your heart. And I bless you and your wife to have a son. But there is one condition – that you name your son after me…"

For a moment the rabbi was confused. Surely the *tzaddik* knew that we don't name children for anybody who is still living. He wanted to say something, but the awe of the whole experience … he found he still couldn't speak. So he just nodded mutely, stayed until after *havdalah*, and then went home to tell his wife: "G-d truly is merciful. The Schwartzer Wolf blessed us with a son."

The next morning the rabbi went as usual to the synagogue for the morning prayers. And as soon as he walked in, he saw that something strange was going on. The *shammes* was going around from person to person, asking everybody to do something. But they all were shaking their heads. The rabbi went over to the *shammes*: "What's the problem here?"

"Nothing to worry about, Rabbi. It's just that somebody died last night, and I'm having trouble getting a *minyan* together for the funeral."

The rabbi felt a shiver of dread. "Tell me, who died?"

"That disgusting woodchopper, the one who lives in the forest. People call him the Schwartzer Wolf..."

Gevalt! The holy, the exalted Schwartzer Wolf...

The rabbi began to cry. He ran to the front of the *shul* and shouted as loud as he could, so that everybody would hear: "My friends, do you know who the Schwartzer Wolf really was? He was the head of the *lamed-vav tzaddikim*, *mamash* the holiest person in our generation!" He told the whole story of what had happened in the forest. And then he said, "And what did we do? We ignored him, we insulted him, we laughed at him, we were afraid of him. *Oy*, we treated him so badly. The least we can do now is to go with him to his final resting place!"

So in the end, everybody in the city went to the funeral of the Holy Schwartzer Wolf. And when exactly nine months later the rabbi's wife had a son, the happy father kept his word to the hidden *tzaddik*, and named his child Schwartzer Wolf after him...

But this is not the end of the story...

Many years later, in 1944, the Holy Belzer Rebbe escaped from the Nazis and came to *Eretz Yisrael*. And his first Shabbos in Israel he was in Tel Aviv.

Now, the *chasidim* of Belz had a special custom. After the meal on Friday night, everybody took their glasses of wine and went up to the Rebbe. They'd tell him their mother's name, and the Rebbe would give each one a special blessing.

On the Belzer's first Shabbos in *Eretz Yisrael*, a very old man – maybe even a hundred years old – frail and stooped and leaning on his stick, made his way up to the Rebbe. The Belzer said, so kindly, "My dearest friend, please tell me your name."

He answered in a hoarse voice, "Schwartzer Wolf ben Chana."

"*Gevalt!*" the Rebbe cried. "Are you a descendant of the first Schwartzer Wolf, the one who was named for the hidden *tzaddik*?"

The old man looked surprised. "Rebbe, I can't believe you know the story."

"Yes, my holy friend," the Belzer said. "I know the story. But there aren't many people left who do. And I'm afraid it will be completely forgotten unless you do something for me..." He turned to his *chasidim*: "Put a chair on the table, and help this man up to sit on it." Then he said to the *Yiddele*: "Please, would you tell everybody here the story, so it will always be remembered?"

So the aged *Yiddele* told all the Belzer *chasidim* the story of the *lamed-vav tzaddik*, the Schwartzer Wolf.

R. Shlomo said that he actually heard the story of the Schwartzer Wolf from someone who was with the Belzer Rebbe on that first Shabbos in Tel Aviv. And he would always conclude with a personal sequel:

Once R. Shlomo was giving a concert in Tel Aviv. And between songs, he decided to tell the story of the Schwartzer Wolf. Suddenly somebody in the back row began to shout and wave his hands. R. Shlomo stopped, and asked the man what he wanted. So the Yid *stood up and began to speak – and R. Shlomo couldn't believe what he said:*

This man was a teacher in B'nei Brak. And in his class was a little boy who was named Schwartzer Wolf. Gevalt! The boy was the great great grandson of the old Yiddele, *the Schwartzer Wolf who told the story to the Belzer Rebbe!*

And then R. Shlomo would beg us always to keep telling the story, to keep remembering the Schwartzer Wolf. Because there are Schwartzer Wolf's everywhere we go. Sometimes they are revealed to us, like this boy. And sometimes they are so hidden – sometimes, like the lamed-vav tzaddik, *they mamash seem to be the opposite of holy. We have to have the eyes to see...*

You know, sometimes we walk the streets of the Holy City of Jerusalem, and we pass people who seem to us disgusting, vulgar, maybe even frightening. But – gevalt! – we have to be so careful. Because they just might be lamed-vav tzaddikim.

You never know...

Opening The Gates

Illustration:

"He ran ... into the nearby forest... And there, burying his face against a tree, he broke down, crying..."

"When the Gates are Locked"

G-d is always opening gates for us – so many kinds of gates. Sometimes we see the gate, know that it's open, and go right through. But sometimes we're afraid to go in, afraid to find out what might lie on the other side. And then there are times when we don't even realize the gate is there...

There were so many occasions when Israel could have fixed the whole world. We could have brought real peace. The gates were open wide ... but we didn't see them. We missed our chance...

Can you imagine the kind of gate the Ribbono Shel Olam *opened for us when we stood at Mount Sinai and received the Torah? We were* mamash *on such a high level that we could have changed all of history. We could have gone right into* Eretz Yisrael; *we could even have brought the Messiah. According to the Gemorah, at that moment there was no longer any death in the world. We had entered the inside of the inside of the deepest, holiest gate. But – gevalt! What did we do? We walked out. We made the Golden Calf. It's as if we were saying to G-d, "We're not interested in Your Gates."*

Every time we do a mitzvah, *G-d opens the gates for us to do more good deeds. Why don't we go through? We seldom do. So often we're just walking around in circles, never taking advantage of the openings in Heaven... In our relationships with people, we should always be opening gates for each other, especially for our families – our husbands, our wives, our children. How many people get divorced because one of them closed the gates? Or how many times are we too busy to see that our children are opening for us the gates of their hearts?*

Sometimes a shlepper *comes up to us on the street, holding out his hand. Do we have any idea how many gates we might open for him if we give him a dollar? Or maybe we see people who are strangers, and we want to turn away. We want to shut our doors, seal our gates: you're not one of us, I don't know you and I don't think I want to. But do you know what might happen if we open our hearts to them, if we welcome them with love? We just might change their lives...*

Why don't we enter the gates? Because – yes, maybe we see that they're beautiful. But we don't think they're what we need. We don't think they're for us. It's true we each have our own unique thing to do in this world. We each need special help and guidance, our own special gates. But the real Gates of Heaven are there for every one of us...

May we all recognize when the gates are open. And may we know in our hearts: "This gate is for me. If I just take one more step, who knows how far I can go...?"

The Munkatcher Passport

You know, we have so many boundaries, so many borders. On the one hand, that's the way it has to be. We all need to define our lives, whether as nations or as human beings.

The problem begins when we become protective, when we start being possessive. We say, This is my territory. Don't cross my border. Then the boundaries become walls. We feel safe as long as we stay inside our borders … and keep everybody else out.

We all know about the boundaries between countries. You can find them on any map. But there are many other kinds of borders — between one person and another, between husbands and wives, between children and their parents. And sadly enough, there are also boundaries that seem to separate us from G-d.

That is why there is no peace in the world. Because we can't get through each other's walls. We don't know how to cross the borders.

Do you know what we need? We need a Munkatcher Passport…

A chasid once came to R. Levi Yitzhak of Berdichev and said, "Holy Master, I hate to bother you, but I have to travel to Lublin and I don't have a passport. I know I could go to the police and get one. But you know what happens to a Jew here in Russia. The moment the police know about him, it means nothing but trouble! I don't want the authorities to know I even exist…

"Please, Rebbe, is there some way you could help me get the passport I need?"

The Berdichever said, "Wait here." He went into his private room, and came out a few minutes later holding a blank piece of paper. "Here's your passport," he said, giving the paper to the *chasid*. Then, seeing the expression on his student's face, he added, "Don't worry. With this passport you won't need anything more."

Can you imagine how much faith it takes to come to a border and hand the guard a blank piece of paper? But this *chasid* was on the level; he had absolute trust in his Rebbe. He ran home, packed his things, and set off for Lublin. When he came to the Polish border, he took a deep breath, said a silent prayer, and handed the soldier the Berdichever's passport.

The officer studied the blank paper for a moment, and then started saluting the *chasid*: "What a privilege – to meet such an exalted person. It's the greatest honor of my whole life! On behalf of the Polish government, I'd like to offer you whatever help I can on your journey. Perhaps a horse and carriage would make your travels more comfortable?"

Now this *chasid* was a poor man; he'd *mamash* never ridden in a carriage in his whole life! Wherever he went in Poland, he showed the Berdichever passport, and all the gates were instantly opened. He was treated like a king. His trip was a *gevalt*, and he returned home *b'shalom*, in peace.

Many years later, in 1935, a Munkatcher *chasid*, a *Yid* with long *peyos* and a thick beard, was also in trouble. He had to go to Germany right away. He had a passport, but with the Nazis, he knew an ordinary passport wouldn't be enough to keep him safe. He didn't know what to do, so he went to his Rebbe for help.

Now the *Heilige* R. Chaim Eleazer Shapiro of Munkatch was one of the greatest Rebbes in Europe at the time. Not only was he a *tzaddik*, a Holy Master, but also a *mohel*, a ritual circumciser. You know, if the person who does the circumcision is very holy, the baby doesn't feel any pain. It just feels natural to him, like G-d intended it to be. When the Munkatcher served as *mohel*, he did the *bris* so fast that the human eye *mamash* couldn't follow the movements of his hands. And the baby never cried. People believed that any baby he circumcised would be holy all his life...

But even the *Heilige* Munkatcher seemed surprised when he heard his *chasid's* problem. "Certainly I will pray for you to have a safe trip," he told his desperate follower. "But I don't know what else I can do for you."

"It's not that I don't trust your prayers, Rebbe" the *Yiddele* answered. " But I'm so afraid... Do you remember the story you told us about the passport R. Levi Yitzhak gave to his student? That's the kind of thing I need. Please, Rebbe – make me a passport like that!"

"The Berdichever Rav was the holiest of the holy," the Munkatcher replied, shaking his head. "Maybe he was high enough to give a Berdichever Passport. But what makes you think I am on such an exalted level?"

"I know you can do it," the *chasid* cried. "I'm sure of it! Rebbe, please – I'm *mamash* begging you. I wouldn't come to you if it weren't so terribly important. I really HAVE to go to Germany, and I'm so afraid I won't make it back. Rebbe, for the sake of my wife and children, please help me!"

"Alright," the Munkatcher sighed. "I'll try. Wait for me here." And he went into his private room.

Now, to go to Lublin from Berdichev, to Poland from Russia, was one thing. But for a *Yid* to go from Munkatch, Hungary to Germany in 1935 – and back...

The Rebbe stayed in his room for three hours. When he finally came out, his eyes were red and swollen, and his holy face was streaked with tears. He handed his *chasid* a blank piece of paper. But the paper was wet – soaked with the tears of all our years in exile. The Munkatcher said, "The truth is, our generation is not really worthy of this passport. Since it's such an emergency, I'll give it to you – but only if you promise me one thing. You must never tell anyone about it as long as I live."

"I promise, Rebbe," the *chasid* said eagerly. "I'll never tell a soul!" So the Rebbe gave him the Munkatcher passport.

The *chasid* came to the German border. The Nazi on guard looked at his sidelocks and beard, and demanded with a sneer, "Where's your passport?" The *Yiddele* gave him the blank piece of paper. The Nazi took one look at it, and his whole expression changed. "Sir, I am so honored to meet you," he cried. "You are probably the greatest person ever to visit our country. Please give me the privilege of assisting you on your journey. Here is a letter to the chief of police of every town in Germany. They will take care of you and protect you...'

The *chasid* stayed in Germany for over a week. The Nazis gave him a car and driver; they even paid for him to stay in the best hotels everywhere he went. He returned safely home, and true to his promise to the Rebbe, he never told anyone about his Munkatcher passport.

The Munkatcher Rebbe left this world in 1936. Before he passed away, he told his followers, "Heaven has shown me that a great dark cloud of evil will soon cover the world. There is nothing I can do to prevent it. And I don't want to be here when it comes…"

Three years later the *chasid* suddenly became very sick. When he saw the doctor shake his head, he knew he would not live much longer. So he called his whole family to his bedside and said, "Before I leave this world I have to tell you a very holy secret…" He told them the whole story of the Munkatcher Passport, and then he said,

"This is my last will and testament. When you bury me, I want the Munkatcher Passport to be in my hand. Because if the Rebbe's paper got me across the most dangerous border in this world, who knows what gates it will open for me in the World to Come…"

Have you ever seen people dancing on Simchas Torah? There are no borders between them, no walls. They are just all together, rich and poor, old and young, parents and children. Do you know why? On Simchas Torah we take out the Torah, but we dance before we read it. While we're dancing, it's as if the Torah is blank. What is G-d giving us? A Munkatcher Passport…

Have you ever learned Gemorah? *The Talmud starts on page two; the first page has no writing on it. It's a blank page. For us to learn Torah, G-d has to give us a Munkatcher Passport.*

You know, at the beginning of a wedding the groom covers the eyes of his beautiful bride. She can't see anything. He is giving her a Munkatcher Passport. Then the bride walks around her holy groom seven times. No one can see anything happening. What's going on? She's giving him back her own Munkatcher Passport.

And did you ever go to the Holy Wall in Jerusalem? On one level it's just a wall. You think there's maybe not much to see. But when you pray by the Holy Wall, something happens to you. Suddenly, gates are open.

Because G-d is giving you a Munkatcher Passport…

When the Gates Are Locked

very Shabbos crowds of *Yidden* came to be with the *Heilige* R. Yerachmiel, son of R. Yaacov Yitzhak, the Yehudi HaKodesh – the Holy Jew. There was no way R. Yerachmiel himself could pay for all the food, and most of his followers were too poor to help. But luckily one of his *chasidim* was a rich man. This *Yiddele* covered most of the expenses for Shabbos, and generally supported the Rebbe's Court.

Then one day, sadly enough, the rich *chasid's* luck changed. He suddenly lost almost all of his money, and found himself barely able to support his family, much less help the Rebbe.

Now, it's really hard suddenly to become poor, especially when you're used to living like a rich man. But the worst thing is that people who were your friends when you were wealthy don't want to know you anymore. Overnight, neighbors whom the *Yiddele* had known all his life wouldn't give him the time of day. His heart was *mamash* broken.

His wife tried to cheer him up: "Why don't you go spend a Shabbos with R. Yerachmiel? You know he'll always be your friend. He'll still be glad to see you, and you'll sit next to him as usual, in a place of honor. You'll see, it will make you feel better."

The *Yiddele* decided she was right. He really was feeling very hurt and sad. And it probably would help if he felt he was appreciated for something other than his wealth. So the next Shabbos he went to the Rebbe. He was sure R. Yerachmiel would welcome him warmly and say, "R. Avramele, I'm so happy to see you. And I'm so sorry about what happened. How can I help you?"

But *gevalt*, was he wrong!

The Rebbe acted as if he didn't see him. No one else even said hello to him. The *Yiddele* thought of all the hundreds of rubles that he had given R. Yerachmiel's *shammes* to pay for Shabbos. Now the *shammes* pretended not to know him, not to recognize him. Avramele couldn't believe this was happening. Didn't these people have the slightest bit of gratitude for all that he had done for them, even if he couldn't do it any more?

All Friday night poor Avramele was completely ignored. Forget about sitting next to the Rebbe. He didn't even get a piece of *challah* from the Rebbe's table. Avramele was beside himself. He had supported these people for years, had taken care of them so they could study Torah. And now it was like he didn't exist. Even the Rebbe… What kind of Rebbe was R. Yerachmiel anyway, if he and his followers rejected a person just because he was poor?

"I was such a fool," Avramele thought. "I *mamash* believed R. Yerachmiel was the holiest of holy. But now I see that he is really the lowest of the low. All he cares about is money!" He wanted to march right up to the Rebbe and tell him off. But it was Shabbos, and Avramele knew there is no place for anger on the Sabbath. So he decided that first thing on Sunday he was going straight in to see the Rebbe and tell him to his face that he was the biggest fake in the world.

Early Sunday morning Avramele appeared at R. Yerachmiel's door. "I want to see the Rebbe."

The *shammes* didn't even look up from what he was doing. "Go stand in line with the rest of the *shleppers*."

For Avramele, this was the greatest *chutzpah* in the world. When he'd had money, the *shammes* had never made him wait to see R. Yerachmiel. He was so disgusted he wanted to walk out and go home. But he had things to say to the Rebbe that couldn't wait.

So what could he do? Avramele stood in line with everybody else. But there were so many people … and the line moved so slowly … and there was *mamash* no air in the crowded hall. After an hour he'd only moved forward about an inch. He just didn't have the strength for this! After another half an hour he'd had enough. So he left, thinking, "I'll wait for the Rebbe outside. At least there I'll be able to breathe."

Avramele paced back and forth in front of R. Yerachmiel's house for another two hours, rehearsing how he would tell the Rebbe exactly what he thought of him. But when he finally saw R. Yerachmiel come out on his way to the *Beis Midrash*, his anger dissolved into pain. And all he could do was call, "Rebbe, please Rebbe … help me!"

But R. Yerachmiel didn't even glance at him. He only reached into his pocket and took out some coins. Without once looking Avramele in the face, he counted out fourteen pennies, which he dropped into the poor *Yiddele's* hand. Then, without a word, he walked away.

Avramele had never been so humiliated in his whole life. Fourteen pennies? You don't give fourteen pennies as charity to even the lowest beggar! For Avramele, this was *mamash* the end. He ran away from R. Yerachmiel's house and into the nearby forest. And there, burying his face against a tree, he broke down, crying:

"*Ribbono Shel Olam*, what's happening to me? First I lost all my money, then all my friends, and now my Rebbe. G-d in Heaven, is there anyone in the world I can trust? I believed so much in these people, but they all let me down. Master of the World, after everything that's happened, can I even have faith in You?" And he sobbed and sobbed from the depths of his broken heart.

Suddenly he felt a tap on his shoulder. He looked around through his tears. There was a little Polish boy standing next to him. The boy said, "Hey, Mister. I'm selling these packages. They're one penny each. Do you want to buy them?"

Avramele almost laughed. Here he was, *mamash* at the lowest point of his life, and this kid was trying to peddle him some junk. "No thanks," he muttered, and tried to turn away. But the boy pulled on his arm: "Please, mister..."

Avramele thought for a moment. Maybe he could get rid of this pest and the Rebbe's humiliating charity, all at the same time...

"Okay," he said. "But I only have these fourteen pennies..."

"That's just the right amount," the boy exclaimed. "Because I have here exactly fourteen packages at – like I said – a penny apiece."

Avramele froze in shock. Fourteen pennies, fourteen packages... Could it be? In a daze, he dropped the coins into the boy's hand and took the parcels. With trembling hands he ripped them open. And – *gevalt, gevalt!* Each one contained hundreds of ruble notes!

Avramele couldn't believe his eyes. He was twice as rich as he'd been in the first place! And suddenly he understood that the Rebbe had given him the fourteen pennies for this very purpose. So even before going home to celebrate with his wife, he ran straight back to R. Yerachmiel.

This time everything was different. All the *chasidim* he passed smiled at him and said hello. The *shammes* greeted him like a long-lost friend and immediately showed him into the Rebbe's private room. And R. Yerachmiel threw his arms around him and cried, "Avramele, I'm so happy to see you!"

"Rebbe, please! I can't take this anymore! What's been happening to me?"

R. Yerachmiel smiled. "*Baruch Hashem*, thank G-d, now I can explain. I want you to know, it was decreed in Heaven that you should lose all your money, and there was nothing I could do to help. I wasn't strong enough to open the gates for you. So I decided to go through the back door.

"The decree was only that you should be poor. Nothing was said about you losing your Rebbe. So I said to Heaven, 'This man is my dearest friend, my faithful *chasid*. I need him, and he *mamash* needs me. But I'm telling you, Heavenly Court, I absolutely refuse to have him as my follower as long as he is poor!'

"And to show Heaven that I meant what I said, I forbade my followers to spend time with you or even speak to you. I ordered my *shammes* not to allow you to see me as long as you had no money.

"And so, Avramele, I forced Heaven to cancel the decree, and to put you back on your feet again!"

You see what it is — there are different ways of opening the Gates of Heaven. Sometimes all you have to do is push a little button, and the gates open right away. But for this to work, you have to know where the right button is, and sadly enough, most of us have no idea. We need G-d to shine a little light on us, and reveal to us all the buttons in Heaven.

But sometimes there is no button, or at least we can't find one. All we see are heavy locks. What can we do? One way is to try to break down the gates…

Once a man came to the Holy Baal Shem Tov and said, "Rebbe, my son is very sick. Please, pray for him that he should get well." The Besht closed his holy eyes and sat very still for a moment. Then he said, "Wait here." He ran out of the room, and returned a short while later with ten men who everybody knew were the top thieves in the city. With this *minyan* he recited psalms for the sick boy, then he turned to the anxious father and said, "Go home. By the time you get there your son will be well."

The Holy Baal Shem's *chasidim,* who had been standing there the whole time, were beside themselves. Finally one of them spoke up: "Rebbe, we know that you are so holy that you not only know good people, but also those who maybe aren't on the same level. But for something as important as healing a sick child, why didn't you take us for your *minyan* – or at least ten decent men? Why did you need ten criminals, ten thieves?"

And the Holy Baal Shem Tov answered, "Let me tell you – I saw that all the Gates were not only closed to this boy, they were locked tight. So I needed ten thieves to pick the locks ... to break open the Gates of Heaven."

And then there are times when we can't break open the Gates. We try as hard as we can, but we're mamash *not strong enough. Then we have to find another way...*

 Yiddele once came to R. Dovid Dinover, the son of the Holy B'nei Yissas'char, and said, "Rebbe, I'm *mamash* at the end. My wife and I have been married for almost twenty years, but we don't have any children. Please bless us to have a child."

R. Dovid Dinover shook his head. "I'm not the one you should be talking to. You need my *chasid,* R. Feibush of Tosh. He's really a very big Rebbe in his own right, and is the top man for blessings to have children. Somehow he manages to open all the gates. As a matter of fact, he's coming here next Shabbos. Invite him for a Sabbath meal, and ask him for the blessing you need."

So when the Tosher Rebbe arrived in town the following Friday, the man rushed out to meet him. "Rebbe, please do us the honor of eating with us on Shabbos."

"I'd be delighted," the Tosher answered. "I'll come for lunch. It's a promise."

The next day R. Feibush arrived at the man's house. The *Yiddele* and his wife were so happy he'd come. They tried to show him to a seat at the table, to engage him in conversation. But the Tosher didn't seem to be paying much attention. Instead he started walking back and forth, from room to room, looking around him intently. At first the confused couple followed him silently as he roamed through the whole house. They had no idea what he was doing, but they had too much respect for him to ask any questions. R. Feibush's face shone with love and compassion, but his holiness also inspired great awe.

Finally the *Yiddele* couldn't stand it any more. "Rebbe," he cried. "What are you looking for?"

"For children's toys, a baby's crib – any sign of a child in the house."

"*Oy*, Rebbe," the man answered, and there were tears in his eyes. "Sadly enough, we don't have any children. That's one of the reasons we invited you here…"

R. Feibush didn't let him finish. "I'm very sorry," he said. "I'm afraid I'll have to leave. You see, I have a very strict rule. I never eat in a house where there aren't any children."

"But Rebbe," the *Yiddele* protested. "You promised that you would have Shabbos lunch with us!"

"You're right," the Tosher said. "I did. So I'll just have to come back again next year." And with that he walked out of the door.

As soon as he was outside, R. Feibush lifted his eyes up to Heaven and cried, "*Ribbono Shel Olam*, I *mamash* did promise these people I'd have a meal in their house. And I've never broken a promise in my whole life. Master of the World, You have to help me keep my word this time too. You have to give them a child!"

Do you understand how deep this is? Mamash, the deepest depths. The Tosher Rebbe knew that the Gates of Heaven were closed to this couple. And he also knew that G-d wouldn't make him be a liar… He found a way to come in through the back door.

So many times we can't make things happen the direct way. The front door is locked. Or we can't even find it. So we have to beg G-d, "Ribbono Shel Olam, please let me in. If I can't get through the front gate, please show me the back door…"

There's another story…

nce a very rich man came to the Holy Radzyminer, R. Yaakov Arieh Guterman. "Rebbe," he begged. "You've got to help me. My heart is *mamash* broken, and my wife is beside herself with sadness. You see, we've been married for so long, and we don't have any children. Please Rebbe, bless us with a child."

The Radzyminer immediately asked him, "How much money do you have?"

"Rebbe, of course I'll give you a big contribution for your help. But what does my wealth have to do with a blessing for children?"

The Rebbe only repeated the question: "How much money do you have?".

So this time the rich man told him. And the Holy Radzyminer said, "Bring it all to me."

The rich *Yiddele* had no idea what was going on, but he did as instructed – he brought the Rebbe all his money. The Radzyminer put the packet of rubles behind some books on a shelf in his private room. Then he said to the rich man, "I bless you to have a child."

Less than a year later, the *Yiddele's* wife gave birth to a son. They were so happy, and so grateful to the Rebbe. The boy grew up and became a big genius in Torah learning. All the *Yidden* in the city saw him as the perfect *shidduch* for their daughters, and soon he was engaged to a wonderful girl, the sweetest of the sweet. But his father needed money for the wedding and to support the holy couple – he had given all his wealth to the Rebbe when he had gotten the blessing and had been a poor man ever since. So what did he do? He went back to the Holy Radzyminer and said,

"Rebbe, I'm sure you don't remember me, but I was here many years ago and…"

"I remember you," the Rebbe interrupted. "And I know why you've come." He went over to his bookcase and took out the *Yiddele's* packet of money. "I've been saving this for you," he said. "Here's the money you need for your son."

"Rebbe," the *Yiddele* said. "It's not that I'm not grateful, but I don't understand."

"It's really very simple," the Holy Radzyminer explained. "When you first came to me, I saw that all the Gates of Heaven were closed to you. So I went through the back door. I took your money and set it aside for your child's wedding. And then I said to G-d, '*Ribbono Shel Olam*, I have here the money for the wedding of this man's son. So, quick! Send the boy down to the world.'"

At the beginning of a wedding, the groom covers the face of his holy bride. Then he's hidden from her. It's hard for her to see him. But he's still standing right there. Do you know what he's telling her? If you can't see the door in front, look for the back door. And there you'll find me...

May all the gates – the front doors and the back doors – always be open to all of us...

You're not Bankrupt
If You
Know How to Pray

Everybody knows that the Holy R. Yaacov Yitzhak Horowitz was called the Seer of Lublin – and for a very good reason. His eyes were so holy that he could not only see everything that was happening in the world at that time, but could also look into the future. So on Yom Kippur he knew exactly what Heaven had decreed for all of his *chasidim* in the coming year. Often he chose not to say anything. But sometimes, when he thought they were strong enough to handle it, he told his followers what was in store.

One Yom Kippur, the Seer turned to R. Simchah Bunim of Pshis'cha, one of his closest students, and said, "It has just been decreed in Heaven that this year you will go bankrupt."

Now, the Pshis'cher was a really top pharmacist. He had a drugstore, and at that time he was very rich. But he knew that once Heaven issues a decree, there's nothing you can do. He returned home from Lublin, and sure enough, right away his drugstore started losing money. So he thought, "Why should I wait until I *mamash* have nothing left? I might as well close my business now." So he shut his pharmacy, gave whatever money he had to his wife, and decided to go to Warsaw. There he took a room in his favorite hotel, the place where he had always stayed when he was wealthy. And since he had no business to take care of anymore, he just remained in his room all day, praying and learning.

And you know, it's a funny thing. Everybody insists that poor people pay all their bills right away. But with rich people nobody worries if they don't pay exactly on time, because they have so much credit. R. Simchah Bunim was well known in Warsaw. Everybody thought he was still rich. So he stayed in the fine hotel for weeks, eating and drinking whatever he wanted, without paying a single penny.

But after a couple of months, the Pshis'cher started finding polite notes in his mailbox: "It has come to our attention that you haven't paid for your room for the last eight weeks. We would appreciate it if you would take care of your bill at your earliest convenience."

So he went to the hotel clerk and said, "Please tell the management that I'm so sorry about my bill. I've had so much on my mind, I totally forgot. But they shouldn't worry. I'll cover everything very soon."

A few days went by. Then there was another note. It seemed the hotel management was getting anxious, because this one was not so polite: "Your bill is now more than two months overdue. We insist that you pay it immediately!" R. Simchah Bunim didn't even bother to reply. Finally one day, as the Pshis'cher was learning in his room, there was a knock on his door. It was a bellboy delivering a note from the top man at the hotel: "I demand that you pay everything you owe us – today! Or else!"

This time the Pshis'cher was a little bit worried. He didn't let it show; he calmly said to the bellboy, "Please tell the manager that I understand. Right now I'm busy with something very important." And he really was – he was learning Torah! "However, if you return at six o'clock, I'll take care of everything."

But as soon as the porter was out of the room, R. Simchah Bunim closed his eyes and started to pray: "*Oy*, G-d in Heaven, what am I going to do? Everybody here knows I'm a *Yid*. If they think I'm cheating the hotel it will bring such dishonor to Your Holy Name. But I *mamash* don't have the money. I was trusting You to take care of things. Master of the World, You've got to fix this for me…"

And he went back to his learning.

At one o'clock that afternoon, there was another knock on the Pshis'cher's door. "*Gevalt!*" he thought. "The bellboy's come already. Now what am I going to do?" He opened the door a tiny crack and looked out. Thank G-d it wasn't the porter – it was a different kind of messenger, in a smart uniform with gold trim. R. Simchah Bunim accepted the letter the man handed him and opened it. And this is what it said:

"Someone told me you're in town and I couldn't believe my luck, because I need your help. I just fired my accountant – the stupid man lost me thousands of rubles because he couldn't even add – and I need to replace him immediately. I've heard you're a top man when it comes to business, so I'm offering you the job. I'll pay you anything you want. Please send your answer back with my valet. Signed, Madame Temeroff."

The Pshis'cher couldn't believe his eyes. Everybody knew about the Temeroffs. Most Polish *Yidden* at that time were very poor, but they were *mamash* millionaires, maybe even billionaires! The husband was a great *talmid chacham*, a Torah scholar, who spent most of his time in the *Beis Midrash*, learning. His wife ran all their businesses and had made all their money. And now this same Madame Temeroff was offering him a job!

G-d was already answering his prayer, right?

R. Simchah Bunim took a pencil and wrote on the back of the note: "I have the skills, you have the cash. I'll only help you if you make me your partner." He folded up his answer and handed it to the messenger. Then he went back to learning Torah.

The day passed slowly. The Pshis'cher kept checking his watch. It was three o'clock, four o'clock, five. Still no word from Madame Temeroff. R. Simchah Bunim started getting nervous. At five thirty there was a knock on the door. "*Oy, Ribbono Shel Olam,*" he thought. "If the hotel bellboy is early, I'm really in trouble. I still don't have the money!" He opened the door and couldn't believe what he saw. Madame Temeroff herself was standing there.

"Simchah Bunim," she said. "I *mamash* couldn't believe your answer to my note. What *chutzpah*, to demand to be my partner! But at the same time, I was impressed by your daring. So I decided to come in person to find out what kind of person you really are. And now that I've seen you, I can tell that you're exactly the man I need!"

So the Pshis'cher and Madame Temeroff became partners. He told her about his trouble with the hotel, and she was happy to pay the whole bill. Then R. Simchah Bunim returned to Lublin, and went straight to see the Holy Seer.

The Seer only had to look at the Pshis'cher to know everything that had happened. He smiled at his *chasid* and said,

"So you see, Simchah Bunim, you're not bankrupt if you know how to pray. But there's one thing I don't understand. Why didn't you immediately grab the chance to become Madame Temeroff's accountant? You *mamash* didn't have a single penny. Where did you get the strength to hold out for more?"

"Holy Rebbe, it's really very simple. I could see that G-d was just beginning to open the Gates for me. And I wanted to make Him open them really wide!"

The Holy Amshinover Rebbe, R. Yaacov Dovid, the son of the holy Vorker, loved this story about the Pshis'cher, and often told it to his followers.

Then one day an Amshinover *chasid* also went bankrupt. He had spent all his money buying a wagonload of furs for three rubles each, hoping to sell them for ten and make a huge profit. But the price of furs fell suddenly to only two rubles, and instead of getting rich, the poor *Yiddele* couldn't even make back his original investment. He had a wife and hungry children to support, and he didn't know what to do. So he went to his Rebbe for advice.

"Go to this city and wait," the Holy Amshinover told him, naming a nearby town. "You'll see, G-d will help you."

First thing the next morning, the *chasid* took his wagon full of furs and went to the city the Rebbe had mentioned. And since he had nothing really to do there but wait, he went to a coffee shop and had a cup of coffee. And then another cup, and then another. Because what do you do when you order a cup of coffee and don't have the money to pay for it? You tell the waiter to bring you another one. By the afternoon the *chasid* must have had fifty cups of coffee. The waiter couldn't decide if he was penniless or crazy – or both!

Suddenly, at about four o'clock, the door to the coffee shop burst open and a Polish army officer – *mamash*, a general – strode in.

"Who is the owner of the wagonload of furs I saw outside?" he demanded in his most commanding voice.

The *chasid* swallowed hard. "Uh … sir … that would be me."

"I want to buy your furs," the general announced. "I was ordered to go to Warsaw to purchase furs for the army. But Warsaw is very far away, and your furs are right here. The price of furs in Warsaw is only two rubles, but I would pay you more for saving me the trip. Name your price."

The *chasid* knew he could ask for three rubles to cover his original costs. Or he could ask for four or five, to make a little profit. But instead, he took a deep breath and said, "I want ten rubles each."

"Ten rubles! I can't pay that kind of money! I'll just go on to Warsaw…" The general hesitated. "I'll tell you what I'll do. I'll give you eight."

"No way. It has to be ten."

"You must be out of your mind! I'm telling you, nobody will pay that." The general shook his head in disgust. "I'm not going to waste any more of my time on somebody as crazy as you..." And he turned around smartly and marched out of the coffee shop.

So what did the *chasid* do? He asked the waiter for another cup of coffee, without a ruble to his name.

The *Yiddele* sat in the café until late that night, waiting for the miracle the Rebbe had promised him. But nothing happened. At a quarter to twelve the waiter finally said, "I'm sorry, my friend, but I'm about to close. You'll have to leave. And you have to pay for all that coffee!"

The *chasid* closed his eyes in despair and whispered, "But Rebbe, you told me if I came here G-d would help me..."

At just that moment the door crashed open. The general was back, so drunk he could hardly stand up. "Hello again," he said, slurring his words so badly the *chasid* could barely understand him. "You know, I've been thinking. I don't have the strength to go to Warsaw." He laughed drunkenly. "To tell you the truth, I've had so much to drink I don't think I can even ride my horse. So I'll tell you what – I'll give you the ten rubles. But let's settle the deal fast, before I pass out!"

So the *chasid* sold his furs for ten rubles each, and became a rich man. Then he went back to the Holy Amshinover and told him what had happened. The Rebbe listened to his story and said, "*Mazel tov*, my friend. I knew G-d would help you. But I *mamash* don't understand you. You see the *Ribbono Shel Olam* opening the gates, and you bargain with Him? Maybe the general was right ... maybe you really are crazy! He offers you eight rubles a fur – more money than you've ever had in your life – and you refuse? What in the world made you hold out for ten?"

And the *chasid* answered, "Rebbe, I'll tell you. I remembered the story about R. Simchah Bunim, and I was only doing what the Pshis'cher said. I saw that G-d was beginning to open the Gates – and I held out for Him to open them all the way!"

But I Can Cry With You

A man once came to the Holy R. Yitzhak Vorker and cried, "Rebbe, I'm *mamash* desperate. My child is so sick, he may even G-d forbid be dying! Rebbe, I'm begging you, please pray for my son to get well."

The Vorker sat very still. He closed his holy eyes and rocked back and forth for a while. Then he looked at the *Yiddele* and said sadly, "I'm so sorry to tell you, but all the Gates of Heaven are closed so tightly there's nothing I can do to open them. You might as well go home."

The father buried his head in his hands and began to sob. But what could he do? He climbed back onto his wagon and started on his way home, crying the whole time. He'd been travelling for about half an hour when suddenly he heard the sound of another wagon chasing after him. He turned around. It was the Holy Vorker himself.

The Rebbe pulled up beside the *Yiddele*. "Stop your wagon here," he said. "I have something to say to you." They reined in their horses, the Vorker helped the father down from his wagon, and they sat together on the grass by the side of the road.

"After you left," R. Yitzhak went on, "I couldn't stop thinking about you and your son. You seemed so sad – it *mamash* broke my heart. Then I realized … I may not be able to help your boy, but at least I can cry with you."

And the Vorker put his arm around the *Yiddele*, bowed his holy head, and began to sob from the deepest depths of his heart.

To his surprise, the father realized that the Rebbe was crying harder for his son than he himself had ever cried for anything in his whole life. So he started sobbing even more.

The two men sat crying together for a long time. Suddenly the Rebbe lifted his head, wiped away his tears, and smiled. Then he laughed out loud.

"Do you by any chance have some wine in your wagon?" he asked the astonished father.

"Yes, I do."

"Then bring it fast," the Vorker said in a hearty voice. "We need to say a '*L'chaim!*'"

The *Yiddele* had no idea what was going on, but he hurried to bring the wine and two glasses. The Vorker poured for both of them: "*L'chaim*, my friend, *l'chaim*!" And the bewildered father echoed, "*L'chaim...*"

"I know you must think I'm crazy," the Rebbe went on, "crying one minute, laughing the next. But it happened so quickly, I just had to celebrate. It's *mamash* a miracle! A minute ago – thanks to our tears – the Gates suddenly opened. Your son will live! *L'chaim*! To Life!"

Do you know how G-d opens the Gates of Heaven? He never opens them wide all at once...

Let's imagine the gate you need is bolted shut. Then G-d hears your prayers and He does just one thing. He turns the key in the lock. From the outside, the gate doesn't look any different. So if you're impatient, if you knock on the gate and it doesn't open immediately, then maybe you'll give up and walk away. Or perhaps you'll pace around a little, smoke a cigarette, and come back to the gate again ten or fifteen minutes later. But the gate looks the same. You can't tell anything's changed. So you think your prayer hasn't been answered, and leave in despair.

But if you stay there, leaning against the gate the whole time with your ear to the lock, you can mamash *feel it when G-d turns the key. And then you know that the door is starting to open...*

The Gates of Heaven should always be open to our prayers...

U'teshuvah U'tefillah U'tzedakah

Repentance, Prayer and Charity

Illustration:

"But one stone ... stands alone outside the gates of the cemetery, under a tree..."

"Yossele the Holy Miser"

Everybody knows that on the High Holy Days, each individual Yid – and Am Yisrael as a whole – are judged by the Heavenly Court. The Court puts all our merits, our good deeds, on one side of a Heavenly scale, and on the other side are all our mistakes. If our merits outweigh our transgressions, then we are inscribed for blessing for the coming year. And G-d forbid, if the opposite is true…

But you know, even if the scales should tip against us, there is still hope. Because, as we say in the davening *on both Rosh Hashanah and Yom Kippur:* u'teshuvah u'tefillah u'tzedakah *– repentance and prayer and charity – cancel any harsh decree…*

Teshuvah

You know, there is a kind of teshuvah *that comes from the Tree of Knowledge. I realize I did wrong, I* mamash *regret what I did, and I decide to try to do better. So I make a little list of all my mistakes, and another list of how I can improve my behavior.*

It's all very sweet, very beautiful. But then there's another level of teshuvah. *Imagine that I love somebody very much. Then, sadly enough, I do something to hurt that person's feelings, and we stop being close. We* mamash *become strangers. And I feel so bad, completely broken. Suddenly, the question isn't so much whether what I did was right or wrong. It's much deeper than that. I just miss my friend with all my heart. So I go to him or her and cry, "I love you so much. Please let me return, let me come back. I just want to be close to you again."*

You know, every time we do wrong, we build a wall between ourselves and G-d. We mamash *shut the Ribbono Shel Olam out of our lives. Then suddenly we realize what we've done. And we miss G-d so much. We miss the Torah, we miss Yiddishkeit, we miss being holy. So we start to cry out from the deepest depths of our hearts, "Master of the World, I know I made so many mistakes. And I don't even have an excuse. But I'm* mamash *begging You, please take me back. Please let me come home to You."*

And this is really the highest teshuvah of all…

Tefillah

We usually think of prayer as asking G-d for something. But it's much more than that. The deepest depth of prayer is that we are making a connection. Through the simple act of praying, just in itself, we connect ourselves so closely to G-d...

Once a chasid *asked his Rebbe, "What should I pray for on the High Holy Days? What should my* tefillah *be, every day of my life?"*

And his Rebbe answered, "Every day we pray for what we think we need — a decent livelihood, good health, children, our soulmate. On the Days of Awe we confess before G-d, admit all our mistakes, and ask for forgiveness. But we should do all this very quickly. And then we should say:

"'Please, Ribbono Shel Olam, let all the world come to know You.

"'Please let all people get together as one.

"'Please show each of us our own holy purpose.

"'And please help us serve You with all our hearts and with all our strength.'

"This is the prayer we should never stop praying. We have to keep it in our minds, in our hearts, until our very last moment on earth.

"Because this is the real prayer, the real tefillah, *of a Jew..."*

Tzedakah

And then we come to tzedakah, *to giving charity...*

How are we supposed to give tzedakah? *Let's say we're walking down the street, and a* shlepper *comes up to us. He's dirty and ragged, maybe he even smells. He says, "Oy, oy — I'm so hungry. I'm* mamash *at the end. Could you give me a couple of dollars?" Or maybe he doesn't say anything, he just holds out his hand.*

So what do we do? We take out our wallet, and — trying not to look at him — we give him some money. Then, without a word, we walk away. And we feel so good because we think we've just fulfilled the holy mitzvah *of giving charity to the poor.*

That's all cute and sweet. But it's not enough. Because maybe, with the charity we have given him, the shlepper *can feed his body. But have we given him anything to feed his soul?*

There's a teaching from the Holy R. Yitzhak Vorker: G-d didn't take us to Mount Sinai and give us the Torah just to tell us to give a beggar some dollars or shekels. Yes, it's important to give him money. But we have to do more than that.

We have to give him back his pride, his self-confidence. We have to revive his soul. We have to say to him:

"Sweetest friend, maybe today you are poor and you need me to give you ten dollars. But I promise you that soon you will be so rich you'll be able to give another Yid *ten times that much."*

You see what it is, when you give somebody tzedakah, *at that moment you have the power of a Rebbe. You are* mamash *on the level to say to G-d,* "Ribbono Shel Olam, *I want You to make this man so wealthy that tomorrow he'll be able to give charity to everybody else!"*

Karliner Minchah

There is a prophecy in the Book of Amos (8:11) that says: "Behold, days are coming ... there will be a hunger in the land. The hunger will not be for bread, and the thirst will not be for water, but to hear the words of G-d."

You know, we are living in such a hungry world. But the saddest thing is, so many people have no idea what it is they're really hungry for.

Sometimes we're walking down the street, and a person comes up to us: "Can you tell me the time?" We look at his arm; he's wearing a watch. He's not asking about hours and minutes. He's really saying, "Time is running out, my life is passing by. I mamash *don't know what to do with myself anymore. Can you give me one kind smile, one holy word, to keep me going?"*

Or somebody asks us for directions to a certain place. He has a map, and anyway the place he wants is only two blocks away. He could find it on his own. Do you know what he's really saying? "I'm so lost, I don't know where I'm going in my life. Can you show me the way to find what I'm missing in my heart, in my soul?"

And that's really what prayer is all about. I'm saying to G-d: "There's an emptiness in my heart. I'm so hungry ... hungry for something beautiful, something real. I'm starving for one holy word, for one message from You — for one moment's revelation of Your light..."

ery late one afternoon, R. Aaron the Second of Karlin said to his followers: "Prepare the wagon. We're going for a ride." One of the *chasidim* said, "But Rebbe, it's time for the afternoon prayer. Shouldn't we *daven minchah* first?"

"We're not *davening* here today," the Rebbe answered. "We have to go to another place. Fast! Get on the wagon."

So all his followers climbed with R. Aaron onto the carriage, and they took off. Can you imagine it — at least twenty *chasidim* hanging onto one small wagon that wasn't made to hold even half that many! As they passed through one small town after another, the people turned to stare.

Now everybody knows that the Karliner *chasidim* always offered the afternoon prayer very late. But there's a limit to everything, even lateness. The night was getting darker and darker, and the *chasidim* were starting to get worried. They didn't like to bother the Rebbe, who certainly knew how late it was. But finally one of them couldn't stand it anymore:

"Rebbe, we've *mamash* got to *daven minchah*. It's so late, maybe already too late…"

But R. Aaron only said, "Soon, soon. We're almost there."

They kept driving and driving, through towns and villages, over hills and past thick forests. The night was becoming darker and darker, but strangely enough, there also seemed to be more and more light. The moon looked so big, the stars so bright. The Rebbe's followers thought the world had never been so beautiful. But it was also getting later and later. Finally one of the *chasidim* said,

"Rebbe, we've really got to pray!"

"One more minute," the Rebbe answered. "When we get to the next village, we'll stop."

As they entered the next town, R. Aaron told his driver to pull over in front of a little *cretchma*, a little inn. While the Rebbe waited, the *chasidim* jumped down and knocked on the door. And a very old man came out. It was impossible to tell how old he was – certainly seventy, perhaps ninety, maybe even one hundred and twenty. He didn't seem at all surprised that twenty strangers were knocking on his door late at night. He just smiled at them and said,

"*Shalom*, friends. What can I do for you?"

"We're students of the Karliner Rebbe and we need to *daven minchah*. Could we possibly come into your inn to offer the afternoon prayer?"

"But of course! It would be my greatest honor."

Now, there's one other thing you should know about the Karliner *chasidim*. They put all their hearts and souls into their *davening* – and also all their voices. They *mamash* shouted and yelled when they prayed. The Holy R. Asher of Karlin once asked his father, R. Aaron the First,

"I know it's important to pray really loud. But how loud is loud enough? Suppose somebody's coming at me with a knife and I'm screaming for help? Is that yelling loud enough for prayers?"

And his father answered, "Well, that's all right – for the beginning. But after that, you have to pray so much harder … and so much louder!"

So here were R. Aaron the Second and all his followers coming into the old *Yiddele's* inn and starting to pray. The *chasidim* knew that this was no ordinary *minchah*, and not just because it was so late. The Rebbe had gone to so much trouble to get to this inn, they knew it had to be a very special place. So they prayed with all their hearts and all their strength, even more than usual. They were crying and shouting, *mamash*, at the top of their lungs.

And you know, it's very quiet in a little village at night. The Russian peasants living around the inn went to bed very early. It was a warm summer's evening, and all the windows of the *cretchma* were open. And the *chasidim* were *davening* so loudly that their voices carried clearly in the still night air, and could be heard from very far away. So the sound woke up all the peasants. They couldn't understand any of the words, all they heard was the shouting. And shouting in the middle of the night meant only one thing to these simple people: there must be a fire. Because a fire in a Russian village at that time … about one hundred years ago … was the greatest danger possible. It could *mamash* destroy the town! So all the little peasants jumped out of their beds, and – many still in their pajamas – grabbed buckets of water and ran toward the *cretchma*.

But when the peasants got to the inn, they dropped their buckets and stood still, staring. Before them was indeed a fire. But not the kind of fire they expected – and feared. This was not a fire that destroys, not a fire that drives you away. It was a fire of love, a fire of joy. This was a fire that brings people together … a fire of prayer.

Now everybody knows, the Holy Ishbitzer teaches that G-d gave His Torah only to us, not to the other nations. So when a *Yid* is learning Torah, a non-Jew sitting next to him isn't inspired to join him. But it's different with prayer. If a person is *mamash davening* with all his heart and soul, even someone who doesn't understand the words is so moved that he also just has to pray.

So when the peasants saw the Karliner *chasidim* pouring out their hearts to the Master of the World, they also started yelling and shouting in their loudest voices, crying out to G-d as they never had before. The *chasidim* finished *minchah*, and began to dance and sing. And the peasants danced and sang with them. There was absolute unity – and so much joy, so much love in the air. R. Aaron stood on one side, marveling at the sight of his *chasidim* dancing hand and hand with the Russian peasants. "*Ribbono Shel Olam*," he whispered. "Surely this is what it will be like when the Messiah comes!"

After a while the peasants ran home to bring fruit for the Rebbe and his students, and they all ate and drank together. Then R. Aaron announced that it was time to leave. The peasants all hugged and kissed the Rebbe and his followers, and escorted them to the wagon. It was *mamash* not to be believed! And you know, if there is still some love here in our broken world, maybe it's from that afternoon prayer.

The old innkeeper also walked with the *chasidim* to the wagon, and stood by its side as they prepared to leave. And just as they were about to drive away, the Rebbe turned to him and said, "So? What do you have to tell me?"

"Rebbe, I've been waiting so long for you to come," the old *Yiddele* answered. "You know, today is my one hundred and seventh birthday. Exactly one hundred years ago, the Holy Baal Shem Tov came to this inn with his followers. I was just a boy then. My grandfather ran the inn. And it was just the same as today. The *chasidim* arrived very late, and wanted to offer the afternoon prayer. They *davened* with all their hearts. They shouted and yelled and danced and sang. And the peasants came running and joined them. They all prayed together, danced and sang together. Their voices became one voice, and I thought the sound of their love must have broken through to the highest Heavens. Then they all ate together, and hugged and kissed each other.

"Finally the Baal Shem Tov said it was time to leave. And just before they drove away, the *Heilige* Rebbe called me over. He put his holy hands on my head and said,

"'My dear little boy, please listen to me. Exactly one hundred years from now another great Rebbe will come with his *chasidim*. They will also *daven* the afternoon prayer. They will shout and cry and sing like we did today. The peasants will again come running to join them, and they will all pray and sing together.

"'Please remember, my sweet child – please tell the Holy Master we were also here before…'"

You see what it is – our parents, our grandparents … our great-great grandparents – left us a message: Please only go where we were before. Please only go to the kinds of places that our Three Holy Fathers, our Four Holy Mothers, the Holy Baal Shem Tov would have visited. And when you stand and pray by the Holy

Wall, listen for the voices of all the holy broken Yidden *who poured their hearts out to G-d there before you...*

Someday all of us, all the people of the world, will get together in Yerushalayim. *And we will all pray and dance and sing together, because the Holy City of Jerusalem is the gate of prayer for the entire world. As the Prophet Isaiah says: "My house is a house of prayer for all the nations..."*

Let the day be soon when the world will be one...

Yossele
The Holy Miser

Our Rabbis teach that we should try to be like G-d. Just as the Master of the World is merciful, we should be merciful. Just as He is slow to anger, so we should try to control our tempers.

But do you know what is the most G-d-like act of all? Giving. When we give to others generously, from the deepest depths of our hearts, we are, mamash, so close to G-d...

n the city of Cracow there is an old cemetery. Most of the gravestones are beautifully engraved, even though they are worn and battered by time. But one stone is unlike all the rest. It stands alone outside the gates of the cemetery, under a tree. And engraved on it is one single line: Here lies Yossele, the Holy Miser.

It was the year 1550. The Jews of Cracow all lived crowded together in a miserable ghetto. Most of them were so broken, so oppressed, so poor. Only one *Yiddele* in the ghetto, Yossele, had a lot of money. So you'd think he would use at least some of his wealth to help his poor brothers and sisters. But sadly enough, that wasn't the case. Because Yossele was the biggest miser in the world.

In his whole life Yossele never gave one ruble to help a fellow *Yid*. Everybody thought his heart must be made of stone. You know, a miser is not really part of society, especially Jewish society. One of the most important *mitzvos* is giving charity. If you're not giving, especially if you're very rich, then nobody wants to have anything to do with you. So nobody ever wished Yossele "Good Shabbos" or "Good *Yom Tov*," or blessed him with a good year. In fact, nobody spoke to him at all. When he went out onto the streets of the ghetto, the other *Yidden* usually moved away. But some people, especially the children, threw stones at him, and called him a filthy miser to his face.

One day word spread through the ghetto that Yossele was dying. Members of the burial society immediately ran to his house. Now really it is the work of the burial society to take care of the funerals of all Jews, whether they are liked or not. But this case was different. When the members of the society came to Yossele's bedside, one of them said,

"Yossele, you know that you don't have long to live. This is your last chance to do *teshuvah*. In your whole life you've never helped one single Jew. Give us some money now. We'll use part of it to pay for your grave, and give the rest to the poor. Maybe that way you can atone for being such a miserable miser."

Yossele just looked at them. "I guess I can afford to give you fifty rubles."

"Fifty rubles! Yossele, you have hundreds of thousands of rubles. You can afford to give us a thousand, at least!"

"No way. Fifty rubles and that's it!"

"Yossele, where you're going, what use do you have for money? How can you be so stingy, so selfish?"

Yossele didn't even answer. He just closed his eyes and lay back on his bed.

Now the members of the burial society were really getting angry. "Yossele," one of them cried. "If you don't give us a thousand rubles, we won't bury you!"

Yossele just smiled. "So what? All my life I took care of things by myself. Somehow I'll take care of that too."

The members of the burial society couldn't believe their ears. They were so shocked that they all got up to walk out. But that moment was Yossele's last. With his final breath he said "*Sh'ma Yisrael Hashem Elokeinu Hashem Echad* … G-d is One," and left the world. The members of the society stood looking down at him for a moment. "Well," one finally said, "I guess he died happy, thinking about all the money he saved." And they turned around and left the house.

The men of the burial society did just what they'd said they would. Yossele died on a Sunday night. No one buried him on Monday or Tuesday or all day Wednesday. Finally on Wednesday night one of his neighbors had mercy on his poor wife and children. He waited until almost midnight, so nobody would see. Then he loaded Yossele onto his wagon, drove to the cemetery, and buried him outside the gates, under a tree.

Now, the chief rabbi of Cracow at that time was a very holy man, *mamash* a great *Kabbalist*, by the name of R. Kalman. Late that Thursday night, as R. Kalman was sitting and learning, there was a knock on his door. It was one of the poorest *Yidden* in the ghetto. "*Heilige* Rabbi," he said. "Forgive me for coming so late. But I have nowhere else to go. Please … could you give me some money for the Holy Shabbos?"

"Of course, my sweetest friend," R. Kalman answered. "It would be my greatest honor. But tell me, I've known you for years and you never came to me for money. How have you been managing until now?"

So the poor *Yiddele* told him, "Rabbi, I haven't had a job for twenty years. No matter how hard I've tried to make a living for my family, nothing has ever worked out. But for all these years, every Thursday morning I would find an envelope under the door of my broken-down house. On the outside of the envelope was written: '*Lekoved Shabbos*', in honor of the Sabbath. And inside were five rubles, just enough to bring some light into my wretched life, some hope into my broken heart. But this week – I don't know what happened, I don't know why – that envelope didn't come…"

"My dearest friend, I understand," said R. Kalman, although he didn't really understand at all. "And I'd be so happy to help you. Here. Good Shabbos." And he handed the *Yiddele* five rubles. The poor man thanked him with all his heart, and turned to leave. But just then, there was another knock on the door. It was a second *shlepper*, who said,

"Rabbi, I'm *mamash* desperate! Please give me some money for Shabbos…"

R. Kalman looked from one poor *Yiddele* to the other. "I'm more than happy to help you, sweet *Yid*, but tell me one thing. Why haven't you ever asked me before?"

"Rabbi, I'll tell you the truth. Every Thursday morning for the last ten years, I've found an envelope with two rubles under my door. But not today, not today…"

That night, one after another, all the poor *Yidden* of Cracow came to R. Kalman's house. There were so many of them that they completely filled the room. All of them asked for money. And they all told the Rabbi about an envelope. Sometimes the envelope contained ten rubles, sometimes five, sometimes two. On the outside of each envelope was the same message: *Lekoved Shabbos*, in honor of the Sabbath. And all the envelopes had come on Thursday morning … until that day…

Now R. Kalman was really puzzled. Someone had taken care of all these people for years, and then suddenly stopped that very day. Why? What was different about that particular Thursday? Then – *gevalt, gevalt*! Suddenly everything was clear. It had been Yossele, Yossele the Holy Miser!

R. Kalman buried his head in his hands. "We were so blind," he whispered. "And we were so cruel to him. We didn't even give him a decent funeral." He looked up and saw all the poor people staring at him. He told them who he thought had been helping them, and then he asked,

"Am I right? Did you know Yossele? Did you ever meet him? And if you did, there's still one thing I don't understand. How did he know your names, where you lived? He gave different amounts of money to each of you. How did he know what you needed?"

The poor *Yidden* all looked at each other. One turned to the man next to him and asked, "Did you ever...?" His neighbor just nodded: "And did you...?" The first man also nodded. Finally one of them said,

"Rabbi, I can really only speak for myself, but I think it's the same for all of us. This is what happened:"

Once my wife and children were *mamash* starving. And I had nowhere to go to get money for food. I didn't know what to do! Then suddenly I thought of Yossele. Maybe I could get through to him just one time. Maybe, just maybe, he'd help me. So I gathered up all my courage and knocked on his door.

Yossele welcomed me so sweetly, with so much love. He invited me in and said, "Please, sit down and tell me all about yourself." Then, to my surprise, before I could say a word, he picked up some paper and a pencil, and started to ask me questions. And he wrote down all the answers. He said,

"My dearest friend, could you tell me your name?"

"My name is Avramele."

"Sweet Avramele, where do you live?"

I told him, and he wrote it on his paper.

"What do you do for a living?"

"I carry water."

"Oy, Avramele, that's such hard work. And do you have any children?"

"Yes, eight. Three boys and five girls."

"Avramele, so many children? How do you feed them? Can you make enough money, carrying water, to take care of them all?"

I just hung my head, too ashamed to speak, to tell him why I'd come.

" Avramele, my heart *mamash* aches for you. You must all be starving! Tell me, how much money do you need a week for your family?"

And he seemed so sincere, he seemed to care so much, that I opened my heart to him and cried, "Yossele, if only you would help me! We're so poor, my children are so hungry. If only I had five rubles a week…" And I started to cry.

Yossele didn't say anything. He just patted me on the shoulder, and left the room. I thought he'd gone to get me some money, but instead he came back with some wine and cake. He invited me to eat with him, and we talked about all kinds of things.

Then suddenly Yossele seemed to go crazy! He started shouting at me, "Who do you think you are, coming to my house like this, invading my privacy, asking me for charity? Did you really think that I, Yossele, would give you any of my precious money? Well if you did, my friend, you're sadly wrong!"

And you know, Yossele was a very strong man. He *mamash* picked me up, put me over his shoulder, and carried me to the door. Then he threw me down the steps of his house. And all the time he was screaming,

"Get out of here! And don't ever come back!"

What could I do? I went home and told my wife, "All the stories about Yossele are true. He really is a miser. He wouldn't give me a thing."

And here the poor *Yiddele* started to cry. "But I should have suspected," he sobbed to R. Kalman. "I *mamash* should have known. Because that Thursday morning there was an envelope with five rubles under my broken door, *Lekoved Shabbos*, in honor of Shabbos…"

R. Kalman looked at the rest of the poor people. "Is this what happened to all of you?" They silently nodded. R. Kalman started sobbing from the deepest depths of his heart. "I can't believe it!" he cried. "Yossele supported all of you. He kept your children alive. And not only didn't we bury him. We never even spoke to him, we never tried to get to know him. Your children, the very children who owed their lives to him, threw stones at him and called him names!" And he cried and cried. Then he looked up and said, "I want you to spread the word to everyone in the community. And I'll also announce it on Shabbos in *shul*. I am declaring this Sunday to be a fast day. Tell everyone to come to the synagogue. We have to ask Yossele for forgiveness."

Early that Sunday morning all the Jews of Cracow came to the *shul*. And they all started crying and praying: "Yossele, how could we not have seen? Yossele, we were so narrow, so closed, so cruel! Please forgive us, please bless us…" They stayed in the synagogue all day, not eating or drinking, just *davening* with all their hearts. But in the very late afternoon R. Kalman turned to the people and said, "It's not enough. I don't think we've gotten through to him yet."

So R. Kalman went to the front of the *shul*, opened the Holy Ark, and cried from the depths of his soul, "Yossele the Holy Miser, please hear us! Please give us a sign that you forgive us!" Then he fell unconscious to the floor.

The people thought their rabbi was dying – or worse. He lay so still, they couldn't even tell if he was still breathing. Everybody began to cry and wail. Then suddenly R. Kalman opened his eyes and looked around, like he was waking from a dream. "Help me up," he said to the people nearest him. And when he was on his feet, he cried out in a loud voice, "*Yidden*, listen to me. While I was unconscious I saw Yossele. But he looked so different. He was shining, *mamash* radiant with light. And he said to me,

"'R. Kalman, please tell everybody to stop fasting. Tell them all to go home. They don't have to ask me for forgiveness. This is the way I wanted it. I wanted to fulfill the *mitzvah* of *tzedakah* in the highest way – by giving without anybody knowing except the Master of the World, the One Who knows everything…'

"I said, 'But Yossele, we didn't even give you a funeral. You must have felt so sad, being buried alone.'

"And in my vision, I saw Yossele smile. 'Holy Rabbi,' he said. 'What makes you think I was alone? Let me tell you, Abraham, Isaac, Jacob and our Four Holy Mothers were there with me. King David walked on one side of me, playing his harp. And Elijah the Prophet was on the other side, carrying a candle…

"'R. Kalman, please tell all the poor people that I thank them so much for coming to my house. I thank them for sharing with me from the depths of their broken hearts. You know, I'm sitting here in Heaven between our Holy Father Abraham and our Holy Mother Sarah. You'd think I'd have everything I'd ever dreamed of. But there's one thing I miss. In Heaven there are no poor people, no way to give, no one to help. I'd give up all of *Olam Habah*, all of Paradise, if I could have just one more Thursday morning to slip envelopes, *Lekoved Shabbos*, under those broken doors…

"'Tell the poor people I miss them…'"

And then R. Shlomo would tell us a personal sequel to the story of Yossele the Holy Miser:

n the mid 1970's R. Shlomo was invited to represent the Jewish religion at a weeklong ecumenical conference. Each religion was assigned one night to host all the others, and Judaism, as the oldest religion, was the host on the first night.

Everyone gathered in a big hall for a kosher meal. No matter what their differences might be, all the people there treated each other with great *kavod*, with utmost respect. There was such a wonderful spirit of unity, openness and love. R. Shlomo, eager to meet everybody, circulated all around the room. He felt particularly drawn to one assistant bishop who was standing alone in a corner, a little bit apart from everyone else. There seemed to be something very special about this man – he was *mamash* shining. So R. Shlomo went right over to him and asked his name.

"Joe," the bishop said, a little hesitantly. "My name is Joe."

After the meal R. Shlomo presented a program on Judaism. And although it hadn't been his original intention, he decided to tell the story of Yossele the Holy Miser. All his listeners were deeply moved, and as R. Shlomo looked out over his audience, he saw that many people were crying…

The next night it was the Catholics' turn to be the hosts. Right before they were to begin their presentation, Joe, the Assistant Bishop, sought out R. Shlomo – who was sitting quietly at a table – and said, "The Bishop sent me to find you. He wanted you to know how much the story you told yesterday touched his heart. And I – I don't have the words to express how much it meant to me. Please, we were wondering if you could tell that story again tonight?"

Of course R. Shlomo agreed, and he told the story of Yossele a second time. And again everybody's eyes were filled with tears.

The last night of the conference, R. Shlomo was scheduled to give a big concert. And just before he was to go on stage, Joe the Assistant Bishop came up to him again: "I know you'll think I'm crazy, but I really have to hear that story one more time. After the concert I'll tell you why it's so important to me."

So R. Shlomo again told the people about Yossele the Holy Miser. And again everybody cried from the depths of their hearts.

After the concert R. Shlomo and Joe the Assistant Bishop went for a walk. For a long time they strolled along in silence. Then, suddenly, Joe stopped. He turned to R. Shlomo and said:

I have a confession to make. I didn't tell you the truth. My name isn't really Joe. It's Yossele from Cracow...

I want you to know, my mother was in the Dachau concentration camp. She was half-dead when an American soldier found her. For some reason he immediately liked her, so he took her with him to America, and took care of all her medical expenses until she was well. Then he asked her to marry him, but he had one condition. He insisted that she never tell any children they might have that she was Jewish. It broke my mother's heart, but she loved him. So she agreed.

My father's a very religious Catholic, and I always went to Catholic schools. So, as you can see, I became an assistant bishop. And I was very happy with my life until...

A few weeks ago my mother called me and said, "Joe, I'm very sick. The doctors have told me I only have days left to live. Please, can you come to see me right away? I can't leave the world until you know my story..."

I rushed to her bedside. My mother looked at me with tears in her eyes and said, "My sweetest son, it's time for you to know the truth. Your name isn't really Joe, and you're not really a Catholic. You are Yossele, Yossele from Cracow – and really, you're a Jew...

"You see, I named you in honor of my father, one of the richest Jews in Cracow before the War. Ah, my father was such a holy *Yid*, so giving, so kind. Our house was like the tent of our Father Abraham, always open to the poor. I can't remember a time when there weren't needy people eating, even sleeping there. My father always said he was just following the example of our ancestor, Yossele the Holy Miser, for whom he was named..."

My mother told me about the Holocaust, about what had happened to her. She told me about her promise to my father. Then she said, "But now I need you to know where you really come from, who you really are..." And she told me everything she knew about how holy it is to be a Jew. She told me about Shabbos and all the holidays, about Rosh Hashana, Pesach, Simchas Torah. She told me all about her parents, my *Zeide* and *Bubbe*. We talked for three days. And when she had no more strength, she held my hand tightly and said, "My son, you have to promise me – you'll always remember that you're not really Joe. You're Yossele from Cracow."

The next day my mother left this world.

I was beside myself – *mamash* so broken and torn apart inside. Until a few days before I'd known myself as Joe, the devout Catholic, the assistant bishop. I loved my career, and I'd put all my heart and soul into it. Then suddenly I find out that it's all a lie. I'm not a Catholic, I'm a Jew. And my name isn't Joe, it's Yossele from Cracow. I just didn't know who I was any more.

One night I couldn't sleep, thinking about this whole thing. So I started to pray, "G-d in Heaven, who am I? Am I Joe, or am I Yossele from Cracow? Please, Lord, You have to help me. Show me who it is that You want me to be!" My eyes filled with tears as I thought about my promise to my mother, so I cried, "Okay, Lord, this will be my sign; if I ever hear someone say the words 'Yossele from Cracow,' I'll know You want me to be a Jew."

Mamash the very next week I came to this conference. And right away, on the first night, there you were, R. Shlomo, standing up on the stage and not only saying the words "Yossele from Cracow," but actually telling the story of my ancestor, Yossele the Holy Miser! I couldn't believe it. I knew it was my sign from Heaven, but I was still afraid. It's such a big change, you know. It means starting my whole life over again. That's why I asked you to keep telling the story…

Tonight, when you spoke about Yossele, I swear I could see my mother standing behind you on the stage. I could see the tears rolling down her cheeks, and hear her prayers. Suddenly it was clear to me that G-d had sent you on her behalf, to remind me that I'm not Joe anymore. I'm Yossele, Yossele from Cracow. And I knew what I had to do…

Yossele took something out of his pocket. It was an airline ticket, from New York to Tel Aviv. He said, "I bought this last week, but until tonight I didn't know if I would use it. Now I'm sure. I'm leaving first thing tomorrow. It's a one-way ticket; I'm not taking anything with me, and I'm not coming back. I'm going first to New York and from there to Israel. If I'm going to learn how to be a Jew, I think the best place to start is in our own land…

"You're the only person I'm telling about this, and after tonight you won't hear from me for a long time. I know my father will be frantic when he finds out I've disappeared; he'll look for me everywhere. I don't want him to know that my mother broke her promise and told me about being Jewish, because, after all, he really did save her life. But I promise that if

G-d is good to me, if I meet a Jewish woman I want to marry, I will go to the Holy Wall in Jerusalem the night before the wedding and write you a letter…"

Time went by, and R. Shlomo heard nothing from Yossele. But he never forgot him. Whenever he went to Jerusalem he searched the faces of all the people he met, hoping to see him. But then again, how could he recognize him? Surely Yossele didn't look the same. He probably had a beard, maybe even *peyos*. And certainly he wouldn't be wearing a big cross anymore. So R. Shlomo couldn't find him anywhere.

Then one day, five years later, when R. Shlomo walked into his office in New York, there was a letter waiting for him. On the front of the envelope was R. Shlomo's name; on the back was written, "From Yossele, once Yossele from Cracow, now Yossele from the Holy City of Jerusalem…"

R. Shlomo tore open the envelope. Inside there was a letter:

"To the holiest of the holy, my dear R. Shlomo. I can never thank you enough for helping me find out who I really am – for showing me that I wasn't ever Joe, that in my heart I was always Yossele from Cracow. I never met my *Zeide*, my grandfather, but I imagine that I look like him – I have a long beard and *peyos*, I even wear *tzitzis*. I learn Torah, I love the Holy Shabbos. And tomorrow night, with G-d's help, I will marry a girl … *mamash*, the sweetest of the sweet, so beautiful, so holy … who in my heart of hearts I know is so much like my grandmother, my *Bubbe*.

"So I'm sitting here tonight by the Holy Wall – it's a dark night, there's no moon, but by the *Kotel* there's always G-d's light – and I'm keeping my promise. I'm writing to thank you. I want to bless you to keep being such a holy messenger. Please keep reminding all the Joe's of the world that they're really not Joe. They're Yossele, Yossele from Cracow…

"With love from Yossele, thanking G-d for all His blessings at the Holy Wall in the Holy City, *Yerushalayim*."

Giving Rebuke

Sometimes people come up to us and say, "You know, you'd really better take a good look at yourself. You did this wrong, you messed that up." They list all our mistakes for us, and then they say, "So, you'd better fix yourself. You mamash had better do teshuvah."

These people think they're our friends. They think they're helping us. But what do they really accomplish? Even if what they say is true, they just make us feel bad about ourselves. They take away our self-respect and make us feel guilty – not only about our mistakes, but about our very lives.

The truth is, you can't make people into better Jews, into better human beings, by making them feel guilty. The Heilige R. Nachman of Breslov says that if doing an aveira – a sin – is bad, making people feel guilty is mamash evil. Because guilt kills the spirit, and takes away all our strength...

Everybody knows that when the Jewish People left Egypt, they met Amalek, who attacked those Yidden who were weak and tired. Amalek is the source of evil in the world. And this is his secret. Amalek doesn't have to try to get us to sin. All he has to do is point out to us everything we've already done wrong. He makes us feel so low he takes away all our strength. Then he laughs and tells us that it's really okay, we can fix it all by repenting, by doing teshuvah. But he's made us feel so weak and tired, what kind of teshuvah can we do?

Do you know what we need? Somebody who can rebuke us, can help us do teshuvah, without taking away all our holy pride. Or maybe we need something even deeper, the deepest depths. Have you ever known people who are mamash holy, who are on a really exalted level? To be in their presence is a little like going to the mikvah. We feel like we're immersed in holiness, in something so very beautiful. And when we leave them, it's like coming out of the ritual bath. We feel purified, cleansed – and we're ready to begin to live new and better lives...

R Yaacov Yitzhak Horowitz, the Holy Seer of Lublin, was the greatest student, and really the successsor, of the *Heilege* R. Elimelech of Lizensk. They studied together as Master and pupil for a long time, and then one day R. Elimelech said to the Seer, "I've taught you many things, but there is one very important lesson which you cannot learn from me. The only one who can give this over to you is my brother, the Rebbe Reb Zussia."

The Seer had no idea what his Rebbe was talking about, but he followed R. Elimelech's instructions without question. He traveled to the Rebbe Reb Zussia and repeated what his brother had said. The Seer expected R. Zussia to reveal to him some deep mystical secrets, or some new way of approaching the *Gemorah*. But instead R. Zussia just smiled and asked,

"Tell me, when you want to get a person to do *teshuvah*, what do you do?"

The Seer thought for a moment. "Well, I ask them about their lives … about the *mitzvos* they keep, how much they help other people. And – *oy vey*! The ugly stories I hear, the number of sinful things people have done! *Gevalt* – sometimes I *mamash* can't bear to listen to it!

"Then, first I try to get the person himself to recognize all his mistakes. I drop gentle hints – but to tell you the truth, this approach doesn't usually work very well. People, you know, are so terribly blind when it comes to taking an honest look at themselves. So I really have no choice. I have to tell the person the sorry truth to his face. I say,

"'*Oy*, my friend, do you realize what you've told me? You did such-and-such, which is *mamash* forbidden. And that, which you did last year, is also not permitted.' And I list for them everything they've done wrong. After which I say, '*Gevalt*, Brother *Yid*, do you realize how terrible this is? Your whole life is *mamash* one sin after the other. You'd better do *teshuvah* fast!'"

"And does this work?" the Rebbe Reb Zussia asked quietly.

"Well, not always, but sometimes. Well, at least occasionally…"

"And do you know why it doesn't work more often?" R. Zussia inquired more forcefully. "Do you realize what you're really doing to these people? You're pulling them down, you're pushing their faces into the mud! You make them feel so low, you take away all their self-confidence. After that, how can you expect them to have the strength to do any fixing?"

"So how do you do it?"

"Ah," R. Zussia answered. "I do it in a different way altogether. I don't say anything harsh to them. Just the opposite. I encourage them, say comforting words to them. I try to be their friend. And then I pray for them. And I pray so hard that I open the gates for Heavenly light to shine into their hearts. Then they don't feel bad about themselves. And they don't have to struggle to do *teshuvah*, to begin a new and better life.

Because when a great light from Heaven is pouring into you, you *mamash* can't do anything but serve G-d…"

You know, there are two kinds of teshuvah – *the* teshuvah *of Moshe Rabbeinu, and the* teshuvah *of Aaron HaCohen, Aaron the High Priest.*

The level of Moses is to admit our mistakes and then to say to G-d, "I regret what I did. I promise I won't do it again."

Ah – but the teshuvah *of Aaron HaCohen – Aaron is the priest who walks into the Holy of Holies on Yom Kippur. He atones for the whole Jewish people. But he doesn't say anything. He just burns incense. And do you know what that incense is? It's the Clouds of Glory that protected Am Yisrael in the desert. Do you know what it means to have the Clouds of Glory around you? It means you are surrounded by G-d's love…*

To do Moshe Rabbeinu's teshuvah *may be very difficult, but it is something we have to do alone. Nobody can do it for us. But to do Aaron's* teshuvah *I need a good friend. Sometimes when people know they've done wrong, they're so broken, so discouraged. They need one person to support them, to give them back their pride. They* mamash *need a friend who surrounds them with love…*

You know, when we received the Torah, Moshe went up onto Mount Sinai. But Aaron stayed at the foot of the mountain. Why didn't Aaron also go up?

Moses went up alone because the teshuvah *he brought down is one we have to do on our own. But Aaron had to stay with the people. You can't take clouds of glory – you can't take love – for yourself. Someone has to give it to you…*

A Real Jew

It's not easy to be an emesser Yid, *a real Jew. It's one thing to be like everybody else – an apple among apples, a bagel among bagels. But to be* mamash *real ... to be a Jew on the deepest inside level ... ah, that's another thing altogether.*

Look at the world we're living in. The world says – whatever you do, don't be real. When it's the "right" thing, put on a smile. Or if it will be pleasing, bring tears to your eyes. Say hello or invite somebody to a party ... but only out of good manners. Don't really mean it. And never let anybody see that you're broken, or mamash *full of joy. Let your wedding be as somber as a funeral, and a funeral as festive as a wedding. Because above all, you should never open to anyone the deepest depths of your heart.*

And it's the same thing when it comes to Yiddishkeit. You know, some people go around saying "Baruch Hashem, thank G-d," all the time. No matter what question they're asked, the answer is always "Baruch Hashem." Maybe somebody is sick as a dog. A friend notices and says, "Hey, brother, you don't look so good. How are you feeling?" And the first person answers, "Baruch Hashem." Or you see somebody whose eyes are red and swollen. It's clear he or she has been crying. And you ask, "Are you all right?" What will be the reply? "Blessed is G-d – Baruch Hashem."

Now, sometimes saying "Baruch Hashem" means you're really on a very high level. You see G-d's Hand in everything that happens to you and you accept His Will with love. But sometimes people say "Blessed is G-d" one time too many. It sounds a little bit suspicious. It sounds like maybe they're hiding what's really going on inside of them behind the mask of faith in G-d...

But the truth is, the Master of the World doesn't need us to say "Thank G-d" all the time. He doesn't need us to hide our pain or our joy. What does the Ribbono Shel Olam actually want from us? He wants us to be real...

This is one of the deepest teachings of the Holy R. Menachem Mendel of Kotzk. We all know it's important to do mitzvos, *to fulfill G-d's commandments. But for Kotzker chasidim there's a deeper question: Where is your service of G-d coming from? Are you keeping His Law out of habit, or are you doing* mitzvos *with all your heart?*

You see what it is – sometimes the most important thing is not how much good or bad you do, but how much light lies hidden in your deepest depths. What is permanent inside you?

If the inside of your insides is mamash *shining, then maybe you can open the gates for G-d's light to fill the whole world. Maybe you can help bring the*

Messiah. But you have to be connected from the inside. Because everything we do has to flow from the very core of our beings...

So in Kotzk, nobody would ask you what kind of Jew you are, how much Torah you know or how many laws you keep. Kotzker chasidim *only wanted to know one thing. Are your actions coming from the soul of your soul, from that place deep inside all of us that only knows the deepest truth, the holiest reality? In other words, they would ask, are you for real? Are you a real Jew...?*

On one particular night of every year, R. Yitzhak Zelig Morgenstein of Sokolov, the great-grandson of R. Menachem Mendel of Kotzk, would have a special feast for all his *chasidim*. They would eat the best food, drink the best wine. And then the Rebbe would say: "We're here tonight to honor the *yartzeit* of Moshele the Water Carrier. I've told you his story a thousand times, but please forgive me – *lekoved* Moshele, I must tell it again..."

When I was very young, I became the Rabbi of Sokolov and moved here from Kotzk. Now, I was a very strong Kotzker *chasid*, and my holy great-grandfather had given over to me one teaching which he told me always to remember: What does G-d love the most in the world? Only that which is real. So when I came to the synagogue my first Shabbos in Sokolov, I was looking for only one thing: a real Jew.

I walked up to the front rows of the shul, where all the great scholars and the rich, important people were sitting. Certainly they were special, maybe even on a very high level. But did they seem to be for real? To tell you the truth, not so much...

I made my way through the whole synagogue, greeting everyone. I walked among all the poor people sitting way in the back. All the *Yidden* were beautiful, the sweetest of the sweet. But did they seem real? Sadly enough, not to me. It *mamash* broke my heart to think I'd have to spend the rest of my life in a place where there wasn't one real Jew.

Then, just as I was about to leave the shul, I saw one *Yiddele* sitting all alone behind the stove, reciting the Psalms. He was just a simple Jew. But I couldn't believe it! He was *mamash* real! He was praying with all his heart. And he was shining with G-d's light.

I decided that this was the one man in town I had to get to know. So I went right over to him and held out my hand: "My dear friend, I'm the new rabbi here. Could you tell me your name?"

He didn't even look up from his prayer book; he only mumbled, "I'm Moshele, Moshele the Water Carrier."

"Moshele, I'm so happy to meet you. Tell me about yourself."

Silence. He just kept saying his Psalms.

I kept trying to get Moshele to talk to me, but he wouldn't answer. Maybe he didn't think I was real enough for him. Finally I guess he lost patience. He closed his book of Psalms and walked away.

After that I tried so many times to get to know Moshele. It was really important to me. He was the most real *Yiddele* in the whole city. But I could never get him to respond. Maybe he was so humble that he just couldn't believe that the new rabbi wanted to have anything to do with him. Whenever I saw him in shul, I always made a special point of talking to him, asking him how he was. But he would just say, *"Baruch Hashem,"* and go on with his *davening.*

One winter's night, many years later, I took a long walk, all the way to the outskirts of Sokolov. And on my way back I noticed a broken-down shack that was shining with light. I was curious, so I went closer and looked through one of the cracked windows. Behold – it was Moshele's house! He seemed to be having some kind of a celebration. He was standing in the middle of the room, holding a glass of wine, and all the simple *Yidden* of the city ... all the tailors, wood-cutters and water carriers ... were dancing around him and singing at the top of their lungs. And again I could see that Moshele was *mamash* glowing.

"Gevalt!" I thought. "Maybe this is my chance to get to know something about Moshele." So I went around to the front of the hut and knocked on the door. When Moshele saw who was standing there, his face turned very red. He showed me inside without saying a word, then managed to stammer: "I ... I ... Holy Rebbe, I never dreamed you would ... I mean ... I can't believe you've come to visit me ... I don't deserve such an honor..."

"Sweet Moshele," I answered. "Really it is MY honor to be in your holy house. But tell me something. I saw from the road that you are having a party. What are you celebrating tonight?"

And it seemed that none of the other guests knew the reason for the party either, because they all gathered around Moshele as he told this story:

"Rebbe, I want you to know, my parents died when I was very young. I never had a real home; I slept on the streets and begged for food. Sometimes I would go to the synagogue, and kind people there taught me how to pray a little bit, and how to recite the Psalms. But that's all I ever learned – I never had anybody to teach me more.

"As I grew older, my body got very strong. So I started to carry water. I didn't make very much money, but at least I didn't have to beg anymore. Then I met the most wonderful woman and we got married. Holy Master, you should have seen my wife when I married her. She was so beautiful; *mamash*, she looked like a queen. We had seven children, the cutest of the cute, the sweetest of the sweet. When they were born, they looked like little angels.

"But my wife isn't beautiful anymore, and my children don't look like sweet angels. They're thin like sticks from hunger, and their eyes are always red because they cry so much for food. I work as hard as I can, *shlepping* water, but I can't earn enough to take care of them. Rebbe, they *mamash* break my heart. I can't bear their hunger, their sadness, their pain…

"Now you know, every morning at three o'clock I bring water to the synagogue. And that early I'm all alone in the *shul*. Do you know what I do? I open the Holy Ark and I start to cry:

"'*Ribbono Shel Olam*, it's me, Moshele the Water Carrier from Sokolov. Master of the World, please listen to me. I'm so broken, I *mamash* can't live like this any more. I can't stand the pain. My wife is so hungry, my children are starving…

"'G-d in Heaven, please send me a thousand rubles. If I could have that much money just one time, I could feed my family. I could start my life over again. Please, I'm begging You…'

"Rebbe, I've been doing this every day for so many years. At the beginning I was sure G-d would answer my prayer, that somehow the money would come. But nothing happened. To tell you the truth, I started to wonder if G-d was really listening to me. But I kept doing it anyway, maybe just out of habit.

"Then yesterday morning, when I went to deliver the water, I saw a package lying on the floor of the synagogue, right by the door. I picked it up and opened it, and – Rebbe, I couldn't believe my eyes! Inside were exactly one thousand rubles, cash! I ran to the front of the *shul*, tore open the Holy Ark, and shouted,

"'Master of the World, forgive me for losing faith in You. Now I know it's true – You do hear, You do answer everybody's prayer. You just do it in Your own time, in Your own way. *Ribbono Shel Olam*, in the name of my wife and children, thank You so much for having mercy on us all…'

"I was *mamash* so happy that I danced around in a circle in front of the Holy Ark. Then I thought for a moment and said, 'You know what, G-d in Heaven. I don't want anybody to know about this for a while. Let it be a secret between You and me for three days...'

"I thought about going right home with the money. You know, now I wouldn't have to carry water any more. But then I thought about all the people who depend on me for their water; I couldn't just let them down because G-d had blessed me. So I continued on and finished my rounds for the day. Rebbe, usually my work is so hard, the water is so heavy to carry. But yesterday I *mamash* danced through the streets. And usually I feel so broken that I don't want to talk to anybody. But yesterday I said hello to all the people I passed, and gave them all blessings. Then I went home. And, *gevalt!* – my wife looked as beautiful to me as on the day we got married. My children looked like angels again. I'd never been so happy in my life!

"Last night I went back to the synagogue for the evening prayers. And before I even got inside, I could see that something strange was going on. The widow Chanale was standing by the door, crying from the deepest depths of her heart. You remember, Rebbe, her husband passed away a few weeks ago, and we all collected money for her and her ten children. We gave her a thousand rubles. And now she was crying, 'I've lost all the money! I know I had it here in *shul*. But I can't find it anywhere. It's gone!'

"I knew immediately what had happened. I went to my usual place behind the stove, but I couldn't pray. I was so broken, *mamash* so angry at G-d. 'Master of the World,' I shouted silently. 'How can you be so cruel? For years and years I've begged You for a thousand rubles. But did you have to take Chanale's money in order to answer my prayer? Are You testing me? Well, I'm telling you right now, I'm not giving the money back. I found it, it's mine! I need it, my wife and children need it. Get Chanale another thousand rubles!

"'And G-d, one more thing. I'm never coming back to *shul* again. I can't serve a G-d who is cruel. I don't even want to know You anymore!'

"And I walked out of the synagogue, intending never to return.

"I went home. My wife looked worn and tired again, my children so sad. I lay down on my bed and buried my face in the pillow. I didn't want anybody to see how hard I was crying. Rebbe, things had been bad for me before, but this time I was *mamash* at the end. I needed those thousand rubles so much, but I couldn't stop thinking about Chanale and her children. They had nothing, nothing at all ... and nobody but me to help them. I just didn't know what to do. I was so confused, so broken. All I wanted was to die!

"I couldn't sleep the whole night. Then, at about midnight, I thought I heard a voice. At first I was afraid somebody had broken into the house, so I got up and looked around. But no one was there. Then I heard the voice again. It seemed to be inside my head. Rebbe, I swear to you, it was my soul talking to me. And my soul said,

"'Moshele the Water Carrier, what are you doing? All your life you always prayed. You always turned to G-d, you always trusted Him. And now, when you *mamash* need help the most, you push the *Ribbono Shel Olam* away? Moshele, talk to G-d again. Pour out your heart to Him like you always did before…'

"And Rebbe, I started to pray like I never had in my whole life: 'Master of the World, I don't know what to do with this money. G-d in Heaven, please – one time let me *mamash* hear Your voice. Tell me what You want of me. And give me the strength to do whatever You say is right.'

"I kept crying and praying for a long time. Finally I didn't have anything left to say, and I fell back, exhausted, onto the bed. And then, out of the silence, I heard another voice, different from the first one – loud, strong and clear. Rebbe, I knew it was the *Ribbono Shel Olam* speaking to me. And He said,

"'Moshele the Water Carrier, get up, get dressed, and – fast! – take the thousand rubles to Chanale. The money belongs to her, not to you.'

"I want you to know, Holy Master, at that moment I felt such complete peace, such absolute bliss. To hear G-d's Voice actually speaking to me … could there be a greater joy in the world? I got up and did as the *Ribbono Shel Olam* had said. I ran right to Chanale's house, and even though it was the middle of the night, I pounded on her door and yelled as loud as I could, 'Chanale, I found your money!'

"Rebbe, I wish you could have seen Chanale's face when I put the thousand rubles into her hand. I'll tell you, all the money in the world is worth nothing compared to what I saw in her eyes when she said to me: 'I thank you in the name of my children.'

"This all happened early this morning. I'm so happy, Rebbe. I feel so good. So tonight I'm celebrating. Tonight I'm thanking G-d for answering my prayer, and for helping me have the strength to give the money back. And mostly I'm thanking the Master of the World for giving me the incredible *z'chus*, the unbelievable privilege, of actually hearing His Holy Voice…"

At this point the Sokolover Rebbe would raise his glass of wine and say to his *chasidim*, "Here's to Moshele the Water Carrier. Did any of you ever hear G-d's Voice? I met one *Yid* who did – Moshele the Water Carrier. Did any of you ever know somebody who was *mamash* real? I did. So here's to Moshele the Water Carrier, a real Jew!"

Today so many people say, "I wish I could talk to G-d, but I don't know how to pray." Do you know what their problem is? They're not in touch with their insides, with their souls.

But when you're mamash *connected to your own life-energy, then suddenly all the gates of prayer are open. And the strange thing is – not only can you talk to the Master of the World from the deepest depths of your heart – but the more you* daven, *the more you feel alive...*

When the Messiah comes, what will be his deepest revelation? That G-d hears all our prayers. He is always listening to us, even if we're not aware of it. And when it is clear to us that the Master of the World hears every word of our prayers, then suddenly nothing is hopeless anymore...

The Holy Apter's Accounts

There is a story about the Holy Apter Rav, R. Avraham Yehoshua Heschel. His chasidim once asked him, "Rebbe, we hate to bring this up, but we really need to know. When your one hundred and twenty years on this earth are over ... may you live long ... what should we write on your tombstone?"

And the Apter answered, "When I get up to Heaven, the Court will ask me: 'Did you daven with all your heart?' And I will have to admit, 'I prayed as hard as I could, but the truth is, I could have done better.'

"Then the Court will ask, 'And your learning?' And I will have to reply, 'I studied the Torah as often and as deeply as I was able, but the truth is, I could have learned more.'

"Finally the Court will ask me, 'Did you really love G-d's people, the Jewish people, from the deepest depths of your heart?' And to this question alone I will be able to answer, 'Yes, I did.'

"So that is what you should write on my tombstone: Ohev Yisrael, *the one who really loved Israel..."*

nce a poor *Yiddele* came to the Holy Avraham Yehoshua Heschel of Apt and cried, "*Heilige* Apter Rav, I'm *mamash* at the end. I owe this Polish nobleman one thousand rubles. He's threatening to kill me if I don't pay him by the end of the month, and not only don't I have the money, I have no idea how to get it. Rebbe, can you help me? What should I do?"

The Apter Rav scribbled something on a piece of paper and handed it to the poor man. "Take this, my friend," he said. "Then pack fast and go to Warsaw. There's a rich man there who is like my private banker. Give him this letter. It tells him to give you the money you need from my account."

So the poor man went immediately to Warsaw. He knocked on the door of the rich man's house, and handed him the Apter's letter. "I'm so sorry to bother you," he explained, 'but the Apter Rav told me to come to you. He sends you his greetings, and instructs you to give me one thousand of the rubles you are keeping for him."

"The Apter Rav?" the rich man exclaimed. "Of course I've heard of him, but I've never met him in my life. And I'm certainly not holding any of his money. The whole idea is ridiculous! But ... I can see that you're poor. So here, I'll give you ten rubles as *tzedakah*."

"Ten rubles!" the poor *Yiddele* cried. "But the Holy Apter said you'd give me a thousand. It's *mamash* a matter of life and death!" He tried to argue, but the rich man slammed the door in his face. So what could he do? He went back to the Apter and told him the whole sad story.

"I'm so sorry, my sweetest friend," the Apter Rav said kindly. "But don't lose hope. There's another rich man – in Brode – with whom I also have an account. Here, give him this note…" he went on, scribbling again on some paper, "…and he'll give you the money."

So the poor man set out again, this time to Brode, and delivered the Apter's letter to the rich man: "The Holy Apter Rav sends greetings to you and asks that you give me one thousand rubles from his account."

"The *Heilige* Apter Rav! *Gevalt* … to think he'd send greetings to me! What an incredible honor! You know, I've never actually seen him, but I know he's *mamash* one of the greatest of all the Rebbes. And if he says he has an account with me, well, it would be my greatest privilege to be of service to him – and to you. Here, sweet friend, are your thousand rubles."

The poor man was overjoyed. He ran right back to the Rebbe to thank him, then to the Polish nobleman to pay off his debt. And so his life was saved.

Meanwhile, the strangest things happened. From the moment that he gave the thousand rubles to the poor *Yiddele*, the rich man from Brode started getting richer and richer until he was *mamash* a millionaire. While the rich man from Warsaw … not only did his business go bankrupt, but the night after he turned the poor man away, a fire completely destroyed his house and he lost everything. He had no choice but to become a beggar, going from town to town, asking for charity.

One day the man from Warsaw found himself in Apt, so he went to the Rebbe's court and stood in line with the rest of the *shleppers* appealing for *tzedakah*. The Apter Rav noticed him there and took him aside. "My friend," he said. "I know you once were rich. And I know that you need help. But charity isn't really the help you need. Let me ask you, didn't you ever wonder why you suddenly became so poor?"

The man from Warsaw began to cry. "Rebbe, I've thought of nothing else since the night my house burned down. Please, can you tell me what happened? Why am I being punished like this?"

"It's not exactly a punishment," the Holy Apter answered. "But tell me, do you remember a poor *Yiddele* who came to you, asking in my name for one thousand rubles?"

The man from Warsaw nodded.

"You told him I had no account with you," the Rebbe went on. 'But there's something you should know. When my soul was about to come down into this world, G-d said to me, 'You are going to be a great rabbi, and many poor people will come to you for help. You will want to take care of all of them, and for that you will need a great deal of money. So I am going to make you very rich so you can give to everyone.'

"But I said to G-d, '*Ribbono Shel Olam*, I don't really want to have to deal with finances and business. I won't have enough time left for learning and teaching Torah. Yes, I'll need access to money. But please, don't give it to me directly. Choose some people to act as my bankers. Let them keep my money on account – they can even use it for themselves, as long as I can withdraw it from them whenever I need to.' And G-d agreed.

"You, my friend, were one of the people G-d chose to take care of my money. That's why you were so rich. But you refused to honor my account, while another rich man was happy to do as I asked.

"So the night that you turned the poor man away, my money was taken away from you, and deposited instead with the rich man from Brode."

Head in Paradise, Feet in Hell

You know, there are two kinds of Rebbes, two kinds of holy people. There's the kind of tzaddik who spends most of his time in the Beis Midrash, learning and teaching the Holy Torah. He wears a clean black kapote and a big gartel. His peyos are down to his shoulders and he has a long beard. He only talks to his students and other Rebbes – and to those needy people who come to him for help. And when he goes out on the street, his eyes are half-closed. He's afraid he might see something forbidden, so he doesn't look at anything – or anyone. Two of his students have to lead him around.

When people see him, with his downcast eyes and his two gabba'im, they nod and say, "Gevalt, is he holy! That's just how a tzaddik should look."

Then there's another kind of holy man. He's always late for davening. He sits and learns and teaches his students, but only part of the day. What's he doing the rest of the time? He's out on the streets, looking for people to help. He stops by a poor man, but he doesn't just give him money. He talks to the shlepper for a while, maybe even holds his hand. He sees children crying and stops to ask what's wrong. A little boy is lost, so he takes the child home. He tries to fix things between a little girl and her parents – or between a husband and wife. So maybe his clothes aren't always neatly pressed, and his shoes are maybe a little bit scuffed. Because he doesn't have time to worry about things like that. He only worries about taking care of Yidden…

When people see him talking to a beggar, they shake their heads: "He can't really be holy if he hangs out with such people!" They look at his clothes: "How can a tzaddik go out in public looking like that?" But you see what it is – the first kind of Rebbe is so busy guarding his purity that he walks with his eyes closed. He passes people by without noticing them, which means he's blind to their pain. So maybe on the outside he is holy, but inside…?

And the second kind of Rebbe – the one who runs around helping every Yid – for him it's just the opposite. Maybe his outside looks a little bit unkempt, a little bit coarse. But his insides … ah, his insides are shining.

Because the truth is, learning Torah and protecting our own holiness are very high ways of serving G-d. But if in addition we also go out of our way to help our brothers and sisters – to love all of Am Yisrael – then our service is so precious before the Master of the World…

The Holy R. Yosef Shaul Natenson of Lemberg was *mamash* one of the greatest Torah geniuses of his generation. Learning Torah was his whole life, and he sat in the *Beis Midrash*, immersed in Holy Books, from early morning until late at night.

One day, while R. Yosef Shaul was sitting in his private room, learning as usual, there was a knock on his door. He thought it was one of his students delivering a message, so he called, "Come in." But when he looked up from his *Gemorah*, to his surprise, a *shlepper* dressed in filthy rags was standing just inside the door.

R. Yosef Shaul recognized the man immediately: "Efrayim? Efrayim, my dearest friend, can it really be you? I haven't seen you for so long – since you moved away. But I never forgot you. I've thought of you often, remembering how we learned together when we were young. Last I heard, you had married the daughter of a very wealthy man. In fact, I thought you were rich yourself. And now, to see you like this! What in the world happened to you?"

"*Oy*, Yosef Shaul, what didn't happen! I lost all of my money, and now I'm just what I seem … a poor beggar. And if that wasn't enough, my daughter just got engaged to the most wonderful boy, and I don't have a single ruble to pay for the wedding. I didn't know what to do, and then I thought of you. You have an important position here, and you know so many people. For the sake of our old friendship, would you help me raise two thousand rubles for my daughter's wedding?"

"My heart breaks for you, Efrayim, really it does. If I had enough money, I'd give you what you need in a minute. But I'm not a rich man. And you know, so many poor *Yidden* come to Lemberg to ask for help, there is no way I can go around trying to collect money for all of them. If I did, I'd never have time for my learning. So I've made it my policy not to go out to raise money for any one person. If I make an exception for you, people will think I've relaxed my rule, and I won't have a moment's peace."

"Yosef Shaul!" Efrayim cried. "I *mamash* can't believe what I'm hearing! I'm not just some ordinary *shlepper* asking for a handout. I'm Efrayim, your oldest friend. We've known each other all our lives. We swore we would always be friends. And you won't break some silly rule for me? Maybe I never knew you at all…" And he began to cry.

"You're right, Efrayim," R. Yosef Shaul sighed. "This is a special case. And I really am your friend. All right, I'll help you. I'll talk to some of the rich people in Lemberg. It may take me a few days, but I'll try to raise the money for you."

That very night R. Yosef Shaul set out for the home of the richest man he knew. But just as he started up the steps of the house, he saw Efrayim coming out of the door. "Efrayim!" he called in surprise. "What are you doing here?"

"Collecting for my daughter's wedding, of course!"

"Did he give you anything?"

Efrayim laughed. "All of ten rubles!"

"What did you expect, Efrayim? R. Yosef Shaul exclaimed. "You're a stranger in town. To these people you look like any ordinary *shlepper* – while I'm well known and respected. People will listen to me, I can explain things to them. Look, you asked me to help you, and I've agreed. But you're just complicating things by trying to collect on your own. How can I get people to donate a lot of money if they've already given something to you? So do yourself a favor. Go somewhere and wait. By Thursday I hope I'll have the two thousand rubles for you."

But Efrayim only looked at him strangely and said, "Yosef Shaul, I know you mean well. You do what you can do. But I also have to do what I have to do." And he turned and walked away.

So R. Yosef Shaul continued on into the house of the rich man to try to collect some money. But in his heart he was very annoyed with his friend Efrayim.

Early the next day R. Yosef Shaul went out again – this time to the house of the second wealthiest man in the community. And again, just as he was about to knock on the door, Efrayim walked out. This time the rabbi was really angry:

"Efrayim, didn't you hear anything I said last night? I hope at least he gave you enough money to make your interference worthwhile."

"Well, I got more than last time – twenty rubles."

"Efrayim, you've *mamash* got to stop doing this. You're making it impossible for me to help you. I promised you I'd raise the money. I told you I hope to have it by Thursday. I'll meet you at the *Beis Midrash* that night and give it to you. Until then, please have a little patience. And stay out of my way!"

Again Efrayim just looked at him intently and said, "Yosef Shaul, you do what you can do, and I'll do what I have to do."

Everywhere R. Yosef Shaul went to try to raise money, he found that Efrayim had been there just before. Even so, by some miracle, by Thursday he had actually collected the two thousand rubles. So that night, feeling very pleased with himself, he went to the *Beis Midrash* to meet his friend, as they had arranged.

For several hours the rabbi waited, glad to be alone and get back to his learning. Then, as it got later and later and Efrayim still hadn't arrived, he started getting annoyed. "All the trouble I went to, collecting this money for him, and he can't even bother to come on time!" But after waiting all night with no sign of Efrayim, R. Yosef Shaul's irritation turned to concern. "Maybe something happened to him," he thought. "He wanted this money so much, he wouldn't just not show up to receive it." Then he had another thought. "*Oy vey* – maybe I really insulted him when I told him not to try to collect himself. Maybe I hurt his feelings so much that he doesn't want to see me. Or maybe he thinks I was so annoyed with him that I wouldn't keep trying to help him. *Gevalt*, what did I do?"

Every night for a week R. Yosef Shaul waited in the *Beis Midrash* for Efrayim, but his friend never came. By now he was frantic with worry, so he sent his *shammes* out to search the town for him. But Efrayim was nowhere to be found. R. Yosef Shaul couldn't imagine what had happened to him.

The next morning, after another sleepless night, R. Yosef Shaul arrived at the synagogue a little late for the morning prayers. And as he walked in the door, to his amazement he saw Efrayim standing in a corner of the *shul*, asking everyone near him for money. The Rabbi rushed over to him and cried,

"Efrayim, thank G-d you're back! I've been so worried … I was *mamash* afraid something terrible had happened to you. My dear old friend, I'm so sorry if I hurt your feelings when I asked you to stay away while I was collecting the money. I realize now that I shouldn't have spoken so harshly. But look – *Baruch Hashem*, I got the whole two thousand rubles." And he started pulling ruble notes out of his pockets and dropping them on the table.

Efrayim looked at him, then at the pile of rubles. "You can keep the money, Yosef Shaul," he finally said. "The truth is, I don't need it. I'm still as rich as I ever was. I never really lost my fortune."

"But Efrayim! I just don't understand. Why did you beg me for help? Why did you send me chasing all over town to collect money you don't even need? You must have known how uncomfortable I felt, asking the members of my community for charity for you. And surely you realized how much time this whole thing was taking from my learning. Why did you play such a trick on me?"

"I had my reasons," Efrayim answered. "Let me tell you the story:"

You were right, my dear friend. I did marry the daughter of a very rich man. Her father set me up in business, and I became very wealthy myself. So there I was ... with lots of money and a beautiful wife whom I loved very much. You'd think I had everything. But there was one problem: my wife and I had no children.

I went around from Rebbe to Rebbe, asking for a blessing to have a child. Finally I came to one Holy Master, and I stayed to learn with him for a long time. In the end I became one of his closest students – and not only because, after his blessing, my wife and I had a son. He was *mamash* the holiest person I have ever met, and the Torah he taught me was the deepest of the deep.

Sadly enough, suddenly my Rebbe got very sick, and there was nothing anyone could do. I was with him right before he left the world, holding his holy hand. I *mamash* didn't know what I was going to do without him. At almost his last moment, I finally blurted out, "Rebbe, I love you so much. I can't tell you how much I'm going to miss you. Would you do me one favor? Would you come back and tell me how things are for you in the World to Come?"

My Rebbe smiled at me and whispered, "Yes, my dear Efrayim. I'll come back to visit you Shabbos night." And shortly afterwards, he passed away.

The first Friday night after that, I couldn't sleep. I was sure that was when my Rebbe had said he'd come to me. But nothing happened. The next Shabbos I stayed awake as long as I could, but I was so tired and sad, I must have dozed off. Because suddenly I opened my eyes and there was my Rebbe, standing next to my bed. And he looked so beautiful, just as I'd thought he would. He was *mamash* shining with Heavenly light. I couldn't take my eyes off him, gazing into his holy face. Then I happened to glance down at his feet. And I couldn't believe my eyes. His feet were as black as coal!

"Holy Master!" I cried. "What happened to your feet?"

"Ah, my dear Efrayim," my Rebbe said sadly. "When I came up here to Heaven, the Heavenly Court started to judge how well I'd used my body in *olam hazeh*, in this world, to serve G-d. They saw that I'd used my head to learn Torah, my mouth to pray, my heart to love other *Yidden*, my hands to do *mitzvos*. And every part of my body that was judged to be worthy immediately became filled with holy light. It all went very well – until they came to my feet. Then the chief of the Heavenly Court looked at me sternly and said,

"'My friend, you did much good in your life. You studied Torah, you davened, you loved other people. But one thing you didn't do. You never went out of your way for another Jew. When poor *Yidden* came to you for help, you blessed them from the deepest depths of your heart. But you never actually walked around to help them get what they needed. So I'm afraid your feet never did one *mitzvah* in your whole life.'

"Here the head of the Court pointed at my feet. I felt a burning pain, and when I looked down, my feet were black. Efrayim, I'm afraid that even if my head is in Paradise, my feet, sadly enough, are in hell…"

I began to cry. I couldn't bear to see my Rebbe like this; it *mamash* broke my heart. Suddenly I knew what to do. I jumped out of bed and shouted, "Holy Master, I can fix this for you! I'll become your feet! In your name I'll walk all around for two years, collecting money for the needy."

And I want you to know, Yosef Shaul, that is how I have spent my life from that moment until today. I've traveled everywhere, to every city and town I could find, raising money for the poor. Mostly, of course, I wanted to help my Rebbe. But I was also curious about other Holy Masters; I wanted to see if they were any different, if they bestirred themselves to help. But sadly enough, I soon realized they were all the same. They were happy to pray, to give a *bracha*. But would they run around and *mamash* do something to solve somebody's problem? To tell you the truth, not so much…

Then I found myself in Lemberg, and I remembered you. So I came to check you out. And I discovered, my dearest friend, that you are like all the rest. You are happiest when you can sit in your room with your books. Your head maybe does a lot of holy work, but your feet…?

So I forced you to go out and help me – and made it really hard for you, got in your way whenever I could. I wanted you to have to exert a lot of effort, to have to go to a lot of trouble – so you could fix your feet while you still had the chance.

Efrayim was silent for a moment. Then he gave R. Yosef Shaul that same intense look and said, "So, my oldest friend, now that you've finally learned to walk, I'm begging you: Don't ever stop!"

You know, sometimes our feet are waiting for our heads to tell them what to do. But it says in the Torah that G-d blessed us for the way we walked behind Him in the desert. All the time our heads were telling us, "You're crazy! There's no water in the desert, no food to eat. Why are you doing this?" But our feet didn't listen to our heads. They just kept on walking.

One of the ways we Jews are holy is that we have holy feet. The holidays of Pesach, Shavuos and Sukkos are called the Shalosh Regalim, the "Three Feet," because, in former good days, on those three festivals our feet carried us to the Beis HaMikdash to serve G-d. On the Shalosh Regalim our feet helped us become holy again.

Now, you might ask, how can feet be holy? Our feet are mamash the lowest parts of our body, attached so much to the ground. But you see what it is … if when someone asks us for a favor we jump up to do it with joy – or when our baby cries in the middle of the night we run right away to take her in our arms – then our feet are the holiest things in the world!

Do you know what the word "exile" really means? That we only move our feet according to our heads' instructions.

But to be free … ah, when we're free, our feet don't ask any questions, they just keep moving. Because they're not only connected to our heads. Our feet are mamash connected to G-d…

Nothing
And Everything

You know, it's a funny thing. Imagine that you're sitting at a table in front of a thick juicy steak. You're mamash hungry as a dog, and gevalt! The meat looks so delicious, you can't wait to start eating. So you take a big bite. And you want to spit the food out in disgust. The meat has absolutely no taste!

Maybe the problem isn't with the steak. Maybe the problem is that the person who gave it to you is a stranger, or even somebody you don't like so much.

Now imagine that somebody gives you a little piece of fish or maybe a crust of dry bread. Doesn't sound so delicious, right? Ah … but if the person giving it to you is someone you love with all your heart, it mamash has a flavor that is out of this world.

Sometimes you go to a restaurant and eat soup. And sometimes you eat soup that someone made for you with so much love. What's the difference? It's really very simple. Is it outside soup, or inside soup? Is it mamash your soup, or is it just soup?

Let's say that a person goes to a French restaurant and orders soup. Is he jumping out of his skin with joy because he's sitting there eating soup? No, because it's just ordinary soup. He chose it from the menu, so he eats it and he pays for it.

Now imagine that this same person comes home and his wife is waiting for him with soup that she made herself. Ah, it's another thing altogether. Because if somebody who loves you gives you soup that was made just for you, then it's really your soup. Eating it not only fills your stomach; it also fills the deepest depths of your heart with utmost simchah, with so much joy.

And then you mamash don't need anything more…

Everybody knows that the Rebbe Reb Elimelech of Lizensk was never totally in this world; he always lived somewhere between heaven and earth. Just before he passed away, he was very sick, and could not eat. His son, the holy R. Lazer, got very worried. "Father," he begged. "Please listen to me. I'm so afraid for you. As long as you are still in this world at all, you have to eat! Isn't there anything I can bring you that you would like?"

"Ah, Lazer – if you could only bring me some of the soup that Malkale, the wife of Avramele the water carrier, once made for me … that is the only food I think I could swallow."

R. Lazer immediately ran to the broken down shack of Avramele the water carrier and knocked on the door. When Malka answered, R. Lazer cried, "Malkale, fast! My holy father is very sick. Please tell me how to make the soup you once gave him. It's all he'll eat!"

To R. Lazer's surprise, Malka started to cry. "I'm so sorry," she sobbed. "Let me tell you the story…"

You know, my husband and I are just poor, simple Jews, not learned or on any high level. But we love and honor your holy father so much, and we were always dreaming that maybe, one day, the Rebbe Reb Elimelech would come to visit us. But of course we never had the *chutzpah*, the audacity, to actually invite him.

Then, a few weeks ago we saw your father walking down our street. Avramele thought this might be our big chance. So he ran outside to speak to him. Now my husband is really a very shy man, and he didn't know what to say or how to invite the Rebbe to our house. He just stood there, silently, as your father passed by.

But the Rebbe Reb Elimelech is so exalted, he knew exactly what my husband wanted. He said, "Avramele, it's so good to see you. Is there something you're waiting for, something, maybe, that you want to tell me?"

Still all Avramele could do was stammer, "Uh, Rebbe … uh, do you think … uh, could you maybe…?"

"Of course, my friend," the Rebbe finished for him. "I would be so honored to come to your house. I just wish I had known that you wanted to invite me. I would have visited you before!" Now, I had always known that my husband, for all that he's just a simple *Yid*, is really a very holy man. And when I saw that your father treated him with utmost *kavod*, with so much honor, I knew the Rebbe also realized that, in the depths of his soul, Avramele is *mamash* the holiest of holy.

The truth is, R. Lazer, our house is usually filled with sadness, hunger and pain. But when R. Elimelech came in, it felt like *Gan Eden*, like heaven. Avramele and I were so happy we didn't know what to do with ourselves; my husband was *mamash* shining from one end of the world to the other. Neither of us knew what to say to your holy father, but it really didn't matter – we were just so glad he was there. The three of us sat together quietly at the table, and it was absolutely beautiful! Suddenly Avramele jumped up from his chair and cried, "Malkale, what's going on here? Quick, bring some food for our holy guest!"

I ran into the kitchen. All at once I remembered that we had no food in the whole house. We ourselves hadn't eaten in three days. I didn't know what to do. I looked around the kitchen. All I saw was a fire burning in the stove. I filled a pot with water and put it over the fire. Then I took a spoon and started stirring the water. And my tears fell into the pot as I prayed,

"Master of the World, You know the truth. If I had all the best food in the world, I would make the most delicious soup for R. Elimelech. But I have nothing, *mamash* nothing at all.

"G-d in Heaven, You have everything. Everything that exists comes from You. In Your storehouse in Heaven You have every kind of food and every kind of taste. *Ribbono Shel Olam*, I'm *mamash* begging you. Please put into this water a taste of Paradise, a taste of *Gan Eden*..."

R. Lazer returned to his father and said, "I just went to see Malka, and she told me what kind of holy soup she made for you."

The Rebbe Reb Elimelech smiled and said to his son, "Then you understand, Lazer. With regular soup you can nourish the hungry. But with soup like Malka's you can *mamash* bring people back to life."

You see what it is — lots of times, sadly enough, we think, "Maybe some things are possible, but what I need is totally impossible. And how can I pray for something which realistically can't happen?"

Do you know what that means? It means we only believe a little bit in G-d. Because if you mamash trust in G-d, nothing is impossible. The Holy R. Mottele of Chernobyl says something very deep: Anybody who thinks for one second that there is anything that G-d cannot do is really a pagan. He or she mamash has no faith in G-d at all.

When we pray, we're above the order of this world, above the question of possible or impossible, even beyond the order of the Torah. Let's say, G-d forbid, that a person is terribly sick. According to derech hateva, the natural order of things, he's likely to die. And still I'm praying, "Ribbono Shel Olam, please change the normal course of things, and let my friend get well!"

Maybe someone hears our prayer. He shakes his head: "Oy, your friend is mamash at the end. Healing him will be really hard, even for G-d."

What does that mean, hard for G-d? About whom are you talking? A water carrier, a woodchopper, a janitor? What could be hard for the One, the Only One, the Creator of the World?

Or imagine that you did every sin possible. According to the order of the Torah, you're the lowest of the low. Yet here you are, praying, "Please, Master of the World, I'm begging You. Fix my soul. Let me be close to You again." And if you mean what you're saying, if you're crying out from the deepest depths of your heart, then G-d will help you, will take you back. Because if you think there is anything that can make you a stranger to G-d, then – gevalt! You have no idea what G-d is all about…

And this is the difference between asking another person for a favor, and asking for something from G-d. When I'm talking to other human beings, I can't ask them for everything I need. If I don't have a penny to my name, I can't have the chutzpah *to ask a rich man for a million dollars.*

But with G-d, it's exactly the opposite. When I have absolutely nothing, that's the time to ask the Ribbono Shel Olam *for everything,* mamash *everything in the world…*

nce there was a group of holy *shleppers* who wandered around from place to place, begging for food. But they were so dirty, their clothes were so torn, that most people didn't even want to look at them – and turned them away. They were lucky if they got some stale bread. But how long can grown men live on one loaf of bread? So, sadly enough, they were always hungry … *mamash* almost starving.

Finally their leader said to the others, "We can't go on like this. If we don't get some food in the next town, I'm afraid we'll die. We have to figure out a better way to sustain ourselves, come up with some kind of a plan."

They sat together in silence for a few minutes, thinking. Then one of them said to the others, "Listen, the only people who are always welcome in a town are the great Rebbes and their followers. Everybody fights over who gets to invite them for a meal. So I have an idea. Maybe you…" he continued, pointing to the leader "… could pretend to be a Holy Master, and we could pose as your students…"

The leader smiled. "You know," he said. "If we clean ourselves up a little bit, it just might work."

And since none of the beggars could think of anything better, that was what they decided to do. They even made up a name for themselves. Their leader would be called the Trich'er Trich'er Rebbe, and they, of course, would be the Trich'er Trich'er *Chasidim.*

As the beggars came close to the next town, they sat down to plan their entrance. They decided that, after they washed themselves and their clothes at a nearby river, two of them would go ahead of the others to announce the approach of the famous "Trich'er Rebbe." And the rest would follow immediately after with their "Holy Master."

Needless to say, when the word got around that a great, if unknown, "Rebbe" was paying the town a visit, everybody came out to greet him. And as the one beggar had predicted, everybody competed for the honor of inviting the "*chasidim*" for a meal. Finally the beggar-*chasidim* went home with one of the richest Jews in the city, who fed them his best food, offered them his best wines, and treated them like kings. For the starving beggars, it was *mamash* the answer to all their prayers.

After the meal, the rich man turned to the supposed "Rebbe" and said, "Holy Master, I have to tell you the truth. There's a reason why I invited you here today. My baby daughter is very sick. The doctors are afraid she may be dying, and they say there's nothing they can do. Rebbe, I've heard that people like you can *mamash* do miracles. So I'm begging you, please help me. Save my child!"

The beggar-*chasidim* turned white as sheets. The "Rebbe" buried his head in his hands in despair. How had their great plan gone so wrong? They were so ashamed that they wanted to cry out, "Can't you see who we really are? We're nothing, much lower than you are. We're just pretending to be holy because we were so desperate for food. How can we possibly help you?"

But of course they said nothing. How could they admit they were imposters? The townspeople would *mamash* stone them. Silently the "*chasidim*" all looked at their "Rebbe." He nodded slightly, then followed the rich man into the baby's room. There he took out a book of the Psalms, sat down by the child's bed, and asked to be left alone.

The "Rebbe" stayed in the baby's room for more than an hour. When he came out, his eyes were red and swollen and his face looked gray and tired. Still he smiled at the rich man and said, "*Baruch Hashem*, your daughter is out of danger. Not only will she live, but she'll be absolutely fine."

The rich man jumped up and rushed into his baby's room to see the great miracle for himself, with all the "*chasidim*" following closely behind. And when the father saw that the child was indeed well, he began to weep with joy. But the beggars had a very different reaction. They started to mutter and whisper to each other, "What's going on here? How can our leader have possibly cured this little girl? We've known him for so long, we thought he was just a *shlepper* like the rest of us. Could it be that he really is holy, that he can *mamash* do miracles? Then why has he been hiding his power from us all this time?"

The beggars managed to keep their mouths shut until the grateful father had thanked the "Rebbe" for his help, they all had thanked him for the meal, and they were back on the road. Then the "*chasidim*" grabbed their leader and shook him, all shouting at once: "Okay, now tell us the truth! Are you a beggar, or are you a Rebbe? How in the world did you heal that child? And if you can really do miracles, why didn't you help US? How could you have let us starve for all these years?"

Their leader looked at them sadly. "I'm no Rebbe," he answered softly. "I've always been just what I seemed – a poor *shlepper* like all of you. But when I went into that child's room … when I saw that beautiful girl and felt the strength of her father's love … I felt so helpless I thought I would die. I wanted so much to help her, but I knew there was nothing I could do. So I started to pray:

"'*Ribbono Shel Olam*, I know I'm nothing. Not only am I just a poor beggar, I'm also a liar and a cheat. And now this father has put his child's life in my wretched hands…

"'But the truth is, Master of the World, this rich man only thinks he's depending on me, on my supposed power. Really, he's looking for You. You're the One he needs, the Only One Who can perform a miracle and heal his child – because You are everything. The problem is, he doesn't know how to find You. So he's asked me, a lying, worthless beggar, to be his messenger.

"'*Ribbono Shel Olam*, I know I'm not worthy of this man's trust. But please, don't punish him because of me. I may be a liar, but he is a good and loving father. Please let his daughter live...'

"And, as you saw, G-d was merciful. The child was saved..."

Sometimes we think we're nothing but worthless shleppers, *the lowest of the low. But the truth is, we can still be messengers, go-betweens with G-d. Because if we cry out to the Master of the World from the deepest depths of our hearts, we too can work miracles...*

Mine is the Silver and Mine is the Gold

Everybody knows how important it is to give tzedakah, *charity. But what does the* mitzvah *of giving to the poor really mean?*

Once there was a great Rebbe, R. Shimon Skernovitcher. He mamash *had thousands of* chasidim. *But every Thursday night, the strangest thing happened. R. Shimon disappeared. No matter how many people were waiting to see him, he was nowhere to be found. And nobody had any idea where he had gone.*

One Thursday some of his followers decided to try to find out what was going on. Early in the evening they hid in some bushes outside the Beis Midrash, *hoping to see the Rebbe when he left on his secret business. Sure enough, after several hours R. Shimon came out and hurried away. So his students followed him.*

The Holy Skernovitcher moved quickly through the streets of Warsaw, the chasidim *sneaking along behind him. Soon he turned into one of the poorest neighborhoods in the city. And, of course, he was immediately surrounded by needy* Yidden *asking for* tzedakah. *But the Rebbe didn't just give some money to a beggar and then walk on. He stopped by each poor* shlepper *and said, "My sweetest friend, I would be so happy to help you. But I really can't give you charity. I can only give you this money as a loan."*

The beggar would look at him in surprise. "A loan? Rebbe, you would really give me a loan?"

And R. Shimon would say, "Yes, of course. Would you accept a loan from me? I have so much faith in you, I know you'll be able to pay me back."

With a huge grin on his face, each beggar would happily accept some rubles as a loan, and the Skernovitcher would go on his way.

After watching the Rebbe do this for a while, the chasidim *decided they'd seen enough. They went back to the* Beis Midrash *to wait for R. Shimon. And when he finally returned very late that night, they confronted him with what they had learned:*

"Rebbe, we have to admit we followed you tonight and saw what you were doing. But really, how could you tell all those poor people you were giving them loans? You know full well they'll never be able to repay you. Why didn't you just give them some charity and let it go at that?"

"Why? I'll tell you why! It's not just that those beggars don't have any money. They've also lost all their hope, all their faith that their lives can ever be better. They're so broken, mamash *in despair.*

"Do you know what it means to them when I, the Rebbe, offer them a loan? It means that I believe in them ... that even though now they've fallen to the lowest place, I have faith that they can get back on their feet again.

"Listen to me! I've taught you a lot of Torah. But this is the most important thing I'll ever tell you. It's not enough to hand a beggar a few rubles. You mamash *have to do more than that. You have to give him back his self-respect, to show him that you believe in him, even if – especially if – he no longer believes in himself…"*

The Holy R. Menachem Mendel of Rimanov was one of the greatest of the *chasidic* Rebbes. And at one time he had a very special follower, a beggar named Eliezer. Now Eliezer was as poor as he was holy and sweet, so when his daughter became engaged to a really special young man, he had no way to raise the thousand rubles he needed for her wedding. He thought and thought, trying to come up with a plan to get the money. And finally he realized what he had to do. There was only one *Yid* in Rimanov who was wealthy enough to give him the whole thousand at one time. He'd have to go to this rich businessman and ask for help.

So Eliezer screwed up his courage and knocked on the wealthy *Yiddele's* door. "Kind Sir," he said. "I'm Eliezer the beggar. I really hate to bother you, but I'm *mamash* at the end. I have no money to pay for my daughter's wedding. Do you think you could possibly loan me one thousand rubles?"

The rich man laughed in his face. "LOAN you a thousand rubles? Who do you think you're kidding? How in the world could someone like you ever pay me back? If you'd come to me honestly, asking for *tzedakah*, I might have been willing to help you. But to pretend that you want a loan…" And he laughed and laughed. Then he saw how much he'd hurt Eliezer's feelings. So he said, "Okay, I'll tell you what I'll do. If you can get somebody trustworthy – and with enough money – to sign as a guarantor for your 'loan,' I'll give you the money. But without that guarantee … sorry, my friend, you're out of luck."

With that the rich *Yiddele* turned to go back into his house, sure that Eliezer would get the message and go away. But Eliezer surprised him by saying, "I accept your proposal. Let's fill out the contract for my guarantor." So the wealthy man wrote out an official document that the undersigned would pay back the thousand rubles loaned to Eliezer the *shlepper*.

Eliezer took the paper, and ran straight to the *Beis Midrash*. He opened the Holy Ark and leaned inside. "*Gevalt, Ribbono Shel Olam*," he moaned. "What have I done? I don't know anyone who could be a guarantor for this loan. All my friends, all the people I know, are poor *shleppers* like me." He buried his head in his hands and began to cry:

"Master of the World, I *mamash* need this money, for my daughter's sake. Maybe You would guarantee this loan for me?"

Suddenly Eliezer picked up a pen and signed the contract himself. And this is what he wrote: "*Li hakesef, ve'li hazahav, ne'um Hashem.*" (Haggai 2:8) Now this passage from the Bible is usually translated: "Mine is the silver, and Mine is the gold, says the L-rd." But "ne'um" literally means "signed," not "says": "Mine is the silver, Mine is the gold, SIGNED G-d." Eliezer looked at what he'd written, straightened up, and set out again for the rich man's house.

When the rich man saw that Eliezer was back, he thought at first the beggar had come to admit that he couldn't find a guarantor. And he was prepared to be generous and give him some *tzedakah* ... if not the whole thousand rubles, at least something. But when he read the contract that Eliezer handed him, he couldn't believe his eyes. His first reaction was: "What *chutzpah* ... to forge a name, and G-d's Name at that!" – and to slam the door in Eliezer's face. But almost despite himself, something impressed him about this poor *shlepper*. Maybe it was his love for his daughter, maybe it was his naïve faith that G-d would really help him repay the loan. Whatever the reason, he found himself saying,

"Okay, my friend, I accept your guarantor. Here's your money."

And he handed Eliezer one thousand rubles, absolutely sure that he'd never see a penny of it again.

Now you know, according to Torah law, if no time limit is stipulated, then a loan must be paid back within thirty days. Four weeks after he gave Eliezer the money, a messenger appeared at the rich man's place of business. The wealthy *Yiddele* didn't happen to be there at the time, so the messenger left an envelope with his assistant. And on the envelope was written: "Repayment of your loan to Eliezer the beggar."

When the rich man came in some time later, his assistant said, "Someone was here to see you and left you this. It's the repayment for the loan you made to some *shlepper* named Eliezer." The businessman opened the envelope. And inside were the full one thousand rubles.

The wealthy *Yiddele* sat down at his desk, staring thoughtfully at the envelope and the money in his hands. "Well, what do you know?" he said to himself. "Eliezer may be just a poor *shlepper*, but he *mamash* has integrity! He must have spent hours ... maybe even days ... begging on the streets to come up with this money. Or – maybe he borrowed from somebody else to pay me back." Suddenly he found himself feeling sorry for Eliezer: "It must have been so hard for him. And really, he didn't have to go to all that trouble, he should have known I didn't actually expect him to repay the loan..."

All at once, the businessman got up and rushed out of his office. He had to find Eliezer! He had no idea where the poor *shlepper* lived, so he wandered all over the city until he finally spotted him begging on a street corner. "Eliezer," he called, running over to him. "My sweetest friend, thank you so much – I received the envelope with the thousand rubles. But I feel so bad that you had to take out another loan just to pay me back."

Eliezer just stared at him: "I *mamash* don't know what you're talking about."

"I'm talking about the envelope you left at my office."

"I never brought you any envelope."

"Well, someone did. Somebody left me an envelope containing one thousand rubles, saying it was repayment for your loan. You mean, it really wasn't you?"

Eliezer shook his head.

"And you haven't got any idea who it was?"

Another shake, no.

"Then what's going on here?"

The two men looked at each other in silence. Finally Eliezer said, "Maybe we'd better go to the Rebbe..."

So the rich *Yiddele* and Eliezer the beggar went together to see the Holy Rimanover. R. Mendele looked at the envelope; he closely examined what was written on it. He looked at the thousand rubles, turning the money over and over in his hands. He closed his eyes and sat very still, lost in thought. After a few minutes, he opened his eyes, took the envelope and pressed it to his holy lips. Then he turned to his two waiting visitors and said,

"I want you to know, this envelope is from Heaven, and the money was sent to you by the Master of the World Himself. Eliezer, when you signed G-d's Name on your contract, you caused such a tumult on High. The Heavenly Court was so moved by your faith that the *Ribbono Shel Olam* would guarantee your loan, that it decided to repay the money on your behalf. And all the *tzaddikim* – Abraham, Isaac, Jacob, even Moses Our Teacher – wanted to be chosen to deliver the rubles to the rich man. But in the end the honor went to the great messenger ... the one who will announce the coming of the Messiah ... Eliahu HaNavi, Elijah the Prophet.

"And you," the Rebbe went on, turning to the rich man. "If you had only had as much faith as Eliezer, if you had only believed that G-d would indeed repay you – you would have had the incredible privilege of actually meeting Eliahu HaNavi when he delivered your rubles. But since you didn't take Eliezer's Guarantor seriously, yes, you received your money. But you weren't worthy of seeing Elijah's holy face."

The rich man covered his face in shame. "Rebbe," he cried. "I can't believe what I've done, what an opportunity I missed! It will haunt me all my life. And now that I know the truth, what should I do? I can't keep such holy money. I could never use it for myself. Maybe, Rebbe, I could give it to you...?"

So the rich man gave the thousand rubles to R. Menachem Mendel Rimanover. Nobody knows what the Rebbe actually did with the money. But his *chasidim* said that when he died, he left his successor, R. Hershele, the envelope delivered by Elijah the Prophet that once contained holy money from Heaven.

You know, when we walk on the street, we usually look straight ahead. We don't look down at our feet. But if sometime, we do glance down at the ground and see a scrap of paper – gevalt! We have to be so careful. We shouldn't just step on it, and we mamash *shouldn't throw it away. Because maybe it's an envelope dropped by Elijah the Prophet. And maybe in that envelope is a contract that is signed:*

"Li hakesef, ve'li hazahav, neum Hashem: Mine is the silver, and Mine is the gold, signed, The Master of the World."

The Holy Vitebsker
at the Kinneret

bout two hundred years ago there was a terrible famine in *Eretz Yisrael*, in the Land of Israel. The situation was particularly bad in the north, in Tiberias and Tzfat, where hundreds of *Yidden* were *mamash* dying of starvation. So the leaders of those communities got together and decided to send a *shaliach*, a messenger, to the Jews of Russia, to try to raise money to buy food. Everybody waited anxiously for the messenger to come back, but a long time went by and he didn't return. And nobody knew what had happened to him.

At that time the Holy R. Menachem Mendel of Vitebsk was living in Tiberias. Now, R. Mendele had a special custom – he always went to the Kinneret, to the Sea of Galilee, right before Shabbos to *daven minchah*. One Friday afternoon he went to the Kinneret as usual, but he didn't start to pray. He just sat down on the shore and stared at the waves. And he looked so sad that the *chasidim* who were with him became very worried. Still, he was, after all, the Rebbe, and they didn't like to disturb him. So they just sat down on the sand beside him, and they all silently watched the water.

Time went by, and still R. Mendele didn't *daven*. One of the *chasidim* dared to whisper, "Rebbe, don't you think we should pray?" But R. Mendele didn't answer. He just kept staring into the Kinneret. It got darker and darker. The Rebbe still refused to move. His followers couldn't understand what was happening.

Suddenly, just before it was totally dark, R. Mendele stood up. He stretched, he smiled, he *mamash* laughed out loud. Then he turned to his *chasidim*: "Thank you so much for waiting for me. Come, let's *daven*." And he led them in the afternoon prayer with great *simchah*, with utmost joy.

After the *davening* one of his followers said to him, "Rebbe, I hope you won't be offended but I can't help but wonder. First you were so sad, and now you're so happy. What's going on?"

And R. Mendele answered, "Do you remember the messenger we sent to Russia, to collect money for food? We'd received word that he had succeeded in his mission and was on his way home. Then he suddenly disappeared, and we couldn't find out where he was or what had delayed him.

"Today, just as I came here to the Kinneret, Heaven showed me the whole story. When our messenger reached Istanbul, the Turkish Pasha arrested him and confiscated all the money he had collected. There was no way he could get the money back – or return home.

"Now, everybody knows that the Holy Wall in Jerusalem is the gateway to Heaven for all our prayers. Everybody's prayers, from all over the world, have to come first to the *Kotel*, and from there they go up before G-d's Holy Throne. But what most people don't know is that before going to the Holy Wall, all of our *tefillos*, all of our words before G-d, have to go to the *mikvah* to be purified. And the *mikvah* for all the prayers of the world is here – the Kinneret, the Sea of Galilee.

"When the Kinneret saw that the Pasha had taken our messenger's money, it decided that it could not allow so many Jewish lives to be lost. So the Sea of Galilee went on strike. It absolutely refused to cleanse or purify anybody's prayers until the Pasha released both our *shaliach* and the money.

"This caused a big commotion in the Heavenly Court. One side said that everybody, even the Pasha, has free choice, and the Kinneret had no right to try to interfere with what he was doing. And on the other side was the Sea of Galilee, which just kept saying, 'I cannot stand by and let the starving *Yidden* die. I will not serve as the *mikvah* for one single prayer until the Pasha relents and the Jews get their money!'

"The battle between these two sides has been going on ever since our messenger disappeared. Today, Heaven let me watch as the Court made its final decision. You see, the world can't exist if its prayers don't reach G-d. And the prayers can't go up without first being purified.

"The Kinneret held out, and in the end, it won. Heaven finally influenced the Pasha to change his mind; I just heard him announce: 'Release the messenger. Let the money go on to Israel to save the suffering Jews.'"

You know, sometimes we meet people, and even though we may never have seen them before, when we're with them we feel very pure. That means our prayers went together into the mikvah *of the Sea of Galilee.*

Or sometimes we meet somebody for the first time – somebody who is mamash *a total stranger. And right away we start sharing the deepest depths of our hearts with this person. This means our prayers met at the Holy Wall.*

And then there are times when we see other people, even from far away. Maybe they are only walking past us on the other side of the street, but we feel like we know them, we know their heart and their soul. Do you know what that means? It's a sure sign that our prayers ascended together before G-d's Holy Throne.

Because when our prayers meet each other and become one, that's the deepest closeness in the world...

Good Shabbos, Good Shabbos

Illustration: _____

"What's the last finishing touch before the beginning of the Sabbath? The woman of the house kindles the Shabbos lights. It's the strongest fixing in the world."

"The Light of Shabbos"

You know, there's the outside of Shabbos, and then there's the inside of Shabbos. The Sabbath is Yom Menuchah, *a day of rest. So we don't go to work, we don't drive a car; we don't talk on the phone, do the laundry, cash a check. Yes, maybe that's a kind of rest. But it's only the outside of Shabbos,* mamash *the outside of the outside of the outside.*

During the six days of the week we're so busy we don't know what to do with ourselves. We're always rushing around – got to daven *fast – can't stop for breakfast, it's time to go to work. Oh no, the car broke down. Got to get it fixed. Where's that taxi? Gevalt, I'm going to be late...*

And it's the same in our relationships with people: this one is angry with us, this one isn't speaking to us. Our children won't listen to us ... and, nebach, *our relationships with our husbands and our wives...*

To make it very short, during the week all we want is peace and quiet, and some rest. And then comes Shabbos...

Shabbos – a real Shabbos – is a totally different world. We're mamash *in another place. It's like we've completely changed our address ... maybe not on the outside, but on the inside. You see, when G-d drove Adam and Eve out of Paradise, He allowed part of their souls to stay in* Gan Eden. *Now everybody knows that Adam and Eve contained within them the souls of all the* Yidden *who would ever live. So part of all our* neshamos *also remained in the Garden of Eden...*

On the Sabbath, the Master of the World gives us back this part of our souls. This is the neshamah yeterah, *the extra soul of Shabbos.*

So every week, on Shabbos, we have the chance to return to Paradise. We are able to receive a Heavenly peacefulness and serenity – a Shabbat Shalom. And we can feel complete, and really at rest...

The Last Few Minutes
Before Shabbos

Did you ever wonder where we, the Jewish people, get our strength? We've suffered two thousand years of exile, two thousand years of oppression and pain. And not only are we still around, we're back in the Holy Land, in the Holy City of Jerusalem. What gave us the strength to hold out?

The truth is, G-d gave to us Yidden – and only to us – a special vitamin: Shabbos.

Shabbos is the strongest vitamin you can imagine, because it doesn't just nourish the body. It mamash heals the soul. On Shabbos, new energy flows down to us from Heaven in the absolutely purest way. But we can't receive this spiritual nourishment in soiled, impure vessels. Before Shabbos we have to cleanse ourselves. We have to make ourselves fit to receive Shabbos light.

And this is the holy work we have to do in the last few minutes before Shabbos. These moments are mamash a little bit like Yom Kippur. Because we have to try to fix ourselves. We have to repair our relationship to our families – our wives, our husbands, our children – and to everyone we love. And most of all, we have to try to connect to the Master of the World from the deepest depths of our hearts...

But you know, it isn't easy to do this cleansing, this purification. A lot of people can't do it on their own. So for them, for all of us – purity and holiness shine down from Heaven one minute before Shabbos...

 any people think that when a *tzaddik* passes away, his influence in this world disappears. But really, it's just the opposite: His power *mamash* increases. And the place where we can feel his holiness the most is at his *kever*, his grave.

When he was a young man of sixteen or seventeen, the Holy R. Shlomo Halberstam of Bobov traveled to the burial place of the *Heilige Rebbe Reb Elimelech* of Lizensk, who had left the world eighty or ninety years before. And *gevalt!* He felt R. Elimelech's holiness so strongly that he went up to some people nearby and said,

"You know, I've come from far away to visit R. Elimelech's grave. And I'd really like to learn more about him. I know it's been a long time, but is there anyone I could talk to who *mamash* knew him?"

One old man spoke up: "Well, it has been almost a hundred years, but ... yes, I think she's still alive. There's an old woman here who used to work for the Holy R. Elimelech. She must be ninety, ninety-five years old by now. I believe she helped out in the Rebbe's kitchen when she was a young girl."

"*Gevalt!*" the Bobover cried. "Do you think I could meet her?"

"Of course," the people said. "We'll get her for you." And they brought the elderly woman to see R. Shlomo.

"Dear lady," the Bobover said to the gnarled, wrinkled old woman who appeared before him. "Please forgive me for troubling you. But I heard you used to work for the Holy Rebbe Reb Elimelech. Please, tell me all about him."

"To tell you the truth," the old woman answered, "my memory isn't as good as it used to be. It's been so many years since I worked for the Rebbe, and you know, I was very young at the time. I don't really remember very much."

"That can't be true!" the Bobover cried. "To have the privilege to work for – to be close to – R. Elimelech, one of the holiest of all the Rebbes … surely you must remember something! Tell me anything – a single word, one experience you had with him…"

The old woman smiled, lost in her past. Then she said, "Well there is one thing that has always stayed with me:"

When I was only nine or ten years old, I was a dishwasher in the Rebbe's kitchen. There were lots of us working there, and the truth is, we didn't always treat each other so well. I mean, we were all fairly young, and we were under a lot of pressure – sometimes hundreds of *chasidim* came to be with R. Elimelech for Shabbos. So we got impatient with each other, yelled and shouted at each other. For a little girl like me, sometimes it was really hard to take…

But every Friday afternoon, right before Shabbos, something happened that made up for everything else. The Rebbe Reb Elimelech himself would come into the kitchen. I was always so excited to see him – he was so holy, *mamash* shining with light. He would stand just inside the door to the kitchen, and you wouldn't believe what he said:

"My precious friends, do you know how important you are to me? Everybody says that the work I do is holy. But without your help, I could do nothing at all. Dear children, I'm here to ask you: Did I do anything during the week that hurt your feelings, that made you feel bad? Maybe I didn't treat you with enough respect? If so, I'm begging you to forgive me. There's no way I can go into the Holy Shabbos if I feel I've hurt any of you sweet young people…"

And – the first time this happened I *mamash* couldn't believe my eyes – the Rebbe would start crying from the deepest depths of his heart. Then he would come up to each one of us on his big kitchen staff, and say, "Please tell me you forgive me. I promise that next week I'll be better to you."

Can you imagine it? The *Heilige* Rebbe Reb Elimelech, the holiest of the holy, asking us – simple kitchen workers, the lowest of the low – for forgiveness! So of course, all of us who REALLY didn't treat each other so well would start crying ourselves, apologizing to each other, and promising to treat each other better. It was unbelievable! You know, R. Shlomo'le, people think they know what Yom Kippur is all about. But if you were never with R. Elimelech in the kitchen just before Shabbos, you *mamash* know nothing about Yom Kippur at all…

And that's not all. After he left the kitchen, the Rebbe would go find his wife and children. He would gather all of his children around him and say, "I want you to know, you are the most precious gift the Master of the World has ever given me. And it *mamash* breaks my heart to think that maybe I didn't treat you well during this past week, that I might have hurt your feelings even in the smallest way. Please forgive me if I didn't love you enough, if I didn't take care of you the way G-d takes care of all of us, His precious children."

And he would hug and kiss each one of his children with so much love. *Gevalt*, there is no way I can ever describe the way R. Elimelech asked his children for forgiveness every week before Shabbos…

And then the Rebbe would go find his holy Rebbetzin and would say, so gently and so sweetly, "My dearest, holiest wife, please listen to me. You know what our rabbis teach us: On *Erev Shabbos* every husband and wife have a chance to fix the mistake that Adam and Eve made on the first Friday afternoon of creation. Do you know what was their biggest problem? Not that they ate from the Tree of Knowledge. It was that they blamed each other afterwards. So, my sweetest wife, I'm *mamash* begging you … we shouldn't blame each other. I'm so sorry if I hurt your feelings, if I wasn't good enough to you. Please forgive me if I didn't treat you the way you deserve to be treated – like a princess, like a queen…"

"I want you to know," the old woman said to R. Shlomo Bobover, "those last few minutes before Shabbos in the house of the Holy R. Elimelech gave me a strength which has lasted all of my life…"

You know, sometimes you might see two Yidden. *One of them you think is* "Shabbosdik," *the other one, not so much. Now, it's the Sabbath for both of them. They both have to observe all the laws. But the second* Yiddele *only keeps* Shabbos *because it's the seventh day of the week — so he has no choice. But the* Shabbosdik Yid … ah! He keeps Shabbos *with so much joy, because he feels its holiness and* mamash *receives its light.*

So right before you go into Shabbos, *it's really important to say: "*Ribbono Shel Olam, *I have the intention of receiving upon myself — upon my body, my soul and the soul of my soul — the* kedushah, *the holiness of* Shabbos." *If you forget, you can also make this declaration after the Sabbath has already begun. And what happens if you omit it altogether? Yes, it will still be the Sabbath. But it won't be an inside* Shabbos, *only an outside one.*

You see what it is, before the Sabbath begins we not only have to fix ourselves and our relationships with other people. We also have to fix our relationship to Shabbos *itself. And we do that by saying just these few simple words. You know, to fix a car or a stove or even bake a cake can take a very long time. But all you have to do is say a few words, and if you say them with utmost sincerity, you can* mamash *draw down upon yourself the inside of the inside of the holy Seventh Day…*

The Light of Shabbos

According to the Rabbis, the Sabbath lights that our Mother Sarah kindled on Friday night kept burning for all of the following week. Now, maybe we're not on the level of Sarah Imeinu ... maybe the physical flame of our Shabbos candles burns out after a certain number of hours. But the spiritual power of our Sabbath lights – ah, this is so strong that their fire can mamash *illuminate our lives from one* Erev Shabbos *to the next.*

Still, you know, there is a big question. In the Talmud, Shabbos itself is called a torch. The Sabbath has its own light, the light of G-d. What can our little flames add to G-d's Great Light? Why do we even kindle our own Shabbos candles?

You see what it is ... G-d's light is so beautiful, so holy, that it's mamash *beyond us. It's a little like looking at a painting by a great master, maybe Rembrandt or Van Gogh. We don't really have the vessels for such immense beauty.*

But the light of our little Shabbos candles is like a painting done by our own children. Imagine that your child brings home a simple little drawing. Maybe you can't tell exactly what it is, maybe it's hardly more than a scribble. But to you it's so beautiful that it mamash *touches you in the deepest depths, and fills you with so much joy...*

And this is the secret of our Shabbos lights. We are all G-d's children. And the fire of our little candles is so infinitely precious in the eyes of our Father, the Master of the World...

Everybody knows about the holiness of the great Rebbes, the Holy Masters. But nobody talks so much about their wives. These *Heilige Rebbetzins* were very hidden, but like their husbands, they too were the deepest of the deep, the holiest of the holy.

There was a time in the life of the Holy Seer of Lublin when, sadly enough, he was *mamash* very poor. Things got so bad that one Friday afternoon the Seer's wife had just enough money to buy wine for *Kiddush*, *challah*, and some fish. But she also needed two candles for her Shabbos lights, and each candle cost a penny. Now, today two cents doesn't seem like very much, but for the Seer's Holy *Rebbetzin*, it might as well have been a million rubles. Because she had absolutely no more money. She searched the whole house – once, twice, three times – hoping to find a penny or two that might have fallen on the floor or rolled under the table. Nothing. The *Rebbetzin* was beside herself. She buried her head in her hands and started to cry:

"*Ribbono Shel Olam*, how can there be Shabbos without my Shabbos lights? Master of the World, You've got to help me – I *mamash* need a miracle. Please send me the money to buy candles for the Holy Sabbath."

The *Rebbetzin* waited anxiously all Friday afternoon, praying for her miracle. But nothing happened. Finally, she couldn't stand being in the house any longer. She ran outside and stood on a street corner, crying bitter tears: "G-d in Heaven, it's almost Shabbos. What am I going to do?"

Suddenly a big carriage pulled by eight horses came racing down the street, driving very fast. When it reached the corner where the *Rebbetzin* was standing, the driver pulled on the reins very hard, and the horses jerked to a stop. The *Rebbetzin* recognized the driver immediately; he was one of the wealthiest Jews in Lublin, a very handsome young man who was known as a real "playboy". The rich man didn't know the Seer's wife. Still he leaned down from his seat high on the carriage and said:

"My dear lady, what's wrong? Why are you crying so much? I can't bear to see someone in such pain. Please, let me help you."

And the *Rebbetzin* saw that this man might be a "playboy" on the outside. But on the inside, he had a heart of gold. She said, wiping away her tears,

"Kind sir, thank you so much for stopping. And I really hate to ask you, but … do you think you could give me two pennies, so I can buy two candles for the holy Shabbos?"

"Just two pennies? You know, I'm really very rich. Let me give you more, here's ten rubles."

But the *Rebbetzin* just shook her head. "No – I mean, it's really very good of you, but I can't accept more than two pennies. I wouldn't even ask you for that, except that it's *Lekoved Shabbos*, for the honor of the Sabbath…"

"If you're sure…" the rich man said, and handed her the two pennies.

The *Rebbetzin* looked at him for a long moment, and then she said, "You'll never know how much this means to me. And I can never thank you enough. But one thing I can do for you. I bless you with the light of Shabbos, with the light of Paradise. It should shine into your heart for the rest of your life."

The rich man touched his cap in respect and farewell, and continued on his way. The *Rebbetzin* hurried to buy her two candles, and so, on Shabbos, the house of the Seer of Lublin glowed with holy light.

That night the *Heilige* Seer went to *shul* to *daven*. Now, most of us are doing well if we can just pray the whole evening service with *kavanah*, with real concentration. But the Seer of Lublin … when he prayed, his soul *mamash* took off and went straight up to Heaven. This particular Shabbos, when he got to the Upper World, he saw that the Heavenly Court was in an uproar. And as soon as he appeared, the head of the Court called to him:

"There you are, Seer of Lublin. We've been waiting for you. You know, we're used to you making trouble for us by blessing *Yidden* who are absolutely not worthy. But this time it's your wife, your *Rebbetzin* – she's following your example. Do you know what she's done? She's blessed this "playboy" – this do-nothing pleasure seeker – with the light of Shabbos! Now you tell us, does he deserve such an honor? Just look at him now, see what he's doing…"

The Seer looked down toward earth. And there was the rich man, driving along fast in his carriage. He had an appointment with one of his fancy ladies, and he was already very late.

"Do you see?" the Head of the Court shouted. "He's driving on Shabbos! And can you imagine where he's probably going on this, the holiest of days?"

"I have to admit, you're absolutely right," the Seer replied. "But let me ask you: why do you think he lives like he does? It's because he doesn't know any better. He's never tasted the beauty of Torah, he's never felt the light of Shabbos. Here, I have an idea. Bless him with Shabbos light for just one hour, and let's see what he does then."

And the Heavenly Court reluctantly agreed.

So Heaven opened all the gates for the rich man. And suddenly the "playboy" felt something new come into his heart, something high and exalted. All at once the world seemed so beautiful, so deep; life itself seemed so meaningful, so holy. He looked at himself, at his life-style, and it was as if he really saw himself for the first time. "*Oy, Ribbono Shel Olam*," he cried. "What have I been doing with my time? I've *mamash* been wasting my life!"

The rich man reined in his horses and sat still for a minute, confused. He was clear that he wanted his life to change, but he didn't know how to begin. Then he thought, "I know where to go…" He turned his carriage around and drove back to the street corner where he had met the *Rebbetzin*, saying to himself, "It's time I learned how to keep the Sabbath. And what better place to begin than the house where my Shabbos candles are burning…"

Nobody knows this man's name. But he *mamash* became one of the top students of the Holy Seer of Lublin, as well as one of the greatest rabbis of his time. And the holiness of his Shabbos light still fills the whole world…

You know, the last thing G-d created during the Six Days of Creation was woman. With the creation of Chava … Eve … our world was complete. And it will also be women who put the finishing touches on the tikkun hagamur, *the final fixing of the world before the coming of the Messiah…*

It's the same thing when it comes to Shabbos. What's the last finishing touch before the beginning of the Sabbath? The woman of the house kindles the Shabbos lights. It's the strongest fixing in the world.

And in that last second before Shabbos, at the time of that deep tikkun, *something very special happens. At that moment, there are no walls between these holy women and their husbands, their children. There are no barriers between them and all of Israel, between them and the whole world.*

And at that moment, there are no walls separating them from G-d…

adly enough, today we live in a world where so many couples split up, and so many hearts are broken. But in former good days, it was a different story. One hundred and fifty years ago, in the time of the Holy R. Yisrael of Vilednik – one of the greatest students of R. Mordechai of Chernobyl – such things rarely happened. So the Holy Viledniker was very surprised when he heard that the wife of one of his students had left her husband and gone back to live with her parents.

The Rebbe immediately sent word to his *chasid's* wife that she should come to see him. And when she appeared he said, "My dear, I'm sure you have your reasons for doing what you did. But I have to tell you, your husband *mamash* misses you. He loves you so much, he spends all day and all night in the *Beis Midrash* reciting the Psalms and praying you'll come back to him. So in his name, I'm begging you – go home to your husband and try to work things out with him."

The woman began to cry. "Rebbe, I didn't leave my husband because of any trouble between us. And really, I also love him very much. But you see, we were never able to have children. And a house without children … without the sound of babies crying, of little ones laughing … is *mamash* not a home. It's just a lonely, empty building. I couldn't stand the pain of it anymore, it was like living in the ruins of the Holy Temple. So I went back to my parents…

"Holy Master, if you want me to go back to my husband, please bless us with children. No, more than that. Please bless me to have a son like you!"

The *Heilige* Viledniker smiled and said, "I'm happy to bless you and your husband to have a child. But the truth is, in order to have a son like me, you have to be a mother like my mother. Let me tell you a little bit about my holy mother:"

I pray that it will never happen to any other child, but my father passed away when I was only seven and my brother was just five years old. My mother had to take care of us on her own. *Gevalt!* She worked so hard, and she was so good to us, so loving, so sweet…

Very early one morning, my mother called to me and said, "Sweet Yisrael, my dearest son, I feel so sick. I want to pray, but I'm *mamash* too weak to get out of bed. Could you please bring me my prayerbook?"

Right away I ran and got my mother her *siddur*. She took it in her trembling hands, but she didn't open it. Instead, she began to cry, "*Ribbono*

Shel Olam, I want so much to pray to You. But I'm too sick. My head hurts so much I can't even read the words of the *davening*.

"Master of the World, if it were just for me, I wouldn't bother You. But I'm so worried about my children. You know that they have no one else in the world, I'm the only one who can take care of them. And if I'm really sick, G-d forbid, or something even worse, I don't know what will happen. So please, for the sake of my children, save my life. Let me get well!"

And I swear to you, five minutes later my mother got out of bed and started making us breakfast. She was completely cured!

Now, let me tell you one more story about my mother. You *mamash* can't imagine her *kavanah*, her intense concentration, when she lit her candles before Shabbos. She cried so many bitter tears, she called out to G-d from the deepest depths of her heart. You know, I was just a little boy, but I've remembered it all my life. I've always thought that the only person who prayed harder than my mother at that moment must have been the High Priest in the Holy Temple on Yom Kippur…

One Shabbos, my mother was bending over her candlesticks, her hands covering her eyes, crying like her heart was broken. I guess her tears must have fallen on the candles and put out the flames. Because when she opened her eyes, her candles were no longer burning.

I didn't actually see what happened – I was in the other room at the time. But suddenly I heard a terrible wail. And when I ran to see what was wrong, there was my mother, sobbing: "Master of the World, how can I enter the holy day of rest without my Shabbos lights? But my candles have gone out, and it's already Shabbos. So I can't light them again…

"*Ribbono Shel Olam*, I *mamash* can't live without Sabbath light! So I'm begging You, please rekindle my candles. G-d in Heaven, bless me with the light of Shabbos!"

"I swear to you," the Holy Viledniker told his *chasid's* wife, "that at that moment I saw a radiant, shining, holy hand come down from Heaven. And – in the *z'chus* of my holy mother, it rekindled the lights of Shabbos."

The Baal Shem Tov's
Olam Habah

The Midrash says that Dovid HaMelech, the Holy King David, woke up every night at midnight. He lifted his eyes to Heaven and prayed: "G-d in Heaven, I have only one request – to hear the heartfelt prayers of Your holy people, Am Yisrael."

So the Ribbono Shel Olam *would take King David up to a very high place, where he could hear all the cries of the Jewish people, and of everyone in the world. Dovid HaMelech would stand there, listening to all those prayers, all those cries, and that is when he wrote the words of* Tehillim, *the Book of Psalms.*

You know, most people think that a tzaddik, *a holy person, is someone who carefully observes all the* mitzvos. *But if he doesn't hear other people crying, maybe most of him is holy. But his ears? Definitely not...*

The truth is, the greatness of the Jewish People is "Sh'ma Yisrael – Hear, Israel." The deepest holiness of us Yidden *is that we can hear somebody cry, even if they're far away...*

ou know, when we travel, we drive our car (or, in former good days, we guided our horses) to wherever we want to go. But for the Holy Baal Shem Tov, it was a completely different thing. His driver, Alexi, would sit with his back to the horses, facing the Holy Baal Shem. And the horses – automatically, as if under Heavenly direction – would take the Rebbe to the place he needed to be. So the *chasidim* often had no idea where they were heading. And sometimes even the Holy Baal Shem himself not only didn't know where he was going ... he wasn't even sure for what holy purpose he had been sent to that particular destination.

One Thursday afternoon the Holy Baal Shem Tov said to his students, "Bring the carriage. We're going away for Shabbos."

The *chasidim* knew better than to ask questions. They harnessed the horses, climbed into the wagon with the Rebbe, and they took off, with Alexi facing the Holy Baal Shem as usual. They had traveled all night when, early Friday morning, the horses began to slow down. The *chasidim* saw a beautiful palace in front of them, and thought that must be where they were going. But the horses passed the palace and stopped a short distance away, in front of a broken-down hut.

The *chasidim* looked at the *Besht*, waiting for instructions. But the Rebbe seemed uncertain, even hesitant, as if he didn't know what to do next. Suddenly the door to the hut opened, and out stalked a huge, fierce looking man. His clothes were dirty, his hair wild and unkempt. And the look on his face! The *chasidim* drew back in fear. They were sure the man must be a gangster or a thief, maybe even a murderer. The frightening stranger strode right up to the wagon and demanded, in a loud rude voice,

"What are you doing here?!"

The Baal Shem answered, almost timidly. "Please, sir, could we possibly stay with you for Shabbos?"

"No way, my friend!" the big *Yiddele* almost shouted. "I know all about your kind. It takes you hours to *daven*, hours more to make *Kiddush*. By the time you sit down for the meal, it's already three o'clock in the morning. Me, it takes me five minutes to pray, another minute to make *Kiddush*. Then I eat a fast meal and hit the bed. You're crazy if you think I'm going to waste my time waiting around for you."

"Please, sir. We have nowhere else to go. I promise we won't bother you..."

"Well..." The man thought for a minute, then seemed to make a decision. "Okay, here's the deal. I'll let you stay, but only on one condition. You have to do everything exactly the way I do it or I'll kick you out, even if it's in the middle of the night. And there's one thing you need to know right from the start: I *mamash* don't like people like you!" Suddenly, the man started insulting the Baal Shem Tov, yelling at him and abusing him in language not fit to be repeated.

And through it all, the *Besht* – still looking confused – just sat on the wagon without saying a word.

When the gangster *Yiddele* had finished his shouting and cursing, he led the Rebbe and his followers into the hut. The *chasidim* looked around them in disgust. The place was *mamash* filthy. The dirty dishes on the table looked like they hadn't been washed in a week. And this was where they were supposed to spend the Holy Shabbos? They again looked at their Rebbe, sure that he would protest, or better still, walk out. But the Baal Shem, with a resigned look, sat down silently on a dusty broken chair.

All Shabbos the Holy *Besht* was *mamash* miserable. He could barely *daven* – by the time he'd finish one blessing with his usual concentration, the *Yiddele* was ready to eat. He couldn't make his own special *Kiddush*, or give over any Torah to his students. He couldn't do anything at all to celebrate the Sabbath. The rough *Yid* mostly ignored the Rebbe and his followers, deigning to speak to them only to order them to hurry, or to heap more abuse and curses on them. And the Baal Shem accepted all of it quietly, still not saying anything. The *chasidim* couldn't understand why their Rebbe was acting like this.

After *Havdalah* the gangster vanished. The *chasidim* couldn't wait to get out of there, but the Holy Baal Shem again seemed confused, as if he wasn't sure why he'd come in the first place, or what he was supposed to do now. He was slowly leading his followers back to their carriage when suddenly the door of the palace next door opened, and a beautiful young woman started walking toward them. The *chasidim* thought she looked like a queen – or like one of our Four Holy Mothers – with her regal posture and her exquisite serene face. And they noticed the Rebbe looking at her strangely...

The woman came up to the Baal Shem Tov and said, "Holy Master, I would like to invite you to share the Feast of King David – the fourth meal of Shabbos – with my husband and me." And she led him and all his students toward the palace.

Inside, the table was set with the finest dishes, and little candles were burning everywhere. The *chasidim* were entranced by the beauty of the scene, but the Holy Baal Shem couldn't seem to take his eyes off the woman. Finally she met his gaze and said softly,

"Holy Rebbe, *Heilige* Baal Shem Tov, don't you know who I am?"

And the *Besht* answered, "I thought ... yes, it IS you. You're Feigele, the orphan girl who worked in our kitchen many years ago. Why, you couldn't have been more than nine years old at the time. And just look at you now! But I don't understand..."

Feigele interrupted him, and her eyes were filled with tears. She said, "Holy Master, I can't tell you how much it means to me that you recognized me. Because I *mamash* owe you so much. I was just a poor orphan, all alone in the world, until you and your wife took me in. You were both so good to me, took such good care of me. And you're right, I helped your Holy *Rebbetzin* in the kitchen.

"You know, I was so happy in your house. But then something happened:"

One day while I was living with you, I got head lice. And the *Rebbetzin* had to comb the lice and all the eggs out of my hair. To this day I don't know if she did it too roughly, or if maybe I was just very sensitive. But it was *mamash* so painful, and I started crying,

"*Rebbetzin*, please stop. It hurts so much!"

And your wife answered, not unkindly, "Please, Feigele, be still. Have some patience. You know this has to be done."

But I couldn't stop crying. "*Rebbetzin*," I sobbed. "Then please, at least do it more gently. It's too much for me, I can't stand all this pain!"

But she just kept combing. And you, Holy Rebbe, you were standing there the whole time, watching – and you kept silent. You saw, you heard that I was crying. But you didn't do anything to help me, to comfort me. You never said a single word.

Not long afterwards, I left your holy house. I wandered around for a while, not knowing where to go or what to do. And then, some years later, I met my holy husband…

Feigele paused, as if waiting for something. Suddenly, the door of the palace swung open, and a man walked into the room. The Baal Shem Tov and all the *chasidim* stared at him. They couldn't believe their eyes. It was their host for Shabbos, but he looked so different. If before his clothes had been torn and dirty, and he had acted like a gangster or a thief, now he wore a long white robe and was *mamash* shining with light. It was clear to the *Besht* and all his followers that they were in the presence of a very holy man. They watched in awe as the *tzaddik* walked up to Feigele and stood quietly beside her.

"*Heilige* Baal Shem Tov, I'd like you to meet my husband, the head of the *lamed-vav tzaddikim*, the thirty-six hidden holy people," Feigele said. And then she went on with her story…

Soon after my holy husband and I were married, he said to me, "My dearest wife, there is something I have to tell you. I know how much the Holy Baal Shem Tov helped you when you were young. But I just learned that because of you, he has lost his share in the World to Come. For when he stood by silently while you were crying, as his wife combed out your hair, a Voice announced in Heaven: 'Since the Baal Shem Tov didn't hear that young girl's pain, there is no place for him in *Olam Habah*…'"

Rebbe, I couldn't believe what my husband was saying. It made me so sad, my heart was *mamash* broken! I love you so much, and I couldn't bear the thought that because of me you should suffer such a terrible punishment. I begged my husband, "You're so holy, you have such influence Above. Please, isn't there some way you can fix things for the Holy Baal Shem Tov? Can't you get Heaven to restore his portion in the Coming World?"

My husband thought for a minute, and then he said, "I think maybe there's a way…"

Of course you know, Rebbe – there is one thing in this world that is on the level of *Gan Eden*, of Paradise. Shabbos! Shabbos is "*mei'eyn Olam Habah*," a taste of the World to Come.

So my husband said to the Heavenly Court: "You know, except for this one lapse – I do admit it's a big one but even so – the Baal Shem Tov is really a very holy man, probably the holiest man alive. It doesn't seem right to punish him so harshly. So I have an idea. Suppose that on one Sabbath he receives none of the light of Shabbos. If that Sabbath is for him as bitter as a fast day – more like *Tisha B'Av* than Shabbos – if he absolutely does not feel any trace of *Gan Eden* … could that fulfill his punishment of losing his share in Paradise?"

After much deliberation, Heaven agreed that this could be enough. But the head of the Heavenly Court had one question: How exactly would it come about that you, Rebbe, would experience such a Shabbos?

"Ah," my holy husband answered. "Just bring him to me for one Sabbath. I'll take care of the rest…"

So Heaven had you come here for one Shabbos. And my husband pretended to be the coarse man you first met. He interfered with your *davening*, prevented you from learning. He cursed you and mistreated you. He *mamash* took the essence of Shabbos away from you, and kept you from tasting one bit of Paradise…

Here Feigele looked up at her husband. He nodded. "And I'm so happy to tell you, Holy Rebbe, that it was enough to fulfill the decree against you. Your suffering on this Shabbos was enough to fix your soul. Because my holy husband just heard another Heavenly Voice that announced:

"'We hereby return the Holy Baal Shem Tov's share in *Olam Habah*…'"

The truth is, maybe we should all be a little bit worried. Do we hear other people crying? Do we feel the pain of all of Israel, of the whole world? Are we in danger of losing our share in the Coming World because we don't hear each other cry?

But you know, we also have – if we dare say such a thing – a little bit of a complaint against G-d:

Ribbono Shel Olam, You tell us to try to be like You, to act like You. And since You are known as the Merciful One, this means we must have utmost compassion – not only for each other, but for Your entire world...

Master of the World, every day we pray to You. We pour our hearts out to You, cry out to You from the deepest depths of our pain. We need Your help so much! But sometimes that help seems slow in coming, and then we begin to wonder if You really hear our cries...

G-d in Heaven, if You want us to hear others crying, please show us that You hear us when we cry out to You. Please have mercy and answer our prayers...

The Bliss of Shabbos

The Yid HaKodesh, the Holy Jew, used to say, "Some people enjoy eating meat on Shabbos. Some people like fish. And some people, when they eat on the Sabbath, only taste Shabbos."

Right before Shabbos, the Holy Karliner would say, "Ribbono Shel Olam, I have wine for the Sabbath. I have chicken, challah, fish. But, Master of the World, how can I get Shabbos for Shabbos?"

You see what it is, the Sabbath has two levels, two faces. There is sh'miras Shabbos, "guarding Shabbos" – holding ourselves back from the thirty-nine kinds of work that we are forbidden to do. This is very beautiful, a very high way of being in Shabbos. But that's only one face. There is also the bliss of Shabbos … Oneg Shabbos.

In Hebrew there are two words that mean joy … simchah and oneg. You know, so many things in olam hazeh need tikkun, need fixing – physically and spiritually. We're living in a world that isn't finished, isn't whole. Still, sometimes we feel like we're maybe a little bit closer to fixing our souls, to repairing our own private worlds. It may not be the tikkun hagamur, the ultimate fixing, but at least it's a beginning. So we're happy.

The beginning of our tikkun as a nation was when G-d took us out of Egypt. So we celebrate Passover with a lot of joy. When we received the Torah on Mount Sinai we got a little bit closer to our fixing, so there's even more joy on Shavuos. And after Yom Kippur, after we've spent a whole day trying to correct our mistakes, we have Simchas Torah. It's the highest happiness. This is the level of simchah.

Oneg, bliss, is a taste of the End, of the absolute, complete tikkun. And this is what we receive on Shabbos … Oneg Shabbos, a joy that is even deeper than Paradise. On the Sabbath we can feel a little bit what it's like to have a mended soul, to live in a world which is whole. And the truth is, not only does this give us so much joy on the Sabbath itself, it also gives us the strength to work on ourselves during the six days of the week. Because once we've tasted what it's like to be shalem, to be whole, we not only know the repairs we want to make, but we want so much to make them…

On Shabbos our fixing is in the air. But unless we reach out and take it, nothing will happen. Entering Shabbos is a little like walking into a hospital. You can say, "Doctor, please help me!" Or you can say, "I'm really just a tourist here, I just stopped by to see what's going on. I'm only passing through." A lot of people do that, you know. They don't want to be fixed, they want to stay the same.

And the thing is — really being in Shabbos means you won't ever be the same again. Because on the Sabbath we're receiving the utmost holiness. Not holiness after it has come down to this world, but kedushah like it is in Heaven. Shabbos showers upon us the deepest fixing in the world, and we can taste the completeness, the bliss and the peace of the World to Come.

But to actually receive this inside of the inside of Shabbos ... ah, that is mamash a gift from Heaven...

verybody knows that for the Holy R. Chaim Tirer of Chernovitz, everything was *mamash* Shabbos.

Imagine that someone would come up to the *Heilige* Chernovitzer and say, "Holy Master, please tell me the meaning of '*bereshis*.'" "*Bereshis*" is the first word of the Torah. It literally means "in the beginning." But R. Chaim would laugh and answer, "How can you ask me such a thing? Of course '*bereshis*' means Shabbos – always Shabbos, only Shabbos!"

Or maybe somebody would ask, "R. Chaim, please explain the meaning of '*barah*.'" Now "*barah*," the second word of the Torah, means "created." But the *Heilige* Chernovitzer would exclaim, "What does it mean? What do you mean, what does it mean? Don't you know? It means Shabbos!"

For him, Shabbos was everything!

And on the Sabbath itself, as soon as his wife lit her candles, an amazing thing happened. R. Chaim seemed to grow five feet taller. A look of absolute bliss would come over his holy face, and he would shine with Heavenly light. Everybody who saw him knew that he was *mamash* in another world.

Now, at the time that R. Chaim was the Rebbe in Chernovitz, about two hundred years ago, a *Yiddele* named Moshe Dovid was living just outside the city. He was just a simple Jew, he could hardly read or write. When he came into town to *daven* on Shabbos he always sat in the last row of the *shul*, and everybody mostly ignored him.

This Moshe Dovid was so poor, his family had almost nothing. You know, sometimes what a person has is just sufficient to keep him from dying, but not enough for him really to be called living. Moshe Dovid's nine children were always hungry, *mamash* on the brink of starvation.

One day the poor *Yiddele* said to his wife, "You know, we've got to do something! This is no life for our children. I don't have any idea how to go about it, but we've got to save some money. If we both worked really hard, didn't sleep, ate even less than usual, maybe we could manage to put aside, let's say, five hundred rubles. Why, with that much money we could even buy our own farm. We could grow our own food. Our children wouldn't be starving any more!" He started getting more and more excited. "Maybe we could grow so much food that we could sell what we didn't use ourselves. We could *mamash* become rich! What do you say? I know it won't be easy. We won't be able to buy anything new for a long time, but will you try with me?"

And his wife agreed.

So Moshe Dovid and his wife worked day and night at any kind of job they could find. They starved themselves and their children, eating even less than before. And they bought almost nothing. They saved every penny they could. It broke Moshe Dovid's heart to see his children with old ragged clothes and empty stomachs, but he clung to his dream. And, *gevalt! gevalt!* After several years they had *mamash* managed to save five hundred rubles!

Immediately, Moshe Dovid started looking for his farm. But you know, you don't buy the first place you see. You have to shop around a little. Moshe Dovid spent a week looking at farms in the countryside around Chernovitz, but by late Friday afternoon he still hadn't decided which one he wanted. So, without going home first, he headed straight into town for the *Erev Shabbos davening*.

Moshe Dovid was so lost in his thoughts about his farm that he had almost reached the synagogue before he realized that he still had the five hundred rubles in his pocket. And, of course, on Shabbos a *Yid* doesn't carry money. Now where do you go if you need a safe place to leave something over the Sabbath? To the Rebbe, of course. So a few minutes before Shabbos, Moshe Dovid knocked on R. Chaim Chernovitzer's door:

"*Heilige* Rebbe, I'm so sorry to bother you right before Shabbos. But I need your help..." He told him all about the money he had saved, and about his search for a farm. "So, Holy Master, that's why I've come. Do you think maybe I could leave my five hundred rubles with you until after the Sabbath?"

The Holy Chernovitzer studied the simple Jew standing before him. "What a special *Yiddele*," he thought. "So pure, *mamash* so holy. And he's completely hidden, totally unrecognized." He said to Moshe Dovid, "Of course, my dearest friend, I'd be delighted to take care of your precious money. But tell me, do you have a place to eat for Shabbos?"

"Why, Rebbe … uh … no … I wasn't invited anywhere … I thought I'd try to walk home…"

"But Moshe Dovid, your home is so far away and you must be tired after traveling around all week, looking for your farm. Please, would you do me the honor of spending Shabbos with me?"

Moshe Dovid couldn't believe it. To spend a whole Shabbos with the Holy Chernovitzer! It was beyond his wildest dreams! He and the Rebbe were still talking about arrangements for the Sabbath when there was another knock on R. Chaim's door. The Chernovitzer called, "Please come in," and a woman entered the room, sobbing from the deepest depths of her heart.

"Holy Master," she cried. "Please help me, I just don't know what to do. Surely you remember my husband, Avramele, who passed away several months ago. Everybody, including me, thought Avramele and I were very wealthy. And our daughter is engaged to the son of one of the richest men in Chernovitz; in fact, the wedding is next week. Well, just a few days ago I suddenly found out – Avramele never told me! – that he had lost all our money. When he died we were actually very poor. Which means that I have no way to pay for my daughter's wedding! I'm so afraid that if the rich man, the father of the groom, finds out about this, he'll call off the engagement. And my daughter loves his son so much – that would *mamash* break her heart…

"Rebbe, please forgive me for bothering you so close to Shabbos. I was just too proud to come to you before. But the wedding is so soon … I just can't handle this alone anymore … I'm *mamash* at the end…" And she cried and cried.

For a moment the only sound in the Chernovitzer's room was the poor woman's weeping. Then suddenly Moshe Dovid said, "Rebbe, I can't stand such pain. We've got to help her. Let's give her my five hundred rubles!"

R. Chaim cried, "No, Moshe Dovid, I can't let you do this! Your wife and children starved for this money. It's your life savings, and your future depends on it. I promise you, we'll find another way to help her."

Moshe Dovid didn't even answer. He just looked at the woman and said, "I'm still young, I have lots of time. I can save more money. But your daughter may never fall in love again. She may never find anyone else she wants to marry. So here – *mazel tov* on the wedding." And he took the five hundred rubles out of his pocket and put it in her hand.

The woman looked at him in wonder and said, "You'll never know how much this means to us. I can never thank you enough." She said goodbye to the Rebbe, and, with a joyful step, started on her way home.

As soon as the door had closed behind her, the Holy Chernovitzer turned to Moshe Dovid and said,

"My dear friend, you are *mamash* the holiest of the holy. Do you have any idea what an exalted thing you have just done? You have fulfilled the *mitzvah* of *hachnasas kallah,* of providing for a bride, in the highest possible way. For that, may G-d make you richer than you ever dreamed possible. And may you live to see the weddings of all your great-grandchildren. But I have another, personal blessing for you…

"Can you imagine, Moshe Dovid, the pain this widow was feeling, alone and suddenly poor? Can you imagine what kind of Shabbos she would have had, not knowing what her future in-laws would say if they knew she had no money, worrying if the wedding would actually take place? Or what her daughter would have suffered, wondering if her groom really loved her, if he would still marry her if he knew she was poor…?

"You, Moshe Dovid, gave Shabbos to these two people. Because of you, they will be able to celebrate this Sabbath with joy. And for that, I give you this special *bracha* – that G-d should bless you with the bliss of Shabbos for the rest of your life."

Moshe Dovid spent that Sabbath in the house of the Holy Chernovitzer. And when he walked into the synagogue alongside the Rebbe, all the people stared. This simple *Yid* – whom, before, everybody had ignored – was glowing with light … *mamash* shining from one end of the world to the other. It was clear that he was not in this world, he was in Paradise. From the time that the Chernovitzer blessed him, every week Moshe Dovid had *Oneg Shabbos,* the bliss of Shabbos.

And within a month, even he didn't know exactly how it happened, Moshe Dovid indeed became very rich, *mamash* a millionaire. He built a *beis midrash* for R. Chaim, called Moshe Dovid's Beis Midrash, that stood in Chernovitz until it was destroyed by the Nazis in the Second World War.

One hundred and fifty years later, the Germans occupied Chernovitz. Sadly enough, all the descendents of Moshe Dovid were sent to Auschwitz. By some miracle every one of them survived. But obviously, all of the family's wealth, passed down from Moshe Dovid, was gone, and when they went to America after the war, they didn't have a penny to their names.

Still, nobody knew how, after four weeks they were rich again. And everybody understood that it was still the effect of the blessing of the Holy Chernovitzer…

So you see, if you want G-d to bless you with Oneg Shabbos, *the bliss of Shabbos, there is one thing you must do: Give Shabbos to somebody else.*

Neighbor Above, Neighbor Below

According to the Gemorah, if Yidden would keep two Sabbaths, the Messiah would immediately come. And everybody is asking, what does the Talmud mean? What two Sabbaths is it talking about?

The Holy R. Mordechai of Chernobyl says the Gemorah is referring to the Shabbos Above and the Shabbos Below. For the Shabbos Below, the most important thing is obeying the thirty-nine laws of the Sabbath – withdrawing from our active world and holding back from forbidden work. This is very beautiful, very deep, very holy. But then there is the Shabbos Above, the exalted light that shines down from Heaven and fills our hearts with joy on the holy seventh day.

Now the truth is, for Shabbos to be whole it has to have both, observing the laws and receiving the light. That's what the Gemorah is saying. If Yidden would keep two Sabbaths – in other words, both guard the laws of the Shabbos Below and rejoice in the radiance of the Shabbos Above – the Messiah would instantly arrive. The question is, where do you begin, from above or from below? How do you teach people about Shabbos? Do you start by telling them: "Don't do this, you can't do that"? Or do you try to open their hearts to the Sabbath Above, Oneg Shabbos, the absolute bliss of Shabbos...?

nce the *Heilige* Baal Shem Tov asked Heaven to show him the reward that would be given to someone who observed Shabbos in the most exalted way. So Heaven took the *Besht* up to the highest place in *Gan Eden*, where even the angels were forbidden to go. And there he saw two golden thrones, shining with light.

The Baal Shem asked, "Whose thrones are these?"

And he was told, "One is for you, if you are wise. And one is for another person you must find..."

The Holy *Besht* immediately set out to find the person who would be his neighbor in Heaven. He ordered his driver, Alexi, to prepare the carriage and they took off, with Alexi, as usual, facing the Rebbe, and the horses running on their own. They traveled for a long time until, as they entered a large city, the horses began to slow down. The Baal Shem looked around. There didn't seem to be a single *Yid* in the whole town. He couldn't understand what was going on. How could his companion in *Gan Eden* be someone from a non-Jewish city?

The horses finally stopped in front of a small house on the edge of town. The Holy Baal Shem knocked on the door, and when a man came out, the Rebbe looked at him in surprise. He didn't have a beard or *peyos*, there was no *yarmulke* on his head. He wore the same clothing as all the people they had passed. In short, he didn't look anything like a *Yid*. Very puzzled, the Baal Shem Tov said,

"My dearest friend, we've traveled a long distance to visit your area. Could we by any chance stay with you for a few days?"

The man readily agreed, and escorted the Rebbe into his house. And as they entered, the *Besht* noticed with dismay that there was no *mezuzah* on the door...

Throughout their stay, the Baal Shem watched the man carefully. He was *mamash* a perfect host. He gave them his best room, and generally attended to all their needs. But he never *davened*, never made a *bracha*, and clearly didn't keep kosher. The Baal Shem was getting more and more upset. This man – certainly not religious, maybe not even Jewish – was going to sit next to him on High? "Perhaps he's a *lamed-vav tzaddik*, a hidden holy man," the Rebbe thought. "Tomorrow is Shabbos. Maybe then he'll reveal his true exalted level..."

But the man didn't keep Shabbos in any way! He didn't pray, he didn't make *Kiddush*, and worst of all, he *mamash* had a big party on Friday night. He and his friends ate and drank. They smoked, played music, sang and danced. In a nutshell, they broke every possible law of the Sabbath, making it impossible for the Holy Baal Shem Tov to pray with his usual deep concentration, or have his usual Shabbos feast. In fact, all he had to eat was the last of the little bread, wine and fish he had brought with him. While the owner of the house had a good time living it up with his non-Jewish friends, the *Besht* had an absolutely miserable Shabbos...

Saturday night, as he prepared to leave, the holy Baal Shem decided he had to find out what was going on here. So he said to his host, "My sweetest friend, you've been so very kind. But I wonder ... I hope you won't mind ... could I ask you one question? You and your friends were celebrating so much Friday night. Was there some special reason for your party?"

"Holy Rebbe," the man answered. "I know you could never tell by looking at me, but the truth is, I'm a Jew. I was kidnapped when I was a small boy and brought to this place. And I'm not allowed to leave the city. My captors told me I'd be killed if I tried to run away and return home...

"I want you to know, I promised myself when I was taken away that I'd never forget that I'm a Jew. But I'm the only *Yid* in this whole area, and I was so young when I was kidnapped, I *mamash* don't know what being a Jew is all about. I have very few memories of my family. But one thing I always remembered: my father telling me that Shabbos is a time to celebrate with utmost joy. And I know our house was always filled with guests on the Sabbath...

"Now, I'm really not a rich man, so I make do with cheap, simple food during the week. I save my money for Shabbos. On Friday night I invite a lot of guests, just like my father used to do, and I have a big party. I serve the best foods, the best wines, and we celebrate in the happiest possible way..."

The Holy Baal Shem looked at the *Yiddele*: "*Gevalt*, what an exalted Sabbath this man has! Knowing none of the laws, and living here all alone, he still *mamash* receives the inside of the inside of Shabbos ... the light, the joy. How could I not have seen it before? What a true Jewish heart he has, what a deep Jewish soul!"

Then he had another thought. "This man really wants to live like a Jew. But he doesn't know how. What if I taught him about *Yiddishkeit*? Then he could keep his promise never to forget where he comes from in a deeper way. And what if I showed him the way a Jew is actually supposed to observe the Sabbath? His Shabbos, as beautiful as it is, isn't complete because he only knows one half, the light and the joy. If I taught him about the other half, *sh'miras Shabbos*, how to keep Shabbos according to the law, then surely his Shabbos would be on an even higher level..."

So the Holy *Besht* opened his mouth to teach the *Yid* some Torah. But to his amazement, no words came out. It was as if something was preventing him from speaking. And then, in his mind, he heard a voice that said, "Holy Baal Shem Tov, think about what you are about to do. It's true that your intentions are the highest. You want to help this simple *Yid* become a better Jew. You want his Shabbos to be whole. But don't you see? He *mamash* believes that by having his party, he is celebrating the Sabbath and carrying on his father's tradition. And this belief fills him with utmost happiness.

"What do you think would happen to this man if he found out that really he has been doing everything wrong – that instead of honoring Shabbos, he is really desecrating it? What do you think would happen to his pure, heartfelt *simchah*? Is it worth it, at this stage in his life and given

his circumstances, to teach him the laws of the Sabbath – if by doing so you destroy his spirit and take away his greatest source of joy?"

So the Holy Baal Shem simply thanked the man again for his hospitality, climbed onto his wagon, and drove away.

nother time the Holy Baal Shem Tov asked Heaven to show him the punishment awaiting those people whose Shabbos observance wasn't on the right level. Suddenly he found himself in the lowest reaches of *Gehinom*, of hell, staring at two burned, blackened thrones.

"Whose seats are these?" he asked.

And he was told, "One is for you – if, G-d forbid, you are not wise. And the other is for someone you must travel to meet."

So again the Holy Baal Shem instructed Alexi to bring his carriage. And this time the horses took him to different city, this one filled with *Yidden*. As they drove through the crowded streets, the *Besht* could hear the sound of children chanting their Torah study, and smell the fragrance of Shabbos food cooking.

The horses stopped before a house which, the Baal Shem Tov discovered, belonged to a big rabbi, the head of one of the largest *Yeshivos* in town. When the *Besht* asked, "My dear friend, could we by any chance stay with you for Shabbos?" the rabbi only nodded his head, and silently led them into the house. There, still without saying a word, he left the Baal Shem and Alexi standing in the hall, and sat down in front of the *Gemorah* that was lying open on a nearby table.

For hours the rabbi remained engrossed in his learning, oblivious to his guests waiting on an uncomfortable bench just outside the room. Only just before Shabbos did he show them a place where they could sleep. Then he quickly left to go to *shul*, with the *Besht* following uncertainly behind him.

When they returned to the house after the Sabbath *davening*, the Holy Baal Shem immediately noticed the *Rebbetzin's* Shabbos candles. They were so short, almost just stubs, that he couldn't help but ask her,

"My dear, forgive me if I'm intruding, but I was wondering, why are your candles so small?"

Before she could say a word, the rabbi himself answered brusquely, "To make sure no one blows them out, of course. Or moves them in order to use their light to read. Surely you know these things are forbidden on the Sabbath." And he turned away and led them to the table for *Kiddush*.

But the rabbi's meal was hardly the joyous Shabbos feast to which the Holy Baal Shem Tov was accustomed. It was very short, and except for the rabbi's brief teaching on the portion of the week, it was almost completely silent. Nobody sang or talked. In fact, it seemed to the *Besht* that the *Rebbetzin* and the children were afraid to open their mouths, or even to move. After the meal, the rabbi immediately sent the children to bed. Then he sat down in a chair and remained there, silent and absolutely still, until he too was ready for sleep.

The whole next day, except for *davening* or eating, the rabbi sat rigidly in his chair. And as for his children — because obviously children can't sit still all day — it seemed that every time they came near, their father was shouting at them: "Don't touch that — it's *muktzah* — you can't play with it on Shabbos." Or, "No, you can't go outside! You might step on an ant, and you know it's forbidden to kill anything on the Sabbath. Or you might, G-d forbid, tear out some grass and leave a hole in the earth, which is definitely breaking Shabbos..."

To make it very short, there was *mamash* not one bit of joy in the rabbi's house the whole Shabbos. Finally, just before *Havdalah*, the Holy Baal Shem couldn't take it any longer. He said to the rabbi, "I'm sorry, but I just don't understand. Why are you yelling at your children like that? And why are you sitting so still, staying so silent?"

And the rabbi answered, "What a question! Surely a great Rebbe like you knows that the laws of Shabbos are very intricate, and very difficult to keep. So of course, as a good Jew, I'm extremely careful not to break even one of the prohibitions. You well know that we are commanded never to speak about weekday matters on Shabbos. But the truth is, this is very hard to do. So I never talk on the Sabbath, lest a forbidden word slip from my mouth. I never go outside, so I won't, by mistake, carry something, or crush an insect, or maybe knock a leaf from a branch or a flower from a bush. And of course, I must also teach my children respect for the laws. I want them to learn the same fear of sin, of punishment and of G-d as I myself possess..." Then he shut his mouth abruptly, as if fearing that he had indeed spoken a forbidden word, and resumed his stiff, silent posture on his chair.

The Holy Baal Shem thought, "*Gevalt*, what a sad, dark day the Holy Shabbos is for this man! It's true, he keeps all the laws. But his fear of Heaven is so great that he's lost all the light, all the joy…" He opened his mouth to tell the rabbi about the bliss of Shabbos, about *Oneg Shabbos*, but again no words came out. And suddenly he remembered a lesson from the Talmud: You should only try to teach someone if you think he will be able to appreciate what you say…

So the Holy Baal Shem Tov stayed in the rabbi's house for *Havdalah*. Then he thanked his host for allowing him to stay for Shabbos, and sadly set out for home.

You see what it is … we need laws, we need regulations and boundaries, in both our physical and our spiritual lives. But the whole matter of laws is very delicate. Without them there's nothing but chaos. But we can become so worried about making a mistake that we're afraid to do anything, we're afraid to move. And then, yes, maybe on the outside we're doing everything right. But on the inside, we become numb. We lose our zest, our joy in life…

Everybody knows it's very important to respect the regulations of human society. And gevalt! How much more so do we have to keep the laws of G-d's Holy Torah. But the thing is, we have to keep them in the right way. And what is the first sign that we are keeping the laws l'shem shamayim, for the sake of serving G-d? When we do the mitzvos with utmost simchah, with a joy that is not of this world…

Chatzkele
Lekoved Shabbos

You know, the Holy Shabbos has a light that is so exalted, so powerful, that even the physical aspects of our lives can be lifted up to a spiritual level. But for this to happen, everything we do has to be Lekoved Shabbos, in honor of the Holy Sabbath. So, before we drink anything else, we make Kiddush over wine, to sanctify Shabbos. And when we eat, we say, "I'm eating this chicken – or meat or fish – Lekoved Shabbos, in honor of Shabbos."

But the truth is, we don't just honor the Sabbath on the seventh day. The great tzaddikim, all during the week, were always looking for a new fruit, a special kind of fish. But they never ate it right away. They saved it for the Holy Shabbos. This way, the Sabbath was with them all the time. Because a real Jew cannot live for one minute ... for even one second ... without being conscious of Shabbos...

You see what it is? Imagine that you love somebody with all your heart. But one day that person tells you that he or she has to go away. You mamash feel so sad, right? You really don't want to let your loved one go...

Everybody knows that Shabbos is our soulmate, the soulmate of all of Israel. So the Sabbath comes, we daven, have our three Shabbos meals, and then Shabbos says, "Sorry, it's time for me to leave." Maybe we argue with her a little bit, sit at our third meal a little longer. But finally we give up and we make Havdalah. We don't want to let the Sabbath leave. But what can we do? We can't say, "Sorry, I'm not part of this world anymore. I'm always staying in Shabbos." Maybe we want to, but...

Yes, it's true that we have to live in this world. We have to earn money, go to our jobs, drive our cars, talk on the phone. Our children have to go to school. But all this is just on the outside, on the outside of the outside. Do you know what the deepest secret of Yiddishkeit really is? Maybe on the outside I go about my life during the six days of the week. But on the inside, I never let go of Shabbos. In the deepest depths of my heart, I stay Shabbosdik all the time. Then everything I do during the week is also Lekoved Shabbos.

And one Shabbos, one very special Shabbos, all of Israel will refuse to make Havdalah. All the Yidden everywhere in the world will lift up their eyes to Heaven and say, "Ribbono Shel Olam, we're mamash begging You. Don't take the Sabbath away from us. We want to stay in Shabbos the whole week. We're telling You, G-d in Heaven – we want to keep Shabbos forever!"

And that is when the Master of the World will bless us all with the Yom She'kulo Shabbos – the Time that is all Shabbos – the coming of the Messiah, may it be soon in our days...

oday, if somebody mentions to us the name "Auschwitz," all we see are the most horrible images of gas chambers and ovens, pain and death. We only know of Auschwitz as a German concentration camp. But in former good days – before the Nazis, may their names be erased – the name of Auschwitz was Uschpitzin, and it was an unbelievably holy *chasidic* city. Many big Rebbes lived there, and one of the greatest, the rabbi of the city one hundred and fifty years ago, was the *Heilige* R. Dov Baer … R. Berishel … Uschpitziner.

R. Berishel wrote a very beautiful *sefer* called *The Three Shepherds*, and in the foreword of that book he tells his own story:

> When I was young, I had the privilege of studying a lot of Torah with very holy rabbis. But even with all my learning, something was missing. I still felt empty inside. I knew what I needed – a Rebbe, a Holy Master. Not another teacher, somebody to give me more information. I was looking for the one person in the world who could connect me to the inside of my insides – *mamash*, to the deepest depths of my heart and my soul. There had to be someone, somewhere, who could show me how to reach the highest place in Heaven.
>
> I was so hungry for a Rebbe that I went to see every one I could find. They were all beautiful, exalted, very holy. They each gave over the highest Torah. But not one was the Rebbe for me. They didn't open my heart, they didn't reach the root of my soul.
>
> Then one day I heard that the Holy R. Shlomo Buchner of Ch'shanov was coming to Uschpitzin for Shabbos. *Gevalt!* The *Heilige* R. Shlomo'le Ch'shanover, one of the greatest Rebbes in the world! He and the Holy Seer of Lublin had learned together with the exalted R. Shmuel Shmelke of Nikolsburg! R. Shlomo'le was one of the few Holy Masters I hadn't visited. But the minute I heard his name, I knew … I *mamash* knew, in the deepest depths … that he was the Rebbe I was looking for. Still, I wanted to be very sure, so I decided to make myself a sign.
>
> Now in those days, every Jew in Uschpitzin was on a very high level. Everybody kept Shabbos, ate only kosher food, prayed three times a day. But there was one *Yiddele*, Chatzkele… Most people thought he was just a simple person. And in one way they were right. He could

barely read or write. He only knew how to daven a little bit and recite a few Psalms. But to me – *gevalt!* What a real Jewish heart he had, what a deep Jewish soul...

Chatzkele was a very big man, tall and strong like a giant. So he was a porter, a *trayger*. All day long he would stand in the marketplace and help people carry their purchases home. But he did so much more than just *shlep* packages...

Imagine that a woman, let's call her Chana, would go to the market on Sunday morning and buy maybe ten pounds of potatoes. Now there was no way she could carry that many potatoes to her house, especially since she lived very far away. So she would call for Chatzkele:

"Chatzkele, these potatoes are *mamash* too heavy for me. Could you help me, could you take them to my house?"

Right away, Chatzkele would come running. He'd lift up the potatoes and put them on his shoulder, no trouble at all. But before he'd start to carry them to the woman's house he'd say, "Chanale, forgive me for asking. But do you think there'll be some of these potatoes left for Shabbos, *Lekoved Shabbos*, for the honor of the Holy Sabbath?"

And – maybe just to make Chatzkele happy, and maybe because it was the truth – Chanale would answer kindly, "You know, I bought a lot of potatoes, even for my big family. I'm sure there'll be plenty left for Shabbos."

Chatzkele would start to smile. His face would shine with joy. He would lift the potatoes up even higher on his shoulder, like he wanted to raise them up to Heaven. And the whole way to Chanale's house he would sing at the top of his lungs:

"*Lek-o-oved Shabbos; Oy, Leko-o-ved Shabbos; Oy, Leko-o-oved Sha-a-bbos!*"

And anybody who saw him knew he was *mamash* in Paradise!

On Sunday, Monday and Tuesday, Chatzkele never carried anything without first asking about Shabbos. By Wednesday and Thursday, he didn't even bother to ask ... that late in the week people were already thinking about the Sabbath. And on Friday – ah, that was his day! Chatzkele would run all around the market, carrying sacks of apples, carrots and onions to all the Jewish homes. And the whole city would echo with the sound of his singing:

"*Leko-o-ved Shabbos; Oy, Leko-o-ved Shabbos; Oy, Leko-o-oved Sha-a-bbos.*"

But the saddest thing is – really, sometimes people can be so cruel! – a lot of the *Yidden* in Uschpitzin made Chatzkele's singing into a big joke. They made fun of him and called him a "crazy idiot". They even made up a mocking nickname for him: Chatzkele Lekoved Shabbos.

But in my humble opinion, Chatzkele was *mamash* the holiest of the holy, and the highest *Yid* in the whole city!

So the sign I chose was this: I knew R. Shlomo'le Ch'shanover had a special custom. Every Friday night, after the evening service, he would say "Good Shabbos" to everybody in the *shul*. I wanted to see how he was with Chatzkele. If R. Shlomo'le could see how special Chatzkele was … if he paid particular attention to him, gave him honor … then I'd know he was the Holy Master I was looking for. But if he ignored Chatzkele, like everybody usually did, and didn't bother to say anything to him, then I'd know for sure that he was not my Rebbe.

❧ ❧

The next Sabbath, the *Heilige* R. Shlomo'le Ch'shanover came to Uschpitzin. And what can I say? It was the highest Shabbos of my whole life! The *davening*, the singing, the dancing – everything was so beautiful, so holy. *Gevalt!* It was *mamash* a taste of Paradise!

After the prayers were over, everybody rushed up to say "Good Shabbos" to R. Shlomo'le. But I noticed that Chatzkele didn't join the crowd around the Rebbe. He just stood in a corner, watching. He looked so sad, totally broken. I thought he was probably so used to being insulted and abused that he couldn't believe that a *tzaddik* like R. Shlomo'le would want to speak to him. I felt so bad for him that I went over and stood by his side.

The Holy Ch'shanover finished greeting all the *Yidden* who were gathered around him. Then suddenly he noticed that there were two people to whom he hadn't yet spoken, Chatzkele and me. So he called to us: "My dearest friends, please come closer. I want to wish you 'Good Shabbos.'" And he held out his hand.

Chatzkele didn't move, so I pushed him a little towards the Holy Ch'shanover. I wanted him to go first, so I could see what R. Shlomo'le would do. Very shyly, Chatzkele walked forward. And I watched as the *Heilige* R. Shlomo Ch'shanover took the holy hand that carried everything *Lekoved Shabbos*.

R. Shlomo'le closed his eyes and stood very still. Then he squeezed Chatzkele's hand tightly and said, very softly,

"My holy friend, would you tell me your name?"

Chatzkele was so bashful, he couldn't even look at the Rebbe. He just hung his head and mumbled, "Uh, my name … my name, it's Chatzkele…"

"Is that your whole name, my sweet *Yid*, or do you maybe have another name also?"

Chatzkele was so ashamed, he bowed his head even more. "I … well … sometimes people call me … I mean, they're only joking, but they call me … Chatzkele Lekoved Shabbos."

"And why do they call you that?"

By now Chatzkele could hardly speak. He almost whispered, "Because … because … because when I carry their packages I always sing *'Lekoved Shabbos'*…"

R. Shomo'le's eyes filled with tears. He held Chatzkele's hand even tighter and said, *"Gevalt,* Chatzkele, how I envy you. To have such an exalted name – *Lekoved Shabbos* – and for such a holy reason. What an honor, *mamash* what an honor! Please, tell me a little about yourself."

"Holy Rebbe, the truth is, there's not much to tell. I never knew my parents. They left the world when I was only five years old. I don't have any other family, so I lived on the streets, making money for food any way I could. Sometimes, late at night, I'd go to the synagogue, and some kind people taught me how to *daven* a little, and how to recite the Psalms. I never learned anything else. But I'm very strong, so I make a living as a porter, a *trayger.* And I have a wife and children… That's all there is to say…"

R. Shlomo'le squeezed Chatzkele's hand again and said, "Sweet Chatzkele, there's one more thing I want to know. Why do you always sing? What are you thinking about when you carry packages singing *'Lekoved Shabbos'*?"

And this time it was Chatzkele who had tears in his eyes. He cried, "Rebbe, I know the beginning, but I don't know how it will end. I know that in the beginning the *Ribbono Shel Olam* created Heaven and earth. I learned about our Fathers, Abraham, Isaac and Jacob, our Four Holy Mothers, about the twelve tribes of Israel. I know the Master of the World took us out of Egypt and brought us to the Land of Israel, where we built the Holy Temple, the place of G-d's Glory, in Jerusalem…

"And – *gevalt, gevalt!* I also know what happened next. We were driven out of our land, the Holy Temple was destroyed, and ever since, *Am Yisrael* has been wandering around the world, in exile, without a home…

"So I know the beginning, and a little bit of the middle. But, Holy Master, I don't know the end. When will our exile finally be over?

When will G-d take us back to the Holy City, to *Yerushalayim*? When will we be able to sing again in the Holy Temple *Lekoved Shabbos*, in honor of the Holy Sabbath?

"So that's why I sing, Holy Rebbe. My song is really my cry, my prayer to the Master of the World. And what I'm thinking is: '*Ribbono Shel Olam, Lekoved Shabbos,* for the honor of Shabbos, let the End be soon; *Lekoved Shabbos,* for the sake of the Holy Sabbath, let the Holy Temple be rebuilt today; *Leko-o-oved Sha-a-bbos…*'"

This time the Holy Ch'shanover couldn't hold back his tears. He began sobbing from the deepest depths of his heart. And he said, "*Oy,* Chatzkele, you *mamash* know the holiest secret of all … that everything we carry, everything we do, everything that happens to us in our lives … everything is all *Lekoved Shabbos,* for the sake of the Great Shabbos to come. If only all the *Yidden* also knew this exalted truth, then the End, the Great Day, the Coming of the Messiah, would *mamash* be so close, so near…"

Then R. Berishel went on to write: "The day after the Holy Ch'shanover left Uschpitzin, Chatzkele also disappeared. I always thought he must have gone with the Rebbe, but I never knew for sure. As for me, I became R. Shlomo'le's follower. I learned with him for many years, I often visited him on Shabbos and the holidays, and eventually I had the honor of being his successor. Whenever I was with the Rebbe I was always looking for Chatzkele Lekoved Shabbos. But I never saw him.

"Then one day, many years later – the Holy Ch'shanover had already left the world and I was the rabbi in Uschpitzin – as I was passing through a little village far away, I saw an old *Yiddele* sitting in the marketplace. And suddenly I heard the most wonderful sound, a song that had always held a place in my heart: '*Leko-o-ved Shabbos; Oy, Leko-o-ved Shabbos; Oy, Leko-o-oved Sha-a-bbos.*'

"I looked again at the old man. *Gevalt!* It really was Chatzkele! And suddenly everything was clear to me:

When R. Shlomo'le Ch'shanover came to Uschpitzin, he made me into his *chasid,* and later I had the honor to become a Rebbe. But Chatzkele – do you know what R. Shlomo'le did with him? He made him into a *lamed-vav tzaddik.* Chatzkele had become one of the thirty-six hidden holy people who keep the whole world going, *Lekoved Shabbos,* until the Messiah comes and brings the End…"

You know, the Holy Nadvorner Rebbe always warned his wife and the people helping her in the kitchen: "Please remember, when you do the cooking for Shabbos, you mamash *have to say all the time: 'Lekoved Shabbos, Lekoved Shabbos. We're preparing this food in honor of the Holy Sabbath.'"*

At the Shabbos meal one Friday night, a chasid *brought the Holy Nadvorner his soup. The Rebbe looked at it, smelled it, then pushed it away. His followers couldn't understand what was going on. They tasted the soup, then said to the Nadvorner, " Holy Master, this is really very good. Please have some." But the Rebbe absolutely refused to touch the soup.*

Some of the chasidim *ran right away to the kitchen to find the Nadvorner's holy wife. "Heilige Rebbetzin," they cried. " What happened to the soup? The Rebbe won't eat it!"*

The Rebbetzin thought for a moment, then she laughed. "Gevalt!" she said. "I think I know what the problem is. There's nothing wrong with the soup. It's just that we hired a new woman this week, a new cook. And I must have forgotten to tell her to say 'Lekoved Shabbos' while she was preparing the food.

"So of course the Rebbe won't touch the soup. Because my holy husband won't eat anything on Shabbos that wasn't made Lekoved Shabbos, *especially for the honor of the Holy Sabbath Day…"*

We should all be blessed that not only our food, but everything in our lives, should always be Lekoved Shabbos, *in honor of Shabbos…*

Tzaddik Yesod Olam

The Righteous Are The Foundation of The World

Illustration:

"And there ... I saw your father, the Holy R. Yitzhak Vorker ... leaning on his staff, staring at the sea..."

"The Ocean of Tears"

How much of the Torah that we have learned can we really say has touched the deepest depths of our hearts? It's possible to know the whole Torah, to study G-d's Word day and night, and still be completely unmoved. It's even possible to talk about G-d all the time, and even while we're mentioning His Name in every sentence, not to be thinking about Him or feeling close to Him at all.

So what's the story here? Why would G-d give us a Torah that doesn't reach us? It mamash doesn't make sense...

The truth is, every word of the Torah contains unbelievable power. The Torah is so absolutely holy and deep that if we received it the way it was given by G-d, it would get right into our bones. And then we would have no choice, we'd have to keep every word.

But the thing is, G-d wants us to have a choice. His whole intention is that we, on our own, choose to observe His Law. So the Ribbono Shel Olam is a little bit hiding. He doesn't hide the words of the Torah. They are open for us to learn. What He's hiding is the deepest depths of the Torah, its dynamic power that is so strong it takes away our free choice.

Still, you know, there are some people for whom the Torah is shining so much that they can't help observing all of it, or at least as much as one can since the Holy Temple was destroyed. These are the righteous, the holy – the tzaddikim.

A tzaddik is somebody who has no choice but to keep G-d's Law. He's mamash beyond choice. Because he has surrendered completely to Hashem's revealed Will, all he wants is to serve G-d with all his heart, with all his soul, and with all his might.

And this is what the Rabbis meant when they said "Tzaddik Yesod Olam", a tzaddik is the foundation of the world. What is a foundation? It's the base upon which everything else is built. You know, when the wind is very strong, a tree may bend in all directions, but it's never detached from its roots. Because that is its foundation...

When a tzaddik learns Torah, the words touch him in his deepest depths. All of his life is built on G-d's Word, and nothing can move him from it. The Torah is the foundation of his life.

Now, everybody knows that nothing can exist unless there are Yidden not only learning, but also keeping the Torah. So when a tzaddik makes Torah the foundation of his life, then he becomes the foundation of the world...

The S'fas Emes and The Soldier

Everybody usually thinks that "holy" means "far out." But the Heilige Ishbitzer *says "holy" really means "right there."*

What is the Ishbitzer saying? That, for example, G-d is called Holy because He's always there when you need Him.

And it's the same thing with the tzaddikim, *the holy Jews. You know, in former good days, what did simple* Yidden *do when they were in trouble? They went to the big Rebbes, the Holy Masters, because the* tzaddikim *were always there for them. Yes, the Rebbes taught the most exalted Torah. They encouraged people to do* teshuvah, *tried to fix their souls. But most of all, they wanted to ease the burden of suffering* Yidden *in this world. What they wanted most of all was to help...*

t the beginning of the twentieth century, Russia and Japan went to war. And sadly enough, the Russian authorities loved to draft young Jewish men, especially *yeshivah* students, into the army to fight the Japanese. These poor *Yidden* didn't want to interrupt their studies, or risk their lives for a country that gave them nothing but trouble. And they knew that their time in the army would be nothing but insult and pain. So what did they do? They went to the Holy Masters, like R. Yehudah Arieh Leib Alter, the *Heilige S'fas Emes*, for help. And the Rebbes would bless them that through some miracle, they would not have to go to the war.

One day the S'fas Emes noticed a young man waiting with all the others for a blessing to be saved from the army. And this *Yiddele* looked so gentle, so sweet, it was clear that he *mamash* wasn't fit to be a soldier. When it was his turn to see the Rebbe, his voice was so low the S'fas Emes could hardly hear him. And all he said, so softly and sadly, was, "Holy Master, I've been drafted."

The S'fas Emes had never seen anybody look as broken as this holy *Yid*. "*Gevalt*," he thought. "He's just a child. He's much too young for all this." Then, turning to the young man he said, " Wait here." He went into his private room, and when he came out a few minutes later, he silently handed the boy a book.

The young man glanced at the title. It was a manual on how to do circumcisions, how to perform a *bris*. The youth looked at the S'fas Emes in surprise. "Holy Master…?" he started to ask. But the Rebbe interrupted him:

"My sweetest friend, listen to me. Read this book, learn how to do a circumcision. And I bless you that even if you do have to go into the army, you should come back safe and whole and *b'shalom*, in peace."

"But Rebbe!" the young man cried. "I don't want to go to war! Bless me that I won't be drafted at all!"

But the S'fas Emes was no longer paying attention. He was already talking to the next person in line.

In the end, the sweet young *Yid* did go into the Russian army, and was sent to basic training. Army life was very hard for him, especially one thing: the other soldiers – peasants, really – were *mamash* SO dirty. Their uniforms were always wrinkled and soiled, their shoes were never shined. They never cleaned their barracks. They didn't know how to stand in straight lines, and they didn't even take care of their rifles. The Jewish boy had always been very neat, very orderly, and he hated living in such sloppiness and filth. He himself was always careful to keep his own things in perfect order and so – *gevalt*! He was the only one in his unit who looked or acted anything like a proper soldier. And whenever he had a few spare minutes, or he felt particularly sad and lonely, he thought of his strange meeting with the Holy S'fas Emes. And, as the Rebbe had instructed, he read the little manual on circumcision from cover to cover.

One day a general came to review the new recruits. He immediately noticed the sorry state of the rooms, the clothes and the rifles, and shouted at the commanding officer: "What's going on here? Is this how soldiers are supposed to be? It's a total disgrace!"

"Sir, I'm really so sorry," the officer said. "To tell you the truth, I'm also ashamed of these men. I've tried to get them to shape up, but… Still there is one soldier I'm really proud of – a Jew. He's always clean and neat, he follows orders well. He's *mamash* a good soldier, despite his being Jewish."

"Is that so?" the general said. "Then bring him to me. I want to see this Jew for myself."

When the sweet Jewish soldier was ordered to report to the Russian general, he trembled in fear. What could such an important person want with him? It couldn't be anything good! Still, he had no choice, so he appeared as instructed at the door of the commanding officer's private office.

The general ushered the boy into the room. Then suddenly, without saying a word, he took out a pistol and pointed it at the young soldier. The poor *Yid* started to shake even harder. The general looked at him coldly and demanded in his most intimidating voice,

"Is it true what they say, that you only eat kosher food?"

The young man was afraid to admit it, but he knew better than to lie. He swallowed hard and answered, "Yes, sir."

The general marched up to him and held the pistol against his chest: "You are now a soldier in the army of the Czar of Russia. And the Czar requires that his soldiers have strong bodies. They must eat all the food they are given. I hereby order you to eat whatever is put before you, kosher or not!"

Suddenly the young *Yid* was more angry than afraid. Eat *treif* food? Never! So he said, in a clear, strong voice, "I'm sorry, sir, but I cannot obey that order. I'm a Jew. I serve G-d, not the Russian Czar."

The general stared at him again. Then he asked, "Is it also true that you keep the Jewish Sabbath?"

This time the young soldier didn't even hesitate. "Yes sir, I do."

"What?" the general cried. "A soldier of the Czar wasting time, taking a day off every week, and in the middle of a war? I hereby order you to work every day!" And he pushed his pistol harder against the youth's heart.

The young Jew knew that this was *mamash* the test of his life. The general could kill him in a second. Still, he squared his shoulders, stood up a little straighter, and answered firmly, "I'm sorry, sir, but I can't do that. There is no way I will work on Shabbos. I may be in the Russian army, but the only One I serve is G-d in Heaven."

Suddenly the general smiled and put away his gun. "It's all right," he said to the astonished *Yiddele*. "I'm not going to shoot you. It's just that I had to be sure. You see, nobody knows this, but I'm also a Jew. I was drafted, just like you, and worked really hard in the army, just like you do. I kept a low profile, and after a while people forgot I was Jewish. And now, as you can see, I'm at the top.

"But my wife just had a baby – a son. And the thing is ... I don't know exactly why, but I want him to have a real kosher circumcision. Now I can't go to a regular *mohel*, because I have to keep his *bris* absolutely secret. If the army remembers I'm a *Yid*, I won't just lose my position, I could also lose my life.

"So I've been looking all over for a Jew here in the army who can do the circumcision quietly for me. And when I heard about you, I thought you might be the one. I'm not really religious, but I do know one thing: A *mohel* has to keep Shabbos and eat kosher and generally observe the commandments. That's why I asked you those questions. I was testing you, to see if you kept the *mitzvos*...

"And now that I see what a good *Yid* you are, I'll make you a deal. I want you to be my *mohel*. I'll sign a pass for you, tell them I need you on my staff, and take you home with me. And after you circumcise my son, I'll give you civilian clothes and you can go on your way."

The young Jewish soldier couldn't believe his ears. *Gevalt*! Thanks to the little manual, a circumcision was something he knew how to do. And for the first time, he *mamash* appreciated R. Yehudah Arieh Leib's true holiness. The Rebbe had such *ruach hakodesh* that he'd forseen not only his own need, but also that of this hidden Jew.

The boy grasped both of the general's hands, lifted up his eyes to Heaven, and cried,

"*Hodu L'Hashem Ki Tov!* Give thanks to G-d, for He is good. And give thanks to his servant and messenger, the Holy S'fas Emes!"

The Silent Rebbe

R. Menachem Mendel of Vorka

Someone once asked the Heilige R. Nachman of Breslov, *"How loud should a person yell when he davens?" And R. Nachman answered, "You have to pray so loud that nobody can hear a thing..."*

Everybody knows the Holy R. Yisrael of Rizhin was mamash *a* gevalt, *the highest of the high. Unlike other Holy Masters, when R. Yisrael davened he didn't sway back and forth, or bend up and down. And he didn't make a sound. Even if you were standing right next to him, you couldn't hear a whisper. He was still and he was silent. But when he was finished with his prayers, on the floor where he had been standing there was always a pool of tears...*

You see what it is – words come from the Tree of Knowledge. They label and define: this is an orange, this is an apple; this is good, this is evil. Words are on the level of garments, of the finite, of head-knowledge.

Ah, but silence ... silence comes from the level of the infinite. When you are silent, it doesn't mean you're not doing anything. It's just that what you're doing is beyond words.

For us ordinary people there are only two choices – either we speak, or we are silent. But with the far-out, really infinite people, it's another thing altogether. When they speak, they don't disturb the silence. Quite the opposite. Their words echo the silence, and make it even deeper...

 You know, all the Holy Masters had different ways of giving over their exalted teachings to their *chasidim*. Sometimes they gave formal lessons or Torah discourses. Or maybe they'd clothe their message in the form of stories or parables. But there was one Rebbe, the *Heilige* R. Menachem Mendel of Vorka, the younger son of the Holy R. Yitzhak Vorker, who was different than all the rest. Not only did he never give classes, he *mamash* hardly ever spoke at all. R. Mendele taught through silence. And so he was called the Silent *Tzaddik*, the Silent Rebbe.

Now it goes without saying that you had to be a little bit extraordinary yourself to be a follower of a Rebbe who rarely talked. Because who wants to sit for hours with a teacher, no matter how holy, who doesn't say anything? Some people would get impatient and think: "What's with this rabbi? I came here for spiritual guidance, to learn some Torah. But I've learned nothing, he hasn't said one word! Who needs this?" And they'd stalk out, never to return.

And others, who didn't understand R. Mendele's ways, completely misunderstood his silence. They thought it meant he didn't know anything, that he had nothing to say. So the "straight" *chasidim* looked down on him, and didn't want anything to do with him.

But still R. Mendele had many followers, infinite, fire people – mostly simple working *Yidden* filled with the greatest hidden holiness. They would sit with their Rebbe for maybe twelve hours at a time, listening to his holy silence. And the whole time nobody in the room coughed, nobody stirred restlessly, nobody even had to go to the bathroom. Everyone was *mamash* out of his body.

It is said that one Shavous R. Mendele sat with his followers all night without saying a word. Right before dawn, just before it was time for the sunrise *davening*, the Rebbe finally spoke. And this is what he said:

"Everybody knows the end of the *Sh'ma Yisrael* prayer. It says, '*Hashem Echad*, G-d is One.' Happy is he who *mamash* knows, in the deepest depths of his being, that '*Hashem Echad*' really means 'G-d is One'..."

And the *chasidim* later testified that when their Rebbe said these words, every cell in their bodies knew, for the first time, what it means to understand that there really is One G-d...

So to those who were on the level, R. Mendele was as exalted as the Holy Baal Shem Tov.

rom the time he was very young, R. Mendele Vorker had a great love for horses. And he had a strange custom. Every day at exactly two o'clock in the afternoon, he would harness the horses to his carriage, take the reins in his own hands, and go for a drive, all by himself.

The Holy Baal Shem Tov once said you can tell a man's character by the way he is with horses. Anybody who can't talk to a horse cannot hope to communicate with other human beings. R. Mendele went a step further. Not only would he never whip his horses, he didn't even have to speak to them. From the moment he picked up the reins in his holy hands, the horses just took off, and without any instructions, went anywhere he wanted.

Hundreds, maybe thousands, of people would gather at his stable every day at two o'clock, to watch R. Mendele go off on his solitary drive. You might think that once he had left, the *chasidim* would go on about their business. But you would be mistaken. All the onlookers waited at the stable until R. Mendele returned. And they said that when they saw their Rebbe heading back toward the stable, no matter how many times they'd witnessed this before, they always shivered in awe. Because the R. Mendele Vorker who was returning home was not the same man who had gone out for a ride only a few hours earlier. He was different, higher, holier. He had more distance behind him, you know.

R. Mendele's holy father, R. Yitzhak Vorker, knew his younger son was not completely in this world. And he was worried about how the young man would cope with such things as making a living for himself and his family. So when R. Mendele was only fourteen years old, R. Yitzhak arranged a *shidduch* for him with a very holy girl – the sweetest of the sweet – who also happened to be the daughter of a very rich man.

Now this girl's father was also a *chasidic Yiddele*, but he tended to be very "straight". He was delighted his daughter was marrying into the family of the great *tzaddik* R. Yitzhak Vorker, but he began hearing strange stories about his prospective son-in-law. So he decided to go to Vorka to find out for himself just what his beloved daughter was getting into. And the first thing he did when he arrived in town was to seek out other "straight" *chasidim* like himself and ask them what they thought of R. Mendele.

"R. Mendele?" one man replied. "You mean the one who never speaks? Well, at least he's honest. I mean, he knows he hasn't got a thing to say that's worth hearing, so he never bothers to open his mouth."

"It's not only his mouth he doesn't open," laughed another person. "I bet he also hasn't opened a holy book in his life. He doesn't know anything!"

"And not only that," a third man injected. "Instead of sitting and learning, like respectable people do, he runs around every day in the forest. They say he communicates with horses without having to say a thing. And everybody knows he's had a pet goat since he was seven years old..."

The rich man had heard enough. He burst into the Holy Vorker's house and announced that the match was off. And then he told the Rebbe just what he thought of his son.

When the *Heilige* R. Yitzhak Vorker heard what the rich man was saying, his face turned very red. Then he became very pale, white like a ghost. Then his face got red again, then white … back and forth like this for a very long time. Finally he spoke:

"My friend, I have to tell you, you're risking your life when you utter words like this about my holy son, R. Mendele. How dare you even think, much less say, that he is not worthy to be your son-in-law? You're *mamash* playing with fire. I want you to know, Heaven was ready to take back your soul for insulting such a *tzaddik*. And I had to work very hard to save you."

Now it was the rich man's face that turned deathly white.

"You have to promise me you will never say anything like this again," the Holy Vorker continued. "And in return I'll also make you a promise. Not only will you be proud of R. Mendele as your son-in-law in this world. You'll be even prouder of him in the World to Come!"

Everybody knows that R. Yitzhak Vorker's oldest son, R. Yaacov Dovid of Amshinov, was also the holiest of the holy. But he wasn't at all like his brother. He gave over his teachings in the usual way – in words. So he attracted as followers many of the "straighter" *chasidim*, and the students of the two brothers were always comparing one to the other.

Several years after R. Yitzhak left this world, there was a big Vorker family wedding. And both R. Yaacov Dovid and R. Mendele, with all their pupils, came to the *simchah*, the joyous occasion. During the wedding feast, the Holy Amshinover gave over many exalted teachings. He was really very holy, and also very learned, so he had a lot to say. But R. Mendele just sat silently as usual, never opening his mouth.

After the *Birkas HaMazon* and the *Sheva Brachos* — the special blessings after a wedding feast, R. Yaacov Dovid's students started whispering among themselves: "It's such a *chaval*, you know, *mamash* such a shame. Our Rebbe, the Amshinover, is so learned. He gives over such high teachings while his younger brother doesn't say a word. It must be true what they say – he doesn't know anything, he doesn't have anything to tell us. And his followers think he's as holy as the *Heilige* Baal Shem Tov! Isn't that crazy?"

Now, R. Mendele's *chasidim* knew that just to be in the same room with their Silent Rebbe was the highest of the high. But the Amshinover's followers needed words, so they started gathering around R. Mendele, making fun of him, and demanding that he at least say something … anything at all…

But R. Mendele didn't pay any attention to their jokes or their pressure. He just glanced up at the large clock on the wall of the wedding hall and said, "*Gevalt!* Look at the time. It's after two o'clock in the morning! Who can start giving over Torah at such an hour? But it's also too early to go to sleep on such a special night. So what can we do? I know, let's play cards!"

The Amshinover *chasidim* looked at him in horror, then turned around and walked out, taking their Rebbe with them.

After the last one had left, R. Mendele turned to his own followers, who, of course, had remained at his side. "Close the door," he said. "I don't want to be disturbed."

So one of his *chasidim* closed the door. And R. Mendele and his students sat there for hours, in absolute silence.

Mendele's top student and later his successor was the *Heilige* R. Berishel Bialer, who was *mamash* a very holy man. Now the chief rabbi in Biala at that time was a certain R. Nechemiah. He was quite learned, actually a great rabbi. But he was also very "straight." R. Berishel wanted R. Nechemiah to go with him to Vorka to see R. Mendele, and kept inviting him to come for Shabbos. But the chief rabbi always replied:

"Why should I waste my time? People say your Rebbe doesn't know anything, doesn't even know how to learn. And I believe them. Why else is he silent? I mean, if he knew anything, why wouldn't he give it over? And anyway, I have better things to do than sit for hours with a crazy rebbe who never says a word." And he always refused to go.

One day R. Berishel decided to try something different. He went to R. Nechemiah and said, "Okay, so you won't go with me to the Rebbe. But some Vorker *chasidim* and I always have a *Rosh Chodesh* feast here in Biala. At least join us right here in town for our celebration of the new moon. You won't have to travel, it won't take up so much of your time…" And he begged R. Nechemiah so much that the chief rabbi finally agreed.

So the next *Rosh Chodesh* the "straight" chief rabbi of Biala arrived for the Vorker *chasidim's* feast. And as he hesitated by the door, he saw all R. Mendele's followers sitting around a table, drinking big glasses of whiskey. R. Berishel noticed him standing there and came up to greet him, holding a water glass in his hand: "My dearest friend, holy rabbi, I'm so glad to see you. Here, have a drink." He filled the glass full of whiskey, gave it to R. Nechemiah, and waited for him to drink it. Then he refilled the glass and gave it to the chief rabbi again.

Now, for followers of R. Mendele, everything was covered up. Anybody watching his *chasidim* would think they weren't saying very much Torah, they were just sitting and drinking a lot of whiskey.

The thing is, you don't have to be on a very high level to drink fruit juice all night. But to drink whiskey for hours and not get drunk you *mamash* have to have control over your body and over all your senses. The Vorker *chasidim* were very simple people – water carriers, wood choppers, tailors. But inside, inside – on a hidden, secret level – they were the holiest of the holy. For them, the spiritual absolutely ruled over the physical. So they could drink all night and not feel a thing.

R. Nechemiah had a very high opinion of himself as a great scholar and a big mystic. He was sure he was on the level to handle anything the Vorker *chasidim* were doing. But he really wasn't accustomed to drinking, and after downing the two big glasses of whiskey, he was *mamash* out like a light. His head fell down onto the table and he lay there, snoring. And when he woke up the next morning, he was all alone in the room. Everybody else was gone.

Now R. Nechemiah wasn't stupid. It was clear to him that R. Mendele Vorker's *chasidim* didn't get together just to drink. He realized something deep, something holy, had happened while he'd been asleep ... and he'd missed it. "*Oy vey*," he thought. "Here I thought I was such a great person, and what did I do? I passed out after only two glasses of whiskey..." And he decided to come back the next month and try to find out what was really going on.

So the next *Rosh Chodesh* R. Nechemiah again joined the Vorker *chasidim* at their feast. Again, all these hidden people were sitting around a table, drinking from a big bottle of whiskey. But this time the chief rabbi had a plan. He accepted the glass of whiskey that R. Berishel gave him, but, when he thought nobody was looking, he poured it out under the table. As soon as R. Berishel saw that his guest's glass was empty, he immediately refilled it. And R. Nechemiah poured the whiskey out again. Then, acting like he was drunk, he lowered his head onto the table, as he'd done the time before, and pretended to pass out.

As soon as R. Berishel saw the rabbi slumped over the table, he said to one of the other *chasidim*, "Okay, now we can start. Bring me the *Etz Chaim*."

Now everybody knows that the *sefer Etz Chaim* is one of the deepest books of *Kabbalah*, of Jewish mysticism. It's *mamash* deeper than deep, one of the highest *s'farim* anyone can study – and also one of the hardest. And here were all these water carriers, wood choppers and tailors, after having drunk who knows how much whiskey, studying the *Etz Chaim* with R. Berishel all night.

R. Nechemiah – lying there, pretending to be drunk – was actually listening to every word. And he couldn't believe his ears. Here he was, a big rabbi, supposedly a great scholar and *Kabbalist*, an expert on mysticism. And he couldn't understand anything these people were saying! Suddenly he realized that for all his learning, he really didn't know anything at all. The simplest water carrier at the table, the kind of person he had always looked down on, understood more secrets of the Torah, more secrets of the world, than he, the chief rabbi of Biala, would ever know if he lived a million years...

R. Nechemiah was so broken he didn't know what to do with himself. He lay there for hours, pretending to be asleep, until he thought he'd heard all the *chasidim* leave the room. Assuming he was finally alone, he opened his eyes and raised his head, only to find R. Berishel sitting silently beside him. R. Berishel said, "I was watching you, R. Nechemiah, and I know you were only pretending to be asleep. Now tell me, could you hear what we were learning? Did you understand it?"

R. Nechemiah hung his head in shame. "To tell you the truth, R. Berishel, I heard everything. But I didn't understand a word. You know, I thought I was such a great scholar. I thought I had penetrated the deepest depths of the *Kabbalah*. And now I realize that your water carriers and woodchoppers know more than I ever will." And he laid his head back down on the table in total despair.

"My sweetest friend," R. Berishel said to him kindly. "Let me tell you something. These Vorker *chasidim* seem to be simple people, the kind of *Yidden* who know very little, who usually sit in a corner of the *shul* and recite Psalms. But that's just the outside, the outside of the outside. Really they're all great mystics, giants in learning. It's just that they don't talk about what they know...

"And I want you to know, as holy and learned as they are, they're nothing compared to me. And as for me, I'm only a great scholar until I come to my holy Rebbe. When I'm with R. Mendele, it's *mamash* clear to me that I know nothing, nothing at all. So if you want to see somebody who's really on the top level, come with me. Let's go together to Vorka for Shabbos."

And this time R. Nechemiah agreed.

The next Friday R. Nechemiah and R. Berishel traveled to Vorka. Now, some people, when it comes to Shabbos, go to the synagogue, knock off a few prayers fast, and go home. Other people keep the Sabbath in a very holy way. But in Vorka ... can you visualize what a level their Shabbos was on? The Vorker *chasidim* were so high they weren't really in this world even during the week. Can you imagine the way they kept the Sabbath – the day you can taste what it will be like after the coming of the Messiah...?

R. Mendele Vorker had a special custom right before Shabbos. Everybody who had come to Vorka – sometimes maybe hundreds of people – stood in line before him, and the Rebbe shook each one's hand. Of course, when he took your hand, R. Mendele didn't say, "Good Shabbos, my friend. Please, tell me who you are, where you're from, how you earn your living." In fact he didn't say a word. He just looked at you. But, *gevalt!* How he looked... It was clear he could *mamash* see your soul before it descended into this world, and everything about your life after you were born. It was said he could even see all your incarnations, how many times your soul had come into *olam hazeh*. He really saw you, he really KNEW you...

So this Friday afternoon R. Berishel and R. Nechemiah stood in line with all the other *chasidim* to shake R. Mendele Vorker's holy hand. Then somehow the two became separated in the crowd. R. Berishel was anxious to hear what the chief rabbi thought about his meeting with the Rebbe, so he went looking for him. And he finally found R. Nehemiah sitting in the *Beis Midrash*, totally engrossed in learning.

"My dearest rabbi," R. Berishel said. "Forgive me for disturbing you, but please tell me, what did you feel when R. Mendele took your hand?"

"R. Berishel, words can't express…" R. Nechemiah began. Suddenly he stopped, realizing what he had said. Then he tried again: "When R. Mendele took my hand, all at once I saw my whole life up to that moment. And it was clear to me that it wasn't what it seemed. I mean, I always thought I believed in G-d. But suddenly I realized it wasn't real. I *mamash* had no idea what believing in *Hashem* actually means. And you know, I've been learning Torah my whole life. But I always had to work so hard at my studies because for me, the words of the Torah weren't luminous, weren't alive… *Gevalt!* I felt so ashamed, so broken…

"And then, when the Rebbe looked into my eyes, my whole body – every bone, every nerve, every inch of my being – was filled with the most awesome light. And all I wanted to do was learn G-d's holy Word. So I rushed here to the House of Study and opened the first *sefer*, the first holy book I saw. And do you know what it is? It's the *Etz Chaim*…

"Before, when you were learning this *sefer*, I couldn't understand anything. Now every word is shining before me. Every word is shining inside of me…

"Because when I touched your Rebbe's holy hand, for the first time in my life I understood – I KNEW! – that the *Ribbono Shel Olam* is, *mamash*, the Master of the World."

You see what it is … if people aren't sensitive enough to be quiet, they become so deaf they can't hear the holy voice of silence…

The Way Of Loving-Kindness

R. Dovid Lelover

You know, all the great chasidic dynasties had their own special ways of serving G-d. For some it was learning Torah, for others it was davening. And for most of the Rebbes, it was really important to teach their followers and to say a lot of Torah.

But with the Holy R. Dovid of Lelov, it was a different thing altogether. For R. Dovid, the most important thing was loving Yidden, mamash from the deepest depths of his heart.

Now, someone might say there were also other Rebbes who loved Jews the most. There was the Apter Rav, who was called the Ohev Yisrael, the lover of Israel. And R. Levi Yitzhak of Berdichev, who was the defender of every Jew.

But you see what it is – the Apter Rav and the Berdichever also gave over a lot of Torah. But R. Dovid Lelover said very little. He didn't need to. His actions told the whole story…

efore R. Dovid Lelover became a Rebbe, he was *mamash* a beggar, a little *shlepper*, sitting all day in the *shul* in Lublin. Now, in former good days, there was no mail delivery. To get a letter to somebody, you had to find a reliable person to deliver it for you. One day a big rabbi – who happened to be a *misnaged*, a person opposed to *chasidism* – came into the synagogue in Lublin. He looked around, then said in a loud voice,

"I'm sorry to bother you, but this is very important. I have to get a letter to Pieterkoff right away. Could anyone take it there for me?"

Pieterkoff was on the main road to Lelov from Lublin. So R. Dovid the beggar jumped up right away and said to the great rabbi, "You know, I just happen to be going home to Lelov tomorrow. I'd be honored to take the letter for you."

The rabbi looked at R. Dovid Lelover. The man's clothes were torn, and he was *mamash* filthy. He thought, "There's no way I can trust this *shlepper*." And he started to tell him, "Thanks anyway, but…" Then the rabbi stopped himself. No one else had offered to help him, and he really did need to send the letter. So he decided to take a chance.

"You'd be doing me the greatest favor," he finally said. "You see, I'm the rabbi of Pieterkoff. I was supposed to leave for home today, but

I've been delayed. And my wife will be frantic if I don't get back on schedule. I need to get word to her so she won't be worried." And he gave R. Dovid the letter.

Now, this great rabbi had ten children. And sadly enough, his oldest daughter, seventeen years old, was completely paralyzed. In those days, only rich people could afford things like wheelchairs or crutches. If you were poor and couldn't walk, you were *mamash* out of luck. You couldn't really do anything. So this poor girl spent most of her time lying in bed.

The rabbi was delayed a long time in Lublin, and finally arrived home four weeks after he'd sent the letter. And when he opened the door to his house, he couldn't believe his eyes. His paralyzed daughter was standing in the middle of the room. When she saw her father come in, she ran to greet him, and jumped into his arms!

"My sweetest girl!" the rabbi cried, as he gave her a big hug. "What a miracle, to see you like this! How did it happen? Tell me everything!"

"I don't really know what happened," his daughter answered with a smile. "All I know is that several weeks ago, late at night, somebody knocked on our door. It was a beggar, a little *shlepper*, delivering a letter from you. But the strangest thing was, for all that he was dirty and ragged, he was shining with the most radiant light...

"We were all so excited we had a visitor, and everybody ran in to see who had come – everyone, that is, except me. As usual, I was lying in my bed. The beggar seemed surprised to see so many children and started counting heads: one, two, three – up to nine.

"'Nine children!' he exclaimed.

"'No,' little Yossi cried. 'We're ten. There are ten children in our family!'

"'But I only see nine. Where's the tenth?'

"Everybody pointed to the room where I was lying. I had been listening to the whole conversation, so I did the only thing I could, I stretched out my neck so the visitor could see my head. The beggar immediately came into the room and stood by my bed. He looked down at me and there was such kindness in his eyes. He said, 'I bless you to be healthy.' And he left.

"That's all your messenger said. But – *gevalt*! The moment he gave me his blessing, I suddenly felt so much energy in my bones that I couldn't help it. I jumped out of bed and started dancing. And I've been dancing ever since!"

You see what it is ... when a person gives love from the deepest depths of his heart, he can work miracles. And when a person understands the holiness of words, when he speaks only the truth, then everything that he says comes true...

 ne day the *Heilige* R. Dovid Lelover was walking down the street with his top student, the Holy R. Yitzhak Vorker. Now the Lelover was a very friendly person, and it was his habit to say hello to everybody he met. So when he and the Vorker passed a little boy, R. Dovid stopped and said, "Good morning, my sweet young man."

The little boy answered, "Good morning to you, Rebbe." And the Lelover smiled at him and continued on his way.

R. Dovid and R. Yitzhak Vorker were walking slowly along when they heard people running after them. They turned around and – *gevalt!* It seemed to be a large family... a man and a woman – probably a mother and father – several children, and even an older woman, maybe a grandmother. The Rebbes waited for the family to catch up, and then the Lelover asked, "What's going on here? Is something the matter?"

"We're sorry to bother you, Rebbe," the father said, breathlessly. "But we wanted to thank you for curing our son. *Nebach*, he's been deaf since birth. And he's never been able to speak. But he just came home and he was talking! And he can hear!

"We couldn't believe it. We asked our son what happened, but all he said was that someone said good morning to him – and not only did he hear the greeting, he was able to reply. And he's been perfectly fine ever since.

"We asked him who spoke to him. He didn't know who you are, but he described you perfectly. So we came looking for you, to thank you for performing a miracle for our son."

"The truth is," the Lelover said, "I didn't perform any miracles. Let me tell you what happened...

"Imagine what the Holy Vorker and I would have thought if we had said hello to your boy and he hadn't answered us. We would have thought he was rude, totally lacking in manners.

"Now, the *Ribbono Shel Olam* knows that I love every Jew, and I *mamash* hate to think bad things about any *Yid*. So He made your son able to hear and speak, in order to save me the pain of having to believe something negative about another person.

"And believe me, that is the greatest miracle!"

Everybody wants to be holy. But there are two ways to do this. One is to work on yourself all the time – and to guard yourself from anything that might bring you down. This is a very high path, very beautiful, very sweet...

But then there is a second way to be holy, to be a different kind of holy. It's to be ready to give up everything ... your davening, your learning, every high level that you've achieved ... for somebody else. And the truth is, the level you reach when you're willing to make your personal holiness smaller for the sake of another person – this is beyond everything else...

t was Yom Kippur night in Lelov. Thousands of people had crowded into the *shul* to *daven* Kol Nidre with the Holy R. Dovid Lelover. It was already time to begin the prayers, but the Rebbe wasn't there. His *chasidim* looked for him everywhere, but no one could find him. His followers waited for him as long as they could, but they finally had to go on without him.

Later that night, as the *chasidim* were on their way home, they glanced into the window of a house they were passing. And – *gevalt!* – there was R. Dovid! He was holding a baby and talking to two people, a man and a woman, who, his followers assumed, were the child's mother and father.

The *chasidim* ran fast up to the house and knocked on the door. When the father answered they cried, "We're Lelover *chasidim*, and we need to see the Rebbe right away!"

R. Dovid came in, still holding the baby. "What's going on? Why are you all here?"

"Why are WE here?" one of his followers cried. "The question is, why are YOU here? And where have you been all night? We searched for you everywhere, we waited for you as long as we could. Why weren't you in *shul* for Kol Nidre? How could you miss the *davening* on this, the holiest night of the year?"

"It's really very simple" R. Dovid Lelover replied. "I was on my way to *shul* when I heard a baby crying. No, not crying – *mamash* screaming! And the wails were coming from this house. So I knocked on the door. When no one answered – and I found the door wasn't locked – well, I let myself in. And here I found this beautiful baby, all alone, yelling at the top of his lungs. So what could I do? I picked the boy up and held him and walked him until he fell asleep. Then I stayed with him until his parents came home."

"That's all very beautiful," said another of the *chasidim*. "But tell us the truth, wasn't it hard for you? I mean, in *shul* the *davening* is so exalted, so inspiring. And you lead the prayers for thousands of people, while here you were all alone. You gave up Kol Nidre. You *mamash* gave up everything!"

"It was all our fault," the father broke in. "And really Rebbe, we're sorry to have put you to such trouble. You see, our boy almost always sleeps through the night. And we wanted so much to go to *shul*. So once we'd put him in bed, we thought it was safe to go *daven* for just a little while. We never dreamed he'd wake up and cry…"

"None of you understand," R. Dovid Lelover cried. "It wasn't any trouble, and I didn't give up a thing. And I didn't pray alone, I was with this beautiful child. Can you imagine how hard I prayed, holding this baby in my arms? It was the highest, deepest *davening* of my whole life. I *mamash* poured out my heart to Heaven like I never did before.

"You see, *davening* is very important. But it's not the only thing, even on Yom Kippur. Would the Master of the World have been more pleased with me if I had left this crying child alone so that I could pray in *shul*? Wasn't He happy that I was taking care of one of His creatures, as He takes care of all of creation?

"The truth is, I was ready not to *daven* at all. It was enough for me to play with this baby until his parents came home…"

A Wait On
A Street Corner

❧ ─────────────────────── ❧

R. Shimon Skernovitcher

You know, it's the saddest thing. On the inside of the inside, every Yid *is* mamash *holy. Deep within every one of us is a spark of G-d's infinite light. So we all have the potential to live on a very exalted level.*

But so much of the time we don't live up to our potential. What happens to us? How is it that with all our inside holiness, we sometimes fall so low? The problem is, our outsides have absolutely no vessels for our insides, for the exalted light that's hidden in the deepest depths of our beings. So our insides get lost. And then our outsides – our lives in this world – lose their shine…

The Holy Ishbitzer says that a tzaddik *is someone who helps us make our outsides into vessels for G-d's light. With his guidance, our outsides start to reflect our inner holiness. And then we can live the true life of a Jew…*

ou know, everybody talks about the six million. But sadly enough, nobody teaches us who they really were. Such unbelievable people, so many Rebbes, so many *tzaddikim…* One of the biggest Rebbes before the Second World War was the *Heilige* R. Shimon Skernovitcher, a descendent of the Holy R. Mendel Vorker. He was *mamash* the holiest of the holy, and he had hundreds, maybe thousands, of *chasidim.*

One day a *chasidishe Yiddele* came to the Holy Skernovitcher and said, "Rebbe, I live in a little village not far from here. I have three sons and a daughter. And I have to tell you, we're the only Jewish family in town." Because you know, in Poland before the War, a *Yid* often found himself living alone in a city of *goyim.*

"Please believe me, Holy Master," the man went on. "I try as hard as I can to teach my whole family how to be good *Yidden.* But you know how it is – my children need friends, so they've always played with the non-Jewish kids who live around us. It seemed natural. I mean, they didn't have much choice, so I never paid too much attention…

"But now – *oy vey,* it *mamash* breaks my heart – my daughter has fallen in love with a Polish boy. They've actually gotten engaged! And not only is he a Catholic, but my daughter wants to convert for him. She's run away from home and is living in a convent, learning about his religion.

"If that's not bad enough, the boy is a drunkard. When he drinks he gets violent, so he beats her up all the time. And the saddest thing is, my daughter thinks she loves him so much that she lets him do anything he wants to without saying a word…

"Rebbe, the wedding is in two weeks, and I can't let this happen! I have to get my daughter out of the convent and away from that man. But I have no idea how to do it. Holy Master, can you help me?"

Now, the Holy R. Shimon Skernovitcher had so many *chasidim*, he could have asked any one of them to go to this man's town and try to rescue his daughter. But do you know what he did? He took one of his followers and traveled himself to the village where the convent was located. When he got there, he looked all around, and noticed a certain street corner near the convent. He took a pencil, and scribbled a note on a scrap of paper. Then he went up to the first Polish boy he saw walking by and asked,

"Excuse me, but do you go to the church where the women from this convent pray?"

The boy couldn't believe someone who was obviously a Jewish rabbi would ask him such a question, and started to walk away.

"Wait!" the Holy Skernovitcher cried. "This is very important! If you do pray at that church, then I have a deal for you. I'll give you five rubles if you'll deliver this letter when you go there next Sunday. It's to a young girl who's studying at the convent for conversion. See, here's her name…"

At the mention of money the Polish boy was suddenly interested. He reached out for the letter.

"Wait a minute. There's one more thing. You have to make sure nobody sees you give her the letter."

"Okay," the boy grunted. He took the letter, and ran away.

And do you know what the Holy Rebbe wrote? "Starting tomorrow, my *chasid* and I will be waiting for you at this street corner…" and he named the corner he had noticed. "Signed, R. Shimon of Skernovitch."

The *Heilige* Skernovitcher and his *chasid* arrived at the street corner early the next Monday morning. And they never left the spot all that day, all that night, and of all the next day. If one of them needed to go away for a few minutes, the other one stayed there, waiting. If one of them went to sleep, the other stayed awake. But the girl didn't appear. By the second night, R. Shimon's student started getting restless:

"Rebbe, I know you mean well, but it doesn't look like she's going to come. Maybe we should try something else."

But the Holy Skernovitcher said, "No, we will wait."

Another day passed. Now the *chasid* was really getting impatient: "Rebbe, you don't even know if the boy delivered the letter. Maybe he just took the money and threw your note away. The girl may not even know we're here, and we're just waiting for nothing. Let's go home!"

But again the Rebbe only said, "No, we will wait."

Then – *gevalt, gevalt*! Late on the fourth night, the *Heilige* Skernovitcher saw a girl run out of the convent and turn toward the corner where he was waiting. He immediately went to meet her: "My dear, I'm so happy to see you! Thank you so much for coming…"

And the girl said to him, "To tell you the truth, when I first read your note, I got very angry. I knew my father had sent you to break up my engagement and I was already sick of his interference. So I decided there was no way I would come…

"But as the days passed, I couldn't help thinking of you and your *chasid*, sitting here on this street corner. I knew you wouldn't leave – that you'd keep waiting for me, even if it took weeks, months – maybe you'd even wait for me for years! For some reason, that made me miss my parents, my brothers, my former life. And … I don't really know how it happened … I started remembering who I really am, where I really come from…

"Then tonight, I suddenly thought, '*Gevalt*, I'm a Jew! What am I doing in a convent? What am I doing with my life?' And I ran right out to meet you…

"Rebbe, please take me home…"

A Load of Whiskey and One Hundred Thousand Rubles

The Holy Seer of Lublin

The Heilige *Yaacov Yitzhak HaLevi Horowitz of Lublin had the holy eyes of a true man of G-d. He could* mamash *see everything – the hidden depths of the Torah, all the secrets of the world – through his* ruach hakodesh, *his clear prophecy. Nothing,* mamash *nothing was hidden from him.*

Not only could R. Yaacov Yitzhak look into the inside of the inside of every human being, he also could see everyone's past deeds, their past lives, even the root of their souls.

So the whole world called him the Chozeh, *the Holy Seer, of Lublin…*

nce the Holy Seer of Lublin traveled to the Ukraine to visit the *Heilige* R. Baruch of Medzibozh. Now, R. Baruch was the grandson of the Holy Baal Shem Tov, and he considered himself the *Besht's* successor, the top Rebbe in all of Russia. And the Seer was the greatest Rebbe in Poland. So their meeting was like the coming together of two world powers.

R. Baruch wanted to impress the Seer, so he immediately said, "Holy Seer of Lublin, welcome to my city. I want you to know, I am the grandson of the holiest Rebbe who ever lived, the *Heilige* Baal Shem Tov!"

But the Seer answered calmly, "And I want YOU to know, I am the grandson of R. Koppel, one of the holiest Jews who ever lived. Have you ever heard of my grandfather? Let me tell you the story…"

You know, in my grandfather's time, Jews were forbidden to be involved in most businesses. One of the only things they were allowed to do was to sell whiskey. So lots of *Yidden* ran *cretchmas*, little hotels, where they could have a bar and make some extra money from the drinks they sold.

My grandfather, R. Koppel, needed to make a living for his family, so he had one of these little inns. But the thing was, he was the only Jew in his whole city. So, aside from an occasional *Yid* passing by on the road, the only people who came to drink in his hotel were Polish peasants.

Now, in his heart my holy grandfather wasn't a hotel manager or a bartender – really, he was a Rebbe. And he didn't want his bar to be a wild, vulgar, drunken place. So he made a point of talking to all his customers, asking them about their lives, sometimes giving advice.

And slowly, slowly, the peasants responded to his holiness. Whenever they had a problem, they would come to my grandfather. Before long, his *cretchma* was more like a *Beis Midrash* than a bar. And whenever the peasants did something wrong, instead of confessing their sins to their priest, they sought out R. Koppel. And he would fix their souls.

Then a new bishop came to town. He saw that most of the peasants no longer confessed at the church. So he asked some of the local people if there was a problem with the priest. The peasants told him, "No, the priest is fine. But to tell you the truth, we don't need to confess to him. We've found ourselves a Rebbe, R. Koppel, the *Yid* who runs the hotel. We go to his bar at night, drink a little bit, and tell him everything. And he helps us…"

The bishop was *mamash* shocked! Good Catholics confessing to a Jew, calling him their Rebbe? Unheard of! He tried to convince the peasants to come back to the church, but they wouldn't listen. They liked going to my grandfather. Then the bishop started threatening them, telling them all the penance they would have to do if they kept confessing to a *Yid*. But that didn't work either. The bishop was desperate. He had to get his people to stop hanging out with a Jew. He thought and thought, and finally came up with a plan.

Everybody knows that by a certain time on the day before Pesach, a *Yid* has to destroy all his *chametz*, everything made out of grain. Or he can sell it to a non-Jew; then, after the holiday, he buys it back. Now, whiskey is nothing but *chametz*. So, before Passover, my grandfather had to sell the entire stock of his bar to a *goy*.

The bishop waited patiently until a week before the holiday. Then he announced on Sunday in church, "Anybody who buys R. Koppel's whiskey before Passover is doomed to burn in hell!"

This finally made an impression on the peasants. None of them wanted to play around with the idea of going to hell.

My grandfather had a neighbor to whom he always sold his *chametz*. This *goy* would always arrive at the inn at a certain time the day before Pesach, to finalize the deal. That year, my grandfather waited and waited, but his neighbor never came. He started getting worried. It was close to the deadline for possessing *chametz*, and he had to sell his whiskey fast. So he went to the man and cried, "What's going on here? Why didn't you come to buy my whiskey?"

And the peasant said, "I'm really so sorry but I can't help you this year. The bishop told us all that we'll go straight to hell if we buy your whiskey. And I'm afraid – I can't risk it…"

This was the first my grandfather had heard of the bishop's decree. He tried to get his neighbor to change his mind, but with the threat of hell hanging over him, the man wouldn't budge. Desperately, R. Koppel went to other Poles, neighbors, customers in his bar. But the result was always the same. Everybody was too terrified to buy. Meanwhile it was getting closer and closer to the Passover holiday.

My grandfather didn't know what to do. *"Oy vey,"* he thought. "If nobody buys my whiskey, I'll have to pour it out. And I haven't even paid for it yet! The nobleman who's my supplier will demand his money two weeks after Pesach, and I was counting on doing a lot of business during those two weeks, to get the cash. Without whiskey, I have no business. And if I can't pay the nobleman, who knows what he'll do to me... *Oy vey, oy vey!"*

But R. Koppel knew he had no choice – a Jew absolutely cannot possess any *chametz* on Passover. So he went home, loaded the entire stock of his bar on a wagon, and drove to a lake near town. When he got there, he took all the bottles of whiskey and dumped them on the shore. He declared, as required, "Master of the World, this *chametz* no longer belongs to me. It's *hefker*, ownerless, no longer mine."

Then he got back on the wagon and went home to prepare for the holiday.

Now I want you to know, my grandfather was really on the level. All of Pesach he didn't think about his whiskey or the nobleman, not even once. But as soon as Passover was over he went outside his hotel, raised his eyes to Heaven, and cried, *"Ribbono Shel Olam,* what am I going to do now? I don't have any whiskey, I don't have any business, and I don't have any money. My supplier will kill me..." Then he thought, *"Gevalt!* I'd better get out of town fast, before the nobleman finds out what happened..."

Just at that moment one of the peasants passed by the inn. "R. Koppel!" he shouted. "I didn't know you were such a rich man."

My grandfather almost laughed. To be called a rich man at the very time he was *mamash* ruined – it was too much to take! "My friend, I don't know what you're talking about."

"I'm talking about the Cossacks ... the thousand Cossacks guarding your whiskey on the beach! Where did you get the money to pay for them?"

My grandfather ran right to the lake. And he couldn't believe his eyes. Sure enough, there was a full regiment of Polish soldiers, surrounding all his bottles of whiskey. He cried,

"Master of the World, I can't believe You did this for me. It's *mamash* a miracle! But *Ribbono Shel Olam*, even though I know that according to the law I could reclaim this whiskey, You know what it took for me to give it up. I did it all for You, and I did it with all my heart. It was maybe the only time in my life I ever reached the level of giving up everything for You.

"So, G-d in Heaven, if You really want to make me rich, please do it some other way. I *mamash* gave this whiskey to You. Don't make me take it back…"

"And my grandfather told me," the Seer of Lublin said to R. Baruch of Medzibozh, "at that moment he heard a voice calling from Heaven:

"'R. Koppel, forget the whiskey. I'll take care of you in a different way. But more than that, since you were willing to give up everything for Me, your oldest daughter, Mattel, will be blessed with a son. And this son will be the greatest light in the whole world…'

"I want you to know, R. Baruch, that Mattel is my mother. And I am the grandson who was promised to the holy R. Koppel…"

ne day a poor *Yiddele*, a *shlepper*, a beggar, came to see the Holy Seer of Lublin and said, "Rebbe, please help me. I need two thousand rubles right away, and I don't have any way to get it. It's *mamash* a matter of life and death! What should I do?"

The Rebbe looked at the man standing before him, at his dirty, torn clothes, his scuffed, broken shoes. He said, "Wait a moment," and went into his private room. He returned a moment later carrying a fur coat, a *sh'treimel*, and a pair of boots. "Here, take these," he said, handing everything to the poor man. "Put them on, and go to…" and he named a certain city. "Take a room at the best hotel, and G-d will help you."

Now this *shlepper mamash* didn't have a single penny to his name. He started to say, "Rebbe, the best hotel? How will I pay…" But the Seer had already turned away.

So the poor man put on the Rebbe's clothes, went to the top hotel in that city, and asked for a room. The clerk thought he looked so rich, he was probably a very important person. So he showed the *Yiddele* to the best room in the *cretchma* without asking him for money.

Now, the poor *shlepper* had nothing to do in that town but wait for the Rebbe's miracle. He was *mamash* afraid to show his face anywhere in the inn. What would he do if somebody asked him to pay? Besides, his suite was so beautiful, he had never lived in such luxury in his whole life. So he just stayed in his room, *davening* and learning.

A week passed, and nothing happened. The *Yiddele* started to get nervous. What if someone came to ask him to settle his bill? He started thinking, "Why did the Holy Seer send me here? I mean, I know he IS the Rebbe, and certainly he must know what he's doing. But it's taking so much time; how long am I supposed to wait?"

Suddenly he couldn't stand being alone in his room anymore. So he went out and wandered around the hotel. He sat down in the lobby, in a chair that was more comfortable than anything he could have imagined, and found himself talking to the man sitting next to him. This *Yid* was a teacher who'd been hired by the owner of the *cretchma* to tutor his children. The two hit it off right away; they started spending time together, eating meals together. And soon the teacher and the beggar had become good friends.

Another week went by. By now the *shlepper* was really worried. Not only was he no closer to his two thousand rubles, but every day he was more frightened that the management of the *cretchma* would find out he was an imposter and kick him out. Then, one night at dinner, the teacher said to him,

"You know, it's strange! We just met, but somehow I really trust you. I need you to do something for me. I can't tell you how important it is. You'd *mamash* be saving my life!

"You see, I've been teaching the children of the owner of this *cretchma* for a long time. The father and I are very close – we're like best friends.

"A few years ago my friend suddenly came into a lot of money – can you believe it? One hundred thousand rubles! Naturally he told me all about it. He even told me where he kept it ... in his room, under the pillow on his bed..." Because in those days, you know, there were no banks – people kept their money hidden in their houses.

"The thing is," the teacher went on, "some time ago my employer took his whole family on a trip and asked me to take care of the inn while he was away. One day, when I was alone here – I *mamash* don't know what came over me, how I could have done such a terrible thing – I stole his money, took it home with me, and hid it in my own house.

"When the owner of the *cretchma* came back and saw that his money was missing, he went absolutely crazy. *Oy gevalt* – it was such a scene! He called the police and they questioned everybody who was staying in – or had anything to do with – the hotel. Everybody, that is, except me. He considered me such a good friend, he thought I was beyond suspicion…

"To tell you the truth, one minute after I took the money, I was so ashamed, I *mamash* didn't know what to do with myself. I mean, I always thought I was a good, honest *Yid*, and now here I was, no better than a common thief!

"I want you to know I never touched a penny of the money. I still have the whole hundred thousand rubles. I've always wanted to give it back to my friend, but I couldn't figure out a way to do it without his knowing who had taken it. To this day I've never had the strength to face him, knowing how much I betrayed our friendship, his trust…

"For all this time I've lived with such terrible guilt. I think about that money all the time. It interferes with my teaching. I can't sleep at night. I just can't take it any longer. I'm *mamash* at the end…

"Please, I'm begging you. Will you help me? Will you return the hotel owner's hundred thousand rubles? Only you must promise that nobody will ever know I'm the one who took it. You can say a stranger came up to you and asked you to give the money back. Nobody will ever suspect you. You weren't even here when it was stolen… Will you do it?"

And the *shlepper* answered quietly, "Bring me the money tomorrow, and I'll see what I can do."

So the next day the teacher gave the poor *Yiddele* the hundred thousand rubles wrapped in brown paper. And the *shlepper* didn't hesitate for one minute. He went right to the owner of the *cretchma* and said,

"I have something to give you. It will *mamash* make you the happiest man in the world. But I can only give it to you if you promise not to ask me any questions, not to try to find out how I got it. Do you agree?"

The hotel owner didn't understand what was going on, but he answered, "Okay, now what is it?"

The *shlepper* handed him the package. And when the owner of the inn opened it, he couldn't believe his eyes. "*Gevalt!*" he cried. "The hundred thousand rubles that were stolen from me years ago! Thank you my friend, thank you so much!"

Then he looked at the *Yiddele*. "You know," he finally said, "I can tell by your clothes that you're very wealthy. But to have a hundred thousand rubles in your hand – that's a lot of temptation for anyone, even a rich man. Let me reward your honesty by giving you a tenth of this money." And he handed the *shlepper* ten thousand rubles!

So the former poor *Yiddele,* now rich himself, returned joyfully to Lublin, and went straight to thank the Holy Seer. He told the Rebbe the whole story, and when he was finished, the Seer sighed and said,

"I'm so happy for you, holy *Yid*. Now you can pay your debt and start a new life. But to tell you the truth, I'm as happy for myself as I am for you. You see, that poor teacher didn't sleep a wink ever since he stole the money. He was up all night, every night, crying about what he'd done and praying for help to return the rubles.

"And I want you to know, when the teacher couldn't sleep, neither could I, because I saw everything he was doing. I heard all his prayers, felt all his pain. Every time I started to doze off, his cries woke me up again.

"So really it is I who should be thanking you, because since you returned the money for the teacher, I've been able to get a good night's sleep for the first time in years!"

If It's Not Sweet, It Can't Be Torah

R. Hershele Rimanover

The *Heilege* R. Hershele Rimanover was the greatest student, and ultimately the successor, of the Holy R. Menachem Mendel of Rimanov. Now you know, some of the big *chasidic* Masters were themselves the sons of Rebbes, or at least of learned, holy people. They grew up in observant homes and learned in *yeshivos* all their lives. But R. Hershele was the son of a simple tailor. Sadly enough, his father left this world when his son was very young, and the boy was raised by his uncle. Until he was 13, he never studied Torah. He spent his time helping first his father and then his uncle, who was also a tailor. But in his heart he was *mamash* longing for G-d, so after his Bar Mitzvah he ran away to learn with R. Mendele Rimanover.

When he first arrived in Rimanov, R. Hershele was so humble, so hidden, that he served as the Rebbe's *shammes*. He would put wood in the oven of the *shul*, make R. Mendele's bed, bring him his food. And he would wake up at four o'clock every morning, take a broom, and sweep the floor of the *Beis Midrash* so the synagogue would be clean for the morning prayers.

R. Hershele got married when he was around sixteen years old, and the wedding was *mamash* a *gevalt*! Such *simchah*, such dancing! It wasn't over until well after midnight. But at four o'clock the morning after the wedding, there was R. Hershele as usual, sweeping out the *shul*. R. Mendele Rimanover's son went to his father and said, "I think there's something strange about your greatest pupil, R. Hershele. He got married last night, the wedding didn't end until almost two a.m., and still this morning he's back, sweeping the floor. Do you think he's normal?"

And R. Mendele cried, "*Gevalt*! Thank G-d R. Hershele came to sweep out the *shul*. I was afraid he'd be too tired, and I wouldn't be able to *daven* today. Don't you know? When he sweeps the floors he clears the way for all our prayers to reach Heaven!"

About seventy years later, the Holy R. Chatzkele Shinover, the son of the *Heilige* Sanzer, went on vacation to the summer resort of Pistian in Hungary. And the first time he went to *daven* in the *Beis Midrash* there, he was *mamash* appalled. The synagogue was absolutely filthy. So he said to the people in the *shul*,

"Aren't you ashamed? This is a holy place, how could you let it get so dirty? Somebody needs to come and clean it up!"

The next day the Shinover arrived at the synagogue very early for the morning prayers. And he found a little *Yiddele* was already there, sweeping the floor. "My sweetest friend," he said, "I want to thank you for getting up so early to clean the *shul*."

"You know," the *Yiddele* answered, "when you asked us to clean the synagogue, it reminded me of a story I heard when I was young – about R. Hershele Rimanover sweeping the floor of the *Beis Midrash* the morning after his wedding. And I thought, 'I'm not on the level of the Rimanover, and I certainly don't know how to make a path for prayers to reach Heaven. But I do know how to sweep.' So here I am."

The Holy Shinover looked at him and said, "Holy *Yid*, you *mamash* have no idea what exalted fixings you brought about in Heaven by sweeping these floors. Now, I know that you have been married fifteen years, and you have no children. And I'm happy to tell you, Heaven has just decreed that because you came to clean these floors for the honor of G-d's holy place, this year you will be blessed with a son."

You see what it is – sometimes we do something without really knowing the depths of what we're doing. But when we're doing it entirely for the sake of G-d's Honor, our simplest actions can reach the highest place in Heaven...

adly enough, soon after their wedding, R. Hershele Rimanover's wife got very sick. And shortly afterward she passed away. It was *mamash* heartbreaking. But what could R. Hershele do? He poured even more of his heart, his soul and his time into his learning, and when he was twenty-one years old he became the Rebbe of Rimanov.

Several years later, a woman came to see him. "Rebbe," she said, "I'm twenty-three years old, and I've never been married. And I'm an orphan, so I have no one to arrange a *shidduch* for me. Can you help me find a husband?"

R. Hershele studied her for a moment, then replied, "Listen to me. I have to ask you a very serious question. Would you think of marrying me?"

The woman thought the Rebbe was making a joke at her expense, and she started to cry. "Holy Master," she sobbed. "Please don't make fun of me. I'm very sensitive, and to me, this isn't funny. I *mamash* want so much to be married. But you know, I'm not asking for someone on such an exalted level as you…"

"I'm so sorry," the Rebbe said. "I never meant to hurt your feelings. Please, let me explain. Aren't you from…" and he named a certain village.

The woman seemed surprised. "Well, yes."

"You have ten brothers and sisters?"

"Yes, but how…"

"And your father was R. Moshele?"

"Yes…"

"I knew it! Now, tell me one more thing. Do you by any chance remember a little boy named Hershele, the son of the tailor?"

By now the woman was beside herself. "Yes, I remember him. My brothers' pants were always torn, so my mother took them to the tailor to be fixed. And this boy, Hershele, would deliver the mended pants to our house on Friday afternoon, so my brothers could wear them on Shabbos. But Holy Master, what does all this have to do with my *shidduch*? And how do you know so much about me?"

"Because I am that Hershele!" the Rebbe exclaimed. "I'm the one who delivered your brothers' pants! I don't blame you for not recognizing me … I know I look very different. But I recognized you right away.

"I want you to know, every Friday when I brought the pants, I would walk into your house and I would see you and all of your brothers and sisters sitting around the table with your father, learning the Torah portion of the week. Now, you have to remember that I came from a simple family of tailors. We had to work very hard, and we had no time to learn Torah. So what I saw in your house – all you children learning together with your father – was very special to me. And every Friday, when I left your house, I would pray,

"'*Ribbono Shel Olam*, that is how I would like my life to be. Please bless me to marry one of those girls!'

"Now I'm asking you again … and, believe me, this is for real … would you be my wife?"

So the Rimanover and the woman got married, because obviously, she was really his soulmate. And do you know what kind of wedding they had? The Rimanover told his *shammes*, "Here's what I want you to do. Drive to this village…" which he named, "… and you will see ten *shleppers* sitting in the *Beis Midrash* there. Ask them to come back with you; they will be the *minyan* for my wedding.

"Don't tell even one other person that I'm getting married. I don't want anyone else to come. And if anyone disobeys me and dares to show his face – I'll never speak to him again…"

You see what it is, anything which originates in Heaven needs to be covered up a little bit when it comes down to this world. Otherwise it's too strong to receive. When Moshe Rabbeinu, Moses our teacher, came down from receiving the Torah in Heaven, his face radiated so much light that the people around him couldn't take it. So he had to cover his face, he had to wear a veil.

Marriages are mamash *made in Heaven. A wedding between two real soulmates shines with the absolutely greatest light. If it's open to the whole world, its light has to be diluted a little, so it won't be too strong. So if you want to preserve your wedding's Heavenly light you say, "Let's cover up our marriage a little bit. Let's keep it a secret between the two of us…"*

 Hershele Rimanover, like many of the Holy Masters, always wore a *kapote,* a kind of long coat. Now, there were no dry-cleaners in those days, so after R. Hershele had worn his coat for a while, it would inevitably get dirty. His *chasidim* thought, "It's beneath our Rebbe's honor to go out in public in a stained *kapote.*" So every few weeks they'd give him money to buy a new one. But the Rimanover always gave the money to the first poor person who came to him for help.

After a while, the *chasidim* decided, "It's no use giving R. Hershele money. If we want him to have a clean *kapote*, we'll have to get him a new one ourselves." So they secretly took his measurements and had a new coat made for him. And not just any ordinary coat – this one was a *gevalt, mamash* so beautiful, with a fur collar and cuffs.

When they presented their gift to the Rebbe, he was beside himself with joy. "Why, to think you would do something like this for me!" he cried. " I'll wear it on Shabbos!"

That Friday night, R. Hershele walked into the *shul* wearing his new *kapote*. And he looked so holy, so exalted – the *chasidim* were very proud! Then, after the *davening*, everybody went into the dining room for the Shabbos feast. And the Rebbe's *shammes* started to serve the soup. But as he walked in he couldn't take his eyes off R. Hershele's new coat. He was anyway a little bit of a clumsy person ... and he wasn't really watching where he was going ... and – *gevalt, gevalt!* He spilled the soup all over the Rebbe! The beautiful new *kapote* was completely ruined!

The *chasidim* were so upset, they *mamash* wanted to hang the poor *gabbai*. But R. Hershele quieted them with a wave of his hand. And do you know what he said? "Ah, the soup feels so warm..."

You know, the Holy Sanzer Rebbe, who himself had hundreds, even thousands of followers, always went several times a year to spend Shabbos with R. Hershele Rimanover. And he was there the Shabbos of the spilled soup. The Sanzer said,

"The truth is, a person basically has to work on himself his whole life to keep from getting angry. But now I have seen one person who has absolutely cleansed himself of anger. Gevalt, the Holy Rimanover!"

 Yosef Shaul of Lemberg was a great scholar and a very holy man. He was the chief Rabbi of the city and the head of the *Beis Din*, the Rabbinical Court. Once a case involving a poor widow came before R. Yosef Shaul's *Beis Din*. The rabbis studied the matter very carefully, discussing every detail. And in the end, they ruled against the widow.

R. Hershele Rimanover heard about the verdict, and hurried to visit R. Yosef Shaul. He read the *Beis Din's* decision, and then cried, "With all due respect to the Court, this is not correct. Please convene another council of rabbis to reconsider the matter." And he pressured R. Yosef Shaul so much that the Chief Rabbi of Lemberg finally agreed to review the case again.

So another *Beis Din* was called. And, after intense deliberations, the second Court ruled that the first verdict against the widow had been a mistake.

R. Yosef Shaul was really a very big man, and, when he saw that he had been wrong, he was only too happy to admit it. But one thing bothered him. He went immediately to see R. Hershele Rimanover and said,

"For the first *Beis Din*, the other Rabbis and I studied the case for weeks before we made a decision. But you – all you had to do was look at our verdict, and you knew right away that it wasn't right. How could you tell so quickly?"

And the Rimanover answered, "When I read your judgement, I saw that it was very severe. It *mamash* tasted sour. But the Torah, the Word of G-d, is never harsh. It is always sweet...

"I knew then that your verdict couldn't be true. Because if it isn't sweet, it can't be Torah..."

The Gemorah says we were driven out of Israel because people didn't say the blessings over the Torah. So everybody is asking, what brachos *didn't people make? And one answer is, they didn't say "V'ha'arev na Hashem Elokeinu es divrei Toras'cha b'finu – Please,* Hashem *our G-d, make the words of the Torah sweet in our mouths."*

You see what it is, if the Torah tastes a little bit sour to you, a little bit harsh, then you don't want so much to learn it. Because really, who in their right mind is attracted to something that's bitter? The truth is, the Torah itself is always sweet: 'All its ways are pleasant.' So if it doesn't seem sweet to us, the reason isn't that there's something wrong with the Torah. It's our taste buds that are off. That's why we have to say the blessing: "Ribbono Shel Olam, let the Torah be sweet in our mouths." What we're really asking is, let us taste the Torah the way G-d mamash intends it to be.

Then there's something even deeper. Our Rabbis teach us that every letter in the Torah represents a Jew. Every Yid in every generation has his or her own letter. Now, the Torah as a whole can't be sweet unless each letter is sweet as well.

So if you know how sweet the Torah is, then you also realize that all the letters ... in other words, all the Yidden in the world ... are mamash sweet as sugar...

And if you know how sweet Jews are, then you also recognize the sweetness of the whole world. Let's put it this way: If you're a parent and you love your children, then you wouldn't think of putting them in a bad environment. You'd want only the top surroundings for them.

The Ribbono Shel Olam is our Father. All Yidden are His children and He mamash loves us the most. So if G-d put us in this world, then olam hazeh must be a good place for us. Why then do we sometimes experience our lives as a little bit harsh, maybe sour or bitter? You know, when we put sugar in our tea or coffee, it sometimes sinks to the bottom in a big lump. So when we drink the liquid, it doesn't taste sweet. Then what do we do? We take a spoon and stir it up.

It's the same thing with olam hazeh. If it doesn't taste the way we know that G-d intended it to be, maybe we have to add to it a little bit of the sweetness of the Torah – and stir it up. And that way we can wake up the whole world...

The Sun
Will Yet Rise Again

R. Chaim of Sanz

Everybody knows that the Heilige R. Berele of Rodashitz was mamash *the holiest of the holy. People said he performed more miracles in one day than the Holy Baal Shem Tov did in a whole year. Because in Rodashitz, the whole thing was doing miracles.*

Now it was just the opposite in Kotzk. The Holy Kotzker Rebbe, R. Menachem Mendel, put all his energy into trying to bring Yidden to a level of real teshuvah, *of knowing the Absolute Truth. He didn't hold so much by miracles, so he and the Holy Rodashitzer weren't exactly the best of friends.*

But one day the Kotzker got very sick, and nobody seemed able to help him. The doctors tried everything, but the Rebbe kept getting weaker and weaker. R. Mendele Kotzker knew that it would mamash *take a miracle for him to get well. So what could he do? He wrote a* kvittel, *a little note, that said: "Menachem Mendel ben Feige admits he doesn't serve G-d as well as he could. So he can't rely on his merits; he can only beg the Master of the World to have mercy on him and grant him a* refuah shleimah, *a complete healing. But he knows this may not be enough. So he begs you to pray for him as well – to intercede for him in Heaven, to make a miracle for him..."*

And he sent his wife to deliver this note to ... the Holy Rodashitzer.

R. Berele took one look at the Kotzker's kvittel *and said to his wife, "What? Your holy husband says he's not a true servant of G-d? I only wish I served the Ribbono Shel Olam a fraction as well as he does...*

"Tell the Heilige Kotzker he will soon be well. And also tell him this: what is the difference between his work as a Rebbe and mine? He's always working on Yidden, trying to get them to listen to G-d. And I – I'm constantly working on G-d, trying to get Him to listen to us..."

Soon R. Mendel was completely cured. And he sent this letter to R. Berele Rodashitzer: "Heilige Rebbe, thank you so much for your help. I must admit you've changed my mind about miracles. And now I have a question for you:

"Instead of my wasting my time trying to get Jews to do teshuvah, *why don't you just tell the Master of the World to send the Messiah, and save everybody so much trouble...?"*

You see what it is, everybody knows the story of Noah and the Flood.[6] Not only all the people of that generation, but also the animals and even the earth itself were so completely evil that G-d said: "Ketz kol basar ba lefanai – the end of all

---

[6] Genesis, Chapters 6-8

flesh has come before Me." Mamash, *what a heavy thing! It's like the* Ribbono shel Olam *was sitting on His throne in Heaven, announcing to the whole world: "Better get your affairs in order, write your last will. This is it, this is the end…"*

Now, the Gemorah says the generation of the flood was so bad that even teshuvah *couldn't help. So the Master of the World had no choice but to destroy the world and start again. But at the same time we know that it rained for forty years before the floodwaters covered the earth. And during this time people* mamash *had a chance to repent. So how could G-d announce the end before it even started raining?*

The Holy R. Chaim of Sanz gives us one answer to this question. Imagine, he says, that you do an ordinary, everyday sin. Then you can fix it by repenting in an ordinary, everyday way. But if you sinned so much that you have mamash *destroyed the whole world, then your* teshuvah *has to be so strong that you fix all of* olam hazeh *and bring the Messiah.*

Now, everybody knows that the time of the coming of Mashiach is called the Ketz – the End, the End of Days. So, the Sanzer teaches, this is what G-d really meant when he said, "Ketz kol basar ba lefanai." He was telling the Generation of the Flood: "Your sin is so great that regular repentance won't work. The only thing that will help you is teshuvah *on the level of Ketz – teshuvah that can repair everything in the world…"*

Then the Sanzer says something even more far-out. In Hebrew, the word tzaddik *is a combination of the letters of the two words, ketz and dai. We know that ketz means end, and dai means enough, sufficient. What is the Sanzer trying to tell us? That a* tzaddik, *a righteous person, a Rebbe, is dai – enough – to bring the End of days. And he can do this in one of two ways.*

On the one hand, a tzaddik *can be like the Holy Kotzker. Such a Rebbe teaches* Yidden *how to do the kind of* teshuvah *that G-d wanted from the people of Noah's generation – a repentance so deep and so strong it can effect the* tikkun hagamur, *the ultimate fixing, the End. This is a very high level, really very holy.*

Ah, but then there's something else – the way of R. Berele of Rodashitz. Not only is such a tzaddik *able to teach others how to repent. He is dai, enough, to bring the Ketz himself. His davening is so strong, his love of* Yidden *so deep, his service of G-d so exalted, that he can work the greatest miracles and hasten the* geulah shleimah, *the complete redemption, and the coming of* Mashiach – *may it be soon, in our days…*

he *Heilige* R. Chaim Halberstam of Sanz was *mamash* one of the greatest *chasidic* Rebbes. From his earliest youth his heart was always burning for G-d, and he was constantly searching for the right Holy Master to show him how he could serve the *Ribbono Shel Olam* in the highest way.

Once R. Chaim had to make a choice between learning with R. Yaacov Yitzhak, the Yid HaKodesh, and the Holy R. Naftali of Ropschitz. He thought and thought, but he couldn't decide which Rebbe to follow. So he just sat down at a crossroad on the highway and started to pray,

"Master of the World, please send me a sign. Show me where to go."

Two minutes later, a *chasid* came walking down the road. He saw the Sanzer sitting by the highway and said, "Holy *Yid*, what are you doing here in the middle of nowhere? Come, I'll take you with me to meet my holy father." And R. Chaim agreed to accompany him.

The *chasid* just happened to be the holy Zhikover, the son of the *Heilige* Ropschitzer! And this is how R. Chaim Sanzer became a follower of R. Naftali of Ropschitz.

Now it was the Sanzer's way to *daven* very loudly, *mamash* to shout his prayers at the top of his lungs. But the Ropschitzer's students prayed silently, barely making a sound. R. Naftali's *chasidim* were always hassling the Sanzer: "Be quiet! We can't concentrate on our *davening* with all the noise you're making!" So R. Chaim started finding a corner in a hallway – or even a closet – where he could pray alone. He only *davened* in the *Beis Midrash* when nobody else was around.

One day the Ropschitzer wandered into the synagogue at an unexpected time. And he found the Sanzer there, screaming out his prayers from the deepest depths of his heart. R. Naftali was so impressed by his intensity and his love for G-d that he told the other *chasidim* to make sure R. Chaim prayed with their *minyan* – and to let him *daven* any way he liked. And none of the Ropschitzer's followers ever bothered the Sanzer again.

For many years R. Chaim traveled regularly between Sanz and Ropschitz. And he always sent word ahead to R. Naftali exactly when to expect him.

Once the Sanzer arrived in Ropschitz a day later than he had said. The Rebbe came out to greet him: "I was really worried! What happened to delay you?"

And R. Chaim explained, "I was driving down the highway as usual. And just as I passed this *cretchma*, the strangest thing happened. The woman who owns the inn darted into the middle of the road, and lay down right in front of my carriage. We almost ran her over – my driver was barely able to stop the horses in time!

"I jumped down from the wagon and rushed over to the woman. She looked at me and said,

"'Rebbe, forgive me. I didn't mean to startle you like this, but I HAD to get you to stop. Please, come into my inn. I really need to talk to you.'

"So what could I do? I went with her and spent the night at her *cretchma*. Holy Master, I apologize for being late. But that woman *mamash* put her life in my hands just to see me. So how could I not stop?"

You know, there are two very important secrets – the secret of living and the secret of dying. The secret of living is to be in touch with how pure you can be. And the secret of dying is to understand how high you can reach.

Now, dying in this sense doesn't mean to stop living; it means to rise to that level where you mamash *can't achieve anything more. So for the followers of the great* chasidic *Rebbes, the greatest honor in the world was for their Holy Master to reveal to them the secret of dying...*

hen the Holy Ropschitzer left this world, R. Chaim Sanzer and his best friend, R. Shalom HaLevi Rosenfeld of Kaminka, became students of the *Heilige* R. Shalom Rokeach of Belz. One day, after they had been with the Belzer for a while, the Rebbe called the two into his private room and said, "I'm very pleased with your learning – you're *mamash* top students. So I think it's time for me to give over to you the secret of dying. But I have to warn you, you have to prepare yourselves to be worthy of this great revelation."

The Sanzer asked, "So what do we have to do?"

"Fast for three days, and go to the *mikvah* eighteen times a day. Then, after midnight on the third day, come to me and I'll tell you the secret."

So the Sanzer and the Kaminker did as the Rebbe had instructed, and the Belzer told them the secret of dying.

The next day R. Chaim and the Kaminker were walking down the street when they met the Belzer's *Rebbetzin*, Malkale. Now, as much as R. Shalom was on a very high level, his wife was also very holy. In fact, the Belzer once said,

"It's really my wife who made me into a Rebbe. You see, at one time a little tailor lived on the other side of the street across from our house. And he got up every morning at four o'clock to start working. Malka, who anyway wakes up very early, would see him there, already busy at four a.m. So she would shake me out of bed, saying,

"'Shalom, the tailor's already working on his clothes, and you're not doing G-d's work yet? Better get up, fast!'"

Malkale knew that the Belzer had told the Sanzer and the Kaminker the secret of dying the night before. So she went right over to R. Chaim and said, "How did it go? And what do you think of my holy husband now?"

The Sanzer answered, "Holy *Rebbetzin*, I'll tell you. But you have to promise not to be angry."

Malkale said, "I promise. I really want to know."

"Holy *Rebbetzin*," R. Chaim insisted. "It's not that I don't believe you, but this is very important. I want you to think about it carefully, and *mamash* clean all the anger out of your heart."

Malkale was really on the level. She closed her holy eyes, concentrated very hard for a minute, then said, "Okay, I'm ready."

"The truth is," the Sanzer told her, "we already knew the secret. Our Holy Master, the Ropschitzer, had already revealed it to us. But he did it in a very different way."

Malkale looked puzzled. "What was the difference?" she asked. Then, seeing the Sanzer hesitate, she added, "Please tell me – I promise I won't be jealous... What did the Ropschitzer do?"

"Well," the Sanzer explained. "Your holy husband told us to fast and to go to the *mikvah*, so we'd be pure enough to receive the secret. But with the *Heilige* Ropschitzer it went like this:

"You know, every week thousands of people came to Ropschitz for Shabbos, and we didn't have much money. But potatoes are cheap, so we mostly ate *challah*, a little fish, and lots of potatoes for our Shabbos meals.

"The Kaminker and I had the job of preparing all the potatoes every Friday morning. First we peeled the potatoes, then we threw them into a big pot of boiling water.

"One *Erev Shabbos*, while we were hard at work, the Holy Ropschitzer came into the kitchen. He saw us, and immediately started laughing:

"'Ha, ha, ha – peeling potatoes! How wonderful!'

"Of course, you have to understand – the Ropschitzer was always laughing. He was *mamash* from the world of laughter…

"The Holy R. Naftali came over to the Kaminker and me. He stood between us and put his arms tightly around our shoulders, so that our three heads were very close together. Then he reached around my back, picked up a potato that we had just peeled, and threw it into the pot. And the hot water splashed in all our faces.

"*Rebbetzin*, let me tell you – when that potato water splashed on us, it washed our souls so completely – we were as pure as before we were born.

"Then the Holy Ropschitzer said, laughing, 'There's something I want to tell you.' And he disclosed to us the secret of dying.

"Afterwards he laughed one more time, and walked out of the room."

You see, true holy laughter is not of this world, but from the World to Come. It is not a joy drawn from the present, from today – but from the Beyond…

hroughout all his life the Holy R. Chaim Sanzer had a problem with his health, which nobody seemed to be able to cure. He had a lot of trouble with his foot, and it was very hard for him to walk.

Of course, the Sanzer was such a holy man that every mother wanted him to marry her daughter. Finally he agreed to a *shidduch* with a woman who everybody said was very special, the holiest of the holy, the sweetest of the sweet. But when his prospective bride heard about his physical problem, she refused the match. "I'm sorry," she said, "but I really don't want to marry a cripple."

The Sanzer immediately went to visit her and said, "My dear young lady, please look in the mirror."

The woman had no idea what a mirror had to do with the *shidduch*, but she did as she was asked. She stepped in front of a full-length mirror and, as soon as she saw her reflection, began to sob bitter tears.

"What's going on here?" she cried. "In the mirror I'm more crippled than you are!"

"Let me explain," the Sanzer said. "Before you were born, it was decreed in Heaven that you would be lame. But I knew you were my soulmate. So I prayed that our situations should be reversed. And so I was born the crippled one, instead of you…"

Finally the Sanzer's problem with his foot became so bad that he needed an operation. The doctor tried to explain the procedure to him: "I'm afraid this is very painful surgery, but don't worry, you won't feel a thing. I'll give you an injection, something to put you to sleep…"

"I don't want an injection or any kind of medicine," the Sanzer insisted. "You do your thing with the operation, and I'll take care of the pain on my own. But I have to ask one thing: If I don't open my eyes right away after the surgery, please don't disturb me. I may lie there for a long time, but just leave me alone. You have to promise me…"

The doctor tried to argue with him, but R. Chaim was adamant. So in the end, the doctor promised to do as he requested.

On the day of the surgery, the Holy Sanzer was wheeled into the operating room. He got up on the table, lay down, and immediately closed his eyes. The procedure took several hours, and the whole time R. Chaim didn't move a muscle. He never made a sound. He *mamash* looked like he was no longer in this world.

Finally the operation was over, but the Sanzer didn't move. For a long time he just kept lying there, absolutely still, with his eyes closed. Nobody could tell if he was even breathing. At last the doctor got really worried. He said to R. Chaim's family, "I *mamash* hate to say this, but I'm afraid maybe the Rebbe died during the surgery…"

But the Sanzer's children answered, "Just do what you promised our father, and leave him alone. If he said he'd be all right, then he will be, no matter how it looks…"

R. Chaim Sanzer lay motionless for four more hours. Then he opened his eyes, saw the doctor hovering anxiously over him, and asked, "So, how did it go?"

"It went fine," the doctor answered. "Actually, better than I expected. But Rebbe … really, I mean no disrespect … but what did you do? And why did you lie there so long?"

The Sanzer smiled: "Let me tell you, doctor – my Rebbe, the *Heilige* Ropschitzer, taught me a very holy secret – how to feel pure joy…

"You know, in *olam hazeh* we live in a world of reasons. There's a reason for pain – and there also has to be a reason for joy. The only way we can feel *simchah* in this world is for something to happen to us to make us feel happy.

"From the Holy R. Naftali Ropschitzer I learned how to receive the bliss of *Olam Habah* – pure absolute *simchah* that needs no outside cause. Of course, this kind of joy is very difficult to attain, and I can't always reach it. But when you told me I would experience a lot of pain, I concentrated very hard, and went into that place of pure ecstasy … a place where there is *mamash* no such thing as pain…

"So I felt nothing during the whole operation. But there was a problem. That level of joy is so exalted, so holy, it took me a while to make myself leave it and come back into this world again…"

Despite his troubles with his own health, the *Heilige* Sanzer was famous for his ability to cure others. Hundreds, maybe thousands of people came to him to be healed.

One day a wagon stopped in front of the Sanzer's house, and a *Yiddele* carried another man – very old, and obviously very sick – inside to see the Rebbe. "Holy Master," the younger *Yid* cried. "My father has tuberculosis, and the doctors say that he *mamash* won't be in this world much longer. Can you help him?"

R. Chaim immediately answered, "Take your father home and give him a cup of strong black coffee."

"What?" the son exclaimed. "Are you insane? Coffee is the worst possible thing for a man in his condition!"

But the Sanzer just repeated, "Take your father home and give him a cup of strong black coffee."

The younger *Yid* didn't know what to do. Finally he thought, "R. Chaim must know what he's talking about – after all, he IS the Rebbe." So he took his father home and gave him some strong hot coffee. And right away, the old man got well.

A few years later, the very old *Yiddele* got sick again. And his son thought, "My father's really too weak to make the trip back to see the Rebbe." So what did he do? He made the old man a cup of strong black coffee. Immediately his father began to cough up blood. So his son loaded him into the wagon, and went back to Sanz.

The Sanzer took one look at the suffering old *Yiddele* and cried, "What in the world did you do to him to make him so sick?"

"I just did what you told me last time – I gave him a cup of coffee."

"What?" the Rebbe shouted. "Are you trying to kill him? Don't you know how dangerous coffee is to a man with tuberculosis?"

The son just hung his head. "Is there anything you can do to help him now?"

The Sanzer looked him straight in the eye. "Take him home, and give him a cup of strong black coffee."

The son shook his head in disbelief. But he took his father home and gave him hot coffee. And the old *Yiddele* was healed.

You know, sometimes we have a very big problem, and we go to a friend for advice. The friend tells us something that sounds very good, very wise. But when we do what he suggested, what happens? Nothing but trouble…

Then sometimes, when we don't know what to do, we go to a Rebbe. He listens to us carefully, and gives us his advice. But many times we don't agree with what the Rebbe says. Maybe we think, "What is he saying? I came to him for help about A, and he's telling me about B. How is this going to help me?" But what have we got to lose? We follow his instructions … and what happens? Gevalt, the greatest things in the world!

You see what it is, everything that happens to us in this world really has its roots in the Upper Realms. Now, as human beings, we can only see what's happening to us here, now; we don't see what's going on in Heaven. So, even if we give the absolutely best advice according to what we see, what we know – sometimes it not only doesn't help, it can mamash *be dangerous.*

Ah, but a Rebbe – a really Holy Person – has a direct pipeline to Above. When he gives instructions, he's talking from a higher place. So his advice, no matter how crazy it may sound to us, can mamash *bring down the greatest blessings from Heaven…*

Because of his bad foot, the Holy Sanzer needed a cane to help him walk. But he used the cane for more than support for his crippled body…

Now, there's one thing you need to know about R. Chaim. Every Friday afternoon, right before Shabbos, he would come home from his learning – and immediately start yelling. He'd run around from room to room, and everywhere he looked, he'd find something that made him angry. So he'd scream: "What's going on here? Why isn't that bed made? Look at the stains on that tablecloth! *Gevalt* – those glasses are filthy! Can't you people do anything right? Is this how to prepare for the holy Shabbos?"

And all the members of his household would run around in circles, trying to fix everything that he said was wrong…

One Friday his family decided they'd had enough. Early in the morning they went all through the house and made sure everything was perfect, so the Rebbe would have no excuse to yell. But when the Sanzer came home and saw that everything was *mamash* in order, he started screaming louder than ever:

"What have you done? I need to yell, and you won't let me! Let me tell you something. The holy light that comes down on Shabbos is too strong for this world to receive. Somebody has to weaken it, dilute it a little. And Heaven gave that job to me…

"When I yell on Friday afternoon, I'm using my anger to cut down that exalted light. Otherwise nobody would be able to receive the light of Shabbos. Do you want to take Shabbos away from all the *Yidden*? So do me a favor – let things go back to the way they used to be, so I can yell as much as I want…"

You see what it is … the Holy R. Chaim Sanzer mamash understood the secret of anger. Usually we think of anger as wrong, as harmful, and we try to suppress it. But the Sanzer knew how to use his anger in the service of G-d.

The truth is, anger really can be destructive. You have to know exactly what to do with it, exactly how to yell. There were only a few Rebbes who were on a high enough level that they were allowed to shout. The other Holy Masters were very holy, but they never spoke harshly or raised their voices. But the Heilige Sanzer was so exalted, not only was he permitted to yell, but also to hit.

And here we come to the Sanzer's holy cane…

Everybody knew that it was a great blessing if R. Chaim hit you a little bit with his cane. It meant you would accomplish everything in this world that you came here to do. Because a blow from his cane cleansed you, and made you so holy that no evil could touch you.

Once a young *Yiddele* was drafted into the army. Now in those days, a Jew in the army wasn't treated like a soldier, he was treated like a dog. He had to do all the worst jobs – scrub the floors, clean the bathrooms, and run around doing errands for everyone. And if he didn't do everything exactly perfectly, G-d forbid what might happen to him… So this young Jew came to the Holy Sanzer and begged him to save him from the draft.

The Holy Sanzer listened to the young man's story. He looked at the boy for a long moment and then, without saying a word, struck him with his cane. And he hit the youth so hard that it knocked all the breath out of him and he fell to the floor.

As the young *Yid* rose dizzily to his feet, the Rebbe said, "You can go now. And don't worry about the army." And he showed him to the door.

A few days later the young Jew was ordered to report to the military. But as soon as the army doctor began examining him, he started to feel dizzy. Then he began having trouble breathing, and collapsed in a dead faint.

The doctor decided that the *Yid* had a serious medical condition, and was completely unfit for the army. And army officers actually carried him home on a stretcher, and *mamash* waited by his side until they were sure there was somebody to take care of him!

The Sanzer's cane was passed down to the dynasty of Bobov. The former Bobover Rebbe, R. Ben Tzion Halberstam, used it only on very special occasions, and the last time was at his daughter's wedding, shortly before the outbreak of World War II. At that time there were thousands of Bobover chasidim, and they all came to see the Rebbe's daughter get married. And maybe the Bobover knew what was coming, because he said,

"I want everybody to line up and walk past me, so I can hit all of you on the head."

Can you imagine it? The Rebbe stood up on a table, and all the thousands of chasidim filed past him, not walking, not running, but mamash dancing with utmost joy. And the Holy R. Ben Tzion hit each one on the head with the Sanzer's cane. Later, the Bobover's son, R. Shlomo, said that even the atonement of Yom Kippur couldn't compare to the cleansing of being struck that night with the Sanzer's stick...

R. Shlomo of Bobov inherited R. Chaim's cane from R. Ben Tzion, and it was his most precious possession. He took it everywhere he went, even when he was running away from the Nazis. Then, one day during the war, he was riding on a train and he put the cane down in the rack over his seat. All at once he saw the Nazis climb onto the train and start rounding up all the Jews. So he quickly opened the window, jumped off the train, and ran away. But in his haste he forgot to take the Sanzer's cane, and it was never seen again.

Still, R. Shlomo always said, a holy cane like the Sanzer's can never really be lost. When the Messiah comes, he will bring it back...

 Yiddele once came to the Holy Sanzer and said, "Rebbe, I'm *mamash* at the end. I have twelve children, no food for them to eat, and not a penny to my name. On top of that, not only is my wife very sick, but so is my mother-in-law. Holy Master, I just don't know what to do. Please help me..."

The *Heilige* Sanzer looked at him for a long time, and then he said, "Okay, I'll tell you what you should do. There's a rich businessman here in town, I'm sure you've heard of him..." and he named the man. "Go knock on his door and ask him for help. He has the reputation of being a terrible miser, but somehow I have the feeling that you'll find a way to get him to give you money. And one more thing – after you see him, come back here and tell me what happened."

So the *Yiddele* went to this miser's house. And then he came back to the Holy Sanzer and said, "You were right, I did get through to him.

He gave me a thousand rubles. But Rebbe – I mean, I'm really grateful for your advice, but if he's such a miser, how did you know he'd help me?"

"Okay," R. Chaim said. "Now, tell me the truth. You don't have a sick wife, do you? You don't have a wife, or a mother-in-law, or even one child, much less twelve. You're not even married! You're *mamash* a liar and a fake – no, more than that, you're a thief – and a good one at that. Now let's be honest – am I right?"

The *Yiddele* hung his head in shame. "Yes, Rebbe," he mumbled. Then he raised his head and looked at R. Chaim. "But I don't understand. How did you know?"

"You see, every time I asked this rich businessman to help a really needy person, he always refused. When you first came here, I smelled something off about your story. It just didn't feel right to me. So I made a little test. I sent you to this rich man. And he was happy to give to you. That's how I knew my first impression was right. Because it's the sad truth of this world that nobody has trouble giving to a fake…"

You know, you can always get all the help in the world for something stupid, something false. You can get lots of money, you can get lots of votes, you can get lots of everything… But for something real…?

It's such a strange thing. When you tell a dirty joke, everybody's quiet and listens intently. But when you want to say or do something important, something holy – ah, sadly enough so often you run into nothing but opposition…

When the Holy Sanzer left this world, thousands of people came to his funeral. And his students noticed a nobleman and his wife standing there, sobbing from the deepest depths of their hearts. The *chasidim* couldn't understand why these people – who obviously weren't even Jewish – were grieving so much for the Rebbe. So they went over to the couple and said, "Please excuse us, but we couldn't help noticing how much you are crying. And we were wondering … why did the *Heilige* Sanzer mean so much to you? Did you ever meet him?"

And the nobleman's wife said, "Let me tell you the story…"

Many years ago one of the Sanzer's *chasidim* was in terrible trouble. He had gone into business with some non-Jewish partners and had made a lot of money. But then his *goyish* associates turned against him, and accused him of being a fraud and a thief. The poor *Yiddele* not only lost all his wealth, but he faced a trial in the criminal court. Now everybody knew how much chance a *Yid* had of a fair trial in a non-Jewish court, and the *chasid* was *mamash* afraid he'd be sent to prison. So he took the little money he had left, and went to see his Rebbe.

He told the Holy Sanzer the whole sad story. And as soon as he was finished, R. Chaim cried, "Hurry, there's no time. Get a ticket for the first class section of the next train, and go home right away!"

"But Rebbe," the *chasid* cried. "A first-class ticket is so expensive! And, anyway, you haven't blessed me not to go to jail…!"

But the Sanzer only repeated, "Buy yourself a first-class ticket and leave right now. *Mamash* immediately!"

And he sent the *chasid* out of his room.

So the *Yiddele* obediently took his last pennies and purchased a ticket for the first-class compartment of the next train home. But with his tattered clothes and his *peyos* and beard, he looked totally out of place amongst all the rich *goyim* travelling in that section. Everybody stared at him, and nobody wanted to sit next to him. So the *chasid* found himself sitting alone in the last row of the car.

After a while, at one of the stops along the way, a man who was obviously a nobleman entered the first-class car. And seeing no other empty place, he took the seat next to the *chasid*. He looked the *Yid* over and then said, "I hope you won't mind my asking, but it's obvious you're not a rich man. Why did you spend all your money on travelling in this first class compartment?"

So the *chasid* told the nobleman all his troubles, how his partners had turned on him and accused him of all kinds of terrible things. Then despite – or maybe because of the fact that the nobleman was a total stranger, the *Yiddele* opened his heart to him and began to cry: "I thought these men were my friends, I *mamash* trusted them. I don't know why they're saying all these things about me – maybe they were jealous because I made so much money, maybe it's because I'm a Jew. But I swear to you that I'm completely innocent of all the charges against me!

"I'm the follower of a very holy man, a Rebbe. So I went to him for help. But all he did was send me away. He told me to buy this first-class ticket and to go home immediately. So now I face many years in prison for things I didn't do..." And he cried and cried...

A few days later the *chasid* appeared before the court. And when the judge entered the courtroom, the *Yiddele mamash* couldn't believe his eyes. *Gevalt*, the judge was the nobleman who had sat next to him on the train! The judge gave no sign that he recognized the *chasid*. He called the court to order, and told the *Yid's* former partners to present their argument. But after they were finished, he jumped to his feet and cried,

"I can't believe you're taking up the court's time on something like this. You have absolutely no evidence, no proof; you have no case at all. In fact, it is the opinion of the court that you are the ones who should be on trial here, not this poor Jew. I hereby order you to repay to this man all the money he lost because of you, plus five thousand rubles for the pain you caused him. And let me warn you, if I ever see your faces in this court again, I'll send you right to jail!" He banged his gavel: "Court dismissed!"

Needless to say, the *chasid* was overjoyed. He ran right up to the judge to thank him. The judge took him into his private office, listened to him graciously and then said, "I'm so happy I could help you. And now there's something you can do for me. Tell me, who is this holy man, this Rebbe, who sent you home on the train?"

"Why, he's the Holy Sanzer!"

"And exactly how do I get to Sanz from here?"

So the *chasid* told him. The judge said, "Thank you, my friend. I wish you well," and ushered him out of his office. And as soon as the door had closed behind the happy *Yiddele*, the nobleman hurriedly packed a few things, caught the next train to Sanz, and went to see the Rebbe.

R. Chaim did not seem at all surprised when a non-Jewish nobleman appeared at his door: "It's so nice of you to visit me, really quite an honor. Tell me what I can do for you..."

"Rabbi," the nobleman said, "I have to tell you, my daughter is very sick. I've had all the best doctors in to see her, but nobody can help her. I'm afraid she may be dying...

"Now, I've been told that you are a very holy man. And you must have great powers if you are on the level to put your follower in the first-class compartment with me. That's why I've come. Can you also heal the sick? Can you help my daughter?"

The Sanzer closed his eyes and sat very still for a long minute. He seemed to be concentrating on something very far away. Then he opened his eyes and said to the judge,

"I'm happy to tell you that I am able to help your daughter. But first, there is something that you must promise me: Nobody else should ever know that I'm the one who healed her. Even after she's well, she must pretend she's still sick, and keep seeing the doctors for six months. She should do everything they tell her, take all their medicines. No one must know that you've even heard of me, much less met me. Do you agree?"

"Of course! I'll do anything you say!"

"Then it's settled. Go home – by the time you get there your daughter will be completely well."

The nobleman's wife paused and took a deep breath. "The judge kept his promise to the Holy Sanzer until his last day on earth," she continued. "Then, right before he left the world, he told his daughter the story of her miraculous recovery. She is the only person he ever told…

"Now, I'm sure you're wondering how I know all this. You see, I am the daughter of the judge who saved the Sanzer's *chasid*. That's why my husband and I are here today, and why we were crying. How could we not cry? If not for the Holy Sanzer, I wouldn't be alive…"

Thousands of chasidim *went to the funeral of the Holy R. Chaim of Sanz. And they were all crying and sobbing,* mamash *in terrible pain. Suddenly one voice could be heard above all the others, wailing, "Oy, what will happen to us now? Our sun has set. And it will never rise again…"*

Then another voice was heard above the din: "Sanzer chasidim, *don't give up hope. And don't despair. Most of you are too young to remember, but I am a very old man. Many years ago I was at the funeral of the* Heilige Seer *of Lublin, and somebody there said the very same thing: The sun has set, and it won't rise again.*

"But the sun did rise … with the birth of our Rebbe, the Holy Sanzer. And although his sun has now gone down, someone else's will appear. The sun will yet rise again…"

Note: The last time this story was told in public was at R. Shlomo's funeral…

The Ocean of Tears

R. Yitzhak Vorker

You know, we are on such a low level that even when we are standing right next to another person, gevalt! – are we still far apart. So it's hard for us to imagine being in touch with somebody who is in another world.

But for the Rebbes, the Holy Masters, it was another thing altogether. For them, from this world to the upper realms was so close, so close...

The *Heilige* R. Yitzhak Kalish of Vorka was famous for his loving-kindness, his compassion for every Jew. To give you an idea of what an exalted level he was on – the Holy Vorker had a little grocery store. If a *Yiddele* came in and said, "I'd like to buy some fish," R. Yitzhak would tilt his head to the side, look at the man, and ask,

"Are you *mamash* sure you want to buy the fish from me? You know, there are a lot of stores around here with very good fish." And he'd list for his customer all the other groceries in the area.

Sometimes the *Yid* would leave and go to another store, thinking the Vorker was either crazy or a very bad businessman. But if he stayed and asked R. Yitzhak again for some fish, then the Rebbe would say, "Okay, if you really want to, you can buy your fish from me..."

Another *Yiddele* ran a grocery on the other side of the street from the Vorker's store. Now R. Yitzhak always got up very early in the morning to open his shop. But first he'd always check that his competitor was also awake and ready for business. And if the other *Yid* was still in bed, the Holy Vorker would bang on his door and shout:

"Friend, it's already morning. People will be coming to buy. Fast, you better open your store!"

One day, R. Yitzhak went to his grocery as usual. But then he returned home early and told his wife, "You know, the craziest thing happened last night. Thieves broke in and stole half of what I had in the store!"

The next day he came home early again: "I can't believe it, the thieves came back again and took everything that was left." He shook his head. "Poor thieves. They had to stay up late two nights in a row..."

Finally, the Vorker closed his grocery. Because the truth was, people didn't come to buy there because of the quality of his products. They really came because of his holiness and the Torah he told them. So he had many more customers than the *Yiddele* across the street.

One day R. Yitzhak was standing outside his shop, and he happened to notice his neighbor on the other side. And *gevalt!* – the man was watching the stream of *Yidden* coming in and out of the Vorker's grocery, while his own store was almost empty. And he looked so sad, so broken, that R. Yitzhak *mamash* couldn't bear it. So he lifted up his holy eyes to Heaven and cried:

"*Ribbono Shel Olam*, I refuse to let You feed me in a way that causes so much pain to somebody else!"

And the next day he closed his grocery for good.

Now the *Heilige* Vorker's way of loving-kindness was very different from the *chasidus* of Kotzk, where the Truth was the most important thing. Still he and R. Menachem Mendel of Kotzk were the best of friends.

Before R. Yitzhak left the world, he promised his son, R. Menachem Mendel, to come back and tell him how things were for him in Gan Eden. But four weeks passed, and his son didn't hear from him. R. Mendele couldn't understand what was going on, so he went to his father's best friend, R. Mendel Kotzker, and said,

"*Heilige* Kotzker Rebbe, I'm so worried about my holy father. He promised to come back and speak to me, if only in a dream. But it's been four weeks, and I haven't heard anything from him. Do you think something could have happened to him in Heaven?"

And the Kotzker answered, "The truth is, Mendele, your father also promised me to come back and tell me what happened to him in the World Above. And I too got very worried when I didn't hear from him. So I went up to Heaven to look for him. Let me tell you what happened:

I went everywhere in Heaven, searching for your father. I went to the palaces of all the *tzaddikim*, all the holy people – of Rashi, the Rambam, Rabbi Akiva. I visited the place of the prophets, and even went to the very highest levels – to Moshe Rabbeinu and our Holy Fathers, Abraham, Isaac and Jacob. Everywhere I went I said,

"I'm looking for my friend, the exalted R. Yitzhak Vorker. Have you seen him?"

And they all told me, "Yes, he was here. But he didn't stay. He went on…"

I didn't know what to do, where else to go. So finally I asked the angels, "Have you seen the holy R. Yitzhak Vorker? Do you know where he went?"

And this time I got an answer; the angels told me, "If you keep going in this direction, you'll come to a thick, dark forest. You must pass through it, and when the forest ends at a sea, that's where you'll find him."

So I kept walking through Heaven, and as the angels had said, I soon came to the darkest, most forbidding forest I had ever seen in my life. I *mamash* wanted to run away, to come back to this world and wait for your father to come to me. But I made myself strong and plunged in. The trees closed in over my head; there was almost no light. The forest seemed to go on forever. And as I stumbled along, I started to hear a strange sound.

Finally I came out of the trees, and found myself on the shore of a sea, an ocean so big I couldn't see the other side. And I realized that the sound I'd been hearing was coming from the waves. But it was not the kind of sound that waves usually make … it was more like a wail, a moan, a scream – full of the most desperate pain. *Mamash*, never in my life had I ever heard waves crying and begging like this…

And there, at the edge of the ocean, I saw your father, the Holy R. Yitzhak Vorker. He was leaning on his staff, staring at the sea. He never took his eyes off the water.

I ran toward him: "R. Yitzhak, my holy friend, what is this place? What are you doing here?"

He turned toward me: "Ah, Mendel, don't you recognize this ocean?"

"No, what is it? What's that sound? What's going on here?"

"Mendel, let me tell you … this is the Ocean of Tears, the Sea of Jewish Tears. I want you to know, Jewish tears are so precious before the Master of the World that Heaven collected every tear shed by *Am Yisrael* through all our long years of pain and exile, and deposited them here. And there were so many tears – so many bitter tears – that they formed this huge ocean…

"When I came here and heard the sound of the waves – *mamash*, the cry of all the suffering *Yidden* since the creation of the world – *gevalt!* I can't tell you how much it broke my heart. And at that moment I made a sacred vow: 'Master of the World, I swear by Your Holy Name that I will not move from this place until You have mercy on Your People, until You turn all the *Yidden's* pain into joy…'"

"And here, Mendele, your father looked at me and said,
"'My dear old friend, I will never leave this Ocean until G-d has wiped away all of Israel's tears…'"

You know, sometimes you're in a house where children are crying. And instead of comforting them, loving them, their parents say: "Stop that crying right now! You're all grown up. Only babies cry!"

Mamash *turns your* kishkes *over, right?*

The truth is, sadly enough, people all over the world are crying. And nobody hears them, nobody helps them, nobody pays any attention.

So what should we do? It's really very simple. Whenever you see tears, don't walk away. Stay right there and say to G-d, "Master of the World, I'm not leaving until You dry up all these tears."

And every time you tell the Ribbono Shel Olam, *"I'm not moving from these tears!" you* mamash *bring a little bit of redemption to the world…*

Have you ever really looked at the Holy Wall? It seems to be made out of big, weathered stones. But the stones of the Kotel are actually made out of tears, the tears of our fathers and mothers, our grandmothers and grandfathers, of every Yid who ever cried in pain. And if you look very, very closely, maybe you'll see that in those holy stones there are six million little tears…

But you know, there is a prophecy. The Master of the World promises to wipe away all our tears. And if you listen very carefully, while you look at the Holy Wall, maybe you will hear the stones of the Kotel singing. Maybe you'll hear those holy tears reminding us that G-d will not forget His promise. He will bring comfort to His people with the coming of the Mashiach, may it be soon in our days…

Reb Shlomo's Vision…

R. Shlomo had a special wish, a wonderful vision:

Imagine little children all over the world.
Their parents have just tucked them into bed for the night,
and their souls are ready to go up to Heaven for just a little while,
to receive the strength they need for the next day.

But the children are having trouble going to sleep.
So their mothers or their fathers – or maybe both parents together
– read them, or tell them, some of these stories.

At the beginning, the children will listen to the stories
with utmost attention.
By the middle, maybe ... hopefully ... they will be fast asleep.

But because of them, these stories will never end...

Glossary

Adam HaRishon: (H*) the first man.

Am: (H) people, nation.

Am Yisrael: (H) the nation or people of Israel.

Aretz: (H) country, land; ground, earth.

Aveira: (H) sin.

Barah: (H) created.

Bar Mitzvah: (H) literally, "son of [the] commandment[s]"; a special ceremony marking a boy's thirteenth birthday, at which time he becomes responsible for fulfilling the requirements of *halachah*, Torah Law.

Baruch: (H) blessed or praised.

Baruch Hashem: (H) literally, "blessed is the Name [of G-d]"; an expression of thankfulness and praise, indicating one's recognition that all fortune comes from G-d.

Bashert: (Y*) intended or destined one, soul mate.

Bas Kol: (H) literally, "daughter of a voice" or an echo; used to refer to a Heavenly voice.

Beis: (H) house.

Beis Din: (H) literally, "house of judgement"; a rabbinical court presided over by three, twenty-three, or seventy-one judges.

Beis HaMikdash: (H) literally, "the sanctified (or consecrated) house"; the Holy Temple in Jerusalem. Historically there were two Temples: the first, built by King Solomon, was destroyed by Babylon in 586 BCE; the second Temple was destroyed by Rome in 70 CE. The third *Beis HaMikdash* will be built by the Messiah, and will stand forever.

Beis Midrash: (H) a house of learning, center for study and worship; sometimes refers to a synagogue.

Bekeshe: (Y) traditional lightweight decorative robe or caftan worn by *chasidic* Jews.

Ben: (H) son, son of.

Bereshis: (H) "in the beginning," the first word of the Torah.

Birchas Hamazon: (H) grace after meals.

B'nei Brak: name of a city in Israel near Tel Aviv, founded by pious Jews from Poland in 1924.

Bracha: (H) blessing.

Bris: (H) literally, "covenant"; the ritual of circumcision performed on the eighth day after the birth of a Jewish male, or whenever the baby's health permits.

---

* H=Hebrew, Y=Yiddish

B'shalom: (H) in peace.

Bubbe: (Y) grandmother.

Burial Society: communal organization – its members attend to all the details of the burial of the dead according to Jewish law.

Chacham: (H) wise; wise man or sage.

Chai, Chaim: (H) life.

Challah, pl. **Challos:** (H) special bread, often braided, used for Shabbos and holiday meals.

Chametz: (H) leavened bread forbidden on Passover.

Chanukah: (H) literally "dedication"; the eight day "Festival of Lights" commemorating the rededication of the Holy Temple and the miracle of the oil after the Maccabean victory over the Syrian Greeks.

Chasid, pl. **Chasidim:** (H) literally "pious one"; a follower of the Baal Shem Tov and the generations of Rebbes and teachers who carried on his tradition (see **Chasidism**).

Chasidic (Anglicized), **Chasidishe** (Y): of or pertaining to the teachings and practices of *chasidism*.

Chasidism: (Anglicized) the religious mystical movement founded by R. Israel ben Eliezer – the Baal Shem Tov – in the eighteenth century, which emphasized prayer and the joy of serving G-d.

Chasidus: (H) the body of teachings of the Baal Shem Tov and subsequent *chasidic* Rebbes.

Chaval: (H) a pity, what a pity.

Chodesh: (H) month.

Chozeh: (H) a seer or prophet.

Chupah: (H) the canopy used in Jewish weddings; can also refer to the entire wedding ceremony.

Chutz: (H) outside.

Chutz La'aretz: (H) literally, "outside the land" – outside of Israel.

Chutzpah: (H) arrogance, audacity, impudence.

Clouds of Glory: supernatural clouds that surrounded, accompanied and protected the people of Israel during their forty years in the desert between the Exodus from Egypt and the giving of the Torah.

Cohen: (H) priest; a descendent of Aaron who officiated in the Holy Temple.

Cohen Gadol: (H) – see **High Priest.**

Coming World: see **Olam Habah.**

Cretchma: (Y) a roadside inn and/or tavern, usually leased by Jews from the local nobility.

Dai: (H) enough, sufficient.

Derech: (H) way, route, method.

Derech Hateva: (H) literally "the way of nature," occurring naturally.

Emes: (H) truth, verity.

Emesser, Emester: (Y) true, real.

Eretz: (H) land (see **Aretz**).

Eretz Yisrael: (H) the Land of Israel.

Erev: (H) evening; the eve of, the day before.

Erev Shabbos: (H) the eve of the Sabbath.

Esrog, pl. **Esrogim:** (H) citron fruit, one of the four species used in the Sukkos ritual.

Four Mothers: the Jewish Matriarchs, the wives of Abraham, Isaac and Jacob – Sarah, Rivka (Rebecca), Rachel and Leah.

Fourth Meal of Shabbos: see **Melaveh Malka**.

Gabbai, pl. **Gabbaim:** (H) synagogue officer or administrator; a rebbe's chief assistant.

Gam: (H) also.

Gam Zu L'tovah: (H) "this is also for the good."

Gamur: (H) finished, complete.

Gan: (H) garden.

Gan Eden: (H) literally, "Garden of Eden," Heaven, Paradise.

Gartel: (Y) belt or sash used in prayer.

Gehinom: (H) hell.

Gematria: (H) a method of discovering the hidden meanings of Hebrew words by calculating and comparing the numerical equivalents of their letters.

Gemorah: (H) the Talmud, compilation of the Oral Torah.

Geulah: (H) redemption, salvation.

Geulah Shleimah: (H) complete redemption.

Gevalt (also Oy Gevalt, Gevaldig): (Y) an exclamation that can be used either positively or negatively to suggest a powerful or overwhelming experience.

Goy, pl. **Goyim:** (H) literally "nation, people," used to refer to a gentile or non-Jew.

Goyish: pertaining to or characteristic of non-Jews.

Ha…: (H) prefix indicating the definite article "the".

Habah: (H) the coming.

Hachnasas: (H) literally, "bringing in," sometimes used in the sense of "providing for".

Hachnasas Kallah: (H) the mitzvah of providing for a bride.

Hakesef: (H) the silver.

Halachah: (H) law, especially Jewish Law.

Hashem: (H) literally, "The Name," signifying the name of G-d; a way of referring to G-d in Hebrew without pronouncing (or writing) the four-letter Holy Name.

Havdalah: (H) literally, "separation or differentiation"; the ceremony marking the end of the Sabbath and holidays, separating them from the days of the week.

Hazahav: (H) the gold.

Hefker: (H) ownerless, renounced, abandoned.

Heilige: (Y) "Holy," an expression of respect and deference used in relation to Rebbes and other special people or objects.

High Holy Days (High Holidays): a reference to Rosh Hashanah, the Jewish New Year, and Yom Kippur, the Day of Atonement.

High Priest (H – Cohen Gadol): the leader of the priests, descendants of Aaron the Priest from the tribe of Levi, who officiated in the Holy Temple. The High Priest alone could perform the holiest of the Temple rites, especially the rituals of atonement on Yom Kippur.

Hodu: (H) thanks, give thanks to.

Holy Ark: the special cabinet or chest in a synagogue in which the Torah scrolls are kept.

Holy of Holies: the innermost, holiest chamber in the Holy Temple into which only the High Priest could enter – and only on Yom Kippur.

Holy Temple: see **Beis HaMikdash**.

Holy Wall: the Western or Wailing Wall (in Hebrew, **Kotel HaMaaravi**) in Jerusalem, the only surviving remnant of the Second Temple.

Hoshana Rabba: the last day of the weeklong festival of Sukkos, which is marked by special rituals and prayers.

Imeinu: (H) our mother.

Kabbalah: (H) literally, "received"; usually used to refer to Jewish mysticism.

Kabbalist: (Anglicized) one who is a master of Jewish mysticism.

Kapote: (Y) silk black outer coat, like a fancy overcoat, traditionally worn by some orthodox Jews, especially *chasidim*.

Kashrus: (H) validity, ritual fitness; usually refers to the Jewish dietary laws.

Kavanah: (H) intention, purpose, concentration, especially in prayer.

Kavod: (H) honor, respect.

Kedushah: (H) holiness, sanctity, sanctification.

Kesef: (H) silver.

Ketz: (H) end.

Kever: (H) grave, tomb.

Ki: (H) because, that, who.

Kiddush: (H) literally, "sanctification"; ceremonial blessing recited over a cup of wine on Shabbos and holidays.

Kol Nidre: (H) literally "all vows"; the prayer chanted at the beginning of the evening service of Yom Kippur, the Day of Atonement, it annuls vows made rashly to G-d.

Kosher: (H) literally, "clean, fit"; usually refers to permissible foods according to Jewish dietary laws. It also is used to refer generally to anything authentic and ritually correct.

Kotel: (H) wall, especially the Western or Wailing Wall in Jerusalem (the **Kotel HaMaaravi**) which is the last surviving remnant of the Holy Temple (see also Holy Wall).

Koved: (see **Kavod**).

Kvetch: (Y) grumble, complain.

Kvittel, pl. **Kvittlach:** (Y) note that a petitioner gives to a Rebbe requesting advice or a blessing.

L'... or Le'...: (H) preposition denoting "to, for."

Lamed: (H) the twelfth letter of the Hebrew alphabet, with a numerical value of 30.

Lamed-Vav: (H) the combination of the Hebrew letters Lamed (above) and Vav (the sixth letter with a numerical value of 6) designating the number 36.

Lamed-Vav Tzaddik, pl. **Lamed-Vav Tzaddikim:** (H) the thirty-six hidden holy people whose merit, according to tradition, sustains the world.

L'Chaim: (H) to life, the traditional Hebrew toast.

Lekoved: (H) for the honor of.

Lekoved Shabbos: (H) for the honor of the Sabbath.

Levaiyah: (H) funeral.

Li: (H) literally, "to me"; mine.

L'Shem: (H) for, for the sake of.

L'Shem Shamayim: (H) for the sake of Heaven.

Lulav: (H) palm branch, one of the four species used in the Sukkos ritual.

Ma'acheles: (H) knife, especially a carving or slaughtering knife.

Madreigah: (H) step, level, degree.

Maggid: (H) a storytelling rabbi; an itinerant preacher.

Mamash: (H) literally, "substance, reality"; used as a term of emphasis, in the sense of "Really!" to indicate something tangible or real.

Mashiach: (H) literally, "anointed" or " the anointed one"; the Messiah, the Redeemer.

Mazal: (H) literally, "constellation"; fate, destiny, luck.

Mazal (or Mazel) Tov: (H) literally, "good luck, good fortune"; used to express congratulations.

Mei'eyn: (H) like, similar, resembling, a taste of.

Mei'eyn Olam Habah: (H) a taste of the World to Come.

Melaveh Malka: (H) literally, "escorting the queen"; a farewell feast to the Shabbos Queen on Saturday night; also know as "The Fourth Meal of Shabbos" and "the feast of King David."

Menuchah: (H) rest, repose.

Messiah: (see **Mashiach**).

Mezuzah: (H) literally, "door post"; the parchment scroll containing the verses of Deuteronomy: 6: 4-9 and 11:13-21, which is affixed to the door post of Jewish homes.

Midah, pl. Midos: (H) attribute, nature, characteristic, quality.

Midrash: (H) interpretations of Scripture through stories, homilies and parables.

Mikvah: (H) ritual bath containing a certain amount of natural water in which a Jew immerses for ritual purification.

Minchah: (H) the afternoon prayer recited between noon and sundown.

Minyan: (H) quorum of ten adult males required in order to recite certain prayers and perform certain ceremonies.

Misnagid: (H) an opponent of *chasidism* who instead emphasizes scholarship and the study of Jewish Law.

Mitzvah, pl. Mitzvos: (H) literally, "commandment," especially one of the commandments of the Torah; also, figuratively, a good deed or action.

Mohel: (H) ritual circumciser.

Muktzah: (H) set apart as untouchable on the Sabbath and holidays.

Musar: (H) ethics, morals; instruction, reproof.

Nebach: (Y) expression connoting "poor thing" or "how terrible."

Neshamah, pl. Neshamos: (H) soul, spirit.

Neshamah Yeterah: (H) additional soul one receives on the Sabbath.

Ne'um: (H) speech; signed.

Niggun: (H) a song or melody, especially a melody without words.

Ohev: (H) v: love or like; n: lover, friend.

Ohev Yisrael: (H) lover of Israel.

Olam: (H) world, universe.

Olam Habah: (H) the world to come.

Olam Hazeh: (H) this world.

Oneg: (H) pleasure, delight, joy.

Oneg Shabbos: (H) the joy or pleasure of the Sabbath.

Oy, Oy Vey: (Y) an expression of ultimate frustration, pain or bewilderment, like "Oh no!"

Pesach: (H) Passover, the holiday celebrating the Jewish people's liberation from slavery in Egypt.

Peyos: (H) sidelocks.

Purim: (H) the holiday commemorating the deliverance of the Jews of Persia from destruction at the hands of Haman and King Ahashverosh.

Rabbeinu: (H) "our teacher."

Rabbi: (H) "my master, my teacher".

Rav: (H) teacher, rabbi.

Reb: (Y) honorary title meaning anything from "Holy Rabbi," for a rabbi, teacher or learned man, to "Mr." as an expression of respect for a simple Jew.

Rebbe: (H) Rabbi, especially the spiritual leader of a *chasidic* community.

Rebbetzin: (H) the title of the wife of a Rebbe or rabbi.

Refuah: (H) cure, healing, recovery.

Refuah Shleimah: (H) complete recovery.

Regel, pl. **Regalim:** (H) foot, leg; occasion, used to refer to the three pilgrimage festivals.

Ribbono Shel Olam: (H) "Master of the World"; i.e. G-d.

Rishon: (H) first.

Rosh: (H) head, beginning.

Rosh Chodesh: (H) the "head" or beginning of the month.

Rosh Hashanah: (H) the "head of the year," the holiday of the Jewish New Year.

Ruach: (H) spirit, soul, breath.

Ruach Hakodesh: (H) literally, "holy spirit," connoting divine inspiration or prophecy.

Ruble: coinage of Russia and the Ukraine.

Safed: city in northern Israel also known as **Tzfat.**

Schneider: (Y) tailor.

Sefer, pl. S'farim: (H) book, especially a holy book.

Sefer Tehillim: (H) the Book of Psalms.

Sh'...(or She'...): (H) prefix denoting which, that, who.

Shabbat, Shabbos: (H) the Sabbath, the seventh day of the week.

Shabbosdik: (Y) referring to, pertaining to or reflecting the qualities of the Sabbath.

Shalem, Shleimah (feminine): (H) whole, entire, perfect, complete.

Shaliach: (H) messenger or emissary.

Shalom: (H) peace; welfare, good condition; greeting, salutation (both "hello" and "goodbye"), the most common Hebrew greeting.

Shalosh: (H) three.

Shalosh Regalim: (H) literally "three feet"; the three pilgrimage festivals, so named because in their honor, in Biblical times, Jewish males were required to travel to the Holy Temple in Jerusalem, usually on foot.

Shamayim: (H) sky, Heaven.

Shammes: (H) a sexton or beadle; the caretaker or guardian of a synagogue; the assistant to a rabbi or Rebbe.

Shavuos: (H) literally, "weeks"; the Festival of Weeks or Pentecost; observed seven weeks after Passover, it commemorates G-d's giving the Torah to the Jewish People.

Shechitah: (H) the ritual slaughtering of animals according to Jewish Law.

Shekulo: (H) that is all, that is entirely.

Shel: (H) of, from.

Shem: (H) name.

Sheva: (H) seven.

Sheva Brachos: (H) seven blessings (of a wedding feast).

Shidduch: (H) match, especially in terms of marriage.

Shiur, pl. Shiurim: (H) lesson, class.

Shlep, Shlepping: (Y) carry or drag, especially heavy items.

Shlepper: (Y) a helpless soul, good-for-nothing; someone without visible means of support, a beggar.

Sh'ma: (H) hear.

Sh'ma Yisrael: (H) the first two words of the central Jewish prayer – **Sh'ma Yisrael Hashem Elokeinu Hashem Echad:** Hear Israel, the Lord Our G-d, the Lord is One – which affirms belief in One G-d and is recited twice daily and right before death.

Sh'mirah (Sh'miras – construct state): (H) guarding, preserving; keeping, observing.

Sh'miras Shabbos: (H) keeping, guarding the Sabbath.

Shochet: (H) a ritual slaughterer.

Sh'treimel: (Y) fur hat worn on the Sabbath and Festivals by many *chasidic* men.

Shul: (Y) synagogue.

Siddur: (H) prayer book.

Simchah: (H) joy, rejoicing; a joyous occasion.

Simchas Torah: (H) literally, "the Rejoicing of the Law"; the holiday immediately following Sukkos which marks the end of one annual cycle of Torah readings and the beginning of the next.

Sukkah: (H) literally, "booth, hut," especially the ritual "booths" which we are commanded to build and in which we are commanded to eat during the festival of Sukkos.

Sukkos: (H) the Festival of Booths or Feast of Tabernacles; the seven day festival following the High Holidays which commemorates the Jewish people's living in booths in the desert after the Exodus from Egypt.

Tallis: (H) prayer shawl.

Talmid: (H) pupil, scholar, student, disciple.

Talmid Chacham: (II) literally, "wise scholar"; a learned man.

Tefillah, pl. Tefillos: (H) prayer.

Tefillin: (H) phylacteries; ritual boxes containing scriptural verses traditionally worn on the head and arm of a Jewish man during the morning prayers.

Tehillim: (H) psalms.

Teshuvah: (H) literally, "return"; repentance.

Teva: (H) nature, natural forces.

Third Meal: the third of the three (evening, morning or noon, and afternoon) meals of the Sabbath.

Three Holy Fathers: the Jewish Patriarchs, Abraham, Isaac and Jacob.

Tiberias: city in northern Israel on the Sea of Galilee.

Tikkun: (H) repair, correction, reformation, improvement.

Tikkun Hagamur: (H) the complete rectification.

Tisha B'Av: (H) literally, "the ninth of (the Hebrew month of) Av," an annual fast day marking the destruction of both Holy Temples in Jerusalem.

Torah: (H) literally, "instruction"; the first five books of the Bible, also known as the Pentateuch or *Chumash*. Can also refer to the scroll on which the Biblical text is written, or to the entire body of Jewish teachings. Without a capital letter, **torah** refers to a teaching, often oral.

Tov: (H) good, beneficial; a good thing.

Trayger: (Y) porter or carrier.

Treif: (H) literally, "torn"; used to designate food that is not kosher and thus forbidden to eat.

Tzaddik, pl. Tzaddikim: (H) righteous or holy person.

Tzedakah: (H) literally, "justice, righteousness"; charity, an act of righteousness.

Tzfat: (see **Safed**).

Tzitzis: (H) ritual fringes attached to a special four-cornered undergarment and to the four corners of the *tallis*.

U'... (also v'...): (H) prefix denoting "and."

Vav: (H) the sixth letter of the Hebrew alphabet, with the numerical value of six.

World to Come (see also **Olam Habah, Coming World**): a reference either to the afterlife, or to the time after the coming of the Messiah.

Yarmulke: (Y) skullcap worn by Orthodox men.

Yartzeit: (Y) the anniversary of a person's death.

Yerushalayim: (H) Jerusalem.

Yeshivah, pl. Yeshivos: (H) school of Torah learning.

Yesod: (H) foundation, basis, source.

Yeterah: (H) extra, additional.

Yid, pl. Yidden: (Y) a Jew.

Yiddele: (Y) the affectionate diminutive of **Yid**; a way of saying "a sweet Jew."

Yiddishkeit: (Y) the body of Jewish teachings; Jewishness, the essence of being Jewish.

Yisrael: (H) Israel.

Yom, pl. Yamim: (H) day.

Yom Menuchah: (H) day of rest, i.e., the Sabbath.

Yom Shekulo Shabbos: (H) the day that is entirely the Sabbath, referring to the afterlife and/or the time after the coming of the Messiah.

Yom Tov, pl. Yomim Tovim: "good day," i.e., a holiday.

Zahav: (H) gold.

Zecher: (H) memory.

Zechus: (H) right, privilege, credit, merit.

Zeh (or Zu): (H) this, that.

Zeide: (Y) grandfather.

Z'l (Zecher Livrachah): (H) "of blessed memory."

Ztz'l (Zecher Tzaddik Livrachah): (H) literally, "may the memory of a holy man be for a blessing".

Biographies

Aaron HaCohen (Aaron the Priest): The older brother of Moses, he was the first High Priest *(Cohen Gadol)*, leading the ritual service in the Tabernacle during the wanderings of the Jewish people in the desert following the Exodus from Egypt. He was especially known as a lover of Israel and a seeker of peace.

R. Aaron the Great of Karlin (1736–1772): A student of **R. Dov Baer, the Maggid of Mezhirech,** he was the founder of the Karliner dynasty and a pioneer of *chasidism* in Lithuania. Although he himself inclined toward asceticism and fasted regularly, he stressed in his lessons the importance of serving G-d with joy. Besides teaching his many students, he also was deeply involved in the social problems of his community.

R. Aaron was succeeded by his disciple R. Shlomo, who also brought up R. Aaron's son, **R. Asher** – who was only nine years old at the time of his father's death. R. Asher later also became Rebbe of Karlin (see **R. Asher of Karlin**).

R. Aaron Rokeach of Belz (1880–1957): He succeeded his father, R. Issachar Dov, as Rebbe of Belz in 1927. Like his predecessors, R. Aaron was both rabbi and Rebbe, active not only as a teacher and spiritual guide (over four hundred students studied at his *yeshivah*) but also in Jewish communal – even political – affairs. From 1940-1944 the Nazis relentlessly pursued him. To elude them he was forced to travel constantly, and twice even had to change his name. He escaped from Europe via Romania, Bulgaria, Greece and Turkey, arriving in Israel in 1944 and settling in Tel Aviv. There he rebuilt the Belzer community, and lived for thirteen years.

In the Holocaust R. Aaron lost his wife, three sons, four daughters, his brothers and sisters, and twenty-six grandchildren. (see also **R. Shalom Rokeach of Belz,** the founder of the Belzer *chasidic* dynasty).

Rabbi Akiva (dates unknown): The son of a proselyte who did not begin learning Torah until the age of forty, he became a great scholar and master of Jewish mysticism. He was one of the Rabbis of the Talmud and the head of the Sanhedrin in the period immediately following the destruction of the Second Temple. Called the "Sage of all Sages," his method of interpreting Scripture and his *halachic* system formed the basis for the development of the Oral Law, and his approach to mysticism influenced the study of *Kabbalah* for generations to come.

Rabbi Akiva died a martyr's death at the hands of the Romans when he defied the Roman ban on Torah study.

Alexander Rebbe, R. Yitzhak Menachem Mendel Danziger (1880–1943): He succeeded his father and teacher, R. Shmuel Tzvi, as Rebbe, and served his community for eighteen years. His teachings stressed the significance of congregational worship and the importance of helping the needy.

At the outbreak of the Second World War, the Rebbe and his family were living in Warsaw. R. Yitzhak refused to abandon his followers and escape to Israel. Instead he remained in the Warsaw Ghetto, working for a time in a shoe factory there.

The Rebbe was murdered in Treblinka in 1943.

Alexei: (short for Alexander). In *chasidic* tradition, he was the non-Jewish, Polish-Ukrainian wagon driver of the Baal Shem Tov.

The Alshich HaKodesh (the Holy), R. Moshe ben Chaim Alshich (1508–1600): He was born in Adrianople (now Edirne), Turkey, and settled in Safed (Tzfat) in 1530. There he received rabbinical ordination from R. Joseph Karo, the author of the *Shulchan Aruch*, the definitive compilation of Jewish Law. The Alshich became a *halachic* authority, taught in two *yeshivos*, and served on R. Karo's Rabbinic Court. Although his major interest was *halachah*, R. Moshe was also one of the most renowned preachers of his time, and a master of *Kabbalah*, Jewish mysticism. A prolific writer, he composed commentaries on almost the entire Bible.

Amshinover Rebbe, R. Yaacov Dovid Kalish (1814–1878): Son of **R. Yitzhak Vorker,** he was a student of **R. Menachem Mendel of Kotzk.** He became a Rebbe in 1840 and settled in Amshinov, where he founded the Amshinover *chasidic* dynasty. To be a Rebbe, he said, one must always be aware of three things: One should feel as if he is sitting on a bed of nails, one must be able to read a petition, and one must regard his supplicants' problems as his own.

Apter Rav, R. Avraham Yehoshua Heschel (1748–1825): A student of **R. Elimelech of Lizensk,** he was known as the "Ohev Yisrael," "Lover of Israel," because he stressed the importance of loving every Jew. He became the rabbi of Apt in 1800, moved to Moldavia in 1809, and finally settled in Medzibozh where he lived for twelve years. His teachings were published in the *s'farim Ohev Yisrael* and *Toras Emes.*

After his death, the Apter Rav was succeeded as Rebbe in Medzibozh by his son, **R. Yitzhak Meir (1776–1855),** who was also a preacher in the nearby town of Zinkov. Hence he was known as the Rebbe of Zinkov.

R. Asher the First of Karlin (1760–1828): The son and ultimate successor of **R. Aaron the Great of Karlin,** he was a disciple of **R. Baruch of Medzibozh** and of the **Kozhnitzer Maggid.** He settled in Stolin, near Pinsk. Thereafter his followers were known as Stoliner *chasidim*, and R. Asher was called "the Old Man of Stolin." He returned to Karlin in 1810, where he died and was buried. He was succeeded by his son, **R. Aaron the Second of Karlin (1802–1872)**.

Avnei Nezer, R. Avraham Bornstein of Sochatchov (1839–1910): A child prodigy who composed original Torah and Talmudic interpretations at the age of ten, the Avnei Nezer was a *chasid* of the "Chidushei HaRim" – R. Yitzhak Meir Alter of Ger – and of the **Alexander Rebbe**. He married the daughter of **R. Menachem Mendel of Kotzk**, who became his primary guide and mentor and greatly influenced his thinking. R. Avraham was a *chasidic* Rebbe who was also one of the leading *halachic* authorities of the nineteenth century. He was the author of the *Avnei Nezer* on the *Shulchan Aruch*, the definitive compendium of Jewish Law, and *Eglei Tal* on the thirty-nine kinds of work forbidden on the Sabbath. His son and successor, R. Shmuel Bornstein, was the author of the popular commentary on the Torah and holidays, *Shem MiSh'muel*.

Avraham Avinu, Our Father Abraham: He was the first of the Jewish Patriarchs and the progenitor of the Jewish people through his son, Isaac. For the Biblical account of his life, see *Genesis* 11:27–25:11.

Baal Shem Tov, R. Yisrael ben Eliezer (1698–1760): The founder of *chasidism*, at first he lived an outwardly unremarkable life. He was an assistant teacher, a synagogue beadle, and a ritual slaughterer. At the same time he often went into seclusion in the Carpathian Mountains, immersing himself in prayer and Torah study. He gained recognition as a wandering wonder-worker, healing the sick, not by magic – but through prayer. Thus he became known as the Baal Shem Tov, the Master of the Good Name – or by the abbreviation, the **Besht**. In 1740 he settled in Medzibozh, where he established a *Beis Midrash* and revealed himself as a Rebbe.

The Baal Shem Tov was a master of the whole Torah. But he focused his attention primarily on Jewish mysticism or *Kabbalah*, which at that time was studied only by an intellectual elite. Believing that mysticism should also be available to the masses, he simplified *Kabbalistic* concepts, reformulating them in more accessible terms. He sought to invest Jewish tradition with fresh vitality and joy, and founded the eighteenth century *chasidic* movement with a message of unconditional love and communion with G-d through joyful prayer, singing and dancing.

There is a misconception that the Besht disapproved of study. The fact is that he put a different emphasis on learning. He stressed that Torah learning should not be simply an intellectual exercise – the lessons of the Torah should be internalized, and should transform its students. He included stories, anecdotes and parables in his teachings, thereby appealing to the heart as well as the mind. His emphasis on the importance of prayer, serving G-d with joy and loving every Jew – as well a deepened appreciation of the piety of the unlearned – attracted both serious students and masses of "simple Jews," who joined him in making *chasidism* a vital creative force for the advancement of Torah. His teachings were continued and elaborated upon by succeeding generations of Rebbes, and his *chasidic* movement flourishes until today.

R. Baruch ben Yechiel of Medzibozh (1753–1811): The grandson of the **Baal Shem Tov**, he studied with the **Maggid of Mezhirech** and **R. Pinchas Shapiro of Koretz**. He was the first Rebbe to stress the concept of royalty, living in a luxurious and regal fashion. Throughout his life he remained faithful to the teachings of the **Besht**, and was hostile to any deviation or innovation in *chasidic* thought.

Belzer Rebbe: see **R. Aaron Rokeach** and **R. Shalom Rokeach of Belz**

R. Ben Tzion Halberstam of Bobov (1874–1944): The son of **R. Shlomo**, the founder of the Bobover *chasidic* dynasty, he was a melodious singer as well as a noted scholar, saying that *chasidus* without a melody is like a body without a soul. He stressed in his teachings the importance of serving G-d with joy, and was renowned for his giving of charity, often paying the medical bills of his poorer students and arranging their marriages. R. Ben Tzion established the Yeshivah Eitz Chaim in memory of his great grandfather, **R. Chaim of Sanz**, and a network of other *yeshivahs* throughout Galicia. His major published work is *Kedushat Tzion* on the Bible and the Talmud.
R. Ben Tzion was murdered by the Nazis in 1944.

Berdichever Rav: see **R. Levi Yitzhak of Berdichev**

Bnei Yissas'char, R. Tzvi Elimelech Spira of Dinov (1783–1841): The nephew of **R. Elimelech of Lizensk**, he was a student of the **Seer of Lublin**, the **Kozhnitzer Maggid**, **R. Mendel of Rimanov**, and the **Apter Rav**. Known for his humility and great love for the Jewish people, he promoted the study of *Kabbalah*, Jewish mysticism, and had a reputation as a miracle worker. R. Tzvi Elimelech was a prolific writer, the author of twenty-nine volumes of Torah teachings. The best known of these is the *Bnei Yissas'char*, a commentary on Shabbos and the holidays as viewed from a *Kabbalistic* perspective.

Bobover Rebbe, see **R. Ben Tzion Halberstam of Bobov, R. Shlomo Halberstam I of Bobov,** and **R. Shlomo Halberstam II of Bobov/Brooklyn**

R. Chaim Tyrer of Chernovitz (1770–1818): A disciple of R. Yechiel Michel of Zlotchov and **R. Avraham Yehoshua Heschel of Apt,** he was Rebbe in Chernovitz from 1798–1807. Known as "the man of the Sabbath" because he derived his greatest joy from the holiness of Shabbos, his *sefer Siddurei shel Shabbos* – the only one of his works published in his lifetime – is considered one of the great *chasidic* classics. His teachings were also published posthumously in *Be'er Mayim Chaim* and *Eretz Chaim* on the Bible, and *Sha'ar Tefillah* on prayer.

In 1814 R. Chaim realized a lifelong dream, and made his home in Safed (Tzfat), Israel.

Chava: Eve, the first woman.

R. Dov Baer (Berish) of Uschpitzin (d. 1838): The greatest student of **R. Shlomo Buchner of Ch'shanov,** he also was a follower of the **Seer of Lublin.** He became a Rebbe in his own right – and the successor of the Ch'shanover – upon the latter's death in 1828. He was the author of the *sefer The Three Shepherds.*

R. Dovid Biderman of Lelov (1746–1813): A student of **R. Elimelech of Lizensk** and the **Seer of Lublin,** he was an ascetic, often fasting from Sabbath to Sabbath. Renowned for his compassion and kindness, he especially loved children, and was even concerned for the welfare of animals. Extremely humble, he rarely delivered discourses. Whatever teachings he did offer were published in *Migdal Dovid* and *Likutei Divrei Dovid.*

Dovid HaMelech, King David: The son of Yishai (Jesse), he was the second king of Israel, the father of King Solomon, and the author of the Book of Psalms. According to our tradition, the Messiah will – and can only – be a descendent of King David. (See the Biblical books of *Samuel I* and *II* and *Kings I*)

R. Dovid Shapira of Dinov (1822–1874): The son of R. **Tzvi Elimelech of Dinov,** the "**B'nei Yissas'char,**" he and his brother R. Eliezer together succeeded their father as Rebbe. His discourses can be found in *Tzemach Dovid* on the Torah.

Eliahu HaNavi, Elijah the Prophet: He lived during the reign of King Achav of Israel, and tried through his prophecy to keep the Jews of that time from worshipping idols and forsaking the Torah. Many miracles are attributed to him: according to the Bible (*Kings II*, 2:11) he did not die, but ascended to Heaven in a fiery chariot. Therefore, our tradition teaches, he continues to help Jews, sometimes reappearing in disguise to offer assistance in time of need, and at other times coming to teach Torah to a select few. A special place is reserved for him at the Passover Seder and at circumcisions, and he will be the one to herald the coming of the Messiah. (See *Kings I*, 16:29–21:29; *Kings II*, 1:1–2:16)

Rebbe Reb Elimelech of Lizensk (1717–1786): Together with his brother, **R. Meshullam Zussia of Annapoli**, he studied first with **R. Shmuel Shmelke of Nikolsburg**, and subsequently with **the Maggid of Mezhirech**. After the Maggid's death in 1772, he became the uncrowned head of the *chasidic* movement for the next thirty years.

The major concerns of R. Elimelech's theology were the nature of a spiritual life, the problem of evil, and the function of the *tzaddik*, the righteous man. He taught that Jews should never hate any Jew, and he himself was particularly concerned with the plight of orphans, delighting in arranging their marriages. He stressed the *mitzvah* of charity to the point that there was seldom any money in his house – because he always gave everything to the poor. His major work, *Noam Elimelech*, a commentary on the weekly Torah portion, is one of the classic *chasidic* texts.

R. Elimelech was survived by two daughters, Merish and Ettel and by three sons – **R. Eleazar**, his successor in Lizensk; R. Eliezer Lippa of Ch'mielnik and R. Jacob, the rabbi of Moglienice.

R. Hershel (Tzvi Hirsch) HaCohen of Rimanov (1788–1847): Orphaned at the age of ten, he was brought up by his uncle, a tailor. Hungry for Torah, he became the attendant of **R. Menachem Mendel of Rimanov**, who became his teacher and mentor. He became Rebbe of Rimanov himself in 1827. Famous as a miracle worker and for his giving of charity, his discourses were published in *Be'erot HaMayim*.

Ishbitzer, R. Mordecai Yosef Leiner (1800–1854): A disciple of **R. Simchah Bunim of Pshis'cha** and **R. Menachem Mendel of Kotzk**, he founded the Ishbitz/Radzyn *chasidic* dynasty in 1839. The Ishbitzer was one of the most original thinkers in *chasidism*. He believed in informed, rather than blind, faith – teaching that the mechanical performance of *mitzvos* is meaningless and that

G-d should be served with intelligence as well as devotion. His teachings were published in his major work, *Mei HaShiloach*.

Kaminker: see **R. Shalom HaLevi Rosenfeld of Kaminka**

Karliner Rebbe: see **R. Aaron the Great of Karlin** and **R. Asher the First of Karlin**

Kotzker Rebbe: see **R. Menachem Mendel of Kotzk**

Kozhnitzer Maggid, R. Yisrael Hofstein (1733–1815): One of the earliest and most important leaders of Polish *chasidism*, he was a student first of the **Maggid of Mezhirech** and then of **R. Elimelech of Lizensk**. In 1765 he became *Maggid* (Preacher) of Kozhnitz and its neighboring towns. He wrote prolifically on the Torah and on tractates of the Talmud; his teachings demonstrate his mastery of *halachah*, and earned him the respect of his contemporaries. The Maggid lived in austerity and was renowned for his giving of charity and his concern for the poor – especially orphans, many of whom he brought up in his own house. He was also known for the intensity of his prayer.

The Lelover Rebbe, see **R. Dovid Biderman of Lelov**

R. Levi Yitzhak of Berdichev (1740–1810): Known for his Torah scholarship from his earliest years, R. Levi Yitzhak was known as the *illui*, the prodigy, of Yaraslov. **R. Shmuel Shmelke of Nikolsburg** introduced him to *chasidus*, and he became a student of the **Maggid of Mezhirech**. After serving as Rebbe in numerous Polish towns – where he was harshly opposed by the opponents of *chasidism*, he finally found peace in Berdichev, where he lived for the last twenty-five years of his life.

R. Levi Yitzhak had an unshakeable faith in the inherent goodness of all human beings. He always gave even the most blatant sinner the benefit of the doubt. A passionate defender of the Jewish people, he was known as "the merciful one" because of his great love and compassion for Israel. His teachings were collected in the classic work, *Kedushas Levi*.

The Lubliner: see **Seer of Lublin**

Maggid of Mezhirech, R. Dov Baer ben (son of) Avraham (1704–1772): He was one of the closest students and the successor of the **Baal Shem Tov**. If the

Baal Shem was the soul of *chasidism*, the Maggid created the movement's body – the *chasidic* court – and his court, the first of its kind, became the training ground for such great future Rebbes as **R. Levi Yitzhak of Berdichev**, **R. Menachem Mendel of Vitebsk**, and **R. Aaron of Karlin**. R. Dov Baer taught mainly through discourses, which were collected and published in *Likutei Amarim, Ohr Torah* on the Bible and *Ohr HaEmes*. Under the Maggid's leadership *chasidism* grew into a powerful religious movement which spread throughout Eastern Europe.

R. Meir of Premishlan (1780–1850): A student of the **Seer of Lublin**, he became a Rebbe at the age of thirty-three. He was known as a miracle worker and was famous for his wit and humor. Like **R. Levi Yitzhak of Berdichev**, R. Meir always tried to find merit in the actions of the Jewish people. Stressing in his teachings the importance of giving charity, he spent most of his own income on providing weddings and dowries for poor brides. His teachings were published in the *sefer Divrei Meir*.

R. Menachem Mendel Kalish of Vorka (1819–1868): The younger son of **R. Yitzhak Vorker**, he was a disciple of **R. Menachem Mendel of Kotzk**. After his father's death in 1848, R. Mendel was reluctant to succeed him. Accordingly, R. Shragai Feivel of Makov became the leader of R. Yitzhak's *chasidim* and it was only after R. Shragai Feivel's death that R. Menachem Mendel became Rebbe of Vorka.

R. Mendel Vorker was known as the "Silent Rebbe," speaking little and always concisely, weighing every word. He would spend a whole "night of silence" with his followers without saying anything at all. His *chasidim* said that in Vorka, they served G-d by thought.

R. Menachem Mendel Morgenstern of Kotzk (1787–1859): One of the greatest Rebbes, he was a student of the **Seer of Lublin**, the **Yehudi HaKodesh**, and **R. Simchah Bunim of Pshis'cha**. The Kotzker stressed a quest for absolute truth, insisting that the teachings of the Torah must be internalized and integrated into one's innermost being. He taught that G-d must be served in fear and trembling, and urged his followers constantly to examine their deeds and piety and always to strive for a greater level of holiness, purity and truthfulness. Accordingly, he and his *chasidim* lived a plain and austere life, consumed by their hunger for knowledge of and closeness to G-d.

For the last twenty years of his life the Kotzker lived in seclusion in his study. He destroyed all his writings; his teachings, however, made a permanent impression on the *chasidus* of Sochatchov, Ger and Alexander, and his discourses are found in the works of many of his disciples.

R. Menachem Mendel of Rimanov (1755–1815): A student of the **Maggid of Mezhirech** (whom he met at the age of eleven), **R. Shmuel Shmelke of Nikolsburg** and **R. Elimelech of Lizensk**, he was known for his extraordinary awe of G-d and his passion in prayer. Considered a saintly person and famous as a miracle worker, his students included such outstanding *chasidic* leaders as **R. Naftali of Ropschitz** and **R. Tzvi Elimelech of Dinov**. His sermons and discourses were published in *Divrei Menachem* and *Menachem Tzion*.

R. Menachem Mendel of Vitebsk (1730–1788): A student of the **Maggid of Mezhirech**, his closest friend was R. Shneur Zalman of Liadi, the first Rebbe of Lubavitch – and he contributed to the development of many ideas commonly associated with the Chabad philosophy. In 1777 he left Europe for Israel, living first in Safed (Tzfat), where he established the first Ashkenazi community, and later settling in Tiberias. The core of R. Mendel's teaching was the absolute unity of all existence in G-d, the Source of everything in the universe.

R. Meshullam Zussia of Annapoli (d. 1800): The younger brother of **R. Elimelech of Lizensk**, he was a follower of **R. Shmuel Shmelke** and the **Maggid of Mezihrech**. In their youth, he and his brother went into self-imposed exile, wandering incognito through Poland for three years. He then settled in Annapoli, where he lived in great poverty. R. Zussia was known for his humility, his kindness, his love for every creature, and his total devotion to G-d and to Israel. He would do everything in his power to help a fellow Jew, often travelling great distances to raise money to ransom Jewish prisoners. He strove throughout his life to teach every *Yid* how to develop the spark of holiness in his soul. His sayings and discourses were collected in his classic work, *Menoras HaZahav*.

R. Mordechai of Neshchiz (1742–1800): Descended from a long line of distinguished rabbis, he began his life as a businessman. A student of R. Yechiel Michel of Zlotchov, he was renowned as a miracle worker, and was master not only of the mystical aspects of the Torah but also of the Talmud and the Code of Jewish Law. His Torah commentaries and insights were published in *Rishpei Eish*.

R. Mordechai Twersky of Chernobyl (1770–1837): Known as "R. Mottele," he was the son and successor of R. Menachem Nachum – "R. Nachum the Great" – of Chernobyl. He lived in regal style, maintaining an elaborate *chasidic* court. R. Mottele recommended a broad curriculum of Torah learning that included Bible, Talmud, *halachah* and works of Jewish mysticism, and was the author of *Likutei Torah*. He was survived by eight sons, each of whom established a separate *chasidic* court in Russia.

Moshe Rabbeinu, Moses Our Teacher: The Biblical leader who brought the Jewish people out of bondage in Egypt, received the Torah on Mount Sinai, and brought Israel to the border of the Holy Land. He is the central figure of the Biblical narrative from the beginning of the book of *Exodus* through the Book of *Deuteronomy*.

Munkatcher Rebbe, R. Chaim Eleazar Shapiro (1872–1937): He was both the head of the Rabbinical Court and the Rebbe in Munkatch. He established the Darchei Noam Yeshivah, and was a prolific writer, producing over thirty books. The Munkatcher was also famed as a *mohel*, travelling great distances to perform circumcisions. He was also renowned for his kindness and his consideration for the poor.

R. Nachman of Breslov (1772–1810): One of the greatest of the *chasidic* Rebbes, his mother, Feige, was the granddaughter of the **Baal Shem Tov**. R. Nachman's teachings have several major themes: the nature of the true *tzaddik* and his relationship with every Jew; *teshuvah*, repentance, as the path to service of G-d; the importance of conquering doubt and despair and of serving G-d with joy, and the significance of prayer. He also taught the practice of *hisbodedus* – of privately pouring out one's heart before G-d. Together with his closest student and scribe, R. Nosson Steinhartz, he published the first part of his major collection of teachings, *Likutei Moharan*, in 1808 (the second part was published posthumously in 1811).

For the last few months of his life, R. Nachman lived in Uman, where he is buried. After his Rebbe's death, R. Nosson assumed the major role in perpetuating and defending Breslover *chasidus* and disseminating his Master's teachings. Still, R. Nachman had no real successor, and he continues to be considered the Rebbe to Breslover *chasidim* throughout the world.

Nadvorner Rebbe, R. Tzvi Hirsh of Nadvorna (d. 1801): A student of the **Maggid of Mezhirech**, he was known as an expert in *halachah*, and was the author of *Tzemach Hashem LeTzvi* on the Torah, *Siftei Kedoshim* on the Psalms, and *Milei D'Avos* on Ethics of the Fathers. It was said about the Nadvorner that he brought many sinners to repentance.

R. Naftali Tzvi Horowitz of Ropschitz (1760–1827): A disciple of **R. Elimelech of Lizensk, R. Menachem Mendel of Rimanov,** and the **Seer of Lublin,** he was one of the foremost Rebbes in Galicia. Renowned for his humor and sharp wit, he was considered by many to be the wisest of the Rebbes. A master of mystical interpretations of the Torah, he nonetheless urged his followers to study works of *musar*, the discipline of critical introspection and self-evaluation, as well as *chasidus*. He was famous for the intensity of his original melodies. His discourses were recorded in *Zera Kodesh*, a *Kabbalistic* commentary on the Torah and festivals, *Ayala Shelucha*, and *Imrei Sheffer*. *Ohel Naftali* is a collection of many of his stories. The Ropschitzer was survived by three sons, all of whom became Rebbes: **R. Avraham Chaim**, **R. Yaacov**, and **R. Eliezer, the Zhikover Rebbe**. His closest student was **R. Chaim of Sanz**.

R. Pinchas Shapiro of Koretz (1726–1791): One of the greatest disciples of the **Baal Shem Tov**, he was not only a great spiritual leader, but also closely followed political developments and was deeply involved in communal affairs. Famous for his scholarship and humility, he traveled widely to collect money for poor Jews in Israel. In 1791 he himself set out for the Holy Land, but died during the journey.

Premishlaner: see **R. Meir of Premishlan**

Pshis'cher Rebbe: see **R. Simchah Bunim of Pshis'cha**

Radzyminer Rebbe, R. Yaacov Arieh Guterman of Radzymin (1792–1877): He was originally a disciple of the **Seer of Lublin**, the **Kozhnitzer Maggid** and the **Yehudi HaKodesh**. After the Yehudi's death he became a follower of **R. Simchah Bunim**, and was considered one of the Pshis'cher's three greatest students — the other two being the **Kotzker Rebbe** and **R. Yitzchak Vorker**. He became rabbi in Radzymin in 1848, but only after the Vorker's death did he, at the age of fifty-six, become a Rebbe.

Although miracles played no part in the teachings of the Pshis'cher, the Radzyminer became known as a miracle worker and attracted a large following. He was the author of *Divrei Aviv* on *Midrash Rabba*, and *Bikurei Aviv* on *Genesis, Exodus* and *Leviticus*.

Rambam, R. Moshe ben Maimon (Maimonides) (1135–1204): A philosopher, a physician and a codifier of Jewish law, his *Mishnah Torah,* a code of law and ethics, is universally acclaimed as the greatest masterpiece of post-Talmudic Jewish writing. His other major work, the *Guide for the Perplexed* – an attempt to reconcile reason with faith and Judaism with philosophy – is considered one of the greatest philosophical works of the Medieval Period.

Rashi, R. Shlomo ben Yitzhak (1040–1105): A teacher of Talmud in France, his name is inseparably connected with Jewish learning. Known as the "Commentator of the Torah par excellence," he wrote commentaries on the entire Bible (except the books of *Proverbs*, *Job* and *Daniel*), as well as on the Talmud – and his exegesis on the Pentateuch is the most popular and widely used of all Torah commentaries until today.

Rimanover Rebbe, see **R. Menachem Mendel** and **R. Hershel (Tzvi Hirsch) of Rimanov**

Rivka, Rebecca: The second Jewish Matriarch, she was the wife of our Father Issac and the mother of Esau and Jacob. See *Genesis* 24:15–67; 25:19–26; 27:1–46.

Rizhiner, R. Yisrael of Rizhin (1797–1851): The great grandson of the **Maggid of Mezhirech**, his mother was a granddaughter of R. Nahum of Chernobyl. Orphaned at the age of six, he was brought up by his elder brother, R. Avraham – and upon his brother's death in 1813, the sixteen-year-old Yisrael became his heir and a Rebbe. Ultimately settling in Rizhin, he departed from the austere lifestyle of the early Rebbes and lived in a royal and elegant fashion. Still he identified with the problems of each of his followers, and the doors of his princely home were never closed to the poor.
R. Yisrael had a charismatic personality and an extremely acute mind. He was a great scholar and his remarks were known for their brevity and depth of meaning. His discourses can be found in *Irin Kadishin*, *Orot Yisrael*, *Ner Yisrael* and other works. His six sons, whom he called his "six wings," all established their own *chasidic* dynasties.

Rodashitzer Rebbe, R. Issachar Baer (Berele) of Rodashitz (1775–1843): A student of **R. Elimelech of Lizensk** and the **Seer of Lublin**, he was known as a miracle worker, often giving his petitioners *kamayot*, amulets, to ward off evil. He lived in great poverty, believing that we are only visitors in this world, so it was not really worth obtaining physical objects. R. Berele was a close friend of **R. Avraham Yehoshua Heschel of Apt**, whose discourses he collated under the title of *Toras Emes*.

Ropschitzer Rebbe: see **R. Naftali of Ropschitz**

Sanzer Rebbe, R. Chaim Halberstam of Sanz (1793–1876): The founder of the Sanzer *chasidic* dynasty, he was first a student of the **Seer of Lublin,** then of **R. Naftali of Ropschitz** – from whom he learned a deep appreciation of melody and song – and, later, of **R. Shalom Rokeach of Belz.** Known for his phenomenal memory and Torah scholarship, he stressed that sincerity in prayer should be combined with song and dance and that generosity to the poor was vital to a religious life. The Rebbe was known for his compassion and his personal giving of *tzedakah.* He strongly opposed the royal lifestyle of other Rebbes and he himself gave everything away. The Sanzer's major published work was *Divrei Chaim.*

R. Chaim had fourteen children, seven sons and seven daughters; his eldest son, **R. Yehezkel Shragai,** was known as the **Shinover Rebbe.**

Sarah Imeinu, Our Mother Sarah: The first of the Jewish Matriarchs, she was the wife of Abraham and the mother of Issac. See *Genesis* 11: 27–12:20; 16:1–18:16; 20:1–21:21; 23:1–20.

Seer of Lublin, R. Yaacov Yitzhak Horowitz (1745–1815): The founder of Polish *chasidism,* he studied first with **R. Shmuel Shmelke of Nikolsburg,** then with the **Maggid of Mezhirech,** and finally became attached to **R. Elimelech of Lizensk.** He founded his own *chasidic* dynasty in Lublin in 1808 and his court became the training ground for many future *chasidic* leaders, such as the **Rebbes of Pshis'cha, Kotzk, Ger, Ropschitz,** and **Dinov.** Called "the Seer" (*Chozeh*) because of his ability to see into people's souls, he was highly acclaimed by his contemporaries, while he himself remained extremely humble. The Seer further developed the concept of the *tzaddik* or Rebbe and the importance of his role in helping his followers attain higher spiritual levels, thereby hastening the coming of the Messiah. He was the author of *Divrei Emes.*

Sfas Emes, R. Yehudah Arieh Leib Alter of Ger (1847–1905): Orphaned at the age of eight, he was raised by his grandfather, R. Yitzhak Meir Alter, the "*Chiddushei HaRim,*" the founder of the Ger *chasidic* dynasty. Not one moment in his life was ever wasted. He woke at dawn and spent the entire day in study and prayer. He was the author of the monumental work *Sfas Emes* on the Torah and Festivals, as well as commentaries on *Ethics of the Fathers,* the Passover *Haggadah,* and the books of *Esther, Ecclesiastes, Psalms* and *Proverbs.*

R. Shalom Rokeach of Belz (1783–1855): An ardent disciple of the **Seer of Lublin,** it was at the suggestion of the Seer that he founded his own *chasidic* dynasty in Belz, where he remained for forty years. He was famous for consulting his wife Malka on almost every problem and urged his followers to follow his example in their own families. Known for his devotion in prayer and intensity in learning, his discourses were collected in *Dover Shalom*.

R. Shalom HaLevi Rosenfeld of Kaminka (1800–1852): Known as a genius from his early youth, he was a student of the **Seer of Lublin**, **R. Naftali of Ropschitz**, and **R. Shalom Rokeach of Belz**. He became Rebbe in Kaminka in 1837 and was the author of *Ohev Shalom*.

R. Shlomo Buchner of Ch'shanov (d. 1828): A student of **R. Shmuel Shmelke of Nikolsburg** and the **Seer of Lublin**, he later became a Rebbe himself, and was succeeded by **R. Dov Baer – "Berishele" – of Uschpitzin**.

R. Shlomo Halberstam I of Bobov (1847–1905): The first Rebbe of Bobov, he was orphaned at the age of eight and was brought up by his grandfather, **R. Chaim Halberstam of Sanz**. Serving as rabbi in Auschwitz and in Vishnitz, he established the first Bobov *Yeshivah* and attracted many outstanding disciples. His entire library and all his manuscripts were destroyed in a fire in 1889; his surviving discourses were included in *Kedushas Zion*, published by his son and successor, **R. Ben Tzion**.

R. Shlomo Halberstam II of Bobov/Brooklyn (1908–2000): The son of **R. Ben Tzion**, the second Rebbe of Bobov. Before the Second World War he served as rabbi in Bobov and was also principal of the Etz Chaim Yeshivah there. During the war he was imprisoned in the German labor camp of Bochnia near Cracow. He managed to escape from that camp and from subsequent Nazi purges, and organized an escape route for the Jews of Poland. The Nazis murdered his father, his wife and two of his children. Upon his father's death, R. Shlomo was named Rebbe of Bobov.

After the war, R. Shlomo made his way to New York, ultimately settling in Borough Park, Brooklyn. There he established a network of Jewish educational institutions and introduced a system of *yeshivah* trade schools offering courses leading to jobs in industry. He also founded Kiryat Bobov in Bat Yam, Israel and the *yeshivah* Kedushat Zion, the Holiness of Zion.

R. Shlomo was the Bobover Rebbe from whom R. Shlomo Carlebach heard many of his stories.

R. Shmuel Shmelke Horowitz of Nikolsburg (1726–1778): A student of the **Maggid of Mezhirech**, he became rabbi in Nikolsburg in 1772. Although he did not establish himself there as a *chasidic* Rebbe, he preached *chasidic* doctrines and vigorously defended *chasidism* against attacks by its opponents, thereby attracting such outstanding disciples as **R. Levi Yitzhak of Berdichev** and **R. Yisrael of Rizhin**. He was the author of *Divrei Shmuel* on the Torah. Like the Biblical Prophet Shmuel (Samuel), R. Shmuel Shmelke lived fifty-two years.

R. Simchah Bunim of Pshis'cha (1765–1827): A student of the **Seer of Lublin** and the **Maggid of Kozhnitz**, he settled in Pshis'cha, where he became both an accomplished pharmacist and the closest disciple (and later the successor) of **R. Yaacov Yitzhak**, the **Yehudi HaKodesh**. Just as the **Maggid of Mezhirech** developed the doctrines of the **Baal Shem Tov**, the Pshis'cher interpreted and developed the ideas of the Yehudi, emphasizing the importance of truth, faith and humility in one's service of G-d. Using parables and stories as an important part of his teachings, his writings – published in *Chedvas Simchah, Kol Simchah,* and *Niflaos Rabbi Bunim* – reflect the Yehudi's new approach to *chasidus* which stressed introspection, self-examination and intense Torah study. The Pshis'cher's most famous disciple was **R. Menachem Mendel of Kotzk**.

Sochatchover Rebbe, see the **Avnei Nezer, R. Avraham Bornstein of Sochatchov**

Sokolover Rebbe, R. Yitzhak Zelig Morgenstern (1866–1940): A great grandson of **R. Menachem Mendel of Kotzk**, he was born in Kotzk and was a devoted follower of Kotzker *chasidus*. In 1899 he became rabbi of Sokolov-Poldski, where he established a large *yeshivah*, Beis Yisrael. He became a prominent leader of Agudas Yisrael and was active in Jewish communal affairs in Poland. He was also deeply concerned about the condition of the Jewish community in Israel and urged Polish Jewry to settle there. Most of his writings were destroyed in the Holocaust.

Stretyner Rebbe, R. Yehudah Tzvi Brandwein of Stretyn (1780–1830): He was the greatest disciple of **R. Uri Strelisk**. At the suggestion of the **Seer of Lublin**, he established his own *chasidic* dynasty during the Strelisk's lifetime, and became the leader of many of R. Uri's followers after their teacher's death. Like R. Uri, the Stretyner was known for praying with great ecstasy and devotion. He also had a reputation as a healer.

R. Uri of Strelisk (1757–1826): He studied with many *chasidic* Rebbes, finally becoming the most devoted disciple of R. Shlomo of Karlin. After his teacher's death in 1792, he became Rebbe first in Lvov and later in Strelisk. He hated fame and honor. He and most of his *chasidim* were very poor because, as he explained it, they prayed for true faith and for fervor in their service of

G-d, rather than for worldly goods. R. Uri was called "the Seraph," for his followers saw in him a resemblance to that Heavenly angel who always sings praises to G-d. His closest disciple was **R. Yehudah Tzvi of Stretyn**, and his discourses were published in *Imrei Kodesh* and *Imrei Kodesh HeChadash*.

Vorker Rebbe: see R. Yitzhak Kalish of Vorka

Yaacov Avinu, Our Father Jacob: The third Jewish Patriarch, he was the son of Isaac, the brother of Esau and the father of the twelve tribes of Israel, from whom the Jewish People are descended. See *Genesis* chapters 25, 27–35, 37, 42–50.

Yehudi (Yid) HaKodesh, The Holy Jew, R. Yaacov Yitzhak (1765–1814): A student of the **Seer of Lublin**, after the Seer's death, R. Yaacov Yitzhak became Rebbe in Pshis'cha, where he became known as the Yehudi or Yid HaKodesh, the Holy Jew. His teachings brought about a new orientation in *chasidic* thought. He de-emphasized the striving after mystical experiences and the miracles that were said to occur at the courts of other Rebbes, stressing instead reflective, self-critical discipline, deep feeling and intellectual honesty. He taught that truth was the highest of religious values, and insisted on sincerity and total involvement in prayer, study and every human relationship.
The Yehudi's Court gave rise to a number of important *chasidic* schools, including those of **Pshis'cha, Kotzk, Ger** and **Ishbitz**. His discourses can be found in *Niflaos HaYehudi*, *Toras HaYehudi*, *Tiferes HaYehudi*, and *Keter HaYehudi*. R. Yaacov Yitzhak was survived by three sons: **R. Yerachmiel**, R. Nechemiah Yechiel, and R. Yehoshua Asher.

Yitzhak Avinu, Our Father Isaac: The second of the Jewish Patriarchs, he was the son of Abraham, the brother of Ishmael, and the father of Jacob and Esau. See *Genesis*: 21:1–21; 22:1–19; 24:1–10, 62–67; 25:19–28:5; 35:27–29.

R. Yitzhak Kalish of Vorka (1779–1848): A student of the **Seer of Lublin**, the **Yehudi HaKodesh** and **R. Simchah Bunim of Pshis'cha**, he was known for his gentleness and loving-kindness. He was concerned with every facet of Jewish life in Poland, as well as the economic plight of the Jews in Israel, for whom he actively collected funds. He urged his followers to give charity generously, and established societies in many Polish towns to provide the needy with their necessities for Shabbos. On one occasion his personal intervention helped bring about the cancellation of a decree expelling all Jews from Western Russia.

The Vorker attracted many outstanding disciples, including **R. Yaacov Arieh of Radzymin**. His discourses were published in *Ohel Yitzhak*, and both of his sons – **R. Yaacov Dovid of Amshinov** and **R. Menachem Mendel of Vorka** – became *chasidic* Rebbes.

Yosef, Joseph: Known as *Yosef HaTzaddik*, Joseph the Righteous, he was one of the twelve sons of Our Father Jacob. See *Genesis*: 30:22–24; 37:1–36; 39:1–48:22; 49:28–50:26.

R. Yosef Shaul Natenson of Lemburg (1810–1875): One of the greatest authorities on *halachah* in his generation, he was chief rabbi of Lemberg (Lvov) from 1857 until his death. Although not himself a *chasid*, he had a good relationship with many *chasidic* Rebbes, especially **R. Shalom Rokeach of Belz** and **R. Chaim Halberstam of Sanz**. He was the author of *Divrei Shaul* on the Torah, and *Shoel U'Meshiv* on the *Shulchan Aruch*, the definitive compendium of Jewish Law.

Rebbe Reb Zussia: see **R. Meshullam Zussia of Annapoli**

SOURCES

Chasidic Rebbes, R. Tzvi Rabinowicz, Targum/Feldheim, 1989

The Encyclopedia of Chasidism, edited by R. Tzvi Rabinowicz, Jason Aronson, 1996

The Great Chasidic Masters, Avraham Yaacov Finkel, Jason Aronson, 1992